EMPIRE OF DRAGONS

VALERIO MASSIMO MANFREDI is the professor of classical archaeology at the Luigi Bocconi University in Milan. He has carried out a number of expeditions to and excavations in many sites throughout the Mediterranean, and has taught in Italian and international universities. He has published numerous articles and academic books, mainly on military and trade routes and exploration in the ancient world.

He has published nine works of fiction, including the 'Alexander' trilogy, which has been translated into twenty-four languages in thirty-eight countries, and *The Last Legion*, soon to be a major motion picture.

He has written and hosted documentaries on the ancient world transmitted by the main television networks, and has written fiction for cinema and television as well.

He lives with his family in the countryside near Bologna, Italy.

Also by Valerio Massimo Manfredi

ALEXANDER: CHILD OF A DREAM

ALEXANDER: THE SANDS OF AMMON

ALEXANDER: THE ENDS OF THE EARTH

SPARTAN

THE LAST LEGION

HEROES
(*formerly* The Talisman of Troy)

TYRANT

THE ORACLE

FOR MIRELLA AND DANILO

Those who would take over the world
and shape it to their will, cannot succeed.
The world is a sacred vessel, not to be tampered with.
Those who tamper with it, spoil it.
Those who seize it, lose it.

Lao Tze, *Tao Te Ching*

Many who read the name of Valerian emperor on a
sepulchre believe that the Persians returned the body
of that Valerian that they had captured . . .

Trebellius Pollio, *Historia Augusta*, XXII, 8

ACKNOWLEDGEMENTS

I would like first of all to thank my friend Lorenzo De Luca, who urged and inspired me to write this novel, and guided me with his expertise as a martial arts enthusiast. Without him it might never have seen the light of day. Special thanks are due to Aurelio De Laurentiis, who believed in this story from its conception. I am also grateful to sinologist Rosa Cascino for the constant attention to detail which helped me set my adventure in the China of the third century AD. I would also like to thank Mario Lucchetti of Soldiers, who did extensive research for me regarding the armed forces and weapons in use in the Roman empire at the time of Valerian and Gallienus. The liberties I've taken in adapting his rigorous reconstructions stem solely from the demands of the narrative itself. Thanks too to Laura Grandi, Stefano Tettamanti and Franco Mimmi for reading my pages with such care and patient intelligence, taking precious time away from their daily occupations. Last, but not least, my affectionate thanks go to my wife, Christine. Her exacting and yet creative assistance has had an important role in crafting this work.

VMM

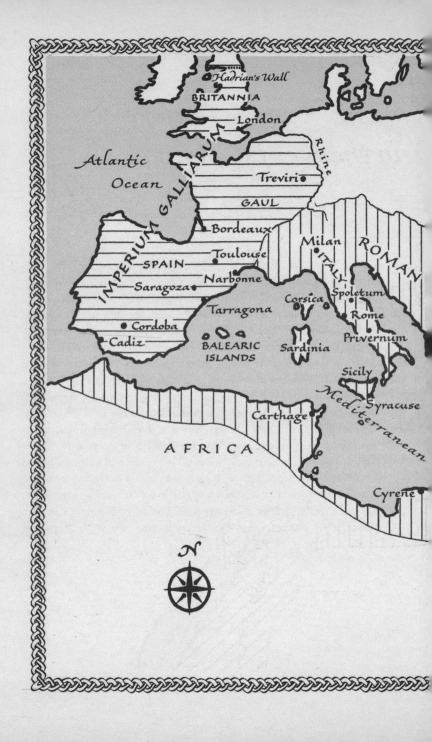

The Roman Empire in the age of Gallienus

AD 260

EMPIRE

Danube

Black Sea

Byzantium

Caspian Sea

Athens

Crete

Cyprus

Sea

Alexandria

LIBYA

KINGDOM OF PALMYRA

Edessa

Antioch

SYRIA

Palmyra

EGYPT

Nile

Red Sea

China
in the age of
the Three Kingdoms

AD 220

N

Chengdu

SHU

Bay of

Bengal

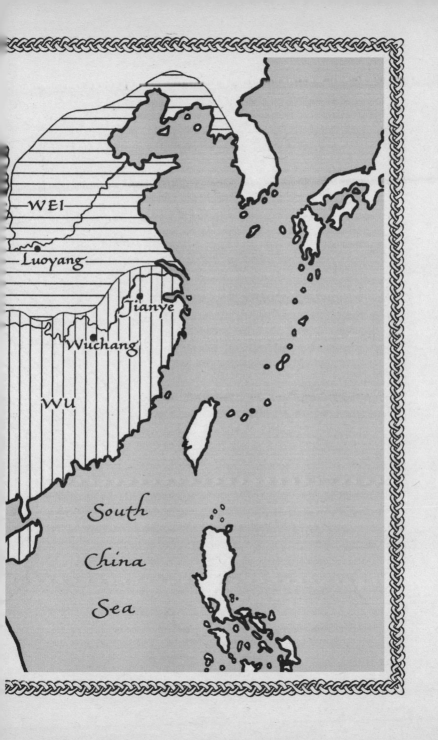

1

THE RAYS OF THE DAWNING SUN bathed the peaks of the Taurus mountains. The snowy pinnacles took on a rosy hue and glittered like gems over the shadowy valley. The mantle of light spread slowly over the ridges and slopes of the great mountain chain, awakening the forests from their slumber.

The stars paled.

The falcon was first to soar up to hail the sun, and his shrill cry echoed amid the rocky cliffs and crags, and down the steep sides of the ravine through which the foaming Korsotes flowed, swollen by the melting snows.

Shapur I of Persia, the King of Kings, of Persians and non-Persians, the lord of the four corners of the earth, was startled by that cry and raised his eyes to behold the wheeling flight of the prince of heights, then turned to the splendidly outfitted Arab thoroughbred his squire had just brought to him. A servant knelt so the king could plant a foot on his bended knee and vault into the saddle. Two more servants held out Shapur's bow and golden-sheathed scimitar, and a standard-bearer took position at his side with the royal ensign: a long flag of red silk bearing the image of Ahura Mazda in gold.

His officers awaited him at the centre of the camp, armed to the hilt, astride horses mantled with precious caparisons, their breasts protected by steel plates. Ardavasd, the supreme commander, greeted him with a deep bow, as did all the others. At a gesture from the king, he touched his horse's belly with his heels and set off. All the other officers fanned out to the right and left of Shapur and together they began to descend the hill.

The sun's light had poured into the valley and touched upon the towers of Edessa, perched high on the barren upland, swept by the winds of the desert.

THE LONG, persistent crowing of a cock greeted the rising sun.

In the courtyard of his house, Marcus Metellus Aquila, legate of the Second Augusta Legion, was already dressed and wearing his armour.

A native of southern Italy, Metellus's bones and muscles had been toughened by long service on all the frontiers of the empire. Years of shouting out orders on the battlefield had made his voice deep and husky and blunted his manner of speaking. His high cheekbones, strong jaw and straight nose gave away his aristocratic lineage, but the simple, unrefined cut of his hair and beard, never completely tamed by a razor, revealed the austerity of a soldier inured to toil and trouble. The amber colour of his eyes and the rapacious intensity of his expression on the eve of a battle made him known to all the divisions south of the Taurus simply as 'Commander Aquila', evoking the proud eagle that his surname signified.

He was just hooking his *gladius* to his belt: obsolete as a weapon, but a legacy from his ancestors that he refused to hang on the wall and replace with a regulation sword. He even kept another hooked to the saddle of his horse, and was famous for saying that with the two of them, he could take out the longest blade.

'A cock's crow in a besieged city is a good sign,' he mused as an attendant fitted the red cloak which denoted his rank around his shoulders. 'If he's survived the hunger we've suffered around here, we'll survive as well.' Metellus approached the shrine of his *lares* and left an offering to the shades of his ancestors, a little one, but even more precious in a period of such penury – a handful of spelt flour – then he prepared to leave.

His wife's voice stopped him: 'Marcus.'

'Clelia. What are you doing up so early?'

'You were going to leave without saying goodbye?'

'I didn't want to wake you. You had such a restless night.'

'I'm worried. Is it true that the emperor wants to meet with the Persian?'

Marcus Metellus broke into a smile. 'It's incredible how women always seem to know the news we try to keep most secret.'

Clelia had to smile as well. 'The emperor has a wife, who has ladies-in-waiting, who have friends . . .'

'Right.'

'Well?'

'I'm afraid so.'

'He'll go, then?'

'It's very probable.'

'But why?'

'He says that peace is well worth risking his life for.'

'What about you? Can't you do anything to dissuade him?'

'I'll speak up if he asks for my opinion, and in that case I'll try to make him change his mind. But once he's decided, my place is at his side.'

Clelia bowed her head.

'Maybe he's just hoping to gain time. Gallienus is in Antioch. In a few days of forced marches he could be here with four legions and lift the siege.' He lifted her chin and saw that her eyes were full of tears. 'Clelia . . . crying as you say goodbye to your husband brings bad luck, you know.'

Clelia tried to dry her eyes. At that very instant they heard the patter of little feet rushing down the stairs and a voice call out, 'Father! Father!'

'Titus! What are you doing here? Go right back to bed!'

'You promised that you'd take me with you to the *palaestra* today.'

Metellus knelt and looked his little boy in the eye. 'The emperor has called me. He's the father of us all, my son, and when he calls we must run to his side. Go back to bed now and try to sleep.'

The child's expression was suddenly serious. 'You'll go away with the emperor and leave me alone.'

Metellus frowned. 'What are you saying? I'll be back, you can be sure of it. I promise I'll be back before nightfall. And you know that a Roman always keeps his word.' He gave his tearful wife a kiss and left the house.

Outside in the street, waiting on either side of the door, were his two adjutants, centurions Aelius Quadratus and Sergius Balbus. The first was Italian, from Privernum. The second Spanish, from Saragoza. Both of their faces were scored by time and the many battles fought in every corner of the empire: rocky faces with thick eyebrows and bristly beards. Quadratus wore his hair very short and was balding at the temples; he was tall and heavily built. Balbus was shorter and darker-skinned, but his eyes were blue and his crushed nose gave away his passion for boxing.

Metellus put on his helmet, tied the laces under his chin, gave them a look and said, 'Let's go.'

They walked down the silent, still-deserted streets of the city with a steady step, each absorbed in his own thoughts, each with a heavy heart.

The cock's crow resounded again and sunlight flooded the street, making the basalt slabs sparkle and lengthening the men's shadows all the way back to the walls of the houses behind them.

At a crossroads they met another small group of officers, who had obviously been summoned by the emperor as well.

Metellus recognized his colleague: '*Salve*, Lucius Domitius.'

'*Salve*, Marcus Metellus,' he was greeted in return.

They continued together to the forum and then walked across to command headquarters. From there they could see the sentry walk up on the battlements. It was time for the changing of the guard: cadenced steps, the metallic clanging of javelins against shields. Salutes given, curt orders barked out.

'The last guards are going off duty,' observed Metellus.

'For today,' Domitius corrected him.

'For today,' amended Metellus, remembering how superstitious his friend could be.

They reached the entrance to the headquarters, where they were met by Cassius Silva, commander of the fortress, messmate and companion-in-arms of many years' standing of Gallienus, the emperor's son.

The praetorians on duty presented arms as the three legates passed and accompanied them inside. The centurions and other officers remained outside.

EMPEROR LICINIUS VALERIAN greeted them personally. He was fully armed and got straight to the point. 'I wish to tell you that I've decided to go to the meeting with Shapur. Last night, a squad of about fifty of our men was dispatched to the right bank of the Korsotes in no man's land. A garrison of Persian horsemen is posted on the other side of the river to guard the territory where the meeting is to take place.

'As you can see, nothing has been left to chance. Our plenipotentiaries have already established the points of negotiation in order to simplify matters.

'Shapur seems willing to discuss ending his siege on Edessa, despite the city's importance as a geographical and commercial nexus between Anatolia and Syria. In exchange he wants a general agreement that redefines the relationship between our two empires and establishes lasting peace. He may ask us to give up some territory in Adiabene and Commagene, without precluding anything. He is open to negotiation. The terms seem good, and I'm ready to go.'

'You've made a wise decision, Caesar,' approved Silva.

Lucius Domitius Aurelian had been frowning from the start and squeezing the hilt of his sword. He was a formidable soldier: having fought in numerous campaigns, he had killed nearly nine hundred enemies with his own hand, carving a notch into the shaft of his javelin each time. He was so quick at unsheathing his sword that he had earned the name *manus ad ferrum* among his men: 'Sword-in-Hand'. He asked to speak. 'I've heard that your son Gallienus is in Antioch, and could be here with four legions in five days' time. Why run this risk now?'

'Because we have enough food for two,' retorted Silva.

'We can ration supplies and make them last. A little hunger never killed anybody.'

'It's not just a question of food,' replied the emperor. 'We can't be certain that Gallienus will arrive, or that it will take him only five days. Our informers tell us that there are Persian cavalry units all along the road from Antioch charged with interrupting our lines of communication and cutting off supplies. No. I will go to meet Shapur. To learn his intentions, if nothing else. If we can lay the foundations of a lasting agreement, all the better. But even if I succeed merely in gaining time and avoiding a large-scale attack while we wait for Gallienus to get here, that will be an achievement on its own. And the fact that it was Shapur who requested the meeting bodes well in any case.'

He turned to Metellus. 'Have you nothing to say, Marcus Metellus? What is your opinion?'

'Don't go, Caesar.'

Valerian looked at him more in surprise than concern. 'Why?'

'There's nothing I like about this. Smells like a trap a mile away.'

'I've taken every precaution. We're meeting on neutral ground, on open terrain. Fifty escorts on both sides, already in place. Nothing can happen. I'm going, I've already decided. And I don't want Shapur to think that the emperor of the Romans is afraid of him.'

He strode out, followed by the other officers.

Metellus fell into step beside him. 'Then I'm going with you, Caesar.'

'No,' replied the emperor. 'It's better that you remain here.' He leaned close enough to speak into his ear. 'I want to be sure I'll find the gate open when I come back.'

'Leave Lucius Domitius. He's the most loyal man I know, he enjoys great popularity among the ranks and he's found himself in such situations before. I'll be more useful to you out there.'

The emperor looked at Metellus and then at Domitius, who was a few steps behind them. 'All right, then. You'll come with me and Lucius Domitius will stay here in the city. Would to heaven that I've made the right decision . . .'

Silva smiled. 'It won't make any difference who comes out with you, Caesar. We'll all be back here having a midday meal in no time, unless Shapur wants to invite you for a bite under that fancy pavilion of his.'

A stableman brought the emperor's horse and Metellus had his own brought around as well. As always, the attendant had already secured his second *gladius* to the pommel of his saddle.

Domitius raised his eyes to the bastions. A soldier on the guard tower waved a red flag: once, twice, three times. 'They're signalling that everything is ready . . .' he said.

A white flag waved from the battlements, from right to left and then from left to right.

'. . . and that all is quiet. Nothing suspicious.'

'Very good,' approved Valerian. 'Now let's move.'

CLELIA HAD MANAGED to put Titus back to bed and was heading towards the house's upper terrace, to see if she could catch a glimpse of what was happening outside the walls, when she heard a noise.

She strained her ears but the house seemed silent, and Clelia thought that she must have imagined it. She started up the stairs but then she heard it again: a clear, pronounced sound that seemed to be coming from the cellar.

Clelia took a candle from the shelf, lit it with the lamp flame and started down to the ground floor. She was troubled by the fact that her husband had already gone and that she was practically alone in the house. What could it be?

She listened intently: the noise was certainly coming from the cellar. She opened the door that led downstairs and began to descend the steps, holding the candle high.

'Who's there?' she asked in a loud voice.

She was answered by a kind of moaning.

7

'Who's there?' she repeated.

Shuffling sounds from behind an iron-clad door. As far as she knew, the door closed off the drainage pipes from an old water heating system that led outside the city, but it had never been opened since they'd lived in the house. She leaned her ear against the door and heard more noises coming from the other side, amplified by the empty chamber beyond. She drew the bolt and pulled hard to open the door, grabbing both sides with her hands. The door creaked, sighed and came loose all at once. Clelia drew back and screamed.

Before her was a man, half naked and covered in blood, who looked at her fleetingly with a distressed expression, then fell back to the ground with an agonized moan.

Clelia realized immediately that the poor wretch was no threat to her; he was dying. She rolled him gently on his side, put her shawl under his head and looked for a glass to give him a little water.

He drank a sip and began to speak. 'We've been betrayed . . . you must tell them . . . warn them . . .'

'Who are you?' asked Clelia. 'Who are you?'

The man was fading fast. 'They took us . . . by surprise and slaughtered us . . . Tell the emperor he must . . . must not go . . . It's a trap . . . It's . . .' His head dropped forward as life left him.

Clelia shivered. She understood instantly what must have happened and what was about to happen if she could not stop the deadly machine the enemy had set in motion.

She ran up the stairs, crossed the courtyard and burst out on to the street. The city was still deserted and Clelia never stopped running.

THE GUARDS opened the city gate and the small imperial procession set off towards the designated meeting place. The sun was already well over the horizon and its rays carved up the arid, rocky landscape around them into swathes of dark and light, scattered with amaranth and terebinth bushes. The Korsotes flowed at their left for a stretch, then curved to the west, intercepting their line of march.

The escort had spent the night securing the ford. They were waiting at a short distance, in no man's land, to escort the procession to the other side of the river, where they would meet Shapur, the Persian king. When they were less than a hundred feet away, a centurion saluted the emperor, and all fifty horsemen moved into position at the ford.

Metellus was struck by something strange and his face darkened. He gestured to Balbus.

'What is it, Commander?' he asked in a low voice.

'White legs.'

'What?'

'Look for yourself. These soldiers were wearing trousers until yesterday. They're Persians, not Romans.'

'Blast it! But where are our men?'

'Probably all dead. You warn the emperor, I'll try to send a signal to Lucius Domitius. We can still get out of this.'

Balbus approached the emperor and whispered into his ear.

Metellus turned his shield towards the sun and began to flash it in the direction of the walls.

Domitius, who was anxiously watching the little group as they made their way to the ford, started as he saw the signals. 'Wh . . . white . . . legs,' he sounded out. 'White legs!' he shouted aloud. 'Persians! It's a trap! The emperor is about to ride into an ambush. Bugler, sound the alarm! Send out the cavalry! Quickly, quickly! Open the gate!'

The legionaries posted at the gate pushed it open again and the bugler sounded the trumpet to muster the cavalry units quartered near the emperor's residence.

In just a few moments, a hundred horsemen had gathered at the open gate, and as many more were preparing to join in as reinforcements, but Cassius Silva, at the head of a squad of praetorians, stopped them. 'Who ordered this sortie? Are you all mad? Halt, halt, I said!'

'I gave the order!' shouted Domitius from the battlements. 'The emperor is in danger. They're about to march into a trap. I'll lead them out myself, immediately!'

'I am in charge of this fortress,' retorted Silva. 'To order a sally now, as negotiations are taking place, is pure folly. The Persians are sure to react violently, and then you'll see our men dead for sure. There is no reason to believe that the emperor is in danger. Close the gate!'

Domitius rushed down. 'What are you saying? This is treason! You will be held accountable for this decision!'

Silva nodded at the praetorians who were with him. 'Legate Lucius Domitius Aurelian is under arrest for insubordination until further orders. Seize him! And you,' he said to the soldiers on guard, 'close that gate.'

The praetorians surrounded Domitius, who was forced to hand over his sword, and they took him away. The soldiers began to pull the heavy gate shut.

Clelia, panting, had just arrived at the guard station and had witnessed the scene. She felt her heart sink. Her husband was out there and knew nothing of what was happening, while in here they were conspiring against him!

She looked around in distress, saw a stableboy leading a horse by the reins and didn't hesitate for an instant. She ripped her gown from the knee down and gave the boy a hard shove. As he fell to the ground, she leapt on to the horse and spurred him towards the gate.

The horse reared up before the closing gate and his front hoofs struck the wood and pushed it back open. Clelia urged him on and he flew off at a gallop.

The emperor and his guard were close to the ford now and the sham escort was waiting at the river bank. No one had made a move, but a plan was ready. 'As soon as all the soldiers are on the other side of the river,' said Metellus, 'we'll turn around and race back towards the city. We'll have enough of an advantage over them to allow us to reach it in safety.'

'As long as they open the gate for us,' said Balbus warily. 'If they received our message, I don't understand why they haven't come out to help us.'

He had not finished speaking when Quadratus interrupted him. 'Look, they must have got it. There is someone coming from the city. But . . . wait . . . it's a woman!' he exclaimed.

Metellus turned towards the walls and was dumbfounded. 'It's Clelia! It's my wife!' he shouted.

The sham escort had already begun to cross the river.

The emperor signalled to Metellus. 'Go!'

He set off at a gallop; Clelia was hurtling towards him and shouting something. She was nearly halfway between him and the walls of Edessa and was still racing forward. Suddenly Metellus saw something fly up from the walls, in a wide arc: arrows!

Whistling cut through the air. One arrow, then a second, plunged into the ground. The third hit its target and flung Clelia from her horse.

Metellus charged towards her, jumped off his galloping steed and gathered her into his arms. She was still breathing. The arrow had pierced her back and was protruding from her breast. Her dress was soaked with blood.

Metellus clutched her to him, weeping with rage and grief, kissing her wan lips, her forehead, her hair.

'It's a trap,' murmured Clelia. 'The escort was murdered . . . Silva is . . . is . . . Marcus, please, save yourself . . . Go back to our son . . . He's all alone . . .'

'I'll go to him. I promise.'

Clelia's head dropped and darkness veiled her eyes. Metellus felt as if he had died with her.

He looked over at the gate of Edessa, which was still obstinately closed, and made out a red cloak fluttering on top of the walls: Silva. It was surely him. Metellus turned towards the ford and saw that the fight was already raging: the emperor was surrounded!

At that sight, Metellus steeled himself and regained his determination and presence of mind. He scattered a handful of dirt over his wife's body as a symbolic burial, swallowed his tears and leapt on to his horse, spurring him madly towards the banks of the Korsotes river.

He burst between the ranks of the fraudulent escort brandishing two swords, one for each of two Persian warriors, who keeled over into the river as Metellus descended upon the others with dreadful violence. He struck out in every direction, stabbing, piercing, gouging, mangling, splitting bones and skulls, opening the way towards his encircled emperor.

More Persian warriors were arriving from every direction and Metellus realized that he had no more than a few moments in which to open an escape route for Valerian. But when he turned, he saw the emperor being flung from his horse and landing in the water in the middle of a tangle of enemy soldiers.

Metellus gave a yell – 'Save the emperor!' – and surged forward like a battering ram: he jumped off his horse and hurled himself bodily against the enemy while rallying his men. 'Balbus, Quadratus, to me!'

The two centurions flanked him like a couple of mastiffs. They rose up like towers on either side of him, their shields striking down anyone who dared approach, their swords impaling all assailants. They mowed the enemy down, trampling the fallen or nailing them with the bottom edges of their shields. Valerian defended himself tenaciously, but he had to fight against the swirling river current as he was fending off enemy blows. He lost his balance and was about to be cut down by a Persian who had just lifted his javelin when Metellus appeared behind his attacker and lopped off both his arms with two lightning-fast swipes, then pushed him into the current like an uprooted tree trunk. He moved in at the emperor's side. With Balbus and Quadratus providing cover, he had Valerian mount his horse and then smashed the flat of his sword against the animal's rear. The thoroughbred raced off towards the city.

Valerian rode at breakneck speed, conscious that his men were sacrificing themselves to save his life; he was determined to call out all the forces in Edessa to rush to their aid and make the Persian pay for his deceitfulness. But a squad of enemy horsemen emerged unexpectedly from the gorge to his right, in which the river flowed, then fanned out to the west, cutting him off from the city.

He wrenched his horse in the opposite direction, thinking that he could reach one of the Roman outposts on the road to Nisibi, but a line of infantry appeared before him all at once, as if vomited up by the earth, and barred his way.

Valerian did not slow down for an instant. He pushed his horse into a formidable leap and flew over the line of foot soldiers. He landed on the other side and spurred his mount on ever faster, convinced that he was safe, imaging how he would avenge the blood of his valorous combatants but his thoughts were suddenly cut short at the sight of an immense array of cavalry and infantry rising from the line of hills in front of him. Shapur himself was at the centre of the fluttering purple standards which unfolded over an enormous front, closing off every passage and every road.

The emperor of the Romans understood that he had no way out and turned back towards the ford to die with his sword in hand beside his men, to end a blameless life with an honourable death. But, just as he was about to throw himself into the battle still raging at the ford, the trumpets blared and the Persian soldiers withdrew, leaving the Romans alone at the centre of a circle of armed men.

Panting with exhaustion and dripping with blood, the soldiers of the little squad prepared to receive their emperor, who had not succeeded in saving himself.

Marcus Metellus Aquila emerged from the river and drew his men up along the bank to face their destiny.

2

SHAPUR TOUCHED THE HORSE'S flanks with his heels and advanced unhurriedly towards the small group of Romans.

Valerian motioned for his men to stay where they were and went forward alone, on foot, towards his adversary. The Persian wore finely embroidered semi-transparent silken trousers and his long moustache was curled upwards. The elaborate mitre on his head was adorned with ostrich feathers and the sword hanging at his side was sheathed in gem-encrusted gold. The Roman was covered with mud and dust, his breastplate disjointed and his tunic torn. Deep cuts on his arms and legs oozed blood.

Shapur made a gesture and two of his guards ran over to the emperor of the Romans and shoved him to the ground, forcing him to his knees.

Metellus rushed forward, shouting, 'Leave him alone, you cowards! Fight me, you barbarian, if you've got the guts! Get off that horse! I'll pull off those feathers and make you swallow them, you bastard, you son of a whore!'

But a net soared over his head and snared him like a lion in a trap. The others were surrounded and disarmed.

Shapur barely gave them a glance. He nodded to his men and went off, passing between the files of soldiers, towards the camp he had left before dawn.

Through the mesh of the netting that imprisoned him, Metellus noticed a strange figure: a man, or maybe a boy, given his slight physique, dressed in a style of clothing he had never seen. His face was hidden by a black scarf that left only his eyes uncovered: long, slanting eyes of a deep black colour. They exchanged a fleeting, intense look before the mysterious person melted away into Shapur's retinue.

The prisoners were dragged to a tumbledown hut and shackled hand and foot, one after another, beginning with Valerian. Metellus looked at his chained emperor and could not hold back his tears. They were then bound to one another and lined up behind Balbus, the centurion; he was tied to the saddle of the last of the horsemen who would be taking them to their destiny. There were ten of them, besides the emperor and Commander Metellus: the two centurions, Aelius Quadratus and Sergius Balbus, a ranking *optio* named Antoninus Salustius and seven legionaries: Lucianus, Severus, Rufus, Septimius, Publius, Aemilius and Martianus.

They walked the whole day under the scorching sun without eating or drinking; they were not allowed to stop until after sunset. They were given bread and dates, and a little water. As night fell they lay down among the rocks to rest, without even a rag to protect them from the bitter cold.

The emperor had not said a word since he had been forced to kneel before his enemy, and he was huddled in a lonely heap now, his back to a rock.

Metellus was overcome by his wife's death, which he still refused to accept, and tortured by the thought that he might not see his son ever again. He had never in his whole life found himself in a state so near desperation. And yet the sight of his emperor – a man who had dedicated his whole life to the service of his state and his people, who had fought with incredible bravery despite his years and who had been unbearably humiliated by the enemy – made him lay aside his own grief and pity the man's abasement.

He went to comfort him. 'You have nothing to reproach yourself for, Caesar. You put your life at risk in the hopes of achieving peace. Fate betrayed us. It could have happened to anyone.'

Valerian slowly turned his head towards him and raised his

shackled arms and bleeding wrists. 'Do you really believe that it was adverse fortune that brought this about?'

Metellus did not answer.

'Do you think they didn't see us from the walls of Edessa?'

'I think they saw us, Caesar.'

'And did you wonder why no one came to our aid? Why the cavalry wasn't sent out to defend us?'

'I can't explain it,' replied Metellus. 'But I'm certain they must have been forced into making such a choice.'

'I think instead that someone deliberately decided to abandon us to our fate, and that that someone was sure he would never have to account for his decision,' said Valerian darkly.

'You mustn't let your thoughts run away with you, Caesar,' reasoned Metellus. 'When we lost contact, we also lost the ability to understand the sequence of events. Anything may have happened. Perhaps it was evident from the top of the guard towers that rescue would have been impossible. Someone may have decided not to risk sending out exhausted, malnourished troops in a hopeless endeavour. But I'm convinced, Caesar, that they have a plan. Mark my words, they'll show up and free us in a matter of days. I know Lucius Domitius: he's a man who fears nothing and nobody. If he didn't come out – for reasons we cannot imagine – it means that the sortie has merely been put off. He could reappear at any time, trust me. He could be behind those rocks down there, see?'

Valerian stared at him with a look full of dismay. His face, hollowed out by strain and hardship, was a mask of stone. 'There's no one behind those rocks, Commander. No one. And no one will come looking for us. That's why I asked you to stay behind.'

Metellus bowed his head, wounded by those words. 'How can you say that?'

'Because the command of the fortress was in the hands of Cassius Silva.'

'I know what you're saying. I didn't want to mention him, because I know he is a personal friend of your son Gallienus, but you see, Clelia, my wife, before she died, said his name.' His eyes misted as he pronounced his wife's name. The wound was too fresh, his pain too great, to control his emotions.

'Your wife,' sighed Valerian, 'sacrificed herself to save us. Uselessly. If the gods heed me and allow our return, I swear that I will raise a monument to her, like the ones to the ancient heroines of our history, to perpetuate her memory and her fame. Unfortunately, in our current state we are slaves without names. And thus we are destined to remain. Silva abandoned us to our fate, and perhaps did even worse . . . I cannot convince myself even now that my own son, Gallienus, schemed with the Persians to arrange this wretched encounter.'

Metellus fell silent. What could he say to a man who just a few hours earlier was lord of half the world, and who was now at the complete mercy of a cruel, duplicitous enemy? A man burdened with chains, tormented by the cold and by his wounds, but above all by the suspicion of the most atrocious betrayal, that of his own son?

It was Valerian who broke the silence, as if he felt guilty for frustrating the attempt of that generous soldier to alleviate his pain and his humiliation. 'You must miss her terribly.'

'I would have preferred to die than to live without her,' replied Metellus. 'We fell in love when we were little more than children, and we ran away together to avoid the marriages that our families had decided for each of us.'

'I understand,' said the emperor, 'and I know that there is nothing that can soothe such a loss. But we must call on our courage and face our destiny like true soldiers of Rome. We must not give our jailers the satisfaction of seeing us beaten, the pleasure of seeing us humiliated.'

Metellus nodded wearily. 'There's one more thing that torments me, that gives me no peace.'

'What is it?' asked Valerian.

'The thought of my son, Titus. What will become of him? Who will protect him? I fear that Lucius Domitius no longer holds any power within the walls of Edessa, otherwise he would have come out for us. My wife is gone. I am powerless to protect the person who is dearest to me in all the world. Just think, I gave him my word that I would be back before nightfall. And I've never broken a promise to him, never in his whole life.'

'That promise was expressing a hope, my friend,' replied the emperor, 'and the fulfilment of our hopes never depends fully on us. But think of it as an oath. The oath of a just man reaches the throne of the gods.

'See that soldier?' he asked, pointing at a young, curly-haired legionary. 'He has just made the sign of the cross. He's making a vow as well. He's praying to his Christian god to save us all and bring us back home. They say he's a powerful god, more powerful than our own. I fear that Jupiter is too tired and too disappointed to do much, after watching the foolishness of men from up on his throne for so many centuries.'

Metellus looked at the soldier: his name was Aemilius and he was from his legion. A good boy, born in Messina, skilled with a sword, a fast runner, an excellent swimmer and no sluggard. Best to have men of courage with him in times of misfortune. He walked over to him. 'How's it going, soldier?'

'Well, Commander, given the circumstances.'

'That's what I like to hear. We must always consider that it could have gone worse. We're alive, we're all together, we're with our emperor. We're the centre of the world, remember that, as long as Caesar is alive and with us.'

Septimius pushed up on his elbows. 'Our men will come to free us, won't they, Commander?'

'I do hope so, but we can't be certain. We are in enemy territory and our best units are back in Edessa, under siege. Where are you from?' he asked, noting the youth's blond hair and blue eyes.

'From Condate, in Gaul.'

'They should send men like you to the northern front. You suffer the heat, and burn with this sun.'

'Well, I've got used to it, sir, but . . . yes, I'd like to go back to my own parts when this mess is over with.'

'My hopes lie in Lucius Domitius Aurelian. If he's given the chance, he'll stop at nothing to liberate us and the emperor.'

'Sword-in-Hand?' said Martianus, a legionary from the Seventh Ferrata. 'There's a man for you. I've never seen a soldier like him. He won't forget us, you can be sure of it. He never forgets his men. I've seen him risk his own skin more than once to bring in a wounded man, or even a dead one.'

Neither Balbus nor Quadratus, the two centurions, said a word. They were past their youth, and had seen it all; they'd learned that it was no use cherishing false hopes in life. They lay apart from the others, their heads leaning on a stone as if asleep, but Metellus knew well that they were wide awake and that nothing that was said would escape them.

'Stay close,' Metellus urged his men, 'one next to another, so you keep warm. It's going to get damn cold tonight and those bastards certainly won't be giving us any covers.'

'I'd rather hold some pretty girl – one of those little whores from Antioch with their firm tits – than snuggle up to a centurion! But I guess you can't have everything in life,' quipped Martianus.

'I've heard of worse fates!' Metellus smiled. 'Anyway, it's better to joke about things than to lose heart. Because from now on we can only count on ourselves. We must survive, men, survive at any cost. This, for the time being, is our only goal. None of us will be abandoned to his destiny; each one of us can count on the help of all the others. Together we can make it, believe me.

'I want you to know something: we're part of the imperial guard now and now, as never before, we must hold fast to our commitment and to our oath of loyalty to Caesar. No one will be allowed to go anywhere unless the emperor can come with us. Is that clear? Any attempt to do so will be punished as desertion and I myself will pronounce judgement and execute the sentence.' He snapped tight the chains that bound his hands.

Then he curled up next to a dry tamarisk trunk, covered his legs and arms with a little sand, and tried to rest. But every time he or any of the men moved, the rattling of their chains made him doubly restless and agitated, because the noise robbed him of his sleep and reminded him that he was a prisoner and a slave. Although he tried to call up all his strength of character, Clelia's expression as she was dying, the face of the son he'd never see again, filled his heart with infinite bitterness.

He prayed to his ancestors to send a sign of their benevolence, he prayed to Jupiter Optimus Maximus to succour the emperor, his representative upon the earth and his highest priest, but he was answered only by the long howl of the jackals that roamed the steppe in search of carrion.

In the end, fatigue won out over his anguish and pain and he fell into a deep sleep.

HE WAS KICKED AWAKE by one of the guards. A servant distributed a handful of dates and their march resumed.

They were heading east, following the southern slopes of the Taurus chain, clearly going towards the interior of the Persian empire, through the harshest and most inhospitable of regions. Water was distributed first to the horses and camels and then to the prisoners, if there was any left. They marched without resting, and anyone who lagged behind was immediately whipped by the guards. It was obvious that no one was concerned about their survival and that their lives had no value. They did not even seem to be worth their price as slaves.

On the second day of their journey, they were joined by another group of prisoners who probably came from the south: they had dark skin and tight curls and wore simple raw-linen tunics. At the centre of the caravan were the camels with the supplies and water bags; the prisoners marched at their sides and were flanked on the outside by guards on horseback. Behind them was a squad of about a hundred warriors, among whom Metellus thought he could make out the mysterious person with the slanted eyes whom he had seen on the day of the battle. He seemed to be free to move along the column as he liked, but Metellus noticed that the Persian soldiers never lost sight of him.

On the third day, the guards took the chains off their feet and this was a great relief, making it much easier to walk and easing the pain of the sores that had formed on their ankles, attracting swarms of gnats and horseflies.

'This is a good sign,' said Metellus to his comrades. 'It means we're worth something to them. They must have plans to put us to work somewhere, and so they're interested in keeping us alive.'

'Look!' cried Septimius at the same time. 'Our gear!' He pointed at the only mule-drawn cart advancing with the column.

'Good blades and good breastplates,' commented Aemilius. 'Why should they throw them away?'

'They're trophies for them. There's the emperor's armour as well,' observed Quadratus.

'If only we could get our hands on them,' said Lucianus, who was half Roman and half Greek, from Nicomedia. 'We could still give these bastards a lesson.'

'Save your breath,' Balbus shushed him, 'for when we get to our destination. Nothing good will be waiting for us there – if we even get there alive, that is.'

The emperor maintained an air of great dignity, despite the privations of the long march. His back was straight, his gaze firm, his brow high. His pure-white hair contrasted with his sun-darkened skin and his proud bearing won him a certain respect from even the guards, who almost certainly knew his identity. He had withdrawn into silence, into a kind of austere inner solitude.

He showed no signs of hunger or thirst, even after hours of fasting, and would wait until food or drink was offered to him; his men never failed him in this respect, trying to honour him in every way possible and to alleviate the hardships of that inhuman journey.

If the guards struck him with a whip or with the shafts of their spears, he bore the pain stoically, without showing signs of weakness or crying out. It seemed that his only goal was to maintain his honour and dignity, more so even than his life.

They walked for over a month, crossing the Tigris on pontoon bridges. The hills of eastern Mesopotamia began to loom before them, and then the pinnacles of a great mountain chain.

'They're taking us to Persia,' said Metellus.

'How do you know, Commander?' asked Quadratus.

'Those are the Elam mountains,' replied Metellus. 'They mark the limits of the Persian plateau which extends for one thousand five hundred miles to the border with Bactriana.'

'Have you been here before?'

'No, of course not, but I've studied the expeditions of Crassus in Mesopotamia, of Mark Antony in Armenia, and most of all, of Alexander.'

Valerian turned. 'They're bringing us to the heart of their empire, from where we're unlikely to escape.'

'You're right,' replied Metellus. 'But I'm sure that your son Gallienus will already be negotiating a ransom. It won't be long now before we're taking this route in the other direction. At least you, Caesar.'

Valerian shot him a glance of proud, aching intensity and said, 'You know that's not true. And, in any case, I would never agree to return on my own.'

For fifteen days they clambered up steep paths. Through the gullies and gorges of the Zagros mountains, through the desolate, stony heights inhabited by a handful of wild nomads who watched from a distance as the column slowly filed past, amid the scuttling of the horses' hoofs and the jangling of the prisoners' chains.

As they ascended, the air became cleaner and clearer and the Mesopotamian plain behind them seemed a yellowish expanse veiled by milky vapours. The vegetation changed at nearly every bend in the road: the palms became smaller and sparser, until they were completely replaced by oleander, tamarisk and broom, and then by majestic cedars and pines. Water roared through the rocky ravines, between walls of black basalt and white limestone, its gurgling further teasing and tormenting the parched prisoners, disoriented by the scorching sun that burned their skin, their eyes, their minds.

Then the plateau appeared before them: endless, blinding, arid and inhospitable, swept by a constant wind that cracked their lips, made their noses bleed and reddened their eyes. They stopped to rest only when a rare oasis permitted it; verdant spots in humid little hollows where dwarf pines, carob trees and every sort of thorny plant grew. The grasses were quite dry and hard and released an intense aroma when the horses and mules trod upon them.

In the evenings, when the guards ordered them to stop at an oasis, there were a few moments of relief for the prisoners, almost of pleasure. The sun descended to the horizon like an immense blazing ball, setting the sky on fire and cloaking the tamarisk and acacia fronds in golden light. The wind ceased or calmed to a tepid breeze, the air filled with the intense fragrance of exotic plants, the spring waters were rippled by gusts of wind, and the long cries of the jackals as they hailed the rising moon sounded like melancholy pleas.

At that hour of dusk, each of them remembered what they had left behind: their comrades, their wives and children, the girls they had made promises to, the elderly parents who would await them in vain. Little by little, as night fell and the sky filled with a myriad stars, that brief moment of solace turned into a stinging sense of anguish and impotence, into dark foreboding.

They would try to react then, imagining the future in scenes which inevitably involved escaping and returning. Or they would repeat the old stories they'd heard tell so many times by old centurions who seemed born wearing armour and a helmet.

'Have you ever heard about the Lost Legion?' Publius, a soldier from the Second Augusta who was born in Spoletum, said one night.

'I have,' replied Rufus, his reddish-haired comrade, a crack javelin-thrower, renowned for his skill in both battle and athletic contests. 'But I've always thought it was just a legend. When an entire division is annihilated, they always have to make up something or say it vanished who knows where, so as not to frighten the troops.'

'No, you're wrong this time,' broke in Quadratus. 'The Lost Legion really does exist – or, that is, it did exist – but no one knows what happened to it.'

'It that so, Commander?' Aemilius asked Metellus, seeking credible support for such a fantastic tale.

'It does seem so,' replied Metellus. 'They say that when Triumvir Crassus was trapped at Carrhae by an army of Parthians from Surena, one of his legions managed to break out at night and avoid being destroyed at the hands of the enemy like all the others. It's said that they succeeded in making it to safety, with their eagle and everything.'

'And then?' prompted Antoninus.

'And then the legion disappeared, as if swallowed up into nothingness. Not a single man ever returned to his homeland.'

Silence fell and for a little while all they could hear was the light breeze rustling the leafy carob branches.

'Well, what do you think became of them?' asked Aemilius.

Metellus shrugged. 'Anything could have happened to them. They may have ended up in one of the deserted stretches that they say exist in central Asia – arid, salt-covered lands that extend for hundreds and hundreds of miles. It's easy to lose your bearings in such a place, what with the blinding light and the salt dust that envelops everything.

'They may have wandered into the territory of savages and been hacked to pieces. Or perhaps they were put to work garrisoning border lines so remote that they were never able to make their way back. But the truth is . . . the truth is . . . we'll never know, I believe. Try to sleep now, men. The march will be even tougher tomorrow.'

The emperor would sometimes assemble his officers: Legate Marcus Metellus Aquila, the two centurions, Sergius Balbus and Aelius Quadratus, and even *optio* Antoninus Salustius, as if to call a session of his general staff. But the order of the day was always the same: the treatment of their injuries, the hunger and thirst they suffered, the disheartenment spreading among the men, the possible escape attempts that must be discouraged since they could only end in capture and atrocious torture.

This was confirmed one day at the height of summer when a Nabataean prisoner who had only recently joined the caravan managed to get away in the middle of a sandstorm. He was recaptured after just three days.

The guards stripped him naked, tied him to four stakes stuck into the ground, then cut his eyelids and urinated on his defenceless eyes. They left him there for the ants and scorpions.

They heard his screams of pain for hours and hours, until the wind carried them away.

Once Metellus had the impression that the mysterious youth he had first seen in Edessa had tried to escape, but it seemed he had only taken a ride on horseback. He made his way up to a mountain ridge, where he was soon joined by a couple of horsemen from their guard. All three remained there to enjoy the sunset, apparently, before returning to their tents.

They arrived at their destination after three long months of marching, all of them, without losses. They were very thin and exhausted by their ordeal, but they were all alive and this seemed like a miracle in itself.

Their destination was a turquoise mine in the heart of Persia, a hellish place called Aus Daiwa. There they would live for as long as possible. And there they would die, one after another, unless a miracle changed the course of their destiny.

3

Shapur raised the siege at Edessa, apparently satisfied with the enormous results he had obtained.

In the entire millennium-long history of Rome, the only event comparable to this defeat was the Carthaginian capture of consul Attilius Regulus during the First Punic War five hundred years earlier. But Regulus was no more than a magistrate – albeit a very high-ranking one – of the Republican order, who had a one-year term and could be replaced. Licinius Valerian was the emperor, the father of the nation: his humiliation and his imprisonment were a catastrophe with unimaginable consequences.

Gallienus entered the city a month later and was greeted by Cassius Silva with full honours, although the circumstances made any kind of celebration unthinkable. The new sovereign was nonetheless hailed by the troops drawn up in formal array and he reviewed them dressed in purple and wearing the imperial diadem. With his top lip folded over the bottom in the piqued expression of a public functionary, his demeanour contrasted greatly with the sumptuous robes he wore and the martial atmosphere that surrounded him. He went to the podium to deliver his first public address.

'Soldiers!' he said. 'What has happened has caused me great consternation and deep pain. The imprisonment of my father is the consequence of the deceitfulness and betrayal of our enemy. You are not to be held responsible in any way, nor are your commanders. I know that many of your comrades were treacherously murdered, and I know that others, including Legate

Marcus Metellus Aquila, fell in combat or were taken prisoner along with my father. Their fate pains us no less than Caesar's misfortune. We pray that the gods may protect and preserve them. I have also learned that the legate's wife, noble Clelia, was killed by Persian arrows as she sought to reach her husband . . .'

'Roman arrows!' yelled out an anonymous voice.

Gallienus continued unperturbed: '. . . an example of heroism worthy of the best tradition of Roman women. Their son will be entrusted to the imperial house, instructed and raised at state expense. I shall immediately commence with negotiations to ransom my father. No sum will be too high for achieving his freedom . . .'

A voice rang out in the vast courtyard: 'It is not with gold but with iron that the honour of Rome must be redeemed, Gallienuo!'

A stunned silence followed. The phrase that had rained down from nowhere, the phrase that they'd all known since childhood, learned at their school desks, pronounced by a Republican hero seven centuries earlier, deeply shocked all those present. Gallienus stared wordlessly at Silva, who was craning his head to see where the voice had come from.

Another man cried out from the ranks, 'Free Lucius Domitius Aurelian!'

More voices joined in, and more still, until the cry swelled into a rhythmic, imperious demand that it was impossible to deny an answer to. Gallienus said something to Silva, who whispered back into his ear. He who aspired to be the new Caesar raised his arm then to request silence, and the shouts slowly died down.

'Legate Lucius Domitius Aurelian was merely temporarily relieved of his duties in order to avoid conflict within the command structure at a moment of great emergency. On the other hand, that moment – with its unhappy result – is behind us now, and there is no longer any reason to keep such a measure in force. Lucius Domitius will thus be reinstated in his rank and his role as commander of the Tenth Gemina Legion.'

Loud cheers rose from the assembled troops. Domitius soon arrived, accompanied by twelve praetorians, and Gallienus himself presented him with his sword. Without saying a word, the legate fastened it to his belt, made a slight bow, then gave Cassius Silva a withering look and descended among his legionaries, taking his place in the ranks like a simple soldier.

GALLIENUS REMAINED in the city for ten days, during which he called a meeting of the commanders in charge of the line of defence on the eastern front. Among them was Septimius Odenatus, a renowned officer who commanded the garrison of Palmyra, a large city on the caravan route east of Damascus. He was also in charge of the auxiliary Osroenian and Syrian troops stationed at the Dura Europus fortress on the Euphrates river.

Lucius Domitius was summoned as well. He had made no secret of his implacable hatred for Cassius Silva, but his huge popularity among the troops made it impossible to marginalize him. Best to find a more prudent method of getting him out of the way, and so Gallienus appointed him to deal with the Sarmatian invasion on the border at the Danube: a dangerous task, and very difficult, given the disproportionate strength of the barbarian troops to his own.

More than a few of those present imagined that the destination had been suggested by Silva himself, who was soon thereafter named prefect of the praetorian guard, an appointment that made him the most powerful person in the empire after the emperor himself. Domitius accepted the charge without batting an eye: Sword-in-Hand would certainly never refuse a call to arms.

Before leaving, he asked to be received by Gallienus. Others were present in the audience chamber: Septimius Odenatus, commander of the Euphrates forces, and his wife, Zainab, famous throughout the East for her extraordinary beauty. Odenatus was so jealous of her that he took her with him wherever he went. Domitius looked into her eyes for a moment and she met his gaze. Then he turned to Gallienus.

'I want you to know,' he began, 'that I consider you regent *pro tempore* while your father is a prisoner, and it is only in this capacity that I recognize your right to give me orders. I will not call you "Caesar", a title which has no significance in your father's absence. I will simply call you by name.'

Gallienus said nothing, but the expression on his face left no doubt about the disappointment and rage that that open challenge had provoked in him. Rage even worse for being impotent: touching Lucius Domitius Aurelian could mean mutiny or worse.

And he went on: 'I will fight as I always have and carry out your orders as best I can. There is only one thing I ask of you: assign me the care of Metellus's son, little Titus. He has lost both of his parents and his mother died a violent death. I will raise him as if he were my own son, and I will remind him every day of his father's bravery and of his mother's intelligence and courage. I will protect him even at the cost of my own life.'

Gallienus frowned. 'Unfortunately I cannot satisfy your request, Lucius Domitius. The line of combat is not a suitable place to raise a child. Your mission is dangerous, and that's precisely why I have chosen you: I know you are one of the best officers of the entire army. That boy needs to be educated and cared for. He will study with the best pedagogues and receive the care that the valour of his father and the sacrifice of his mother have earned for him. I thank you for offering, your request does you honour, but do not hold it against me if I cannot grant your wish.'

Domitius bit his lip, as he was wont to do to control his outbursts of temper, then said: 'I am sure the boy will be treated as he deserves to be. But I want you to keep in mind what I'm about to tell you. If anything happens to him, anything at all if he falls on the stairs or has an accident while playing, or swimming, or if he should fall ill, or even get a stomach ache from eating too much – I will hold you personally responsible and I will hunt you down and demand an explanation, wherever you may be.'

'Do you dare to threaten me?' shouted Gallienus. 'Do you dare to impose conditions on your emperor?'

'My emperor is a prisoner of the Persians and I am sure that you will ensure his return as soon as possible, that you will pay any sum for his ransom, as you yourself declared and solemnly promised. But if I don't see Valerian coming back with his escort in a reasonable amount of time, I will hold you responsible for this also. Farewell.'

He gave Gallienus no time to react, but turned on his heel and walked away between the lines of praetorians, holding his helmet under his left arm and his right hand on the hilt of his sword, as always.

He left with his legion the next day amid the blaring of trumpets and the waving of standards, setting off down the road for Caesarea, and then on to Ancyra and Byzantium, heading for Sirmium, where the general headquarters of the Danubian army was, under the command of Publius Festus, a fine officer and brave soldier.

Gallienus and Silva breathed a sigh of relief when they saw the rearguard of the Tenth Gemina disappearing round a bend, headed north. They left three regiments of the Second Augusta in Edessa and returned to Antioch with Metellus's son.

It was not easy to drag him away. He yelled that his father had promised to return and that he would wait for him; he wanted to be home when his father got back.

One of Gallienus's servants grabbed him by the arm and said, 'Your father is never coming back. He's surely dead by now.'

Titus bit his hand and tried to run away, but he was caught and dragged off as he screamed, kicked and cried.

From Antioch they sailed in midsummer to Ravenna and then Milan, where Gallienus established his residence.

Titus was handed over to the palace master, who was in charge of educating him, but the little boy was completely unmanageable. He refused to eat and would see no one. He hid under his bed so as not to be found and tried continually to escape his prison, so that they finally had to post a guard to keep a watchful eye on him.

Gallienus, already absorbed in affairs of state, was nonetheless worried about the boy, who was rapidly wasting away. He remembered the words of Lucius Domitius Aurelian well, and knew that Sword-in-Hand never made empty threats. He had the child's pedagogue – a shrewish and authoritative old man – replaced by a fifteen-year-old slavegirl.

'Who are you?' asked Titus as soon as he saw her.

'I'm the person who's been assigned to serve you. My name is Tillia.'

'I don't need anyone. Go away.'

'It's me who needs you.'

Titus eyed her suspiciously.

'I'd like to convince you to eat something.'

'I'm not hungry.'

'Your appetite will pick up if you eat.'

'I'm not hungry, I said.'

'If I don't convince you to eat, they'll beat me. The palace master is an old son of a bitch.'

'You got that right.'

'And he likes hurting people.'

'I'll bet he does.'

Tillia came close and sat down beside him. 'I've brought you a cup of hot broth. I made it myself. You'll like it.'

Titus said nothing.

'If you don't eat, you'll die. And when your father comes back, he'll die of heartache. Is that what you want?'

'They told me that my father's already dead.'

'They lied.'

Titus lit up and opened his mouth to ask how she could say such a thing, and Tillia took the opportunity to spoon in a bit of broth.

'How is it?' she asked.

The little boy replied with a question: 'Why do you think

they lied to me? I mean, about my father dying? And what do you know anyway? You're only a slave.'

Tillia gave him another spoonful of broth, taking advantage of the breach she'd managed to open in his defences, and answered, 'Because your father is Commander Aquila. He's a living legend. Everyone talks about him. And everyone says he's been captured by the Persians, along with Emperor Valerian. His body was never found, although they did find the bodies of plenty of men who died that day in Edessa.'

'Were you there too?' asked Titus.

'No. I came later, with Gallienus's retinue, along with the cooks and the stewards accompanying the court. But it happened shortly before I arrived, and there were still soldiers going out to retrieve the bodies once the Persians had gone.'

'Well, what difference does it make? If my father is a prisoner and a slave I'll never see him again anyway.'

'No, that's not true. Gallienus has promised that he'll pay the Persians a ransom to free the emperor. If the emperor is freed, he'll surely come back with your father and the others who were captured with him.'

'And when will this happen?'

'Soon, very soon, I think. Surely they're already negotiating.'

'What if they don't agree?'

'People in power always find a way to agree.'

'I hope you're right. It's funny . . . you sure know a lot of things for a slave.'

'That's normal. Slaves are not considered people and everyone speaks freely around us, as if we were statues, or pieces of furniture. Now, all you have to do is get your strength back, so that the day your father returns you'll be able to give him a big hug.'

Titus finished the broth and then, after Tillia had gone, went to the window and leaned his chin on the sill. He could see the busy scurrying of servants and soldiers in the courtyard below, which reminded him of the fortress at Edessa and the training palaestra where he had often watched his father practising with his sword and javelin. He remembered the caravans that would come from Dura and Damascus, from Palmyra and Thapsacus, from Nisibi and Ctesiphon: the gaily coloured fabrics, the engraved weapons, the glass and the gems, the decorated ostrich eggs, the peacock feathers, the exotic animals. He was homesick for Edessa and homesick for his parents – for his mother, whom he would never see again, and for his father, the hero he admired more than any human being he had ever met. He hoped deep in his heart that he was still alive and tried to imagine where he might be at that very moment; if he was hungry or cold, if his jailers were humiliating him. He watched as the sky darkened in the east and tried to calculate the distance that separated them, then he closed his eyes and tried to picture him, sitting under a palm tree maybe, or perhaps marching through immense far-away lands behind swaying camels. He sharpened all his little-boy senses to try to hear his thoughts and feel the affection he so badly needed.

MILAN WAS HUMID and hazy, always covered by a shroud of fog that only rarely opened to allow a glimpse of the Alpine peaks in the distance. When Titus was allowed to go out with one of his tutors or guardians, he never found anything that really interested him, except for the pedlars' stalls in the forum on market days.

As time passed, Tillia became his only friend, but she was just with him when he was inside the palace. Outside he was always accompanied by men and always closely watched.

One day, while he was in the garden with Tillia, he asked, 'What is a hostage?'

Tillia looked at him in surprise. 'Where did you hear that word?'

'One of my guardians used it, while talking to my tutor.'

'But they weren't talking about you.'

'Oh yes, they were, I think. Why? Is it a bad word?'

'No, not so bad. It means a special guest. A guest who's treated well, but who can't go off whenever he likes.'

'Then it was me.'

'I'm afraid so. But it could be worse, believe me.'

'Maybe. But I still really miss my parents. When do you think I'll see my father again?'

Tillia looked into his eyes. There was an intensity of feeling in them she had rarely seen in her whole life, a hope so strong that to disappoint him would be cruel and to deceive him, vile. She answered, 'It's hard to say. We don't know where Emperor Valerian and his guard are being held prisoner. We don't know how far away they've been taken, or how negotiations are proceeding. I'd say that we could reasonably expect from six months to a year.'

'So long?' asked Titus.

'Time goes quickly, little one. If my predictions come true, we'll be very lucky.'

'But things might still go badly, mightn't they?'

Tillia touched his cheek. 'Ill fortune does exist, I'm afraid. Look at me. I was born a slave and I've never met my parents. Still, I can't tell you how much I miss them, how much I want them. Not a day or night goes by that I don't try to imagine how they look, their voices, even only their names.' As she spoke, she saw the little boy's eyes misting and his whole face take on an expression of distress. She felt bad at the mere thought of what was going through his head and tried to find the words to encourage him. 'But we must trust in the gods and in the virtues of men. Your father is a great man and so is the emperor, I'm told. Great men always take paths that ordinary men don't think of. And you know what else? Good thoughts bring good luck. Isn't there something that your father did, or something he said, that you can take as a good omen? You know what I mean?'

The child drew a long sigh and was quiet for a while. Then he said: 'Yes, there is something.'

'Well?'

'That morning my father said he'd be back before nightfall.'

'That's a beautiful promise.'

'But he didn't keep it.'

'That doesn't matter. It wasn't his fault. It's what you hope that counts, believe me.'

She took him by the hand and brought him inside the palace, where his tutor awaited him for his usual grammar lesson.

LUCIUS DOMITIUS AURELIAN reached Sirmium, in Pannonia, towards the end of August and he and his legion took up quarters in the vast camp built on the right bank of the Danube.

Publius Festus, commander of the Danubian army, greeted him with great cordiality. 'I would never have even hoped to receive such reinforcements. One of the best commanders of the empire! With a legion that's never been beaten: the Tenth Gemina. I thank whoever had such a marvellous idea.'

'It was Gallienus, on the advice of Cassius Silva.'

'You don't seem happy about it. Antioch would have been much better, I imagine, or Alexandria, but you'll get used to it here. Although you won't find many distractions. A game of dice with some centurion when you're lucky.'

'I don't gamble,' replied Domitius.

'Right. So I've heard. Sword-in-Hand is an absolutely upstanding officer. The old-fashioned kind. As you see, your fame has preceded you . . . At any rate, the women are beautiful out this way and like a good tumble.'

'Women are not the issue. When do we attack?'

'What?'

'I asked you when we attack. I'd like to get this over and done with and go back to my base in Edessa. There's much I have to do there.'

Festus was appalled. 'Legate, I don't think you understand what's going on here. Beyond the river are more than seventy thousand barbarians armed to the teeth and well accustomed to fighting on an endless plain on their untiring horses. We're lucky that they haven't crossed over and attacked our positions en masse. We have three legions in all – including yours – and if we had to fight on the open field we'd have no hope.'

'I'm not saying we should send all our forces out at once. I'd like to ask you to let me resolve the situation. Me and my legion.'

Festus shook his head incredulously. 'I wouldn't dream of it! It would be total suicide, and I will need you and your men if those barbarians ever do attack.'

'So, then, what should I do, just sit here and wait?'

'Wait, Legate, wait. And hope they don't cross over to this side.'

Lucius Domitius fixed his commander in the eye. 'I've never waited for anything my whole life,' he said. Then he got up, nodded briefly and left.

4

THE AUS DAIWA MINE was located in an isolated spot on the upland plains, in a completely barren area beaten by a ceaseless wind that never died down before dusk. A well, a couple of shacks for the miners, a mud-brick building for the guards and the armoury were the only structures apparent at first. Until one saw the gigantic mortar for crushing the minerals at the centre of a wide, open square. It was operated by a winch that pulled a rope held taut by a large pulley. The winch was driven by half a dozen bars, each of which was pushed by four men. When the hammer was raised to the highest point on the frame, the pin that locked the winch wheel in place was extracted, the outer wheel was released and turned backwards and the hammer fell hard on the rocks piled up at the base, crushing them. Then the winch was cranked up again, sighing, for another Sisyphean round.

The kitchen was a simple open fire where the troops' food was prepared.

As soon as the caravan of prisoners from Edessa arrived, a jailer greeted them with shoves and kicks, lining them up in front of the shacks. His long lecture in Persian was translated line by line by another prisoner: a bony, toothless old man who said his name was Uxal.

'This is the place where you will die. It doesn't matter when, but it will be here. No one has ever managed to escape from this place: the closest village, as you will have seen as you arrived, is three days' journey away. The next is seven.

'If anyone is tempted to escape, he should know that he will be chased and recaptured within a few hours, and impaled in the middle of the square. Our executioner is highly skilled. He can insert a stake in a man's body and run it through from one end to the other without piercing a vital organ, so that he will live for days.

'Rebellion – any type of rebellion – will receive the same kind of treatment. Simple disobedience or the failure to produce the quantity of mineral required of each one of you will be punished with ten lashes or with three days at the stake with no food and no water. The quantity of rough stones to be produced each day is fifty pounds. At night you will be shackled. By day your chains will be removed so you can work better. The straw in the huts will be changed once a month. When one of you dies, the rest of you must throw the carcass into that crevasse over there.

'This is all you need to know.'

When he had finished speaking, the jailer opened one of the shacks and Uxal accompanied the new arrivals inside: twenty-three men in all, including the twelve Romans.

The old man pointed out their straw pallets and fixed a shackle with a ring to one of each man's ankles. He attached a chain secured to the floor with another ring and a padlock. Uxal fettered himself as well and handed the key over to the jailer, who went out and closed the door behind him.

Uxal gestured for everyone to keep silent until the jailer's steps faded into the distance, then spoke softly. 'Now you can talk, but they mustn't hear you outside. If they hear us, they'll punish us, and I can assure you that that's no laughing matter. Your lives are worth nothing here.'

'How do you know our language?' asked Metellus, who was near him.

'As a boy I spent ten years in the service of a Roman merchant of precious stones who had a warehouse at Buprasium, in the gulf.'

'How did you end up here?'

'The merchant sold me to a Persian nobleman to pay off his

debts, even though I was a free man! I could not stand being a slave and I tried to flee, and this is where they brought me.'

'That means you can survive a long time here,' observed Lucianus. 'You're an old man.'

'Don't count on it,' said Uxal. 'I'm alive because they need me. I'm good at handling the turquoise. If nothing else, that son of a bitch who sold me taught me something that's helped me to survive, if you can consider this living.

'Now, let me explain a few things. Let's start with the food: the miners eat only dry beans and fish meal, which is distributed once a day in the morning. For dinner there's a bowl of murky soup with a revolting taste, whose ingredients I've never been able to guess. All the better, probably. Water is rationed because there's very little of it. Don't drink much during the day, when you're sweating a lot. Drink in the evening, when it's cooler, so your body can use it all. Sometimes the food never gets here because there's been a sandstorm or for other reasons I'm unaware of. When this happens, the jailers eat and we don't. Cockroaches can help you survive, and so can mice. I roast them on the coals from the forge and, let me tell you, they're not at all bad. Otherwise you can eat them raw. You get used to it.

'As far as your attitude: forget you are a man, forget you have a name, a country you come from, a family. Forget you have any honour or personal pride, or you'll be dead before you know it. Never react to provocations, don't ever look a jailer in the eye, don't help a comrade who is ill. Any kind of group solidarity is seen as a threat, as a possible conspiracy.

'These people, who watch us and punish us for nothing at all, often do so only because if something happens their punishment would be as bad as ours, or worse. The Persians have incredible imaginations when it comes to torture . . .'

'I know,' said Metellus. 'I've read Ctesia's *Persian Memories*.'

Uxal shook his head. 'What's that?'

'The story of a Greek doctor who lived at the court of Emperor Artaxerxes.'

'Ah,' replied Uxal. 'Anyway, you in particular have got me worried. You're a soldier, aren't you?'

'We all are.'

'But you more than the others. The way you look is a permanent challenge. Your eyes are defiant. Hide both if you want to live.'

'I have to live,' said Metellus, 'and so do my comrades.'

'Fine. Then do as I've said and you may last a little longer.'

As he spoke, the expressions of the others darkened; the signs of consternation were painted on the faces of those men who had all been accustomed for years to facing the worst dangers, to risking their skins constantly. But the prospect of a life without hope, a life of degradation and humiliation, dragging on for who knows how long only to meet an abominable death, made many of them think of suicide, a much more honourable end for soldiers.

It seemed that Uxal had read their thoughts when he began to speak again after a brief interruption. 'Tomorrow you'll see that hell exists, but remember that there's worse: the third level, the bottom galleries. Whoever ends up down there is branded first, and then never again allowed to see the light of day. Only cadavers come out of those dark tunnels.

'Some of you will probably decide to commit suicide. That's the rule: usually two or three out of ten, but that depends on the type of men you are. I don't know you yet, so I couldn't say. I've seen men crush their skulls against a rock, or throw themselves into one of the wells or run themselves through on their pickaxes. It's a choice I respect. I've considered it myself more than once. But if you want my advice, try to keep going. You never know what the future holds. To tell the truth, I've seen men leave here.'

'How many?' asked Publius.

'Three . . . in twenty years.'

'Not that many,' commented Quadratus sarcastically.

'Depends on your point of view,' replied Uxal.

'And do you know how they managed to get out?' asked Balbus.

'That I don't know.'

'Ransom?' asked Metellus.

'Maybe. But I'm not certain.'

'We are grateful for the warnings and the information you've given us, but I'd say it's best to get some rest now. Tomorrow we begin work in the mine.'

'Don't mention it. We're all in the same shit. I thought you should know the way things are. One last thing: don't trust anybody and don't speak with anyone you don't know. Everyone's a spy here. Ready to sell you off, or report you, for an extra spoonful of soup.'

'You're a spy as well, I suppose,' said Metellus.

'No.'

'And why not?'

'Because I have my dignity. I've never lost it because I've always kept it hidden. Not all men are the same. That's why I've never decided to take my own life. I've met a lot of interesting people in here, after all. Many of them have died, lucky them. Others are still alive.'

'Thanks for the advice. And now, if you don't mind, we should try to get some sleep.'

'Just one more thing . . . a question.'

'Yes?'

'There was a strange rumour going around the camp before you arrived.'

'Oh, really?'

'That's right.' He nodded. 'They were saying that among you is a person of exceptional importance . . .'

Metellus did not bite.

Uxal leaned forward and examined the faces of the newcomers. 'I wonder which one of you is this big fish . . . this great man . . .'

Metellus still did not say a word. Uxal's gaze rested on

Valerian. 'It's you. No doubt about it. It can't be anyone but you . . . the emperor of the Romans. Incredible!' His lip twisted. 'Human destiny makes no sense . . . no sense at all. You who commanded half the world are now less important than this toothless old fellow you have in front of you.'

Metellus, who was closest to him, grabbed his miserable rags. 'That's enough, old man. One more word and you'll never feel like joking again.'

Uxal cracked a half-smile. 'Calm down, General, it's not me that the emperor here has to fear. It's just that I've never seen an emperor before. If I had died yesterday, I would have missed this opportunity.' He lay down on his pallet but continued to mutter to himself, 'Unbelievable . . . Who would have believed such a thing . . .'

Metellus lay down as well. 'Try to rest, men, and try to survive. At any cost. Even suicide is desertion. Remember that.'

IT WAS STILL DARK when they were awakened and their chains removed. A jailer gave each of them a shovel and a pickaxe and Metellus noticed that, as the tools were being handed out, the armed guards were never more than a few feet away, their swords unsheathed. Groups of five men at a time were made to step on a platform tied to a winch with ropes. They were lowered underground to the point where the tunnels branched off. Each man was given a lamp to light up the dark, narrow burrows of the mine.

When the newcomers arrived at the worksite, Metellus took the emperor aside. 'Caesar, you must not strain yourself. There are eleven of us and we're more than capable of producing your share as well. It will only mean a slight effort on our part, but your life is precious, and it is our duty to protect it in every way we can.'

Valerian replied in a calm, firm voice, 'No. Here we are all the same. I will do my part. It is not right that you sacrifice yourselves for me.'

The others insisted as well. 'Caesar,' urged Quadratus, 'you must preserve your strength for the day you will be ransomed. You are responsible for the empire. You are the father of our nation and you must return, whatever the cost.'

'I'm nothing now, my friends. Nothing more than a companion in misfortune. I'm sorry to disappoint your hopes, but if my son had tried to ransom me, we would know something by now. Messages between governors fly much faster than the caravan that brought us here. And now let's get to work. The time we have is barely enough to fulfil the daily task that our jailers have set for us.' He took an axe and began to strike the rock with considerable strength. The fragments flew in every direction.

Metellus, Quadratus, Balbus and Antoninus grasped their own pickaxes and began digging. The others began to gather the fragments, to load the baskets and pile them up in the main gallery where the elevator hoist was. One of the jailers noted the number of baskets per miner, then gave a signal and the hoist rose creaking towards the light.

As work proceeded, the tunnel was invaded by a dense dust which settled on the miners, turning them into white ghosts, stealing away their breath and burning their eyes. The airless atmosphere sucked away their energy and the heat made their toil unbearable.

The day seemed interminable and, when Metellus and the others were lifted to the surface, they could barely stand up. The awful-smelling soup tasted delectable and the water soothing their scorched throats a balm.

'Everything is relative,' Uxal commented after he had distributed the water. 'This stuff would make anyone vomit under normal circumstances, but after such a hellish day, it's not bad, is it?'

'You're right, old man,' replied Antoninus, swallowing the soup with his eyes closed.

'Listen well to what I have to say. Beginning tomorrow, cover your noses and mouths with damp rags, or in a very short while, you'll no longer be able to draw breath.'

Valerian approached him. 'Why are you doing this for us? The man who made you a slave was a Roman. You should hate us.'

Uxal's toothless mouth broke into a grin. He evidently felt very honoured to be conversing on such intimate terms with the emperor of the Romans. 'My master was a son of a bitch before he was a Roman – there are plenty of those everywhere. The reason why I want to help you? I don't know. Maybe because you act and speak like civilized people.'

'We have mines as well, with slaves working them exactly the way we are now.'

'Slaves exist everywhere and they will always exist in some form, but when I travelled in your world I also saw temples, squares, libraries, fountains and aqueducts, streets like nowhere else in the world, public baths with hot and cold water . . . Once I was in a city called Lambaesis: it was bang in the middle of the desert, in the middle of nowhere. Yet there was a library full of books and a market with clerks checking the weights on the scales and the capacity of the wine and oil jars. There were baths and fountains fed with the water of an aqueduct that came from hundreds of miles away. And when I travelled, every night I stopped in a place where there was something to eat, a clean bed to sleep in and soldiers to keep thieves, swindlers and murderers away.'

Valerian was moved. That humble man who had travelled through his empire was recalling the very aspects of civilized living that he had sought to revive during the years he had ruled; the years of his government. 'Your words give me pleasure,' he said, 'even though they are not completely justified. All you know of the Persian world is what you've seen in this hellhole. If you had visited Persepolis, Pasargade, Babylonia, Susa, you'd surely be speaking of them with enthusiasm.'

'That might be,' replied Uxal, 'but each man can only speak of his own experiences. You know, my dream was to be a Roman citizen. Can you believe that?'

'I can,' replied Valerian. 'It's still the dream of many. For what it's worth, I have the power to grant your wish. I have not been deprived of my office and thus, by virtue of the humanity you have shown towards me and my companions, I, Licinius Valerian Caesar, declare you a Roman citizen.'

Uxal glanced at the others with an amazed expression, then looked the emperor in the eye. 'I'm a Roman citizen. Incredible. If they'd told me, I would never have believed it. What can I do?'

Balbus spoke up. 'Well, first of all you can vote and elect public officials, and you can bequeathe an inheritance and the right of citizenship to your children. In case of trial you are entitled to appeal against the sentence and if you are condemned to death you have the right to a rapid execution by decapitation . . .'

'Hmmm . . . all advantages that I fear I'll never be able to enjoy, but I'm happy all the same. Thank you, Emperor.'

Valerian smiled and went to take his ration of food from the bucket.

Quadratus approached Uxal. 'Tell me something, old man, now that we are compatriots. Hasn't anyone ever thought of using his work tools to take out the jailers and the guards?'

'I imagine so,' replied Uxal. 'But no one has ever tried, at least since I've been here.'

'Why, if I may ask?'

'Because after a month in the mine you've barely got the strength to pull yourself out of that hole in the evening and crawl to your pallet of stinking straw. Do you think you'd be able to overcome well-armed and nourished men who greatly outnumber you?'

'I get it,' mumbled Quadratus.

'Good. Now lie down, because the jailer will soon be here to shackle us.'

They heard the sound of a bolt being drawn and Uxal gestured to everyone to stay down. The jailer entered and passed a chain through the rings that each man wore at his ankle, except for Uxal. He then padlocked the chain and left after closing the door at his back.

'Why don't they put you in fetters?' asked Antoninus.

'Sometimes they do, sometimes they don't,' replied Uxal. 'They know that I'd never try to get away. They can tell when someone is resigned to his fate. And where would I go anyway? They'd get hold of me after half a mile tops, and I don't want to end up with a stake through my guts.'

AFTER A WHILE, all the men were sleeping or seemed to be, but Metellus lay there for a long time with his eyes open, thinking of Clelia and of little Titus, whom he missed more with every passing day. He had never found himself in such a hopeless situation and he thought for the first time of how fate can overturn a man's life. He thought of the morning that he had gone out at the emperor's side to face Shapur; he remembered his feeling of foreboding, but he could never have imagined how radically his life would change. That his existence would end at the bottom of a mineshaft, in a dark pit where no one could reach him.

Yet, despite the deep feeling of despair that had taken hold of him, he tried to think philosophically about his fate: just as destiny had so utterly changed his existence once, it might as easily – for reasons which were unimaginable at the present – reverse the course of events again. The important thing was to stay alive and to protect the emperor's life.

He raised his eyes to the ceiling and there, between the cracks of the wooden planks, he saw a star. It shone with an intense, sparkling light and he tried to work out which constellation it belonged to. He was determined to keep his mind occupied, to not let himself be beaten down by despair. He tried to go through every possible escape route in his mind, despite Uxal's warnings. The enemy had taken away their freedom but not their intelligence, or their will or their resourcefulness. Not only were these still intact, but circumstances would hone them to the full. They were powerful weapons that the men would have to keep hidden from their jailers in order to use them to their maximum advantage when the opportunity arose.

For years and years, Metellus had been trained to do battle, to withstand fatigue, pain and privation, but the test which faced him now was more arduous than the most bitter combat, than the most exhausting march, than the most agonizing wound. He earnestly called on his ancestors to succour him in this abyss, then he gave in to weariness and fell into an anguished nightmare: neither awake nor asleep, neither alive nor dead.

5

MONTHS PASSED, MADE UP OF unchanging days, of brutal toil, of deprivation and humiliation. As did the seasons. Autumn, winter, the sun which descended ever lower on the horizon only to began its ascent once again. The shacks were freezing at first, then hot, then scorching, or all three things together depending on whether it was night or day. The sun slowly began to decline again, and the dust of the storms penetrated every crack and covered everything with the same grey colour: men and objects.

The first to die was Aemilius, the Christian, one night in late autumn. It was not the exertion that broke him as much as the confinement, the dark, the beatings. The continuous beatings inflicted upon him by one of the jailers, who had singled him out for no particular reason. In the end, he could not bear the mortification. He stopped eating and let himself waste away, day after day.

His Judaean god had not been capable of freeing him or saving his life. For Metellus and the others, it was normal to think that the gods might not occupy themselves with the plight of men. But not for Aemilius. He thought that his god loved him personally, that he had chosen to suffer two hundred years before under prefect Pontius Pilate to expiate the sins of all humanity. He believed that beyond death there was another life, in which his god would console him for his sufferings. If only that were so, thought Metellus, as inside their hut he closed his friend's eyes.

'Sleep, soldier,' he told him. 'You'll suffer no more. And

wherever you go, take with you the part of our hearts that belongs to you.'

Then he turned to Uxal. 'I have to ask you a favour.'

'There's not much I can do, but ask away.'

'Would you ask the head jailer if we can bury him? Christians want to be buried, as far as I know.'

'Forget it. The Persians believe that the dead contaminate the earth. Which is sacred. They expose their dead on the tops of high towers, like the ones you can see down there on the hill. They call them "towers of silence". The bodies are eaten up by vultures, and the bones slowly decompose in the sun, the cold, the rain and the snow. Maybe they don't have it all wrong. It seems better to me than putting people underground. Anyway, you've got no choice. Throw him into the pit along with the others. It won't make much difference.'

'Of course it makes a difference,' replied Metellus. 'Of course it does. None of my soldiers has ever died without receiving funeral honours from the assembled ranks.'

'You stiff-necked Roman,' grumbled Uxal, 'can't you see what you're reduced to? Can you imagine what you look like? I'd like to have a mirror so you could see yourself. You look a wreck, a . . .'

'I don't need a mirror,' replied Metellus. 'I see myself in the eyes of my men, in their demeanour, in their unhealing wounds. I mirror myself in the unspeakable humiliation of my emperor.'

He then made up a rudimentary litter with two acacia sticks and some runners and nodded to his men, who placed Aemilius's body upon it.

When he saw they were about to leave the shack like this, Uxal stopped them. 'Just a moment, blast you. Do you want to all get killed? Let me tell the guard that you want to accompany your friend's body to the ravine.'

Metellus halted his men.

Uxal came back shortly later. 'You can go, but not before it gets dark. Don't walk in a straight line, mill around as if you weren't up to anything special. Don't show any signs of military discipline and carry his body low, not up on your shoulders. And leave your chief here. It's best he doesn't go with you.'

'All right,' replied Metellus, exchanging a look with Valerian.

They waited until the sun had dipped below the horizon and then went out with their comrade's body. They crossed the camp under the distracted eyes of the guards, who had moved off to the side to eat their dinner, but as soon as they were out of sight, Metellus ordered his men to hoist Aemilius's body to their shoulders and to follow the rough bier lined up two-by-two and walking in step. At the edge of the gorge, they lowered him to the ground.

'Does anyone know a Christian prayer?' asked Metellus.

'I do,' replied Severus.

'Are you Christian too?'

'No. But I was.'

'Then say the prayer. We'll listen.'

Severus bowed his head and began: *'Pater noster, qui es in coelis, sanctificetur nomen tuum . . .'*

When he finished, Metellus prayed as well: 'God of the Christians, receive my valorous soldier, gladden his vision with your light, because he has died in darkness and the darkness would renew his death for all time to come.' He turned to his dead soldier: 'You will be buried, as you deserve.'

He glanced around to make sure that no one was watching, then gathered up a handful of sand. He sprinkled it over Aemilius's body as a ritual burial. *'Sit tibi terra levis, Aemili . . .'* he murmured, and instantly, in his mind's eye, saw his hand scattering dust over Clelia's ashen face and he could not hold back his tears.

The time had come: he signalled to his men, and they tilted the litter towards the gorge, letting the corpse fall inside. They saw him bounce like a disjointed puppet off the hard rock walls and finally crash to the ground with a dull thud.

They looked at each other and read the same question in the others' reddened and weary eyes: who would be next to fly into the ravine?

As they returned to camp, Metellus drew close to Severus. He was thirty-five years old and had served the legion for fifteen, all with an honourable mention.

'Were you really once a Christian?'

'Yes, that's right.'

'Well, why aren't you any more?'

'Because I think that the Christians will change us to the point of making us incapable of defending ourselves and fighting.'

'And you don't think that someone can be a good combatant and a good Christian at the same time?'

'In theory you can, but in reality, no. Each one of us, I believe, would like to give up his arms, but who wants to be first? Act like a sheep and the wolf will eat you, that's what they say in my parts.'

'Mine too,' agreed Metellus.

'What's more, desiring revenge is forbidden for a Christian. You have to forgive your enemies. Can you believe that? What do you think is keeping me alive, Commander? I'm nursing my hate, and it's growing with every hour that passes, and one day I hope to get my hands around one of these jailers, even if just for a few moments . . .'

'That's fine, soldier. Anything that keeps you alive is fine. Hold on to your life tooth and nail. Our time will come, if we are tough enough, bold enough, patient enough. We Romans have a strength that the whole world envies, the strength that has made it possible for us to beat any people we've come up against. It's our *virtus*. And it's only when we forget it that we can be beaten.'

They continued walking until they came within sight of the camp. The night-shift guards were already in the saddle and were patrolling the area on horseback.

Severus stopped a moment. 'Commander.'

'Yes?'

'Will we get out of here?'

'A year has passed and most of us are still alive. That's extraordinary in itself. I think . . . yes, I think we'll make it.'

'Do you mean that they'll pay a ransom to free us?'

Metellus looked him straight in the eye. 'I'm afraid not, soldier. I'm afraid too much time has gone by. If they had wanted to ransom us, we'd be out by now. We have to rely on ourselves.'

By now the others had clustered around as well.

'Do you mean to say you have a plan, Commander?'

Metellus was reluctant to lie to his men, who trusted him blindly, but nonetheless he said in a firm voice, 'Yes, I have a plan.'

When they reached their shack, they were greeted by a hoarse rasping. The emperor was lying on his straw bedding, racked with fever and struggling to draw his breath.

'Martianus,' called Metellus.

Martianus approached and knelt down next to the emperor. He was not a doctor, but he had been a camp orderly for many years. He touched the emperor's brow and said, 'He's burning up.'

'I can see that,' said Metellus in a worried voice.

'It's the change in temperature: it's torrid during the day and freezing at night. You come out of the mine dripping sweat and the highland winds cut you in two.'

'What can we do for him?'

'We need woollen blankets, something hot to drink, steam to open his lungs.'

Valerian opened his eyes. 'Don't worry about me. Death would be a liberation. Do nothing to save my life. You would only prolong my agony.'

'Unfortunately, Caesar, there's nothing we can do,' replied Metellus, 'but that won't stop us from trying, because none of us believes that your time has come.'

Martianus dried his forehead and gave him a little water to drink. He put an ear to his chest and listened for a while to the grating hiss of his breathing. 'Try to sleep, Caesar,' he said, and then turned to the others. 'If each of you will give me a little straw from your litters, I can cover him and keep him warmer.'

The others began to gather straw, but Uxal stopped them with a jerk of his hand. He opened the door a crack and looked out. 'They'll be here any moment to lock the shackles,' he said. 'If they don't chain me up, maybe I can find a blanket. It's risky, but I'll try.'

A cold wind had risen and was whistling between the planks. The men shivered and pulled their threadbare rags close.

The guard arrived and threaded the chain through the rings on the prisoners' ankles but left Uxal unshackled. They considered the old man a collaborator and gave him some freedom of movement. When the guard had gone, Uxal waited until night had fallen and then slipped out. He came back shortly with a sheepskin.

'Here,' he said, 'this will keep him warm enough.'

'Thank you,' said Metellus. 'I won't forget this.'

The wind picked up even stronger and the men huddled together, tugging at their chains, for a bit of warmth.

Metellus was next to Valerian and close enough to put a hand to his brow. He could feel him trembling and hear his teeth chattering under the sheepskin, and he suffered greatly knowing that there was nothing he could do to alleviate his emperor's misery.

'This winter seems to be much colder than last,' he whispered to Uxal. 'How will we protect ourselves?'

'Sometimes they hand out covers or sheepskins, but I have no idea what they'll do with you. I don't know what instructions they've had.'

'Do you mean to say they'll let us freeze to death in this hole?'

Uxal sighed. 'I can't rule it out.'

Metellus thought of his distant home, of the long nights when he slept beside Clelia, and he was flooded by memories of the warmth of her body and the fragrance of her hair. He thought of when he used to go to tuck in his son in the bedroom next to theirs, sleeping under the protection of a little golden amulet than hung from the wall. His heart ached. He felt his strength draining away and feared that discouragement would get the better of him and leech away the energy he needed to go on.

Severus's voice made him jump. 'Commander, you said you had a plan. Do you? Will you get us out of this hole?'

'Leave him alone,' said Balbus. 'Can't you see how ill the emperor is?'

'Let's worry now about how we can take care of him,' replied Metellus. 'Maybe Uxal can bargain for more humane conditions. But when the time comes, yes . . . I'll get you out of here.'

'You've promised,' said Rufus.

'Yes,' replied Metellus. 'Yes, I promise you. But now we have to make sure the emperor gets better. We won't go without him.'

They all fell silent, because their commander's last words somehow negated the first. How could he keep such a promise? How could they escape with a man reduced to such a sorry state?

Valerian was burning with fever and delirious, calling out words without meaning and then drifting into unconsciousness. His breath was getting shorter and shorter, a laborious whistle that was becoming a death hiss.

At dawn, Metellus turned to Uxal. 'This man cannot be made to work today. He can't even stand up.'

'I know,' replied the old man.

'Do you think they'll let him rest?'

'You're asking me? I've never found myself in a similar situation.'

'Help me. Talk to the guard.'

'I'll try. But we have nothing to offer him. Only something to ask. Why should he listen to us?'

'I don't know why, blast it! But you try, all right? Try, damn you!' shouted Metellus.

Uxal muttered something to himself, then said, 'There's no need to raise your voice. You won't resolve much that way. I only hope I come up with an idea before that son of a bitch enters and opens the lock.'

He got up, went over to the emperor and took a long look. Valerian was deadly pale, his eyes black-rimmed and hollow. His body was covered with bruises, his hair filthy and clotted with dust and sweat. Uxal gave a sigh.

At that moment the door creaked open and the guard appeared. He bellowed something in his own language and opened the padlock, pulling the chain from the rings. Uxal muttered something back and the other replied with a shrug. Uxal insisted in a calm and rather detached tone, as if he were merely explaining something.

The man replied with a short grunt and then turned towards Valerian and gave him an oblique look. He turned to Uxal again and spat out a few words.

Metellus shot the old man a questioning look and was answered by a slight nod.

They were soon at the mine entrance, while Valerian had been left behind on his straw bed in the shack.

'What did you tell him?' asked Metellus.

'I said that if he forced Valerian to go down into the mine, he would be responsible for his death and that the spirit of a dead emperor becomes very vengeful and wicked, and would make him die the most abominable death a Persian can imagine: being buried alive in the mine.'

'And he believed you?'

'Maybe not. But why should he take a risk? It's not going to cost him anything; I promised him he'd have the same quantity of turquoise tonight anyway.'

'I'm very grateful to you. I only hope to be able to pay you back one day for what you've done for us.'

'I haven't done much, but I quite like the thought of dispensing favours to an emperor. Doesn't happen every day.'

'No, I'd say not,' agreed Metellus.

Balbus and Quadratus organized the working day so that in the evening the quantity of turquoise would be as much as the whole lot of them had produced together, and of the best quality to boot. They laboured without a pause so there would be no delay at the moment of weighing and they could get back to their shack as soon as possible. Metellus was especially bothered by the thought of the emperor all alone and feverish in that stinking hovel.

And bothered by the thought of his son, which never left him. He wondered whether Titus was thinking of him as well, or had given him up for dead. Merely imagining such a thing made him suffer unbearably.

The worst hours were the last; their muscles, aching with strain and riddled with cramp, no longer responded and every movement required immense effort.

When the time came to be lifted to the surface, Metellus and his men were there for the weighing; the material was well over the required quantity, and of excellent quality as well. No one stopped them from returning to their hut; on the contrary, from the way the guards were speaking, Uxal understood that they were quite satisfied. He began to realize that his friends might survive.

'Did you know the yields would be so high?' he asked Metellus.

'What do you mean?'

'Don't tell me you knocked yourself out just to make your jailers happy.'

'No. I'm trying to get them to understand that it's worth their while to keep us alive, because we ensure better profits than the others.'

'Hmmm . . . simple, but effective. In fact, it's the only reason for them to keep you alive. But I wonder how long you'll be able to keep up such a rate.'

'They might even decide to feed us better.'

'Forget that,' replied Uxal.

But the old man was wrong this time: the rations tasted better that night, and were more abundant. And there was bread along with the soup, for the first time.

Metellus tried to get Valerian to eat something, with no success. The emperor's condition had worsened. He was soaked with cold sweat and gasping for breath. His heartbeat was accelerated and his whole body seemed beset by unbearable fatigue.

Metellus consulted with Martianus. 'What do you think?'

Martianus shook his head doubtfully. 'He might go on a few days, but he may not even last the night.'

Uxal interrupted them. 'You know, I've had an idea. It struck me out of the blue.'

'What is it?' asked Metellus.

'You know that pit that we throw the cadavers into?'

'We were just there.'

'Well, in theory that gully is the bed of a stream which is dry practically all year. I'm not sure where it comes from; the mountains, I suppose. Now, when it rains hard up there or at the end of winter when the snow up on the peaks melts, the gully is sometimes flooded with water. For just a few days, or even just hours, that dry gorge turns into a dark, raging torrent that rushes between the rock walls and boils over the boulders at the bottom. It carries away everything. When the water stops flowing the bottom is clean: no more bodies rotting in the sun, no more bones and skulls laughing in your face with their jaws gaping.'

'I can't see where you're going with this story,' said Quadratus with a snort.

'Nowhere in particular,' retorted Uxal. 'It's just that something happened to me once while I was down in the mine during one of those floods and I was wondering if . . .'

'Gods!' broke in Metellus. 'Shut up, will you? Can't you see how ill he is?'

Valerian's breath came in a weak rattle, his emaciated chest rising and falling, stretching the skin over his ribs and breastbone. His eyes were glassy and he seemed unconscious.

Metellus got as close to him as the chains allowed and he realized the emperor was trying to say something. 'I'm here, Caesar,' he said, taking his hand.

'You must return, Marcus Metellus . . . you must return . . .'

'Not without you.'

'No, it's over, you know that. My son has abandoned me . . .'

'Don't say that . . . We don't know that, Caesar . . . You mustn't lose heart. You must try to get well. We'll help you.'

'I have no breath, son . . .'

Metellus started at that epithet, which the emperor had never used with him in all these years. He knew that the words they were about to exchange would be words of truth. No more piteous lies.

'Listen to me . . .' continued Valerian. 'Gallienus does not have the strength to govern alone. He will let himself be swayed by the Christians. The army will rebel against him . . . You must return and save the empire from disintegration. Promise me . . . promise this to a dying man.'

'I promise you. I will leave nothing untried to obey your orders.'

'Throw my body in the pit and think of nothing but this promise. The rain will wash me and the wind will bury me . . .' Tears streamed down his hollow cheeks. 'It's my fault,' he said, with great effort. 'I should have known. But a father's heart is blind, understand?'

'Do not torment yourself, Caesar. Your suffering will soon be over. Your ancestors are ready to receive you. Free your soul of anxiety, lift your spirit. You are about to become a god and to your shade we shall offer sacrifice in our homeland, under the skies of Italy. I swear to you.'

For a moment only the hiss of the wind between the cracks in the planks could be heard, and then even the wind seemed to die down. In that unreal silence the voice of Marcus Metellus Aquila rang out: 'The emperor is dead.'

6

BEFORE DAWN UXAL LEFT the shack and went to talk in secret with the head of the guards. 'Their emperor is dead.'

'When?'

'During the night.'

'What of?'

'What of? Of exhaustion, what else? They're going to take him over to the pit now, if you have no objections.'

'All right. But remind them of the rules.'

'They know the rules perfectly well. They're not stupid. Send someone to unlock them now. They want to be back before work starts. They have two to make up for now.'

'Well, that won't be a problem for them, will it?'

'Do you know how they manage? Organization. They've created a kind of structure where each one of them does the type of work he's most suited for, because of the way he's built or his natural inclination. This way, they put all their time to good use and don't miss a thing. If the whole mine were organized that way, you'd double production.'

'Interesting. Maybe I should have a little talk with that Roman.'

'If you want, I'll bring him here tonight.'

'I'll tell you when I want to see him.'

'Naturally, my excellent commander.'

'And now get out of my sight, scum.'

Uxal returned to the shack accompanied by the guard who held the key to the lock, who released the prisoners.

Metellus and the others took the same litter they'd used for

Aemilius and laid Valerian's body upon it. Stars still filled the sky and only the mountain crests towards the east were edged with a slight tinge of pink. The men walked in silence along the dusty trail that went to the gully, led by Uxal, who lit the path with a lantern. The wind had picked up again, raw and biting, dragging dry amaranth bushes in search of more hospitable places to put down their roots.

After a while, the trail began to descend towards the pit and the camp disappeared from sight behind them. At that point, Metellus ordered his men to hoist the litter to their shoulders and to proceed in step as if they were still wearing the red uniform of the legion, as if the eagle were guiding them.

When they came to the edge of the crevasse, Metellus ordered them to place the body on the ground. He signalled to Balbus, Quadratus and Publius to help him to uproot some dry tamarisk trunks and stack them. The other men joined in as well, as Uxal tried in vain to stop them.

'What do you think you're doing? Have you all gone mad?'

'Don't worry, old man. No one will notice a thing. The wind is getting stronger and it's blowing from the north. It will carry away the smoke and the smell.'

'But why? What's the point in risking your lives?'

'The emperor of the Romans must have the funeral honours he deserves, or he cannot be taken in by the gods. His ashes must be delivered to the urn.'

'Ashes are ashes!' screamed Uxal. 'You are crazy . . . crazy! You cannot believe this idiocy!'

'You'll see,' replied Metellus.

The woodpile was ready and other branches had been inserted among the trunks to feed the flames. They had prepared a kind of makeshift crematorium and a little clay jar.

'Give me the lantern,' ordered Metellus.

'I wouldn't dream of it!'

'Give it to me or I'll throw you into that pit.'

'Would you really be capable of doing that?' asked Uxal, stunned.

'Without a moment's thought. The lantern . . .' he repeated peremptorily, holding out his hand.

Uxal handed it over, shaking his head incredulously.

Metellus opened the lantern and poured the mineral oil it contained on to the branches, then held the wick flame close. The stack of wood caught fire immediately, stoked by the impetuous highland wind.

'Men!' shouted Metellus. 'In formation!'

The two centurions divided the men into two columns, right and left of the pyre.

Metellus declaimed, emphasizing each word, 'Honour to Licinius Valerianus Augustus, emperor of the Romans!'

The men raised their hands as if gripping the legion's javelins and shouted out, 'Honour!'

Uxal shook his head, disconcerted. He couldn't believe his eyes. Just when things were promising to get better, when his able diplomacy was about to earn some small privileges for the group, this useless and absurd ceremony was going to ruin everything. 'I'm getting out of here,' he said loudly. 'I'll take no part in this craziness. You have no idea of what will happen to you if they find out.'

'Go,' replied Metellus. 'We'll be here for a while.'

Uxal turned on his heel and, when he arrived at camp, tried to slip back into the shack, but one of the guards spotted him.

'Where are the others?' he demanded.

'The others? They're coming. They're still busy with all their prayers and conjurations. You know, there are all those religions in Rome and each one of them has to say something different. They'll be here soon.'

The sun was peeping over the mountain crests and the wind changed direction, bringing a burning smell towards the camp.

'But that's . . .' said the guard in alarm.

'The sentries' campfire. It's so cold this morning,' said Uxal, trying to distract the guard. But the man shoved him aside, sending him rolling to the ground, then ran off towards the gully. Uxal popped up and took off after him at a run, shouting,

'Where are you going? There's nothing going on down there. Stop!'

When the guard arrived the fire had abated and the embers were arranged in a rough circle. 'What do you think you're doing?' he shouted.

'He asked what you're doing,' translated Uxal, who had just drawn up, panting.

'We're just trying to get warm,' replied Metellus. 'We'll be starting back now.'

The guard took a look at the men's faces and knew they had something to hide. He poked the embers with the tip of his sword and saw a piece of half-burnt fabric, with something unmistakable attached to it. 'You've burnt that corpse!' he cried out. 'You've profaned the fire, damn you all!' He turned towards the camp and yelled out, 'Hurry! Out here! Sacrilege!'

Metellus jumped on him to make him stop yelling and wrestled him to the edge of the crevasse.

'No! What are you doing?' cried Uxal, but the other guards, who had heard their comrade's shouts, were already upon them and had the little group surrounded. There was nothing they could do. Metellus let go and got to his feet, panting.

'He has nothing to do with this,' said Metellus, pointing at Uxal. 'It was us.'

'He said I had nothing to do with this,' translated the old man.

The guards closed in on them and chained them hand and foot, dragging them back to the centre of the camp.

'What have you done?' Uxal continued to moan. 'I warned you. I told you not to do this . . . Now nothing and no one can save you.'

'Quit your jabbering, old man,' Quadratus shut him up. 'If we have to die, we'll die and get this whole farce finished with.'

'You don't know what you're saying,' replied Uxal. 'You have no idea of what you're saying.' He shivered inside at the thought of the tortures they'd be subjected to.

The head of the guards stepped forward and reviewed the

chained prisoners one by one. When he was in front of Metellus, he stared into his eyes for a few moments and seemed to move on, but then spun around and struck him violently in the stomach with a club. Metellus bent in two with the pain and, before he had time to react, the jailer gave a sharp blow to the nape of his neck and he dropped to the ground.

When Metellus opened his eyes he saw an indistinct shape before him: a burning globe. As soon as he could focus he realized it was a red-hot branding iron and that the jailer was about to use it on his eyes. They were going to blind him.

In that instant, the awareness of the horror that awaited him unleashed all his remaining energy. He knew that the next few moments were all he had. Metellus yelled out with all the breath he had in his lungs and grabbed the burning iron with his bare hands, ripping it away from the jailer, who was taken totally unawares. He sent it circling and grabbed the other end, pushing it straight into the man's screaming mouth.

The scream ended in the sizzling of seared flesh. The iron then pounded on to the man's head, crushing his skull.

Balbus and Quadratus lunged forward, wielding their chains like weapons. Balbus felled the guard in front of him with a ruinous punch and then, before he could get back up, wrapped his chains around his neck and strangled him. Quadratus sprang at one of the guards, the one who held the keys, and knocked him to the ground. He pressed his chains hard on the man's mouth, like a horse's bit, shattering his teeth and dislocating his jaw. The wretch's shriek of pain was drowned in a suffocating gurgle. The other comrades threw themselves at their jailers with all the vehemence of their desperation. Meanwhile, Balbus, Quadratus and Metellus had seized the weapons of their adversaries and were striking out with awesome blows in every direction. As two survivors fled towards the guardhouse to raise the alarm, Martianus, who had seen the guard with the keys on the ground, jumped him, got his hands on the keys and freed his comrades.

'This way!' shouted Uxal. 'Quick, this way! The armoury!'

The men took off at a run, while fresh guards rushed towards them full of murderous intentions. Quadratus unhinged the bolt on the armoury door with a stroke of his axe and was the first one in, followed by the others. Tens of arrows stuck into the door just instants after they had closed it behind them.

Several moments of interminable silence followed, in which the men from the guardhouse – nearly thirty warriors armed to the teeth – advanced through the thick dust produced by the battle and headed towards the armoury. But when the dust settled, the vision they found before them left them astonished and incredulous. Ten Roman soldiers encased in their armour, swords unsheathed: Metellus, Balbus, Quadratus, Martianus, Publius, Rufus, Severus, Lucianus, Septimius and Antoninus.

Before the guards had recovered from their shock, the Romans were upon them. They fought like furies out of hell, like demons of war, with fierce rage and furious perseverance.

Not a single blow missed its mark, not a single wounded enemy escaped death.

Marcus Metellus Aquila shouted to his men, urging them on, knowing that this superhuman burst could not last and that any failure would leave them at the mercy of their jailers. Each of the jailers had to die; they had to wipe out every last one of them. When, finally, his sword swung through empty air, he realized that they had succeeded in this impossible endeavour. Ten slave labourers, reduced to skin and bones, had exterminated more than thirty well-armed and well-nourished warriors.

They looked at each other in disbelief, panting, covered in blood, dust and sweat. Metellus raised his sword and said with the last bit of voice he had, 'Caesar is avenged.' Then he crashed to the ground as if dead.

All the others collapsed as well, one after another, exhausted. Even a child, arriving at that moment, could have finished them off with no effort whatsoever. They had expended their last spark of energy to regain their lost freedom.

Uxal approached Metellus and shook him. 'This is no time to rest. Come on. Get moving. We have to do something!'

Metellus forced himself to get up and he looked around him The other camp prisoners had gathered in a circle, speechless and dazed, and could not take their eyes off the incredible spectacle they found before them.

'Tell them they're free. Tell them to join us. Together we can force our way through the outer confine and reach safety.'

Uxal shook his head. 'You must be raving! None of them will move. They know that no one can break out of the external limits of camp, and that anyone who gets caught – that is, everyone – will be impaled.'

'You translate what I said!' shouted Metellus. 'In the meantime, you – Rufus, Martianus and Severus – go with Balbus. Throw Persian cloaks on your shoulders and take the guards' places at the outermost posts. We don't want anyone getting suspicious.'

Balbus took the men and assigned them to the most visible guard posts so they would be seen, then returned.

Uxal translated what Metellus had told him to say in all the languages he knew, but the results were as he had predicted. For an instant, his words lit a crazy light in the men's eyes, but very soon one after another bowed his head in resignation. There was a brief buzzing here and there, then silence.

'What did I tell you?' said Uxal. 'They're afraid. When a bird has been kept in a cage his whole life, he won't fly out even if you open the door. The outside world frightens them. Imagine them trying to break out of here, surrounded as we are by a hundred vicious guards.'

'Then we'll go on our own.'

'It's suicide, but I know you're right. This is no life. You're soldiers, so at least you'll die with your swords in your hands. But you should lock up the prisoners first. Someone might think of ratting on you to get in good favour with the guards.'

'Lock them up again?' asked Metellus.

'You've got no choice. It's for their own safety as well. That way no one can accuse them of sedition.'

Metellus ordered Quadratus, Lucianus, Publius and Septimius

to take the prisoners back to one of the shacks. As they were doing so, he turned suddenly to Uxal. 'What were you saying?'

'Me? Nothing.'

'Not just now, before . . .'

'What are you talking about?'

'Last night, in the shack, when I interrupted you. You were talking about the gully flooding once . . . and then what happened?'

'Oh yes. I was in a gallery down on the third level, removing the corpses of some of the prisoners, when I saw that water was seeping out of one of the walls, a lot of it.'

'Are you saying that the wall down there communicates with the bottom of the gorge?'

'Something like that. The water couldn't be coming from anywhere else.'

'Do you think that the point of contact with the gully wall might be outside the confines of the camp?'

'I'm convinced of it, but that doesn't mean I'm sure.'

'Could you find the place again?'

'I imagine so.'

'Let's go then, now.'

He called Quadratus, who was just returning after locking the prisoners up. 'Muster the men, have them bring shovels and axes and follow me.'

Quadratus was quick to follow orders and the others were soon ready, except for Balbus, who stayed behind to work the hoist.

'It's down this way,' said Uxal. After a few steps, he added, 'I should warn you that we'll find people down there. It's not a pretty picture. It's where the lot of you would have ended up.'

They descended a couple of ramps to the second level, then went down a steep stair cut into the rock, until they found themselves in front of an iron door bolted from the outside. Below was a hinged slot, just big enough to pass food through. Uxal drew the bolt, but it took Quadratus's muscle to get the door open. The narrow tunnel before them seemed to descend into the bowels of the earth. The air was foul with an unbearable stench of excrement and putrefaction. They looked at each other in disgust and stepped back, but Uxal shook them out of their stupor. 'Come on, then. Shall we get moving or settle in here and meditate on what the future may bring?'

'Move it,' ordered Metellus.

He was the first to start off down the tunnel, holding his lantern high. At the end, they found themselves in a vast gallery where they were shocked by the vision of pitiful human larvae scratching at the walls with wooden picks by the light of a few lamps. At the sight of a group of men armed in such an unusual way, the toilers all paused from their work and turned towards them. They looked like ghosts: black-rimmed eyes, hollow cheeks, long, unkempt beards, missing teeth, skeletal limbs. They coughed continuously and could barely stand. In a corner, some of them were crushing lumps of mineral in mortars and gathering the turquoise stones in a basket.

'They receive food in proportion to the number of stones they manage to produce. It seems incredible that these poor wretches can still have a hold on life. Most of them have no more than a few months to live anyway in this inferno. Follow me now. It's this way.'

They walked towards another narrow tunnel, which led away from the point where they had entered.

'What do we do about them?' asked Quadratus, pointing at the slaves.

'Forget them,' said Uxal. 'They couldn't walk more than a hundred paces outside of here. The sun would blind them and their skin would be covered with sores. Let them die in peace.'

They advanced about a hundred feet to a fork in the tunnel, where Uxal went to the right. They soon reached another widening of perhaps five feet by three, closed off by a dead end.

'It's here,' said Uxal. 'At least I think it was here.'

'You think?' asked Publius.

'What do you want from me? It happened at least three years ago, if not four. If you're so good at this, why don't you find a way out?'

Metellus made a gesture and moved the lantern close to the wall as the others fell silent. 'It is here,' he said. 'The colour of the wall is a little different. See?'

He placed his lantern on the ground, took an axe and began to dig. The sandstone was crumbly and yielded rather easily to the pick. Septimius and Lucianus took their own axes and started to work the wall alternately, so that the tools were striking uninterruptedly and knocking a great quantity of detritus to the ground. In a short time, all three had to stop, exhausted and panting, but Antoninus took over from the man who was most tired, and the others followed suit so that work could continue.

Uxal would gather up the chunks of stone from the ground as the hole got deeper, and noticed that they were becoming damper and damper. Then at a certain point they became drier again.

'Stop!' he yelled.

'What is it?' asked Antoninus, trying to catch his breath.

'I want you to touch those fragments of sandstone and tell me what you think. I mean, what's wet and what's dry. I don't want my imagination playing tricks on me.'

Metellus picked up the stones he was pointing at, as did Quadratus, Antoninus and Septimius.

'This one here is damp,' said Metellus.

'And this one is much drier,' confirmed Quadratus.

'This one over here is drier as well,' said Septimius.

Uxal scratched his chin. 'Here's what I think: first we found a dry layer, then a damp one, the inside layer I'd say, and now a dry layer again. I think that means we're getting close to the outside wall, which opens on to the gully where it is exposed to the sun.'

'I think you're right,' said Metellus.

'Then we have to risk the highest stakes we've got. If you

continue here, I'll go back and have Balbus hoist me up. We'll collect food and water and come back down with Rufus, Martianus and Severus who are still out standing guard. If my calculations are correct, you will have nearly broken through by then. With a little luck, we'll make it out and have at least a slightly better chance of surviving. If we find ourselves inside one of the guard circles . . . well, we'll have a good feed at least before we head out. Better to die on a full stomach, I say.'

'I think that just might work, old man,' said Metellus. 'Or at least I hope so. Go ahead with your plan. We'll press on down here.'

Uxal groped his way back along the tunnel so the others could keep the lantern. They immediately began their work again, but fatigue was overwhelming them and the need to rest was becoming more and more frequent.

'Let's hope that Uxal and the others get back here soon, or we'll die before we've managed to put a hole in this damned wall,' said Septimius.

'Silence!' Metellus suddenly called out.

'What is it?'

Metellus gestured for them to be quiet and started hitting the bottom of the breach with the tip of his pick. 'Can you hear that?'

'It sounds hollow!' said Septimius, his face lighting up. His thinness gave him the look of an undernourished adolescent.

'Yes, it does, by the gods! Come on, men. Let's give it all we've got!'

They started swinging their axes again, their vigour renewing as the wall began to yield under their blows.

'Stop now,' ordered Metellus. 'We'd be idiots, after all we've been through, to let ourselves be done in by haste and emotion.'

He turned the pickaxe around and started knocking at the wall with the handle, until the thin diaphragm of sandstone crumbled, creating an aperture that allowed a beam of light to filter through.

The men looked at each other in silence, although they felt like shouting with joy. Metellus held an ear to the opening, then widened it enough to stick his whole head out. When he pulled it back in there were tears in his eyes as he said, 'We've done it. We're out!'

7

THE KING OF KINGS, Shapur I, was still in his private apartments for his ritual morning dressing when a messenger was allowed in with a missive of absolute priority.

The man prostrated himself with his forehead to the ground before the sovereign and remained in that position until the vizier signalled for him to rise to his feet and speak.

'My Lord,' he began, 'the Roman died ten days ago. At the Aus Daiwa turquoise mine. I've come to bring you the news in accordance with your orders.'

The emperor seemed disconcerted. He waved away the hairdresser who was curling his beard and asked, 'How did he die?'

'Like everyone who works in a mine. Exhaustion, illness, maltreatment of every kind.'

'Did he say anything before he died?'

The messenger lowered his head in confusion. 'Pardon me, Great Lord, but he died during the night and no one was present except for his comrades, the Romans you defeated and had taken into captivity through the power of your authority. But he couldn't have said much. He had been more dead than alive for a long time.'

'Well, when he was alive, didn't he ever say anything? Didn't he ever plead or beg for deliverance?' The messenger was ready with the reply that he imagined would please his sovereign, but Shapur interrupted him before he could begin: 'The truth,' he said.

'He never said anything. From when he arrived to when he died, he never uttered a word.'

Shapur bowed his head without speaking for a moment, then asked again: 'His body? What was done with it?'

'It was thrown into the gorge, where the corpses of all your enemies who are expiating their wrongdoings in the work camp are thrown.'

Shapur fell silent again, pacing back and forth in his bedchamber, wrapped in a dressing gown of red silk and gold. 'I want his armour and weapons here, in my palace. Why have they not been brought to me?'

The messenger hesitated.

'I asked you a question,' repeated the emperor in irritation.

'The Romans' arms are being held at the camp armoury, but no one ever made a request in the name of the royal palace.'

'The request has now been made.'

'Your Majesty shall not need to ask again. As soon as I reach the camp I will relate your order and the trophy you are entitled to will be brought here in as short a time as possible.'

The emperor made a gesture to dismiss him and the messenger withdrew, walking backwards and bent double, all the way to the door.

Shapur turned to the vizier, an elderly dignitary from a family of ancient nobility who was called Artabanus. 'He said nothing! He did not beg for mercy. He did not ask to be relieved of his intolerable burden.'

'If he had, would you have heeded him?'

'Perhaps.'

'True generosity comes from he who does not wait to be implored.'

'Are you saying that I am not generous? That I am not magnanimous? In my reign I have allowed the spread of both the Greek and the Indian cultures. I have allowed all of my subjects to practise their own religions. Is this not magnanimity?'

'I don't say it is not, My Lord. I'm saying that perhaps the compassion you feel for him now comes from the fact that he is dead. Only now have you realized that no one is safe: even an emperor can fall captive to his enemy and die. And perhaps you're asking yourself whether you would have been capable of dying like him, enduring misery, humiliation and the certainty of having been forgotten. It is not difficult to die in battle with your sword in hand, to die in the sun at the peak of excitement, in the frenzy of combat. It is different to die slowly, in privation, abandoned by all.'

'He died the death he deserved. The Romans are insatiable raiders and plunderers. The entire world does not suffice to satisfy their avaricousness.'

'Some say the same about us.'

'Whose side are you on?'

'Do you have doubts? Have I not served you faithfully my whole life? It is my duty to say things that may displease you. I'm a minister, not a courtesan. The Romans have not always been this way. In the time of your predecessor Osroes, their emperor returned his daughter, whom he held hostage, without demanding anything in return.'

'Hadrian . . .' mused Shapur. 'He was a great man.'

'And he was not alone. What troubles me about this story is that Valerian was deceived, drawn into a trap. If I had been at Edessa, I would have advised you against it. It was not worthy of you. And what he was made to suffer afterwards was unworthy of you as well. After all, Valerian was guilty of no crime. He was merely trying to stabilize the frontiers in a territory that has always been hotly contested.'

'His fate is to serve as a warning. His successors must know what awaits them if they dare to challenge the emperor of the Persians. You'll see that Gallienus will not attempt to move a finger against me.'

Artabanus nodded solemnly and said, 'Gallienus is not a problem. The problem is Septimius Odenatus, defender of the eastern borders. As you were returning from Edessa he was bold enough to attack us. Your booty and your concubines fell into his hands, and you still bear the signs of the wound you received . . .' Shapur wrinkled his brow but Artabanus continued unperturbed: 'His cavalry is not inferior to ours and his infantry is superior. Our army was not capable of defeating him or seizing what he had stolen from you.'

'When I defeat him he will suffer a punishment ten times harsher than what his emperor suffered.'

'That doesn't seem like such a good idea, if I may say so. Odenatus is a great warrior, but he is also very ambitious, and his wife – the beautiful Zainab – is even more so than he. Gallienus is an intelligent man, but weak. My informers have hinted that Zainab is pressing her husband to break away from the empire and establish a kingdom of his own.

'If this should happen, he will necessarily have to come to terms with us. The caravans headed for Palmyra – Odenatus and Zainab's base – have to pass through our territory. It's not worth his while to be at war with us and, all things considered, it's not worth our while either. You have inflicted the greatest humiliation of all times upon the Roman empire. Don't push your luck, My Lord. If Septimius Odenatus breaks away from Gallienus, as I think he will, the empire of the Romans will be greatly weakened, but he alone will certainly not be able to match the power of Rome. We have to pursue our own interests. As long as there is someone in the West who buys the precious goods the East has to offer, we cannot but stand to gain. Kings yearn to achieve glory through war and battles to ensure that their names will live on, but a good minister must occupy himself with making commerce and trade flourish, thus spreading wealth and well-being.'

'I must think it over,' replied the king. 'I will reflect on your words. In the meantime, gather any information that may be useful to us.'

He gestured for the hairdresser to resume his work, and the man began to curl Shapur's beard with a hot iron.

The vizier understood that he was expected to leave and he proffered the ritual question, 'May I serve you in any other way, My Lord?'

Shapur waved him off, but the vizier lingered 'What is it?' asked the king.

'There's something that you've never told me and that I've never managed to learn.'

'What are you referring to?'

'Did Gallienus ever offer you a ransom for his father?'

Shapur motioned for the hairdresser to leave again, then looked straight into the vizier's eyes. 'Why do you want to know?' he asked.

'Simple curiosity. I'm a father myself and I have been a son. I'm interested in knowing whether power can be so important for some men that blood ties and familial love are relegated to second place. What's more, it seemed strange that, as your vizier, I was never informed of any ongoing negotiations. It's a question of state that concerns me directly.'

Shapur continued to stare at his minister with an indefinable expression. 'I should dismiss a vizier who believes that a sovereign may be influenced by blood ties. The supreme interests of the state go well beyond the private interests of one's family.'

'I am not a king. I can allow myself to have emotions.'

Shapur did not respond to this, but said, 'Yes. Gallienus offered a ransom.'

'How much?'

'He did not set a limit.'

'Did you answer him, Majesty?'

'No.'

'Why not?'

'It's a personal matter.'

'Did Valerian ever learn that his son had offered to ransom him?'

'No.'

'Why not?'

'Because I wanted him to suffer as much as he could possibly suffer. For a father, this is worse than torture.'

'So even a sovereign has feelings.'

'I could not exclude this hypothesis.'

'I see. And in this case, his suffering would be greatly exacerbated. Was this a personal matter as well?'

'Yes,' replied the king.

'May I be so bold as to ask what this personal matter was?'

'You may ask, but you will obtain no answer.'

Artabanus nodded without saying anything else.

'And now you may go,' Shapur dismissed him.

The vizier bowed and walked backwards to the door as the king once again entrusted his cheeks to the hairdresser's hands.

ARTABANUS WENT TO his rooms and sat at his desk. The fact that the king had hidden Gallienus's ransom offer troubled him greatly. Shapur keeping him in the dark about such an important matter boded ill for his relations with the sovereign and for the position he occupied. In theory, as vizier he should have been the first to be informed, and he should have conducted the negotiations himself. He pondered over their conversation at length, especially regarding the personal matter that Shapur had hinted at. The king was not obliged to tell him why he had acted in a given way; he could simply have refused to answer him. Perhaps he wanted to let the vizier know that, despite the esteem he had for him, he had preferred or been forced to deal with this matter personally.

Since Artabanus had become vizier, he had never found himself in such a situation. He decided to summon his best informer, an old Nubian eunuch who was blindly faithful to him and who for years had enjoyed the confidence of the queen-mother, the king and many other important court personages. He was called Ardashir, but that may have been the name given to him at court. Perhaps not even he remembered his birth name any longer.

Ardashir arrived rather quickly, given his considerable girth, the result of his castrated condition as well as the fine Indian cuisine that a cook from Taxila prepared for him every day with great skill and refined art.

'How are you?' asked the vizier as soon as he entered.

Ardashir wiped his brow and took a chair, extracting a pheasant-feather fan from his pocket and beginning to fan himself. 'Not too bad for such an old man,' the eunuch replied. 'What is it you want to know, Excellency?'

'There's not one thing in particular, actually. There's something that escapes me and I would like to understand – if I can – what I'm being kept in the dark about in this palace and why.'

'What are you speaking of?'

'The king has only informed me now that Gallienus, the son of the emperor of the Romans, sent him a ransom offer some time ago. I was never told about this. The king refused his offer, purportedly for personal reasons he has not revealed to me. But as far as I know, the king has never met Gallienus personally on any occasion and, what's more, I don't believe he'd ever met Valerian before the ambush at Edessa. Do you know anything about this?'

'No. But instinct tells me there's a woman involved.'

Artabanus smiled. 'Many claim that you eunuchs are the best judges of feminine nature and, if the rumours I've heard are true, the best lovers as well.'

Ardashir sighed. 'Water under the bridge, Excellency, I'm too old for those things any more. But it's true that when you've suffered such cruel mutilation as a mere child, your sensitivity increases greatly – something that women can appreciate. And our caresses may be much more pleasant for them than the often brutal penetration of a male in heat who has all the tenderness of a copulating boar. But, returning to the topic of our conversation, in all sincerity I do not know what these "personal reasons" that the king spoke of could be. That's why I thought of a woman . . . women are always involved somehow.'

'Are you sure that nothing comes to mind that might help me to understand?'

'There is a rumour that has been circulating for some time in certain parts of the court . . .'

'What rumour?'

'That the king, in the course of certain negotiations a couple of years ago, made the acquaintance of the wife of Septimius Odenatus, the Roman general who defends the eastern front. She is a Syrian named Zainab. Her beauty is legendary.'

'I've heard speak of it myself.'

'And such is her fascination that no man who sees her can remain immune to it. At least this is what I've heard said. I've never met her in person, regrettably.'

'But what does this have to do with what I asked you and with what the king told me?'

'Probably nothing. But it's the only personal element – if we can call it such – that I could imagine might involve the King of Kings, the radiant Shapur, our sovereign.'

Artabanus searched in the eunuch's eyes for the meaning behind his subtly allusive expression.

Ardashir began in a different tone of voice, as if he were trying to explain something quite simple to someone a little dull-witted. 'Shall we make a hypothesis? Just a little game, of course. Let us imagine that the king was smitten by this female and was no longer able to rid himself of the thought of her. Imagine that when he received Gallienus's proposal he made a counter-proposal . . .'

'Zainab in place of a sum of money?'

'It's only a hypothesis, mind you. You've said it, Excellency, not me. But suppose for a moment that the hypothesis is valid: many things tally up, wouldn't you say? The king could certainly not make a request directly to Odenatus, who had just recently stolen his plunder and a good part of his harem through a treach- erous attack. But he could demand that Gallienus oblige the general to give up his wife in reparation for the insult suffered by the Persian king. An agreement destined to remain a secret between the two emperors: Valerian in exchange for Zainab.'

'If that were the case,' replied Artabanus, 'Gallienus was therefore unable to compel Odenatus to turn his wife over, and thus the negotiations for the release of Valerian reached a deadlock.'

'Obviously we're talking about a completely imaginary hypothesis,' said Ardashir. 'You know how we eunuchs are: always fascinated by great love stories, precisely because experiences so sublime and at the same time so terrible have been denied us.' He concluded his phrase with a long sigh.

'Of course,' replied the vizier. 'Nothing more than an imaginative hypothesis and a bit of court gossip. I'll keep that in mind. But you understand, my good friend, that in my position I must take everything into consideration, even the warbling of the birds and the sigh of the wind in the royal gardens.'

'Quite true,' replied the eunuch. 'In any case, it has been a pleasure to exchange a few words with you, Excellency. Consider me always at your disposal.'

They left each other with a kiss on both cheeks, and the eunuch made his way towards the door, his flesh quivering at every step.

Artabanus sighed. Ardashir the eunuch had probably found the correct interpretation of what had happened. It explained Shapur's silence as well. The king would never admit – not even to his loyal minister – that he had become obsessed with a woman and that he was mixing fundamental state affairs with a sordid matter of personal passion. In any case, the vizier felt relieved. There was no lack of trust towards him; if anything, what was involved was a kind of shame or perhaps discretion that did not reflect on him in any way. He felt reassured and quite certain that he had received – in an allusive form, naturally – the correct information regarding the mystery of why Valerian had not been ransomed.

He leaned back into his chair and enjoyed a few moments of serenity, then took the papers that his secretary had prepared for him and began to read his correspondence. He jotted a response at the end of each page, stopping only for a short meal at midday, and continued working in complete tranquillity for several more hours. Only the waning of the light streaming in through the window made him realize that the sun was setting and the dinner hour approaching.

His servant would soon enter to tell him that the table was ready and his secretary would come in to remind him of the names of the guests and the reasons for which they had been invited to dinner.

Instead, one of the imperial guards walked in, without even knocking at the door. 'The king wants you.'

The vizier rushed down the corridor and arrived, breathless, at the audience hall, where Shapur was waiting for him. The sovereign spun round as he entered. A glance was sufficient for Artabanus to see that he was furious and that part of that ire would rain down on him.

'Vanished!' shouted the king. 'Disappeared, and no one knows where to!'

'Excuse me, My Lord. Who has vanished?'

'The Romans! Those bastards have vanished without a trace! How it that possible?'

'I . . . don't understand . . . weren't you told that Valerian had died?'

Shapur tried to contain his rage and turned to a man whose presence Artabanus had just noticed. The king motioned for him to speak.

The man stepped forward from the shadows and explained. 'Yes, Valerian died, but there were ten men with him who have disappeared. A cavalry unit entered the camp, alerted by the strange silence that reigned there. They found most of the prisoners locked up together in the same shack, but the ten Romans were missing, and their weapons are missing from the armoury. We've searched for them everywhere, but haven't found the slightest trace. An old convict who had been in the camp such a long time that he acted as an assistant to the guards has also disappeared.'

Artabanus drew closer. 'What about the armed guards?'

'Dead. Killed.'

'The prisoners somehow managed to get hold of their weapons, killed the camp guards and escaped. Where is the mystery?' asked Artabanus.

'There were more than thirty guards, well armed and well fed, and there were only ten of them, prostrated by forced labour and malnutrition. They don't even look like human beings any more when they've been in the camp that long. What's more, the outskirts of the camp are garrisoned by over three hundred men on horseback who control every way out. And not one of them saw a single thing.'

'I don't believe in miracles,' said Artabanus. 'They must have gone somewhere and they'd better be found, or the man in charge of the camp will pay the consequences.'

'The guard in charge of the camp was killed,' explained the messenger, 'but the head of the external garrison has launched an exhaustive search. He's requested reinforcements from the closest units and is combing the area inch by inch. Most of the land is barren and deserted. There's no place they can hide. We're sure to find them, My Lord. Our commander says that he's certain the hunt will be successful. In any case, he wants our lord the king to know that he is not responsible for their escape. The chief guard was to blame for having underestimated the Romans' resolve and he's paid for that with his life.

'It is very probable, My Lord, that at this stage they have already been captured. I left Aus Daiwa ten days ago, as soon as we realized the Romans had escaped. I would not be surprised if another messenger arrived very shortly to tell you that the runaways have been caught.'

Shapur, livid with anger, said nothing: an evident sign that the vizier was expected to take care of the inconvenient matter.

Artabanus gestured for the messenger to follow him. 'Our lord and sovereign has been sufficiently disturbed by your impudence. Come with me and we shall try to make sense of this heap of nonsense.'

But the messenger was reluctant to move.

Shapur ordered him to come closer. 'What more is there? Don't make me lose my patience!'

'My Lord, I must give you more bad news. The guest with the piercing eyes has also escaped.'

'What?'

The messenger replied, trembling, 'At nearly the same time. He had asked to visit a Zoroastrian monastery and was accompanied there by our men, but then somehow he managed to slip out of their sight. The priests had no idea of where he was and when the guards realized he had disappeared it was too late. We have alerted all of our garrisons, from here to the Ocean. He doesn't stand a chance.'

Shapur seemingly no longer had the energy to lose his temper. He gestured for the messenger to shut his mouth and called Artabanus. 'Send a group of couriers as soon as possible to warn our friend to be on guard. He must be told that our guest has fled, and may reappear when he least expects it. Inform him that there was surely a conspiracy involved in his escape, and that he should watch his back. Ensure him of our utmost support in searching for the fugitive, who will be captured as soon as possible, and so on and so on. We cannot afford to lose his friendship. It is with him and with his government that our most important commercial agreements are to be forged in the coming years.'

'Have no fear, My Lord, your message will arrive before any other.'

'I'm counting on you,' replied the king. 'You are the only one I can trust. How is the work at Persepolis proceeding?'

'Very well, Majesty, the work is almost finished. And what a wonder it is! An enormous bas-relief showing Valerian on his knees begging for mercy in front of Your Majesty on horseback, in the splendour of your glory. The inscription celebrates your deeds in Persian, Parthian and Greek.'

'Excellent. Go now, there's no time to lose.'

Artabanus bent low in a deep bow, took the messenger's arm and went out into the corridor.

As soon as they had left the audience chamber, he pushed him roughly up against the wall and hissed, 'The truth, if you want to leave this palace alive.'

The man lowered his eyes and said, 'I left after two days of incessant searching within a range of seven *parasangs* from the Aus Daiwa camp.'

'Seven *parasangs*? They couldn't have covered that much land in two days, given the condition they were in.'

'Several patrols went out even further, but they found no one, not a trace, not a sign.'

'They vanished into thin air, then, as the king was saying.'

'I don't know what to say, Excellency. We turned over every stone and searched every caravan within a range of seven *parasangs* and we found no one. The men on the second ring of guard towers never left their posts and yet they didn't see a living soul go by.'

The vizier took his hands off the man and ordered him to follow him to his private study. 'If they didn't find them far away, they must look for them closer, understand?'

'What do you mean to say, Excellency? We inspected the camp inside and out.'

'Were the other prisoners interrogated?'

'Yes. They said that the Romans locked them up in a shack and that they had no idea where they were headed.'

'Now, listen to me well, if you don't want to end up impaled. Go back to the camp and have all of the sheds, the mine tunnels and the guard routes searched thoroughly. They cannot have disappeared. They may be hidden very close by, waiting until you stop looking before they start moving. Find them and bring them here, do you understand?'

'Yes, Excellency.'

'And get news to me about the guest with the piercing eyes as soon as you manage to locate him. I have to account for him as well.'

'Very well, Excellency.'

'Leave immediately and send me good news as soon as possible, about both one and the other.'

'I will do so, Excellency,' babbled the messenger, white as a sheet.

'Move, then. You don't have a moment to lose.'

The man went off in great haste. Artabanus, back on the balcony of his private apartments, saw him gallop out of the southern gate of the palace and disappear in a cloud of dust.

The vizier immediately summoned the man in charge of the courier service and handed him a message that would have to travel as fast as the wind.

8

METELLUS WAITED FOR his comrades to return with the supplies and for darkness to descend to the bottom of the gully before he widened the hole in the mine wall and finally emerged.

He raised his eyes and saw the sky teeming with stars. He saw the Milky Way crossing his narrow field of vision between the two walls of the deep gully like a bridge of light and he felt tears surge up and wet his cheeks and his breath swelled in his chest like the first breath of his existence, as if he had been born a second time.

He bent down and sank his hands into the dry sand and the pebbles smoothed by the water and the wind of countless seasons. He breathed in the fragrance of a horse-mint bush and brushed the blossoms of a hard little broom plant growing out of the wall. He had the marvellous sensation of seeing and touching the world for the first time.

The suffering of these dreadful years, the loss of his wife, the separation from his son, the death of his comrades and of the emperor: everything seemed to fade away in the sweet air of freedom. He realized that his life had been given back to him, and that he would do anything to defend it. He felt strength and invincible power: he was sure deep down that he could face any trial in life after such a miracle. He felt that he would be able to bend events to his will by means of a new and indestructible determination.

He did not find the stink of death that he had expected, because omnipotent and ever-changing nature had already dissolved the corpses, transferring their substance into other substances, into other ways of being: wild animals, the sun, the wind, the dust . . . In the distance he could see, in the reflected glimmer of the limestone walls, the gleaming white of scattered bones. The bones of so many unlucky wretches, the bones of his companions who had come to die in a distant and desolate land.

Those first instants of regained freedom were so intense that Metellus lost his sense of time and when Quadratus's hand landed on his shoulder he felt as if he was waking from a dream.

'Commander . . .'

He turned to look at his men: they were hairy, emaciated and bore the signs of their inhuman imprisonment on their bodies and souls, and yet a magical light shone in their eyes, a mad light, capable of piercing the black of night. The light of victory over death, over darkness, over desperation.

He embraced them one by one, stared into their eyes burning with emotion and tears, and with every embrace the clanging of breastplates sounded, iron against iron. The embrace of diehard soldiers, ready again for anything, for they had endured it all.

But in that same instant Metellus realized that basking even for a short time in that indescribable joy could mean the end of everything they had achieved. 'Now we have to mask the breach we've opened in the sandstone wall. You, Publius, you're the thinnest of us. You go back inside and wall up the opening, leaving only just enough room for you to get out. We'll do the rest from the outside. But let's eat first, and drink. We need to get our strength back.'

'Slowly,' said Martianus. 'We're no longer accustomed to eating our fill. It may be dangerous to load up our stomachs. Once in Pannonia we freed a prisoner who had lived on nothing but raw turnips for three months. He gobbled down a big chunk of bread with salted pork, and before we knew it he was dead. Be sure to chew every bite to a pulp before you swallow it. Drink in small sips. As soon as you feel satiated, stop. You'll eat less food, more often. If you listen to me, you'll save your skins and build up strength. If you go into a feeding frenzy, you'll die.'

Uxal handed out the supplies that he'd taken from camp; barley bread, pulses, walnuts. And water.

Publius went to work immediately to camouflage the breach and then completed the job from outside with extraordinary skill, continuing to smooth the inner surface with clay for as long as he could get his arm through the hole. He then closed it up with a stone of perfect size. He had been part of the *murarii* for many years and their legendary skill in masonry had remained with him.

At that point they held council. Metellus questioned Uxal, the only one of them who had any knowledge of their surroundings. 'We owe our freedom to you, Uxal, and now our fate still lies in your hands. What can we do? What direction should we take?'

Uxal answered with a certain emphasis, conscious of the role he was assuming. 'My advice is to stay put where we are.'

'What?'

'Exactly what I said. They're going to unleash every single man they have to hunt us down in every corner, track or trail. They'll ransack every caravan and every caravanserai for miles in every direction. When they finally get it in their heads that they aren't going to find anything searching far and wide, they'll come back to search the vicinity, but they won't think of looking for us underground, and even if they do, they won't find anything. At that point, we'll make our move and we'll get as far away as possible. Need I say more?'

'No, that's perfectly clear,' admitted Metellus. 'But will it work?'

'Do we have a choice?'

'No, I'd say not.'

'This place is as safe as we can get because it's contaminated for them and they have a sacred fear of it. It will also give us a chance to recuperate and get into shape for a long march.'

'What about our weapons?' asked Balbus. 'What will we do with them?'

'My first impulse is to say hide them, leave them here, but

that's not necessarily the best choice. A group of armed men commands respect, and having weapons puts you in a position to negotiate or to enforce your will. You can even decide to hire yourselves out as escorts or guards. If the situation is favourable, that is.'

'I don't see us meeting up with any favourable situations for at least a ten-mile range,' commented Antoninus. 'But our armour can be disassembled into segments, and the coats of mail don't take up much space. We'll have to leave the shields behind. They're just too bulky.'

'We'll do that, then,' said Balbus, 'if everyone agrees.'

'When we're ready to start our march,' continued Uxal, 'we'll need some pack animals. Not too far from here there's a pool of water that never dries up, and there's a group of wild asses that go there to drink. I'd see them often from up on high when I came out to dump the waste. We could make a trap. They would be a good means of transport for us and a way to carry our supplies and the weapons.'

Metellus turned to Septimius and Lucianus. 'You were good hunters, as I recall. Find some way to build a few traps so we can catch these asses.'

The two men nodded.

'We'll just have to keep them tied up for a few days and feed them with the forage that grows around here. They'll follow us like lambs. We'll be able to make ropes by braiding the fibres of this plant that grows between the rocks,' suggested Uxal.

Metellus looked over at Antoninus: he was the right man for the job, an engineer from the *fabri* corps. He gave a nod.

'What then?' asked Metellus.

'We'll travel down the gorge,' said Uxal, 'until we find water, and we'll continue until this dry gully turns into a stream and then a torrent. We'll go on until we find a confluence. It won't be an easy march, but at least we'll be out of sight and we'll be using an itinerary that the scouts on horseback won't be able to follow. If I'm not mistaken, west of here flows the Khaboras, which has its source at a beautiful oasis where it will be much easier either to lie low or to find a way out, acting as an armed escort for a caravan, for instance. Those caravans go everywhere, all the way to the heart of Asia. At a day's march from the oasis, we'll be able to board a ship on the river and reach the shore of the Ocean. There, I'd say, we'll finally be safe and each of us can go his own way.'

'How can we repay you?' asked Metellus.

'You already have. As I speak I'm a free man, I'm breathing in this splendid evening air and I'm surrounded by friends. Even if this were my last night on earth, it would have been worth it. But you can take your time thanking me. Lots of things can happen between here and the Ocean shore.'

'True,' replied Quadratus, 'but you're right about one thing: it will have been worth it. I've only just realized that dying as a free man is just as important as living.'

'Remember,' Uxal started up again, 'we'll be doing all this by night. There mustn't be any trace of our passage the next day or they'll track us down in no time. If they were to find us, we'd have no choice but to seek death. If that should ever happen, you must promise me that the first blow of your swords will be for me. If they catch me alive, there'll be no end to my suffering.'

Metellus held out his hand. 'You have the word of a Roman officer,' he said. 'It's worth more than an oath.'

'Good. And now let's look for shelter for when the sun comes up. Two of you go up the gully, another two go down. The first to find adequate shelter will come back to tell the others. Don't make a sound; don't so much as breathe! If they find us, we're dead.'

Metellus sent Quadratus and Antoninus downstream, Balbus and Septimius in the opposite direction.

It was Septimius who first found a cavity behind a rocky spur, well hidden by a slab of limestone. 'When I was a boy,' he said, 'I'd spend the summers up at my uncle's house in the mountains. I'd love searching for caves. I wouldn't miss a single one! Come on. This one's nice and big.'

His comrades followed him as silently as shadows and slipped into the crevice that let them into the cavern. There was dry sand on the floor and they all lay down, exhausted by the prolonged tension, the physical strain and the violent emotions of that long day. Metellus was first to stand guard, flanked by Uxal, who didn't want to leave him alone.

'You don't trust me?' asked Metellus, amused. 'Do you know how many hours I spent on guard duty in the legion?'

'In the legion you were healthy, well fed and strong as an ox. Now you're a real wreck, and you desperately need to sleep. You'd be nodding off in less than an hour if I left you alone.'

'And you won't nod off?'

'Old men don't sleep much. And we like to talk . . . It's a lovely night, Commander Aquila. That's your family name, isn't it?'

'That's right.'

'Well, you don't say! The name of a true soldier, by Jupiter! What else could you have become with a name like that?'

'We say *nomen est omen*: your destiny is written in your name.'

Uxal changed the subject and looked back up into the sky. 'Look at all those stars . . . what a wondrous sight! And to think it's the same sky we had over our heads in camp.'

'Right, but who ever saw it? When we came up from the mines, we were so exhausted that we'd collapse as soon as we finished that vile soup.'

Uxal pointed at a skeleton stretched out a short distance away between two boulders. 'Who could that be?'

'What does it matter? One of the many who died in that inferno.'

'Well, he's finished suffering now. Look at him grin, all his teeth in the air. He's laughing at us, all our scheming, our worrying, all the little tricks we're thinking up to prolong our miserable lives by a mere hair's breadth. He knows that you've got to die and there's not much you can do about it. That's why he's laughing. Don't you think?'

'Maybe. But he's wrong. There's not an instant of our lives

that isn't worth living. Even when I was surrounded by the worst squalor, the fact of living was important for me. The fact of seeing my friends, of seeing the dawn and the dusk, of hearing the birds sing or the jackals howl at night. It's hope that keeps us going. Hope never dies. The hope of seeing my son, for instance.'

'Ah, your son . . .'

'In a few days it will be his birthday. If I were home we'd celebrate. I'd give him his own set of armour – I'd already spoken with a good craftsman who said he'd make it for me. And a military tribune's cloak. How he dreamt of that! He's a good boy, you know. He studies hard, respects his teacher. He's intelligent and affectionate. When I came home from head-quarters at night, he'd run up to me and unhook my sword from its belt, help me unlace my leggings. He'd bring me clean towels for my bath and sit there on the rim of the tub, asking me all kinds of questions.'

Uxal sighed. 'It must be lovely to have children.'

'If you're lucky it is. Have you had children?'

'How? To have children you need a wife. Who'd want someone like me? Sometimes I wonder what they might have looked like. Your son, what does he look like?'

'He's a handsome child,' said Metellus. 'He's got deep black eyes like his mother's, and his skin is soft and smooth, a beautiful golden colour.'

'Isn't he anything like you?'

'Oh, certainly, of course. I think so. His character is like mine, his mannerisms, even the way he walks.'

'You'll find him again,' said Uxal. 'I'm sure of it.'

Metellus didn't answer. His head dropped and he fell silent.

All at once, noises broke through the night air, the echoes of neighing horses, distant shouts. The two men exchanged an apprehensive look.

But almost immediately Uxal gave a toothless chuckle. 'They don't have a clue. Hee-hee-hee!'

'Shut up,' hissed Metellus. 'You want them to find us?'

'Don't worry. They have no idea which way to turn! You know why? If there's one thing they're certain of, it's that no one has ever got out of the third level alive. And that's just how we stole away! By this time they're searching everywhere: in the shacks, in the rubbish dump, in the hay loft. They're checking the prisoners one by one, stripping them down, making them parade before the guards. I saw it happen once, a long time ago. Look!' he said suddenly. 'They've crossed over to the other side.' He pointed at lights moving along the rim of the gorge on the side opposite the camp. 'Do you know how far they've had to go to get over there? I've heard say that the gully is impassable for miles and miles, both upstream and down. That's why they built the camp in that location.'

After a while, the horsemen were swallowed up by the night. Metellus checked the position of the stars and said: 'It's time for the second guard shift. I'll go and wake Quadratus. You should try to get a little sleep yourself.'

When he was able to stretch out on the dry sand, in the natural warmth of the cave, Metellus felt at peace with himself and with his surroundings, and protected in that hidden recess. He slept a deep, albeit brief, sleep.

The light of the sun woke him, and Uxal's voice: 'What do you say to a shave, Commander?'

'What?'

The old man was standing in front of him with a bowl of water, a sponge, scissors and a razor.

'Where did you find those things?'

'When I went back to get food and water, I saw there was plenty of other stuff in the storehouse and I helped myself. In the state you're in, people will be able to tell from a mile away that you're escaped convicts. A nice clean shave will make you look like gentlemen.'

Metellus willingly subjected himself to the torture as Uxal scraped away at his cheeks with a razor that had known better times and with scissors that must have been used to clip sheep.

Despite all that, first Uxal and then all the others expressed their approval and they all lined up to receive the same treatment. That simple rite made them feel somehow that they'd been readmitted to respectable society and seemed almost to bode the return to a normal life.

THEY CAREFULLY rationed supplies during their stay in the cave, thinking of the journey ahead of them, but Publius and Lucianus, who had served in Palestine and Arabia, soon noticed the presence of plants that produced small tubers tasting like hazelnuts which were very nourishing. They would go out after dark to gather them, camouflaging themselves with a coating of dust.

Trapping the asses was no simple task. Ropes were made by braiding plant fibres, nooses were fashioned and snares set, sacrificing a fair number of perfectly good tubers as bait. But in less than three days they had captured three asses, two females and a young male. They were brought, bucking and kicking, to the shelter to accustom them to the presence of humans and to the food they provided.

The men used the same fibres they had braided to trap the asses to make mats which they slept on and which could be used in the future for any number of purposes.

One day Metellus and Antoninus studied a way to climb up the gorge wall, and under cover of darkness they reached the rim, from where they had a view of the Aus Daiwa camp. From their vantage point they could see the agitated comings and goings of a number of patrols. Light signals flashed over the great deserted expanse that stretched in every direction to the horizon. They were still looking for them. They hadn't given up yet.

Metellus decided to wait another couple of days before moving out, since in two days' time there would be a new moon and the cover of complete darkness.

The men swathed the asses' hoofs, loaded their armour on the beasts' backs and covered them with mats. When the last glimmer of daylight had died away, they set off. They were in fine form, thanks to their forced rest and the nourishing food that had sustained them.

They advanced with great caution, worried more about keeping quiet than about covering any great distance. When they stopped at dawn the next morning, they had gone a little over a mile. Their position was critical: they were too close to the camp and without shelter. They would be spotted if a patrol passed on the eastern rim of the gorge.

They decided to separate into three groups, spaced out by about three hundred paces each, so they wouldn't be discovered all together if a patrol should arrive. They continued to advance in the hope of finding a refuge.

Centurion Aelius Quadratus, who was leading the small vanguard, heard the scuttling of hoofs at the top of the gorge and ordered his comrades to flatten themselves against the wall. Antoninus, who was at his side, turned back to warn the others.

Antoninus arrived just in time: an instant later and the group with Balbus, Uxal, Lucianus and the asses would have come into full view. They waited, holding their breath, until they heard the sound of a gallop fading off in the distance, then caught up with the others, who had made ready for the worst, prepared to sell their lives dearly before giving in.

'The gods are protecting us,' said Metellus. 'We'll go forward. We have no choice.'

They covered another mile, protected at times by the shadows cast by the crags and spurs rising on the eastern side of the gully, their hearts pounding at the thought of being seen, until they found a shelter big enough to conceal them from sight. The passage of periodic floods had carved out a section of the crumbly sandstone between two layers of silica, creating quite a deep cavity, tall enough for a man to stand inside. They entered in haste, first the pack animals and then the men, and finally relaxed, allowing themselves a little rest.

Metellus sent Publius and Antoninus to explore the walls. Their task was to find a point from which they could keep watch

over the surrounding territory, the Aus Daiwa camp, if it was
still visible, and the circle of guard towers, which they fervently
hoped were behind them by now.

The two men, wearing only their short tunics, climbed up to
a rocky ledge from which they could continue all the way up
to the rim, and they stood guard for the rest of the day, offering
the others the security of knowing they were being watched
over.

When they climbed back down at dusk, they sensed a certain
excitement among the men inside the cave, and discovered that
Septimius and Lucianus had brought down a male ibex with
their javelins and were skinning him.

'By Hercules!' exclaimed Antoninus. 'The commander was
right about you being good hunters!'

'I'm half Celt,' replied Septimius. 'We learn to hunt boar
before we learn to talk.'

'I'm half Greek,' said Lucianus, 'and I love roasted meat. I
can't wait!'

'Don't even think about it,' retorted Metellus. 'We're still too
close to the camp. The smoke and the smell would give us away.
We'll eat the meat raw. It's just as nourishing that way.'

'Raw meat?' yelped Uxal. 'Not easy for a toothless old man
like me. I'll just have some chickpea flour and water.' But his
companions chopped up the heart and liver with their daggers
to allow him to join in the feast. They cut up what was left and
wrapped the pieces in the fibre mats, hoping to roast or smoke
them as soon as possible.

They joked and teased, but underneath their good humour
lay a palpable apprehension, an irrepressible fear that hovered
among them. The fear that their refound liberty might come to
an end, sooner or later, and that destiny might not give them
the time to take their own lives before falling into their enemies'
hands.

The howling of a jackal saluted a thin crescent moon and
marked the start of the first guard shift for Centurion Sergius
Balbus and legionary Septimius. They took up their positions,

armed only with daggers and swords, in the shelter of two big boulders at the centre of the gully at a distance of about ten paces from each other. They watched in silence, ears straining to hear any slight sound, eyes wide to spot any moving shadow.

Every now and then, Balbus called out to his comrade, 'Hey, Blondie! You still there?'

'I'm here, Centurion,' he'd answer back. 'I'm here.'

9

THE MARCH BEGAN AGAIN at the end of the second guard shift, and after a while the terrain became a little less challenging. The bottom of the gully widened, the sides were lower and their slope was not so steep. The stones they trod had been smoothed by the effects of wind and water, with the dual advantage of facilitating their passage and making it impossible to leave traces that the enemy could possibly use to hunt them down.

The white limestone of the boulders and walls reflected a tenuous light that let them see where they were putting their feet. Before dawn they had covered perhaps three miles in total silence and complete tranquillity. They could begin to hope that the rest of their march might be free of obstacles, but in reality no one dared to believe this, as if everything had been too easy up to that moment.

They found a refuge which kept them out of sight for the day and waited there until evening. Metellus sent Lucianus and Severus, who seemed to work well together, to explore the surroundings and make sure that no one was following them. The two scouts did not have much scope for movement in such a flat and barren region, but they served as a kind of outpost which safeguarded the others from unwanted surprises and could forewarn them of the approach of any Persian patrols or caravans: while the first put them in danger of death, the second could mean salvation.

They proceeded in this way for four more nights until they reached a point at which the gorge widened into a river bed covered with pebbles and gravel, studded with thorny bushes and aromatic plants. They stopped to hold council.

'From here on we're out in the open,' said Metellus. 'Any patrol would spot us immediately. We can neither turn back nor remain sheltered by this gully forever. Uxal is the person who knows the area best, and his opinion will count for more than anyone else's.'

'I don't have much to say,' began Uxal. 'I think our only option is to follow this dry river bed. The banks are still quite high and offer some protection. If there's a problem we'll lie flat on the ground and wait until the danger has passed. The darkness of night still helps to hide us, although the moon is getting much brighter. If I remember correctly, after two or three legs of our journey we should meet up with the trail of the caravans headed towards the oasis and towards the Ocean shore, and at that point our chances of making it will improve daily.'

'By the gods! The man is a true strategist,' exclaimed Balbus in a sarcastic tone. He turned towards Uxal. 'You'll soon be better than Commander Aquila himself.'

'If you have a better idea,' sniffed Uxal, 'no one is stopping you from telling us about it. I say what I know and propose what I think is best.'

'Balbus was joking,' broke in Metellus. 'And I agree with you. We can only hope that fortune continues to assist us. What concerns me is how short we are on food. We'll have run out in just a couple of days, and our water is nearly used up as well. This is the problem we have to deal with.'

'Notice how the vegetation in the river bed is becoming more abundant? That means we should manage to find water soon. If you're worried about food, I think I know where we can find some once we get to the oasis of Khaboras. If we get desperate there's always the asses.'

'Well, then,' said Metellus, 'let's resume our march, and may fortune assist us. The only precaution we can take is to send a man ahead for reconnaissance, and post another at the rear to cover our backs. There's no more that we can do.'

Antoninus was chosen as their scout and Quadratus as rearguard, each at a distance of about half a mile from the little convoy. At the first light of dawn, both men joined up with their comrades to report back.

They continued in this way for two more nights, covering about two *parasangs*, which corresponded to a little more than six Roman miles. On the morning of the second leg, Quadratus appeared at the meeting point with a troubled expression.

'What's wrong?' asked Metellus.

'I've noticed something, Commander. Someone, that is, who seems to be following me.'

'How many of them are there?'

'One.'

'One man alone? Strange.'

'I saw one man. And I'm almost sure he's alone.'

'On horseback?'

Quadratus nodded.

'The Persians move in quite sizeable squads,' broke in Uxal. 'It's practically unheard of for one of them to go out alone, if only because, should he discover something, he would have no way of reporting back without losing contact.'

'You're right,' agreed Metellus. 'So who could it be?'

'I have no idea,' replied Quadratus. 'I saw him in the distance on the top of a hill, once or twice, and then he disappeared.'

'There's only one way to find out,' said Metellus. 'Double back towards him and take him by surprise, in the hour before dawn, if possible. Take Publius with you, he's agile and quick, and try to find out what it is this bastard wants from us. Be careful not to take any unnecessary risks. Don't show your faces. Our aim is to discover his intentions without exposing ourselves.'

'We'll do our best, Commander,' replied Quadratus. 'You can count on us.'

'Good. Rest now for a while, then. You'll set off tonight. Take your swords and daggers – you may need them. At the slightest sign of danger, turn back and try to catch up with us as quickly as possible. We'll wait here for you.'

'Of course, Commander,' replied Quadratus.

He and Publius stretched out on a mat in the shade of a big tamarisk bush. At the end of the last guard shift, they took their weapons and set off in the opposite direction to the route they had been following. They made their way very cautiously, moving low between the sparse bushes, shielding behind ridges and boulders. The dim moonlight made it easy enough to pick out the features of the landscape and the crystal-clear sky shimmered with a multitude of stars. Quadratus abruptly motioned for his companion to stop.

'What is it?'

'Can't you smell it? Smells like burning.'

'You're right. I can smell it now as well.'

'A fire. A campfire. Not too far away.'

'Shall we go and have a look?'

'Yes, but stay low to the ground. We don't want to run any risks.'

Leaving a few paces between them, they advanced with the utmost care, anxious not to make a sound, feeling the ground with their feet and hands to avoid sending stones rolling and revealing their presence. They had covered perhaps half a mile when Quadratus signalled Publius by making an owl's hoot: the signal they were used to using during military campaigns to indicate the proximity of their objective. Publius hooted back and slowly moved in.

Quadratus was pointing his finger at an extinguished campfire which still gave off a vague odour of smoke. Both men took a quick look in every direction, then approached the site.

Quadratus plunged his hands into the ashes. 'They're still warm. He didn't even bother to douse the fire.'

'You're right,' replied Publius, running the ashes through his fingers. 'Maybe he didn't want to waste what little water he had with him.'

'Don't be foolish. Sand will put out a fire. It's almost as if he wanted to lure us here to . . .'

He didn't have time to finish what he was saying. Publius

was nudging him to get his attention. He was gesturing wide-eyed with an expression of fear and astonishment.

Directly in front of them, no more than twenty feet away, was a horseman sitting immobile on his mount. They could make him out quite well in the moonlight: he was slightly built, like a boy. He wore trousers and a tunic and his face was almost completely covered by a strip of black cloth fixed at either side of his face to a kind of felt head-covering of a style they had never seen.

'Is he armed, do you think?' whispered Publius.

'I'm afraid so,' replied Quadratus. 'Don't move. We don't know what's going through his head.'

The horsemen touched his heels to the flanks of his horse and began to slowly circle the two men. The silence of the night was absolute in that moment, yet the sound of the horse's hoofs was nearly imperceptible.

'It's as if he's not touching the ground!' whispered Publius again, and he turned to get a full view of the mysterious horseman.

'Don't move!' hissed Quadratus. 'Do not challenge him. He won't strike us from behind. If you keep twisting around like that, he'll think we're afraid.'

'That's the truth!' admitted Publius between his teeth, and froze to the spot.

The horseman completed his brief circuit around the two unmoving men and the campfire, and stopped again directly in front of them. A bow suddenly materialized in his hands, an arrow nocked into the taut string.

'It's over,' muttered Publius. 'Farewell, Centurion, I'll see you in Hades.'

Quadratus did not answer. He was staring at the tip of the arrow as if spellbound. The horsemen held his aim for a few moments, then slowly released the bowstring. He put the weapon away, spurred on his horse and vanished instantly over the top of a line of hills.

The two men looked each other in the face without saying a word, then headed back at full pelt towards their camp.

They reached their comrades just as dawn was about to break and told them what had happened. Metellus listened attentively, then turned to Uxal. 'What do you think? Who could it have been? Not a Persian scout, that's for sure. Why would he have spared them?'

'No, I don't think it was a scout put on our trail. He would not have stopped at threatening them with a bow, and he wouldn't have been alone. All we can say is that this fellow doesn't want anyone in his way. If he met up with one of us again or if we crossed his path, he wouldn't hesitate to let that arrow fly.'

'I think so as well,' said Quadratus. 'He had all the time he needed to run us through, if he had intended to. He just wanted to make it clear that we should give him a wide berth. And that if he finds us sniffing around his trail again, he won't think twice about striking back.'

'Did you say that he was wearing a kind of black veil that covered his mouth?' asked Metellus.

'That's right, wrapped up around the top of some strange headgear. He was wearing a tunic that crossed over in the front and was fastened by a belt, with trousers and boots.'

Metellus thought immediately of the horseman with the veiled face that he'd seen among the warriors in Shapur's entourage that day in Edessa, and then once or twice again during their long journey across the Persian high plains.

'He's a strange one, all right,' observed Severus. 'He follows us, but he won't tolerate us following him.'

'He's not necessarily following us,' observed Balbus, who hadn't spoken up till then. 'Maybe he's just on the same road. Maybe he's fleeing from someone or something, just as we are.'

'It's possible,' agreed Metellus. 'I don't think he'll give us much cause for concern. Let's continue on our way. We'll move on now, for as long as it stays cool. When it gets too hot, we'll stop in a sheltered spot, if we find one, or we'll build a makeshift shelter ourselves. In marching order, men. We're off.'

He set off first, followed by Balbus and Quadratus. The

second group was formed of Uxal, Septimius and Lucianus with the asses, and the last of Antoninus, Severus, Martianus, Publius and Rufus, who always kept his javelin at the ready, even while marching.

Dawn was not long in coming, announced by a thin pink strip to their left, becoming a luminous arch that put the stars out one by one. The endless barren countryside, sculpted by the half-light and tinted by the mix of midnight blue and rosy dawn, was transformed when the sun appeared. The terrain which had been peopled with fleeting shadows turned into a blinding, chalky waste land, a formless slab above which the shimmering air created dancing apparitions.

When he saw that his men were dripping with sweat, Metellus ordered them to stop and to fashion a shelter from the sun using the mats they carried and some sticks. The asses were let loose to graze on the tamarisk shrubs and on other plants with a globular shape and an intensely green colour which managed to grow in the midst of the stones.

They lay down alongside each other, covered their faces with rags and tried to sleep. Rufus remained on guard along with Publius, who continually scanned the horizon for any sign of life.

'There he is,' said Publius suddenly.

'Who?'

'Him. The archer on horseback.'

'I don't see anything.'

'Over there. See, near the dust-devils. On the top of that hill.'

'You certainly have got good eyesight. Now that you've pointed him out I can see him too. What's he doing?'

'Nothing. He's stock-still in the middle of the desert on his horse.'

'Isn't his brain burning up?'

'Don't ask me. Who knows where he comes from? Who knows who he is? They say that Asia is so big that it covers the rest of the world. There are lands populated by one-legged monsters, and others where the inhabitants don't have faces – just an eye in the middle of their chests.'

'And you believe that?'

'I don't know, but that fellow's nothing like us, I can tell you that. He appeared in front of us as though he'd come out of nowhere. And how do we know what's behind that black veil that covers nearly his whole face? Centurion Quadratus has got guts, you know that, but he turned white as a sheet when he saw that bastard smack in front of us in the moonlight with that arrow aimed straight at him.'

'Everyone looks white as a sheet in the moonlight.'

'Shut up, will you?' Quadratus broke in. 'I'd like to sleep an hour or two, if you'll let me.'

The two men fell silent, but they kept their eyes on the small dark shape immobile on top of the hill.

'If you want to know what I think,' said Rufus in a whisper, 'he doesn't intend to pass us. He's letting us go first so he'll have no surprises.'

'Or he doesn't know where the hell to go and he's following us because he hopes we know the way.'

'Yeah, maybe. Anyway, the commander's right. Let him stew in his own juice, and we'll mind our own affairs. Sooner or later he'll disappear.'

And in fact he vanished as suddenly as he had appeared. Rufus and Publius were distracted for a moment by the asses, who were wandering off, and when they turned their gaze back to the hill the horseman had disappeared in the quivering white-hot air.

TOWARDS EVENING they ate some dry dates and a few walnuts, swallowed down their last ration of water, served by Martianus in a wooden bowl, and set forth again, marching up the dry river bed.

They walked all that night and all the next, with very little food in their stomachs and no water. Their weariness was becoming unbearable. The strain of years of unceasing toil and brutal treatment could certainly not be eased by forced marches and rationed food. They went forward by dint of willpower alone and the steadfastness forged of endless hardship.

Uxal was the one who worried Metellus most: his age, the continuous exertion and the emotions generated by their adventure seemed to weigh more heavily on his frail frame than on anyone else's.

Finally, by the dawn of the third day, the vegetation in the river bed had become so plenteous that Uxal himself urged the others to push on instead of stopping to prepare a shelter for the day.

'What's the hurry?' asked Metellus. 'We've waited so long, what's another day?'

'I'm sure that we're close now,' replied Uxal. 'See those birds? They're finches. They need water every day. You'll see.'

He wasn't wrong. In less than two hours, the temperature had changed markedly and a lush thicket appeared in the middle of the river bed.

'I'll go first,' said Uxal. 'You never know. Wait for me here and stay out of sight.'

He strode off alone and when he returned a little while later his hair and clothes were wet and his mouth was open in a smile that could have been called radiant if he'd still had his teeth.

'Water,' he said.

'Water?' repeated Metellus incredulously.

'And dates, and pistachios. All you want.'

Metellus said nothing, but in his heart he thanked his ancestors and Clelia's beneficent spirit for protecting him. He set off after Uxal, leading the others to the top of a little knoll, and from there he stopped to contemplate the scene of their salvation. He stood and watched as his men ran towards a copse of palm trees and luxuriant tamarisks, and did not dare to believe that another step towards their freedom had been accomplished.

'Water and food,' he mused as he walked to catch up with the others, 'will give us the strength and courage to continue. It can only get better from here on. We'll find villages, markets and caravans that can take us far away from this inferno.'

Metellus thought of his son and it felt as if Titus had always been with him, trusting in his return, sending him the water that he would soon be drinking. He was convinced that the benevolent thoughts of those who loved him could bend events to his advantage, and to the advantage of his comrades.

The water gushed from between two limestone rocks and filled a natural basin all the way to its rim. From there it spilled through a little crack and bubbled down into a cascade that fed a rivulet that trickled away amid shiny pebbles and clean sand.

The men had stripped completely. They cupped the water between their hands and tossed it at each other, laughing like boys, washing away the sweat, dust and filth that encrusted their bodies and hair. Metellus joined in that collective bath after having quenched his thirst. It felt as if all his strength was back and, with it, his faith in the future.

When they got out of the pool it was nearly midday. They stretched out in the shade to dry off and rest, leaving Martianus on guard outside the oasis.

Lucianus noticed that there were animal tracks all around. 'We'll find meat here as well,' he said. 'When night falls, gazelles, ibex and antelopes come here to drink. We'll just lie low and patiently wait for the right moment to strike.'

'Will we be able to light a fire?' asked Severus.

'I think we're out of danger,' replied Uxal. 'We're miles away from Aus Daiwa and it's been such a long time since we escaped. They won't have a clue where to look any more, and besides, this is a caravan route. The smoke of campfires is hardly an unusual sight. We can do it at night, and shield the fire with our mats, or with palm leaves or whatever else we can find.'

'I'm against it,' replied Metellus. 'But if you all agree I'm willing to risk it. We've been sorely lacking sustenance and a joint of roast meat is too great a temptation even for a legion commander.'

The men laughed and then, one after another, surrendered

to their fatigue. They spent the rest of the day gathering figs – they weren't ripe yet, but they were edible – and pistachios to roast on the fire once it had been lit.

Lucianus and Septimius had their comrades move away from the water so they could prepare their trap. Rufus joined them with his inseparable javelin and the three of them waited in silence until darkness fell. The asses were let loose so that their presence would reassure the wild animals.

The wait was longer than expected. A young gazelle approached shortly after sunset but smelled something in the air and sprang away in huge bounds. Next came a jackal, which had a leisurely drink and trotted away. The bigger animals didn't arrive until it was pitch black: an antelope and a couple of ibex. Lucianus aimed with his bow, taking advantage of the faint light of the moon, and let fly. The female ibex, hit in the thigh, tried nonetheless to run away but Rufus was ready and flung his javelin, striking her flank.

The animal dropped to the ground, kicking, while the male and the antelope leapt off, vanishing in the dark. Septimius finished the female off with his knife, skinned her and cut her into pieces. Meanwhile, Uxal was trying to light a fire, nomad-style: rubbing a sycamore stick against the hollow of a dry tamarisk branch. He soon tired, but Balbus and Quadratus took over, quickly learning the technique. After a while, the continued friction caused the tamarisk branch to start smoking and a little flame burst out.

It was the first true meal they'd had after two years of imprisonment, and Uxal had even managed to flavour the meat with a savoury herb that grew between the stones.

'If only we had a little wine . . .' mused Antoninus. 'Can you imagine? I don't know what I'd give for a sip of Massico.'

'We have this water,' said Metellus. 'That's miracle enough.'

'Commander,' said Rufus, 'we'll make it now, won't we? They'll have stopped searching for us by now.'

Metellus broke off a stalk of wild oak and twirled it between his fingers for a moment, in silence, before he answered. 'You always have to put yourself in the enemy's mind. If you were them, what would you do? Would you give up?'

Antoninus did not reply.

'We'll take what comes,' added Metellus. 'Every day is a day gained. We can make it, I do believe that. With every passing hour we're closer to freedom. But they won't be giving up any time soon. We can be sure of that. So douse the campfire, hide the traces, load up the asses and we'll leave.'

They set off and the little column was soon swallowed up by the night.

10

A CARAVAN APPEARED on the top of a hill at a distance of about three or four miles: a dozen loaded camels and a small escort of horsemen. They looked like dark shadows because the sun was behind them, and their route seemed to be running more or less parallel to the one that Metellus and his men were taking, as they continued along the river bed so as not to be noticed. More than once, the commander had strayed several hundred paces to the left or right to check how visible their little convoy was; he was reassured to see that the heads of the tallest men barely emerged from the top of the banks, and were practically indistinguishable in the darkness by anyone who was not aware of their presence.

He had decided to continue to proceed only by night because the strategy had produced excellent results, but they began their march earlier, at dusk, and they kept it up until a few hours after dawn, when the sun rose. In this way they managed to increase the distance covered by each leg up to seven or eight miles.

The waterway at the centre of the river bed widened as they advanced and seemed increasingly like a torrent, surrounded by an abundance of vegetation and visited by many animals, including groups of partridges and bustards that often contributed to enriching the diet of Metellus's men and filling out their frames. Apart from Uxal, they were all quite young and their physiques reacted well, after such lengthy privations, to the scarce but nourishing food they were able to procure for themselves. But what gave them vigour was, above all, their enthusiasm for their refound freedom and their firm determination never to be deprived of it again, at any cost.

They continued to advance with this spirit, always keeping up with the caravan they had sighted. They imagined them to be a group of merchants accompanied by servants, camel drivers and an escort; every night they camped on the shores of the torrent, lighting a fire to cook their dinner.

Halfway through the second leg of their journey, after having seen the caravan, the torrent disappeared suddenly, swallowed up by the earth, and for nearly eight miles they didn't see it again. They had plentiful water supplies, but were always rather short of food.

One evening Quadratus approached Uxal, who was busy roasting something on a stone brought to a red heat in the embers. 'What is that?' asked the centurion. 'It sure smells good.'

'Delicious stuff,' said Uxal. 'Taste.'

Quadratus took some and the other comrades followed suit.

'What was it?' asked Severus when he had finished. 'I've never had that before.'

'Larvae,' replied Uxal.

'Do you mean worms?' exclaimed Severus with a disgusted expression.

'Call them what you like. What's important is that you've eaten,' said Metellus behind them. 'I can't afford to let your energy fail. We need every spark we've got.'

They continued for two more legs of three *parasangs* and were relieved to see the torrent reappear; it never abandoned them again, for the rest of their journey. At the end of the sixth leg, as the day was dawning, they came within sight of an area covered with lush palm trees between which their torrent wound its way until it poured into the Khaboras, a great river which dominated the valley with its glittering presence. It flowed from north to south between two low sandstone banks, where it had carved out a passage. Caravans could be seen everywhere, camped among the palm groves and along the shores of the river, and more seemed to be coming from every direction. On the eastern side of the grove there was a village of low green-brick houses plastered with mud.

'The oasis of Khaboras!' exulted Uxal. 'What did I tell you?'

'I never doubted it,' said Metellus, laying a hand on his shoulder, 'and we're very grateful to you. You, Uxal, are the true leader of this expedition. Without you we would never have managed to get this far. But I'm afraid we're not in the clear yet. These places are crossing points for traffic coming and going in every direction. And no one knows that better than our enemies. I'm certain that among the caravans, or in the village houses, there are Persian spies or even soldiers in disguise.'

'What do you propose we do, Commander?' asked Quadratus.

'I say we send Uxal forward with Septimius and a couple of asses. Septimius will pretend to be a servant, and thus won't need to talk, and he can return here every night to report back to us. When Uxal has negotiated passage with a caravan, we'll come forward and arrange to continue our journey, in the hopes that this time we'll be distancing ourselves from danger once and for all.'

'I think that's a sensible idea. When do we leave?' asked Uxal.

'People who have nothing to hide travel during the day, so I think you should wait for evening before you go.'

The men found a clearing in the shade of the palm trees and went about various activities to while away the time: washing their clothes in the river, carving a stick, honing the blades of their swords or daggers, braiding straw to make a basket.

Publius preferred to backtrack for half a mile down the river bed, along with a companion.

'You're still thinking of that horseman, aren't you?' Rufus asked him.

'You know when you've got a mosquito buzzing around you with that continuous, insufferable droning, and it doesn't bite and you keep thinking, "It's going to bite, it's going to bite" and you can't think of anything else?'

'Yeah, I know what you mean.'

'Well, that's the way it is. I'd give anything to know where he is and what's going through his head right now.'

They reached a rise, a kind of mound in the landscape from where they could look out over a vast sweep of land, but all they saw was a caravan in the distance, probably headed for the oasis of Khaboras.

'I think he's gone about his own affairs. We won't see him again, trust me,' said Rufus.

'I hope that's so, but my heart tells me differently. I'm going to stay out here a bit longer. If you want to return to camp, go ahead.'

Rufus stayed with him, but nothing happened: the horseman did not emerge out of that wide, empty space. And as the sun rose towards the centre of the sky, the scorching surface of the desert created strange illusions, fleeting forms that danced over the bleak contours of the rocks, dust-demons that twisted and wriggled like damned souls under the sun's merciless rays.

'Let's go back,' said Rufus after several hours of futile vigilance. 'We're waiting for a ghost. As I told you, he's gone off on his own.'

Publius grudgingly agreed and the two men walked along the gravelly shore of the torrent in the direction of their camp. 'You know?' he said after a while. 'I'm sure that as soon as we turned our backs, he appeared. That son of a bitch. Somewhere out there in the middle of the desert . . .'

'You're obsessed,' replied Rufus lightly. 'I wouldn't think about it if I were you. He can appear and disappear as much as he likes. All I care about right now is slipping in with some caravan, reaching a port on the Ocean, boarding a merchant ship sailing west and getting back to my house in the Sicilian countryside in two or three months' time. You could come with me if you like. It's a beautiful little stone house, with a stream that turns the grinding stone in the mill. There's an orchard, olive trees, a pasture for the sheep. I keep chickens too. My wife gathers up a full basket of eggs every morning.'

'I live in the country as well,' said Publius. 'Near Spoletum we've got fields of wheat, a nice vineyard and a forest of oak trees where the pigs can root around. I make a mean ham and my sausages are legendary.'

'Don't start me thinking about it!' moaned Rufus. 'It's best not to get our hopes up. We're not out of danger yet. The worst is yet to come, I fear. You heard what the commander said. He thinks this oasis is the ideal place for people to come looking for us.'

Publius wheeled around, as if to surprise someone behind him. Someone who wasn't there.

'Ah!' exclaimed Rufus, shaking his head. 'You won't give up, will you?'

Publius said nothing until they had reached the camp.

The sun-dazzled afternoon passed in a strange, uneasy silence, because each one of them was immersed in his own thoughts, as he considered the dangers of entering such a busy place.

Those among them who had suffered the most in captivity, those who were the least well disposed to living under any kind of oppression – Quadratus and Balbus certainly, but even Septimius, and Antoninus as well – wondered whether it wouldn't have been better to prolong their liberty by choosing to stay in the wild rather than risking everything in a village where they might lose their freedom for good. But they were well aware that they must all share the same destiny and that salvation would be for one and all or for no one, and they knew that their little army had a chief, Commander Aquila, legate of the Second Augusta Legion, one of the most valiant generals of the empire, and the best leader they could hope for.

They sweated in the shade of the palm trees in the heavy atmosphere, and every now and then they'd cast a furtive glance at Metellus to check on his humour, but the expression of their commander, absorbed in planning the moves for the following days, was impenetrable. He was determined to avoid any possible problem and to work out the safest itinerary to bring them to freedom once and for all.

IT WAS NEARLY dusk the next evening when Uxal came back, along with Septimius. He held out a straw bag and exclaimed, 'Bread! I've brought you bread, valiant combatants. What do you say to that?'

'Bread?' repeated Lucianus. 'I think I've forgotten how it tastes.'

'Here it is, mama's boy!' said Septimius, showing him the loaves. 'There's enough here for a whole legion!'

'How did it go?' Metellus asked immediately.

'Well. Not bad, I'd say. We met up with an Indian merchant, a certain Daruma, and Septimius worked for him and earned this sack of freshly baked bread. He's due to leave in a couple of days. He intends to go downriver for a day or two until he reaches a port where he can board a ship and reach the Ocean.'

'Did you tell him about us?'

'I said I was expecting friends who wanted to set sail as well, but that we couldn't afford to rent a ship on our own. I haven't gone into details yet, but I have prepared the ground.'

Metellus turned to Septimius. 'Did you notice anything suspicious? Did you have time to take a look around?'

'Not really. I saw merchants, labourers, slaves, people of all imaginable races: Persians, Judaeans, Armenians, Arabs, Commagenians, Adiabenians. I even found someone who spoke Latin, a Syrian from Hemesa, who told me all sorts of interesting things.'

Uxal began to cut the bread as Lucianus lit a fire from the embers he carried inside a palm-wood container, covered with ash.

'What kind of things?' asked Metellus.

'First of all, that Odenatus, as he was returning home with the legions of Palmyra and his Osroenian auxiliaries, attacked Shapur, stole away the plunder he'd accumulated during his military campaign and inflicted heavy losses on his troops. It seems that Shapur himself survived out of pure luck.'

Metellus looked at Septimius with an uneasy expression. 'That is good news, but how did you come to speak of such a topic?'

'We were drawing water from a well and I heard him speaking Latin to a slave, so I asked him where he was from and he told me. You know how these things go. After a while he was telling me that he was in the provisions convoy when Odenatus caught up with Shapur and gave him a good thrashing before the Persian chariots loaded up with booty could cross the bridge on the Tigris.'

Metellus pounded his fist on his thigh. 'Good job, by Hercules! I wish I'd been there to teach him a lesson, that decked-out rooster, that pompous peacock, that lily-livered son of a bitch . . .'

'I thought the same thing,' continued Septimius, 'and I also thought that if Odenatus had attacked him any earlier we might have been liberated. Maybe even the emperor would have been saved. Who knows!

'Anyway that Syrian knew a lot of things. He said that Gallienus hasn't shown his face in the East, that he has surrounded himself with Christian ministers and that in any case, south of Anatolia, it's Odenatus who's in control, as if he were an independent sovereign.'

'I'm not surprised,' retorted Metellus. 'Odenatus is an excellent general, but he's very ambitious and his wife is even more so. And she's got him wrapped around her little finger . . . What language does this Daruma speak, anyway?' he asked.

'Uxal spoke with him in Persian, but I think I heard him haggling with a Syrian in Greek, if I'm not mistaken.'

'Let's go, then. I want to meet him.'

'Now?'

'No point waiting. We'll eat the bread on the way. Let's go.'

They started walking towards the oasis, where at that moment a multitude of campfires were being lit, casting a reddish glow on the palm leaves that bowed downwards. As they passed, they saw the groups of the various caravans busying themselves with dinner: Arab women with tattooed faces, young Syrian slaves, groups of Armenians wearing long cloaks of light blue, ochre and black over their grey tunics, Indians with smooth hair and crinkly hair, Judaeans with their white linen head-dresses, even Ethiopians. A buzz could be heard everywhere around them, along with the laughter and cries of children scurrying between the palm trunks and hopping the myriad streamlets of the irrigation canals. But neither Metellus nor his men allowed themselves to be distracted by that serene, inviting sight, allowing their eyes to roam only to pick up on any suspicious details.

'That's Daruma's camp,' said Uxal. 'Down there, near the brick houses. Let me go first.'

The others slowed their pace until they were nearly standing still, waiting until Uxal signalled to them that it was safe to approach.

Daruma was at the centre of a clearing where his men were roasting mutton over an open flame. He wore a full-length ochre-coloured tunic that covered his massive frame and fat belly without hiding them. Silver rings dangled from his ears and his hair was gathered at the nape of his neck. He seemed to be about fifty, to judge from the numerous grey hairs that con-trasted with the raven-black colour of his locks.

Metellus greeted the Indian in Greek: 'Chaire!'

'Chaire,' replied Daruma in the same language. 'Welcome to my modest camp, stranger.'

He spoke an Oriental-style koinè, with a strong but indefinable accent, the type of Greek that everyone used from Byzantium to Alexandria, in every warehouse of the Persian Gulf, the Red Sea and the southern coast of Arabia: a language understood mostly by non-Greeks that a Greek from Athens would never be able to speak.

'I imagine that you are the head of your small caravan,' said Daruma.

'My companions have put their trust in me,' replied Metellus, trying to adapt to the expressions of the man before him.

Daruma sat on a mat and invited his guests to do the same. Metellus and his men crouched and then crossed their legs with evident difficulty.

'I have no cushions with me!' said Daruma, smiling 'These mats are much easier to transport on long trips and they take up so little room.'

'The mats are fine,' said Metellus with a hint of embarrassment.

'Your comrade has told me that you're looking for work.'

'I'll tell you why we're here,' replied Metellus. 'We were transporting a load of fabrics and skins to the port of Hormusia when we were assaulted by a band of brigands. We managed to escape with our lives, and later found these three asses, which had fled into the desert when we were attacked. It's a miracle we survived. We've managed to live on what little we could find to eat and drink. We have no money, but we're seeking a passage to the coast, where we plan on taking ship. We can do a little of everything. There are skilled craftsmen, blacksmiths and carpenters among us. We can work as porters or . . .'

A servant laid a tray of roasted meat at the feet of his master, who looked around at his guests. 'You must be hungry,' he said with a peculiar expression, halfway between enquiring and curious.

'Yes,' Metellus said without hesitation. 'We are hungry.'

Daruma gestured to his servant, who passed around with the tray. Each man took a piece of meat and was about to sink his teeth into it with the avidity of someone who hasn't had a decent bite to eat for ages, but Metellus's withering gaze obliged them to make a show of self-control. Metellus took a portion as well and began to eat it calmly under their host's attentive eye. Metellus could feel Daruma's eyes upon them; he knew that he was observing him and his men with meticulous, albeit well-disguised, scrutiny. He realized that there was nothing in their appearance, their expressions, their wary glances that escaped him.

Daruma also had his servant pass round an amphora of palm wine, surprisingly cool and sparkling.

'How do you keep it so cold?' asked Metellus to revive the conversation.

'By continually dampening the vessel that contains it. As it dries, the water cools the amphora and the wine inside. I learned that from the desert nomads, who are accustomed to living in conditions that no city dweller would ever be able to tolerate.'

Metellus thanked him. 'We're greatly obliged to you for your kindness and hospitality. I hope to find a way to pay you back . . .'

'Who are you?' asked Daruma suddenly, staring closely into his eyes.

Metellus hesitated.

'You're not used to lying,' Daruma pressed on, 'or to sitting this way. You're used to giving orders and being obeyed without even opening your mouth. You come from the West, then, almost certainly a military man. A Roman officer, I'd say . . . I'd bet on it, actually. And these, apart from the old fellow, are your men.'

He spoke softly so that only Metellus could hear him. Metellus tried to hide his discomfort, but his right hand started to slip almost imperceptibly under his tunic towards the hilt of his sword.

'You don't need that,' Daruma said without even looking at him. 'It is the custom never to betray one's guests where I come from as well. As long as you eat my bread, you're as safe as if you were in a fortress.'

Metellus put both hands on his knees and drew a long sigh.

'I might think that you were a group of spies sent into the heart of the Persian empire, but I can see from the hardships you've suffered, the scars you're trying to keep hidden under your rags and the terror in your eyes, that you're fleeing from a grave threat. If I said that you're the group who escaped from the Aus Daiwa camp – whom the Persians are searching for in every corner of this region – would I be very far from the truth?'

'What do you expect me to answer you?' said Metellus.

'Nothing. I know I've hit the mark.'

'Why have you offered us your hospitality, then?'

'Pure curiosity. These long crossings are deadly and I never miss an opportunity to occupy myself with someone else's affairs if I find them exciting enough. In any case, I didn't believe a word of what the old man told me, or what you said, although he's a much better liar than you are.'

'And now that you know, what will you do?'

'Do you have children?' asked Daruma, as if he had not heard him.

Metellus looked at him in surprise at the sudden change of subject, but replied, 'A son. But I don't know where he is or what has happened to him.'

'So you don't have a wife.'

'I did. She was murdered.'

'By the Persians?'

'The Romans.'

'The most logical question would be: why remain loyal to these Romans, then? You're a high-ranking officer, obviously, and you must have information that's worth quite a lot. But you would naturally have already sold out if you were so inclined, to save yourself from imprisonment and oppression. I think I understand. You're one of those Romans one sees carved on arches and columns: inflexible, upright, intrepid and a little stupid.'

'That may be,' replied Metellus stiffly.

'Don't let it get to you. I'm just trying to figure out what you're like. I have to get to know who I'm travelling with, don't I?'

'Do you mean that—'

'What's your name?' Daruma interrupted him again.

His way of abruptly jumping from one subject to another was driving Metellus mad, but he replied without hesitation, 'Marcus Metellus Aquila.'

'Pronounced in your language, that must be a name that makes a man tremble just hearing it.'

'It's a name that has never been dishonoured.'

'I'd imagined as much. Now listen. Tell your men they can sleep in that tent down there, near the camels. You'll be my guest.'

Metellus bowed his head. 'I'm accustomed to sharing everything with my men.'

'This time you'll make an exception to please me. I'd say I've earned it.'

'I don't think I'd be able to sleep. I must supervise the guard shifts personally.'

'No guard shifts. This place has already been scoured three times from top to bottom by Persian soldiers. They've turned over every stone. I don't think they'll be back. What's more, my guards don't take kindly to other people doing their job for them. If you don't like it, you can go back to where you came from.'

'No,' replied Metellus. 'I accept and I thank you, in the name of my men as well. Will you take us with you, then?'

'It depends.'

'On what?'

'You'll soon know.'

Daruma got up and made his way towards his tent.

11

Uxal accompanied the men to their quarters and Metellus remained alone next to the campfire for a little while. It was a lovely night, he was the guest of a well-to-do merchant and he had dined on oven-fresh bread, roast meat and cold wine. His men had eaten well and were graciously lodged. There was good reason to hope that Daruma would take them with him and that they might reach the Ocean and, perhaps, return to their homeland. It almost seemed that the long imprisonment, the death of the emperor and of a comrade, the cruel suffering they'd borne, were all just a nightmare, a bad dream destined to vanish with the rising of the sun. But there was one thought that made him harshly aware that everything was real: his undiminished longing for his lost spouse and for the son whose fate he knew nothing about.

He thought of Lucius Domitius Aurelian, of Sword-in-Hand, and trusted that his loyal friend had done everything he could to protect little Titus. Perhaps the boy was living with him, and perhaps Lucius was keeping his memory alive in the child, instilling hope in his return.

Not a single night since he had fallen into captivity, and then since he had escaped, had he lain down to rest without invoking his ancestors to keep watch over Titus, over the son to whom he had broken his promise to return that very day he had been forced to depart on a journey that anyone would have imagined without return.

'Where are you, my son?' he wondered. 'Where are you, boy?' And he asked himself whether Titus, at that same moment, was wondering the same thing: 'Where are you, father?' Perhaps their two thoughts were meeting, unknown to them, somewhere across the arc of the sky, setting aflame a falling star. There, like the one he could see just then, tracing a line of fire in the dark, all the way down to the palm leaves.

ULTIMATELY, he was not deceiving himself. If the gods were listening to his paternal yearnings, they would have seen Titus leaning on the balcony of the imperial palace of Milan and scanning the sky, just as his father was.

Tillia the slavegirl was watching him. He had grown since she had entered his service and seemed somehow to have resigned himself to his condition. He attended the lessons of his tutors, learning Greek, mathematics, grammar and calligraphy. He was treated with respect and accompanied every moment of the day until dusk, when Tillia took over his care.

He saw Gallienus very rarely, only during official ceremonies, and always at a distance. He was convinced that the emperor was avoiding him because he didn't want to answer the question the boy wanted to ask: 'Where is my father? And where is yours?'

He had never seen Aurelian again either: his father's friend, the hero whom the soldiers called Sword-in-Hand. They had received news that he had led the legions beyond the Danube, against the Sarmatians, and that he had killed fifty of them by his own hand in the course of a battle in which over twenty thousand of those barbarians had fallen. But he had been awarded no triumph, as would have been his right, because Gallienus was jealous of him. Or so they said. Instead of being called home, Aurelian had been transferred to Moesia, which was being threatened by the Goths.

It was Tillia who told him those things, because as a young slave she had the opportunity to listen without being noticed, much as if she were a statue or a piece of furniture.

'Why are the barbarians so angry with us?' Titus had asked

his tutor one day, a rhetorician from Treviri with a yellowish beard and hair like straw.

'They're not angry with us,' he had replied. 'They want to be allowed in, because they want to enjoy the beautiful things we have. If you had to choose between living in a cart through the chill of winter and the heat of summer, hardly ever being able to wash, suffering both hunger and thirst, or living in a nice house with food every day, a bath, heating in the winter and fountains that cool the air in the summer, libraries and gardens, which would you choose?

'Do you know how many aqueducts Rome has? Eleven. And do you know how many Milan has? Seven. Do you know how many rooms there are in this palace? Three hundred. And how many libraries there are in the empire? About five thousand, with thirteen million books. And how many roads have been built? Two hundred thousand miles of roads, with a post-house every fifteen miles.

'We're trying to stop them from getting in: when we can with negotiations, when we can't with the army. That's what our generals are doing now in Pannonia and Moesia.'

'One of our generals is a friend of my father's,' Titus said.

'Oh, really? Who is it?'

'Aurelian, Sword-in-Hand. You can't joke around with him, and if anyone hurts me they'll have him to face up to.'

'No one wants to hurt you.'

'Then why are you holding me prisoner in this place?'

'You're not a prisoner. You're a guest. And "this place" is the imperial palace, the most beautiful place in which anyone could desire to live.'

'Well, I don't like it and I want to leave.'

'You're too little.'

'Then why don't you let my father come back?'

But that was a question that no one had an answer to. Not even the emperor.

When Titus spoke about his father, he was gripped by a deep

sense of gloom that his young spirit could not bear. He'd slip away then, no matter what he was doing, and find a place to weep in frustration and sadness until he had cried himself out.

'WHAT ARE YOU thinking of?'

Daruma's voice suddenly boomed out behind Metellus, making him jump. He couldn't have said how long he'd been absorbed in his thoughts. He looked at the fire and saw that only ashes remained. A long time had passed.

'My son,' he replied.

'Do you think he is in danger?'

'Anything could have happened. I know nothing. Not hearing anything at all is almost worse than having bad news.'

'Isn't there anyone who can take care of him?'

'I have a friend, the commander of one of the large combat units of our army. I know that he would do anything to protect my son, but he may be too far away to be able to help him. He may even have died. That's what happens to soldiers.'

'Not generals.'

'He's the kind who stays in front, not behind. Always the first to face the risks he subjects his men to. I've always done the same. We're those upright kind of Romans, a little stupid, as you pointed out.'

'Everyone has defects and qualities. No one is perfect,' Daruma declared.

'I imagine that the Persians are offering a reward for our capture. Aren't you tempted to turn us in?'

'I buy and sell goods, not men.'

'But our presence in your caravan, even for a brief time, represents a serious risk for you. Why should you do it?'

'At the end of dinner, you asked me a question and I answered, "It depends." '

'On what?'

'On what you're willing to risk, you and your men.'

'Everything, in exchange for freedom.'

'Then we can talk about it. If you're not tired, that is.'

'I'm not tired. I'm listening.'

'I'm not here for purposes of trade.'

'Neither am I. Go on.'

'I had an appointment with a person who has not shown up. The agreement was that if in fifteen days he had not come here to the oasis, the appointed place would be shifted further south, to the port on the Khaboras, a two-day journey from here.'

'And so you're ready to go.'

'Tomorrow. Or the next day, at most. The fact that this person hasn't arrived makes me a bit apprehensive and leads me to believe that having a group of armed, experienced soldiers with me might not be a bad idea.'

'Us?'

'Well, you're a little knocked up, but you look like people who have been through hell and survived.'

'Nearly two years at Aus Daiwa.'

'That seems impossible ... In any case, if you're willing to act as an escort for this caravan, I'll feed you and pay you in silver shekels every ten days until we reach our destination. After which you'll be free to go. With the money you'll have earned you can return to your homeland.'

Metellus shook his head.

'You don't like it?'

'You said you had guards. Why would you need us?'

'I lied. I didn't want you to know that my guards are only willing servants. I didn't want you to get any funny ideas. On the other hand, you lied to me as well. When needs must, it's allowed. Well, shall we make this agreement or not?'

'It's fine with me. It's that I can hardly believe it.'

'Maybe I wasn't clear. You'll be risking your lives.'

'What does it matter? That's all I've been doing up to now.'

'What about your men?'

'They'll agree with whatever I decide.'

'It's a deal, then,' said Daruma.

Metellus replied, 'I'd say it's best that I begin right now, given the situation.'

'My men are on watch. I think that's enough for tonight. The moon is so bright you can almost see as well as day. But if it will make you feel safer, go ahead and put one of your men on guard. Your bed is ready in my tent, whenever you like. Good night, Commander Aquila.'

'Goodnight, Daruma,' replied Metellus. 'And . . . thank you.'

Daruma smiled and disappeared inside his tent.

Metellus drew his sword from under his tunic and slung it over his shoulder. He went towards the tent where his men were sleeping and found Balbus awake.

'I imagined as much! Go ahead and finish the first guard shift, Centurion. We're back in service. Daruma has hired us to escort the caravan.'

'You're not joking with me, are you, Commander?'

'Not at all. In exchange for our services, he'll give us food and pay until we reach our destination. A good deal, I'd say.'

'Magnificent! Go ahead and rest. I'll take care of organizing the shifts.'

Metellus made another round of the camp before retiring. The oasis was immersed in silence, the fires had been put out and even the animals were sleeping – the asses, mules, big Bactrian camels, slender dromedaries, all fettered, covered with saddlecloths adorned with red and blue tassels. The murmur of the water running through the canals made a counter-melody to the voice of the Khaboras and her majestic current. The moon roused a sparkle of silver from the canals and every now and then the shadow of a bird of prey would pass among the trunks of the century-old palms, their great wings as silent as nocturnal thoughts.

Metellus returned towards Daruma's tent with the thought of stretching out on a bed of straw for a few hours of true rest, but as he was about to enter he heard snarling coming from the dog tied at the post.

He took a look around. Everything seemed calm. He knew that dogs were able to hear sounds that the human ear could not pick out, or so they said, and he gazed into the distance, beyond the expanse of palm trees to the chalky hills that crowned the oasis to the north. He thought he saw something, like a wisp of barely perceptible fog. But it couldn't be fog . . .

'Dust! Horses!'

The sudden awareness that a squad of horsemen was galloping towards the oasis froze the blood in his veins. Their dream was over, but at least they'd die like men, with their swords in their hands. He ran towards the tents and found Balbus on the alert.

'There's something wrong, Commander. Birds are taking flight, the animals are restless . . .'

'Wake everyone, quickly, to arms! There's a cavalry squad approaching.'

Awakened roughly by the centurion, the men sprang to their feet and gathered around their commander.

'They've come to capture us,' Metellus told them. 'But I will not be taken alive; I will not return to that sewer. If you feel as I do, fetch your weapons and follow me.'

They were all beside him in an instant. The sound of galloping was just starting to be heard, off in the distance.

'No one moves without an order from me. Stay hidden behind these palm trees, near the houses. It is the most sheltered spot. If they surround us, we'll pull back into that alley between the two houses at our backs, and we'll fight them off as long as we can. I have no other plan to propose. It's a choice between quick death and long agony. We must be thankful that we have the chance to choose. All I want to tell you is that I'm proud of you. You are the best soldiers and the dearest friends I could desire. If destiny wants us to be dining together in Hades tomorrow, so be it! Let's go!'

Each man took up his position behind a palm tree so he could see his commander and his comrades as well. Lucianus and Septimius tensed their bowstrings, Rufus brandished his javelin, Publius and Antoninus gripped their swords, and Severus and Martianus their daggers. The two centurions, Balbus and Quadratus, wielded both sword and dagger and glared at the darkness before them, anticipating the direction and the moment of assault.

All the men were dripping sweat as they waited for the fight to begin, the brief, furious fray that would lead to their deaths.

In that instant of spasmodic tension, Uxal's voice sounded. 'Wait. Something's happening. Look over there!' He pointed at a path that crossed the eastern part of the oasis, where they soon distinguished a solitary horseman wrapped in a black cloak galloping by like a fury.

'What in Hades . . .' muttered Metellus.

Before he could even finish the phrase, the cavalry squad stormed in from the north and crossed the oasis at nearly the same speed as the horseman who had just streaked by. In a few moments they had all disappeared from sight, heading south in a dense cloud of dust.

'They weren't looking for us,' said Uxal.

'I guess not,' replied Metellus with a great sigh of relief.

'It was that horseman they were after,' observed Quadratus.

'Did any of you get a good look at him?' asked Metellus.

Publius stepped forward. 'He passed so quickly, in the shade of the palm trees, but I could swear it was the same man that was following us, up until the other day.'

'Don't listen to him, Commander,' broke in Rufus. 'He's obsessed with that horseman without even knowing who he is. He dreams about him at night. He sees him everywhere, even when he's nowhere to be found.'

Metellus turned to Publius. 'What makes you think it was him?'

'That black cape, his slender build, the way he rides. I'm usually not wrong, Commander.'

Uxal interrupted them. 'Whether it was him or someone else, it doesn't matter to us. What does matter is that they've gone, and that they weren't after us. For a moment there I thought it was all over.'

'So did I,' admitted Metellus.

'What's happening here?' A voice rang out behind them.

Metellus turned and found Daruma in his nightclothes.

'A squad of Persian horsemen just crossed the oasis. They seemed to be pursuing another man on horseback who raced through here just before they did.'

Daruma scowled. 'A lone horseman, you say? Did you see him?'

'I did,' said Publius, and he described him as he had to Metellus.

Daruma wrinkled his forehead. 'In what direction was he heading?'

'That way,' Publius said, pointing to a patch of vegetation that extended south along the river.

Daruma sighed and motioned for Metellus to follow him into the tent. 'Sit down,' he said as soon as they entered.

'I prefer standing. I'm more comfortable.'

'I'm worried . . .' began the Indian.

'Do you think it's the person you were supposed to meet up with?'

'It may have been him.'

An excited buzz came from outside, dogs barking, people calling out in any number of languages. The people of the caravans had been rudely awakened by that sudden raid, but no explanation could be found, further increasing the confusion.

Daruma retired briefly into a brooding silence, then said, 'Useless to fret now. There's nothing I can do. But we must depart immediately. Tomorrow. Have your men ready at dawn, dressed and armed. I've had new clothes brought to their tents. We'll be marching day and night, without cease. We must get to the port on the Khaboras as soon as possible. Rest now, for we have a long journey ahead of us.'

Metellus left to give instructions to Balbus and then came back and lay down on the bedding that had been prepared for him. Before he closed his eyes, bone-tired, he realized that he was going from one adventure to another he knew nothing about.

They left at daybreak, as the cocks' crows were just starting to sound through the still-dark oasis. They set out without breakfast; food and drink would be distributed on the road.

They marched on all day under a scorching sun. Daruma was perched on a huge camel, topped by a canopy that sheltered him from the sun; he often wet his brow with a moistened handkerchief. Despite his anxiety, he was not one to give up his comforts.

The Khaboras flowed at a short distance to their right, between shores verdant with palm trees, stands of sycamores and fig trees and profuse oleander bushes.

Metellus had drawn up his men to the right and left of the convoy while Uxal followed, riding one of the tamed asses. As they advanced, they began to see all kinds of craft afloat on the river: some were simply wicker vessels over which tanned ox hides had been stretched and coated with bitumen for watertightness, but others had true wooden hulls with wide trapezium-shaped sails and a double helm at the stern, and were sailing upstream. Sometimes the boats were so close to the shore that they could see the faces of the sailors, intent on their rigging. The calcareous bottom of the river bed was usually quite deep; only occasionally were there shallow banks that sloped down in the direction of the current.

When the banks were lower, they would find villages, the houses made of sun-dried mud bricks. Women with earthenware pots on their heads returned from the river, hips swaying gracefully under their load. Naked brown-skinned children played in the water, shouting and splashing. Those little communities seemed much like any other village on their own Internal Sea, or in Mesopotamia or Egypt. And yet the great imperial powers – here, just as on the shores of their own sea – took the young men from those peaceful communities and filled them with hate and aggression towards the enemy to be fought, whoever that might be, sending them off to war. Each of these powers felt they were in the right, each thought that their own world was the best possible and should be expanded and imposed wherever possible.

Metellus had had such thoughts before, and remembered

them well. But he also remembered that the more he travelled and visited other countries, the more he became convinced that his own world was the only one worth living in. He had never, in any other place, encountered a concept and an idea of man that could be compared to what the civilizations of Athens and Rome had produced. His long, cruel imprisonment at the mercy of an enemy who had no respect for people's rights, no respect for someone who had shown courage, valour and loyalty, had only confirmed this conviction.

He could understand how the others, the foreigners, could be sure they were in the right. But he could not forget that Valerian, his emperor, had lost his freedom and his life because he had trusted his adversary, because he had felt that any risk could be faced to attain and uphold peace in every corner of the known world, from the shores of the Atlantic to the mouth of the Indus.

Absorbed in these thoughts, he marched in silence under the burning sun.

12

THERE WERE NO PARTICULAR obstacles to set them back during
their journey. Towards dusk a small group of armed men who
may have been brigands appeared, but the sight of the impressive
display of Roman weaponry dissuaded them from taking the
offensive, had that been their intention. They rode off on their
dromedaries, disappearing behind a rise in the terrain.

The port appeared the evening of the next day. It was a dusty
city, tucked into a bend of the river, surrounded by palm trees
of every kind and by thickets of red and white oleanders. A small
wharf made of fired bricks sheltered the bend and allowed the
mooring of a good number of vessels.

Daruma advised Metellus and his men to cover their faces
with the cloth they wore swathed around their heads. He was
almost sure that there would be Persian soldiers in the port, or
spies lying in wait to snare their game.

'Scatter,' he said, 'but don't lose sight of one another.' He
showed them a green flag. 'When you see this hanging from the
yard of one of the boats, that means it's ours. You can board it
as soon as night falls, but get on a few at a time, not all at once.
Keep your weapons hidden under your cloaks and don't pick a
quarrel with anyone. Don't speak among yourselves, because if
a spy hears half a word in Latin you're dead. Communicate using
gestures and only when you're sure no one's looking. Remember
that this is the last obstacle standing between you and your
freedom. If you get through today, your imprisonment will be a
distant memory. If you make a false step, it could cost you
everything you've accomplished until now. The last moments

will be the most dangerous. The slightest thing could tip them off: a glance or an expression, a word that slips out at the wrong moment, or in the wrong place. Remember, if you are caught, I don't know you. I've never seen you. Is that clear? And I'll never be able to do anything for you, ever.'

'You've already done so much, Daruma,' replied Metellus, 'and we don't want you risking your life for us. We can take care of ourselves. I'll instruct my men.'

'Fine. We'll separate now, then.'

Metellus and his men decided not to enter the taverns that lined the wharf and not even to buy food from the stalls so as not to attract attention. They ate stale bread and drank water from their flasks as they walked down the crowded streets of the little town with an indifferent air.

The merchants' stands offered a great assortment of wares: dates, unleavened bread baked in brick ovens, dried salted fish as well as the day's catch from the river. There were delicious-looking peaches, along with squashes, melons and little wild pears that looked very hard. There were plenty of animal vendors as well, selling snakes, monkeys, brightly feathered birds of a kind they'd never seen before. The men were fascinated by that spectacle, by the odours of the roasted meats, the exotic condiments and the spices and even the perfumes contained in jars of coloured glass and alabaster.

It was difficult to understand the prices, but it was clear that the perfumes were only for the wealthy; merchants with purses full of silver haggled loudly in every language and then made their deals, buyer and seller both convinced they'd struck a good bargain.

It was the first time that Metellus was travelling as a free man outside the confines of the empire. He had thought many times of making such a journey, but the empire was so vast that by the time you were near the border, you realized it was time to turn back.

He felt out of place, but excited at the same time; the situation gave him a new sensation, a kind of dizziness brought on by the immensity of it all, the lack of confines and limits. He realized that Asia had dimensions that were immeasurable and that a virtual infinity of peoples inhabited it. He thought of those unvarying expanses they had traversed, the deserted plains, the unchanging white of the cloudless skies. He recalled stories of fabulous animals and peoples that he had read in the pages of Pliny and the De Mirabilibus and he realized that those monstrous forms of nature only existed in men's imaginations. As exploration and knowledge achieved the upper hand over fantasy, the monsters had to be relegated to ever more remote regions. Or perhaps the ancient heroes – Hercules, Theseus, Odysseus – had already destroyed all the monsters long ago. Even Alexander must have been disappointed when he got to India and found neither hippogriffs nor chimeras nor mining ants that dug gold out of the bowels of the earth.

Metellus was accompanied by Uxal, who knew the local language and was inconspicuous in the crowd; the Roman listened intently to what was being said, trying to guess at the meaning. At a merchant's stand, his attention was drawn to a toy, a little elephant carved of painted acacia wood with a jointed trunk that swung back and forth. He whispered into Uxal's ear: 'Can you buy that for me? For my little boy, that is.'

Uxal, who was in charge of the group's coffers, entered into long and animated bargaining until he managed to get what he thought was a good price. He paid with a few coins and took the toy. 'You're counting on getting home soon,' he observed when they were out of earshot.

'Why?'

'Because children grow up quickly. He might no longer like the toys you choose.'

Metellus sighed. 'You're right. Time stopped for me when I was taken prisoner. I'll always think of my son as the little boy I left that morning, even if I stay away a thousand years.'

'You know,' Uxal started, 'I think I remember a story like yours in an old poem I heard once. It talks about a man, a sailor,

I think, who returns to his island after many years away, and finds that his son has become a man.'

'The Odyssey,' replied Metellus. 'The poem is called The Odyssey, from the name of its protagonist, Odysseus. He leaves his son a newborn and when he sees him again he's twenty: Telemachus is his name.'

'Right, that's the one I'm thinking of. I hope you see your boy long before he turns twenty.'

'So do I, Uxal,' replied Metellus. 'So do I . . .'

They walked on for a little while in silence as darkness began to fall on the less congested streets and the white terraces of the town. Metellus glanced towards the port and nudged Uxal. 'The green flag,' he said. 'Daruma has found a boat.'

THEY WERE THE LAST to board, after they'd watched their comrades, one by one, cross the wood-and-reed gangway that connected the boat to the mainland.

Daruma had lanterns lit fore and aft and posted two men on guard: one of his Indians, a man called Saraganda, and one of Metellus's men, Antoninus. He had dinner distributed: a variety of foods bought on shore, all very spicy and peppery – salted goat's meat, roasted fish seasoned with thyme and malva, savoury unleavened bread baked in brick ovens and palm wine.

Rowdy laughter could be heard from the other moored boats, where the crews were relaxing after their day's work, noisily carousing and enjoying themselves with girls hired at the port. But the tension was still too high among the Romans, nor did they feel at ease yet with the rest of the crew, about whom they knew nothing. They ate and drank in silence, keeping a wary eye on the shore.

Metellus approached Daruma. 'Who are the men in your crew?'

'They're from Taprobane. There's no danger of them talking – no one here can understand them anyway. And they don't know anyone because they've only been here a few days. But they've been working for me for years and I've always paid them well. You can rest easy.'

Metellus nodded. 'It's just that everything is going so smoothly, it feels too good to be true.'

'Going smoothly?' retorted Daruma. 'That raid in the middle of the night at the oasis seemed normal to you? If the man trying to escape on horseback was the person I was waiting for, he may already be dead by now.'

'You're right,' replied Metellus. 'When you've suffered so long, you become egotistical and think only of yourself.'

Daruma nodded. 'If you want to know what I think, we're not out of danger yet. There are boats sailing downriver with the king's soldiers on board, this port is surely crawling with spies and there are squads of archers on horseback all up and down the river, in small garrisons. You seem to be very import-ant to them, if I've understood correctly. If you want us to continue this voyage together, you'd better tell me the whole truth.'

'What truth?'

'Why there were ten of you at Aus Daiwa. And how you escaped. It's said to be impossible.'

'If I tell you, do you swear you'll never repeat it to anyone?'

Daruma smiled. 'You'd trust the word of a merchant?'

'If you wanted to turn us in, you would have done so already.'

'True. Well, then?'

'Do I have your word?'

'For what it's worth, yes, you have my word.'

Metellus hesitated, then thought that Daruma did have the right to know what risks he was running by offering them hospitality. 'I was the commander of the guard of Licinius Valerianus Augustus, the last emperor of the Romans, who died in prison at Aus Daiwa after being betrayed and taken captive by Shapur at Edessa. After his death, we escaped thanks to the help of Uxal, who brought us to the oasis at Khaboras. You know the rest.'

'Great Trimurti!'

'What did you say?'

'I invoked our supreme Triad, like the one you venerate at your Capitol in Rome.'

'Have you been to Rome?'

'No, although I know someone who has been. But don't change the subject. You are in a fine mess and so am I. You could have told me right away.'

'Would you have taken us with you if I had?'

'No.'

'See.'

'How long ago did you escape?'

'I haven't kept count, but I'd say about a month and a half, or more.'

Daruma sighed. 'A great deal I've made. If they find us they'll skin us alive, to say the least.'

'I know.'

'On the other hand, they haven't caught up with you yet. How did you manage it, without horses, in this barren terrain?'

'We stayed hidden for many days in a place they consider sacred and forbidden: the gully where they throw their dead.'

'A stroke of genius. And then?'

'When we had the impression that they had stopped looking for us there, we started to move out. At night, travelling on the bottom of the gully, until we found water. We followed the stream until we reached the confluence with the Khaboras.'

'I take back what I said about you Romans being stupid. But we must be careful not to ruin it all on this last part of your journey.'

'Will we have to stay here long?'

'At least three days. That was the pact and I've added one day for good measure. I don't want you ever going ashore for the entire time. If you need something, I'll get it for you.'

'All right.' Metellus nodded. 'But there's a problem.'

'What is it?'

'We have a deal with you. You are paying us to escort and

guard your convoy. If we can't show our faces off this boat, how are we to do our job?'

'You'll have your chance, I can assure you.'

'But where? And when?'

'You'll know when the moment comes. Now try to lie low for as long as necessary.'

THEY SPENT THREE DAYS in a state of suspended apathy. The heat in the hours around midday was unbearable. Metellus and his men would sprawl between the rigging, in the shade of the sail that had been stretched out like a canopy to shelter them from the sun, sweating in the oppressive heat instead of taking a dip in the river, which had been strictly forbidden by their host. Only towards evening did a slight breeze bring some relief. Just sitting down to dinner became an important event.

Daruma spent most of his time ashore with two or three of his men, evidently trying to make contact with the person they were expecting. They would return towards dark with straw baskets full of food for the crew. Metellus never asked about the man they were looking for, but he could tell that Daruma was quite worried. Every passing day increased the risk that their presence on board would be discovered, while it diminished the probability that this long-awaited guest might turn up.

On the evening of the fourth day, Daruma made a decision. 'We'll leave tomorrow,' he said. 'If the man you saw on horseback at the oasis of Khaboras was him, he should have been here at least two days ago, seeing that we travelled at the pace of our camels and asses. I can't wait any longer. The last opportunity we'll have to find him will be at the Ocean port.'

'As you like,' replied Metellus. 'I'm sorry that this person has failed to meet up with you. We are ready whenever you are.'

They weighed anchor the next morning just before dawn. The sailors pushed the boat to the centre of the current by sticking their poles into the river bottom, then used the stern rudders only when necessary to maintain their route. Their speed was moderate but constant and the countryside passed before them in a pleasant variety of natural settings. At times they'd see groups of tiny gazelles raise their black snouts from the water in alarm as the boat went by, although they did not run off, accustomed to river traffic as they obviously were. Every now and then they would even see clusters of pink flamingos probing the edge of the bank with their curved beaks in search of food.

Antoninus, Publius, Rufus and the others watched in delight, and even Metellus enjoyed the view that became more varied and spectacular at every bend and every promontory: the ochre and yellow shades in the rock, the tall, lush palms, the fishing and farming villages that multiplied on the river's banks.

'This reminds me of certain areas in southern Egypt...' began Metellus, but he was interrupted by the shout of a sailor perched on the yardarm. The man, dark-skinned and gleaming with sweat, was pointing to a spot on the shore.

'By all the gods!' exclaimed Publius. 'It's him!'

The horseman with the black cloth wrapped around his head was descending a hill towards the river at a gallop. His pursuers soon became visible as well: twenty or so Persian soldiers chasing after him at full tilt. They must have just caught up with him, because their pace was too fast to be maintained for any length of time without exhausting the horses.

Daruma rushed to the railing and shouted, 'It's him! Draw up alongside the shore!'

The helmsman didn't wait to be told twice. He lunged at the bar that connected the stern rudders and thrust it to the right, causing the boat to veer sharply left. At that point the banks were low but steeply angled and the horseman was heading at full speed towards a bend where the foliage had created a vast, dense thicket. Perhaps he was hoping to hide there, but from what they could see his fate seemed sealed.

'Bows and javelins, men!' shouted Metellus, and they rushed to the portside rail, ready to let fly.

The helmsman had shifted the bar to the centre to correct his course and the boat was racing along parallel to the bank now, at a distance of about twenty feet. The horseman seemed to notice their manoeuvring and got as close to the bank as he could, without reducing his speed. The Persians behind him had begun to loose their arrows, which rained around the fugitive with increasingly threatening precision, though they never struck him. It was almost as if he knew what direction they would arrive from and could dodge them at the last moment. Metellus ordered his men to take aim, and two of their arrows hit their marks, felling a couple of the enemy and slowing down the onward rush of the others.

Daruma shouted again, 'To shore!' but the helmsman yelled something back and stayed on course. He was afraid of running aground on the shoals. With unsuspected energy, Daruma grabbed him by the scruff of his neck and dashed him to the planks. He gripped the bar himself and urged the boat ever nearer to the shore. Twice he heard the keel scraping the bottom but the hull held fast and he remained at a distance of eight to ten feet from the bank.

Daruma yelled again, even louder this time. A single word, with a curt, sharp tone, an order, perhaps, or an exhortation in another language.

The horseman reacted to the word, and under the unbelieving eyes of the soldiers and crew he pulled himself to his feet on the horse's back and sprang into an acrobatic leap. He vaulted through the air as if weightless and landed on the boat's deck with a dull thud, his feet and hands wide apart and his knees flexed, stopping in an absolutely static position, as if he were nailed to the planks on the deck.

Daruma immediately turned the boat towards the centre of the river and, as the Persians showered them with a barrage of arrows, Metellus and his men raised the wicker mats as if they were shields, to fend off the worst of the attack. As soon as they were out of range, Daruma turned towards the middle of the deck as if to convince himself he had not been dreaming. The mysterious person was still there, as motionless as a statue, as the crewmen and the Romans circled around him to get a closer look at the prodigy.

Metellus turned to Daruma in amazement and said, 'Is it him?'

Daruma nodded.

'What did you yell out to him?'

'Jump!'

'In what language?'

Daruma gestured as if to say, 'I'll tell you later,' then he drew close to the man who had rained down from the sky. At that moment, Metellus had the distinct sensation of having already seen those eyes. So strange, so long and slanted. And he realized that the stranger was feeling exactly the same sensation. The Roman's mind flashed back to Edessa, to the harrowing moment when Valerian was compelled to kneel before Shapur, and then he stared once more into those incredibly black, sparkling eyes.

Daruma stood in front of the newcomer, folded his hands on his chest and bent his torso down to the level of his waist in a deep bow. The mysterious being stretched into an erect position and joined his closed left fist to his open right hand with a very slight nod of his head. He then walked towards the bow and remained there, staring at the horizon.

Metellus's men looked at each other wordlessly in astonishment.

'I told you it was him,' Publius broke their silence.

'Him who?' asked Rufus.

'The man who was following us in the desert.'

'That may well be,' retorted Rufus, 'but who is he?'

'I'd say "What is he?"' broke in Lucianus, without taking his eyes from the unmoving figure at the bow.

'A man, by Hercules! What else might he be?' replied Antoninus.

'What if he were a god?' said Severus. 'I've never seen a man dodge arrows like that and . . . fly.'

'He did not fly,' shot back Antoninus. 'He jumped.'

'Oh, yeah? You call that a jump? You try. Let's see if you can do it.'

Metellus cut their argument short and gestured for them to quieten down. He approached Daruma. 'Is it really him, then?'

'Praise the Heavens, yes. I'd lost hope.'

'But who is he, if I may ask.'

'A prince.'

'From what country?'

'China.'

Metellus looked at him in surprise. 'China? What's that?'

13

'CHINA?' REPEATED DARUMA with a smile. 'China is the Land of Silk, the country you call Sera Maior on those very approximate maps of yours.'

'Actually they say that some of my countrymen have been there,' said Metellus. 'Merchants, mostly, but perhaps even a delegation. I've heard tell that at the time of Emperor Marcus Aurelius, a magistrate of the equestrian order and a couple of centurions got all the way to their capital. But as far as I know the account of their journey has been lost. Do you know the country well?'

'Fairly well. I go there every two or three years to buy consignments of silk that I resell on the Persian and Indian markets. When the goods get to you in the West, they've already been through many hands and each of us has earned our share.'

'Is that where you met him?' asked Metellus, nodding towards the man sitting at the bow. He was wearing a grey-coloured tunic edged in yellow that ended in a little collar at his neck. He also wore wide trousers and the strangest footwear Metellus had ever seen, similar to what women in Phrygia and Cappadocia wore. He still hadn't got a good look at his face, which was covered by the black veil that was wound around his head as well.

'Yes,' replied Daruma. 'That's where I met him, many years ago.'

'Who is he?' asked Metellus again.

'A prince. A prince of his people, the son of the emperor.'

Metellus thought of Gallienus and a shiver ran down his spine. He felt destiny looming over him, an alien destiny that he wanted to reject but that he was strongly attracted to at the same time. 'And just how was a simple merchant introduced to the sovereigns of that land?'

'It's a long story that I'll tell you some day . . . if we have time.'

'What was he doing with Shapur?'

Daruma hesitated an instant before answering. The boat slid through the water between ever more distant shores. As the width of the river grew, the speed of the current decreased, also slowed by the wind blowing from the south.

'He was sent there as an ambassador,' said the Indian after a long pause, 'and guest. He was to spend several months at the court of the king of the Persians. It had never happened before, but it seemed a very wise initiative. All of the caravans that bring silk to the West pass through Persia, and it could have been very useful to establish a direct relationship between the two countries . . .'

'And since you deal in this sort of commerce, you encouraged the initiative,' commented Metellus without ever taking his eyes off the prince.

His men were watching as well: stealthily, as they spoke among themselves in low voices, or openly and without embarrassment, as one would observe an exotic creature that had come from a distant land. But the alien continued to stare at the horizon, apparently closed in a solitary dimension. As if he had not nearly escaped death just moments ago, as if he had not just done something that no mere mortal could ever do. What kind of man was he anyway? What blood flowed in those veins?

Daruma fell into silence again and the voice of the wind made itself heard, making the ropes vibrate like harp strings. 'The weather's changing,' he said then, as if thinking aloud, before resuming his words where he had left off. 'Yes, I did, but anyone would have done so . . . I suppose. In any case, two years passed and there was no news from the prince.'

'Two years . . .' thought Metellus. More or less the length of time he was in prison at Aus Daiwa. He asked, 'When were those two years up?'

'A few months ago. That's when I set off to seek this . . . encounter.'

So, the day on which Valerian was taken captive outside the walls of Edessa, the prince was a guest, or perhaps he had not yet realized he was a prisoner.

A crewman approached Daruma and pointed at a rise a few miles beyond the western bank. Dromedaries, moving at a run.

'Do you think they're following us?' asked Metellus, turning his gaze in that direction.

'You're asking too much. All I know is that the great king uses dromedaries to send urgent messages through the desert. They're much more resistant than horses and don't need much water. If those men are carrying messages, they may very well concern us, and in that case I'd give every penny in my purse to know what they're saying. But I'm afraid I don't have the gift of second sight.'

Metellus asked nothing more, but his heart sank at the idea that there were still obstacles that could separate him and his men from freedom. They'd certainly find a port at the mouth of the river, a port where ocean-going ships loaded and unloaded goods destined to be transferred to river craft or to land caravans heading west.

West. That had become his overriding thought and his gaze turned insistently towards the path of the setting sun. Towards the west, towards his land.

Edessa: would he ever see her again? Would he see his son? What would he find on his return? He reflected on what might have happened inside the city walls and he thought that his life would be just as much in danger there, in his homeland, as it was now in this foreign land. He would have to use stealth, operate in the shadows, strike with ruthless determination. He was going back to keep a promise, to make up for the error he'd committed. He had acted in good faith, certain that Aurelian would perform his duty and that Silva would be equal to his task as commandant. But he knew all too well that if he had obeyed the emperor, who had asked him to stay inside, he would perhaps have been able to avert the disaster. He could have led troops out to rescue Valerian, or set him free after he had been made prisoner. Or who knows what else.

Alternative, parallel destinies passed through his mind continuously, fed by the remorse that usually remained at the bottom of his conscience, like a crocodile nesting in the slime for as long as the surface was rough, only to rise to the surface and wound his spirit when the waters calmed.

Valerian had entrusted him with an impossible task: to return and re-establish the authority of the state. But he had promised, giving his word to dying Caesar . . . He knew that taking on an endeavour that was too difficult usually meant sacrificing one's life, but he was a soldier and was accustomed to the thought that death is a lesser evil than losing one's honour.

The speed of the current continued to diminish and Metellus watched as the group of dromedaries gained ground to the south and then disappeared over the horizon. There were a great number of boats on the river now, large and small, and traffic increased as they sailed on. Some, like theirs, went with the flow, while others pushed their way upstream, their unfurled sails exploiting the wind blowing from the south.

At a certain moment, when the sun was beginning to set, Metellus saw the prince get to his feet, flexing his limbs in a way he had never seen: his legs and arms straightened out alternately while he opened his hands and extended his fingers first in one direction and then in the other. What strange kind of movements might these be? A dance? A way of stretching one's muscles after long periods of inactivity? And why had he remained so utterly still for so long?

Metellus looked at his men: each one was intent on some small task. Publius was carving a piece of wood with his dagger. Uxal was making spoons out of an acacia branch. Lucianus was mending his clothing with a fisherman's needle. Severus and

Martianus had laid out the disassembled segments of their *loricae* and were checking them one by one and nipping the rings with pincers so none would get lost. Rufus was sharpening the blade on his javelin. Antoninus was making a rudimentary fishing line, aided by Septimius. Balbus was honing his sword with a slow alternating motion and speaking softly with Quadratus.

Inertia was a punishment for them, a source of tedium. The fixed immobility of that alien prince seemed totally unnatural and nearly impossible to them, proof of how the world was infinitely bigger than the Romans imagined it to be, so big that the empire of the Caesars – which extended over all the lands of the Internal Sea – seemed quite a little thing. Such diversity was bound to grow and accumulate in the endless spread of territories, under the bending sky and the changing constellations.

Perhaps, in such distant lands, even the rules of life were different. Perhaps what was good in Rome and Alexandria was no longer good in the land of those small men with their oblique eyes. Perhaps they saw reality in an oblique way as well, according to their own way of understanding and considering. Certainly, such reflections didn't have much to do with him, although he would have liked one day to talk to his son about them, when everything was over.

Daruma's voice distracted him from his thoughts: 'It's ready, Commander.'

'What's ready?'

'Can't you smell it? Dinner, that's what's ready.'

'Gods . . . it's already evening. I hadn't even noticed.'

'You've been absorbed in your own thoughts for a long time. I didn't want to disturb you. When a man has been held prisoner so long, his mind needs to expand its faculties – through imagination, fantasy, dreams. Lack of freedom squashes intelligence, and annihilates any plans you thought you had. The first thing that comes back to you is the past . . .'

'That's true,' replied Metellus, 'with all its ghosts.'

'But the future as well, with all its hopes,' pointed out Daruma.

'Hopes . . .' muttered Metellus. 'I don't have many of those left. But even the faintest hope means life. You can't imagine how we feel, my men and I. We're just slowly emerging now from a deathly torpor. We're gradually regaining the awareness of what we've become, of what remains to us and what has been taken away . . .'

'Eat now,' said Daruma. 'Life will seem better on a full stomach.'

They sat in a circle along with the crewmen who were not involved in operations. The young alien came to join them, sitting on his heels as was his custom. He removed the black veil and revealed his hairless, almost childlike face. His long hair was incredibly black and straight, collected at the nape of his neck with a short leather lace. His mouth was small and well defined and his skin was ashen, with a strange overall pallor. A face that could not redden. Metellus wondered whether that meant it was impossible for him to lose his temper or feel strong emotion. Perhaps he possessed an inborn imperturbability: the ataraxy conjectured by western philosophers.

Uxal came forward and started handing out the brand-new wooden spoons that he had just carved. A galley boy passed out plates and then went round with a big pot full of a stew made from fish, vegetables and legumes, seasoned with oil, saffron and pepper.

The men started to eat hungrily, but Metellus, seeing that the young man with the narrow eyes was not eating, handed him his own spoon with a slight inclination of his head. The other did not reach out his hand to take it, but said a few words in a quiet voice.

'What did he say?' Metellus asked Daruma.

'If you like, I can ask him if he will agree to speak with you. He knows Persian.'

'Who says that I speak Persian?'

'I heard you exchanging words at the oasis with a mule driver.'

'And you've had me speaking *koinè* all this time?'

'I imagined that you wanted to keep a language in reserve, for reasons that did not concern me.'

'What about me?' Uxal broke in. 'It didn't concern me either? You've had me acting as your interpreter for nearly two years like an idiot without telling me that you understand Persian.'

'I speak it as well,' replied Metellus calmly, 'but I wanted that to remain a secret. It wasn't that I didn't trust you, Uxal. When everything is at stake, you can never be too careful.'

Uxal mumbled something and stuck his head back in his plate.

Daruma spoke to his guest in a very respectful tone and then turned to Metellus. 'I've asked him if he will agree to have a conversation with you.'

'You have?' replied Metellus. 'And what was his answer?'

'He agrees. You may speak to him. In Persian.'

'A bizarre destiny . . .' said Metellus to the prince, after having reflected for a short while, 'that has brought us together.'

'Not so bizarre,' replied the prince. 'People like us, who have high responsibilities, never meet by chance.'

'Why do they meet, then?'

'Because they share the same paths. It is easier for two kings separated by great distances to meet than for either one of them to bestow a single glance on the man who cleans his latrine.'

The prince's tone was apparently cold and detached. Metellus tried to switch to a more familiar topic. 'Won't you eat with us?' he asked.

The man answered: 'The quantity of food contained in that utensil is unseemly for a person of good upbringing.' He took two thin sticks from a pocket inside his tunic and began to eat, taking tiny quantities of food from his plate; they were so small that the movement of his jaw was nearly imperceptible.

'By the gods!' said Uxal. 'He eats like a bird.'

'He eats enough,' said Daruma. 'We've all seen how much energy this man has.'

'Exactly,' Metellus joined in. 'I wonder where he gets it from.'

'You'll know in time,' said Daruma.

'Time?' replied Metellus. 'There won't be much of that, I'm afraid. It won't be long before we reach the Ocean shore.'

Daruma dropped the subject.

Uxal stopped talking as well, and for a while an uneasy silence reigned as the men continued to shoot furtive glances at the alien. They noticed that Commander Metellus had also begun to take much more modest quantities of food from his plate, with the tip of his spoon. Then they began to speak among themselves again, in low voices.

'Daruma tells me you come from a great land in the Orient . . .' Metellus began in Persian.

'Zhong Guo,' replied the prince.

'Is that the name of your country?'

'Yes,' he said. 'And yours?'

Metellus hesitated an instant, then replied in Latin, 'Imperium Populi Romani.'

'Where is it found?'

'In the far west. It contains an entire sea.'

'It must be the land we call Taqin Guo. It means western country.'

Metellus thought that the word *guo* must mean 'country' or 'land', since it was common to both words. 'So you know of our existence, as we know of yours. We buy a great deal of your silk. Daruma has also told me that you are a prince,' he continued. 'I would like you to know that we are honoured to share this part of our journey with you.'

The prince acknowledged his courtesy with a slight bow of his head.

'May I know your name?'

'Dan Qing,' replied the prince.

'I'm Marcus Metellus Aquila.'

'Everything seems very complicated in your tongue.'

'It all seems much simpler in yours, but that's surely a superficial impression, both on my part and on yours.'

Metellus noticed that when the prince spoke to him he never broke contact with his eyes, making the Roman feel ill at ease. The prince's gaze seemed enigmatic and inscrutable.

A sudden gust of wind, quite prolonged this time, interrupted their conversation.

'It's coming from the west,' observed Uxal.

'Yes, it is,' agreed Metellus.

'I don't like it,' said Septimius.

'Neither do I,' replied Metellus. 'But that doesn't mean much. The wind is like the fate of man: it can change from one moment to the next.'

Daruma gestured for the galley boy to collect the empty plates and he passed around a jar of palm wine. Everyone took some except for Dan Qing, who drank only a few sips of water. He then stood, made a bow and disappeared below deck.

'I haven't seen the two of you speaking much,' said Metellus to Daruma. 'That's strange for people who have to come up with a plan of escape.'

'Not enough privacy here. I'll go down now and we'll be able to speak freely. Those of you who want to rest will be given mats and covers. It's humid on deck at night, even though it's hot. You don't need me to tell you to keep your eyes open,' he added. 'Small pirate boats might draw up alongside our vessel during the night. They are very fast and very dangerous. And the threat we're fleeing from has not disappeared either.'

'I know,' replied Metellus. 'We won't be taken unawares.'

Daruma went below deck as Metellus rallied his men and assigned the guard shifts. A big red moon hovered over the river, creating a long golden trail on the water, while to the west only a faint reflection of the vanished sun remained.

Dan Qing reappeared around midnight and went to the bow, where he took up the same immovable pose as before. There he remained until dawn. Metellus observed him several times but could not tell whether he was awake or asleep. His position, with his head slightly reclined on his chest, would have allowed either one or the other, but certainly, if he fell asleep from time to time, his was a vigilant rest. No movement escaped him, no change of direction or vibration in the air.

THE NIGHT passed tranquilly. The moon waned after the second guard shift, leaving a sky teeming with stars of a luminosity never seen before, crossed from one end to the other by the white veil of the Milky Way. Metellus took the last shift before sunrise himself, together with Quadratus, and he noticed that at dawn Dan Qing had leaned his head on a coil of ropes, permitting himself a little rest. He showed an almost infantile fragility at that moment, but the bow-shaped curve of his reclining body gave the impression that he could lash out at any moment with the same power he had shown in that astonishing jump on to the boat.

Metellus would have liked to speak with him, to learn more about that remote land from which he'd come, travelling all the way to the confines of the Roman empire. He'd have liked to ask him about the origins of silk. All sorts of nonsense circulated in the West, but the most absurd claim of all was that the fabric was woven by a worm. But he felt reluctant to disturb the prince's intense solitude, although soon each one of them would be going his own way, each towards the world he had left so long ago, and they would never have another chance to talk.

Daruma reappeared at daybreak, wearing floor-length robes made of a light-coloured cloth similar to linen but much thinner. The river was even wider now and the low, sandy banks were even further away.

'We'll be able to see the Ocean in a couple of hours,' Daruma said.

'And our roads will part. I can't tell you how grateful we are . . .' replied Metellus.

'I don't think so,' interrupted Daruma.

'What do you mean "I don't think so"?'

'That we will not part. You will come with me and the prince.'

'You're joking. But we . . .'

'We had an agreement. Is this how a Roman stands by his word?'

'You can't expect us to stay with you all the way . . .'

'To China? Exactly.'

'That was not in our agreement.'

'Of course it was. I hired you as my guard until the end of the journey.'

'This is the end of the journey. The Ocean shore. Even Alexander stopped at the Ocean shore. Daruma, I have left a son, alone, without his mother, in the hands of enemies. Don't you understand? My thoughts were with him when I agreed to your terms. In good faith, I agreed to come with you as far as the shores of the Ocean, and by this good faith I shall feel free of any obligation as soon as we reach the mouth of this river.'

Daruma bowed his head and seemed to reflect for a few moments in silence, then said: 'You owe me your lives, you Romans, and I now demand payment of this debt. And since there is nothing in this world as precious as life, you will have to do what I ask, to repay me at least in part. But . . . this is philosophy! If you set foot in this port, how far do you think you'd get, anyway? You don't have enough money to pay for passage with a caravan.'

'We'll go by sea.'

'But the Persians control all the shipping wharves.'

'It's a risk we'll have to run.'

'If you come with me,' continued Daruma as if he hadn't heard, 'you'll see things that you've never even imagined might exist. You'll see a world that no one from your land has ever seen nor perhaps ever will. You will be paid with such generosity that you won't have to worry about earning money for the rest of your lives. And when it's over, I'll accompany you back to the confines of your world myself. I'll come with you personally or hire trusted guides to do so in my place.'

Metellus's men had gathered at a short distance and watched with apprehension as their commander argued with Daruma.

Even Dan Qing had turned towards them with an expression that finally hinted at something like emotion. Misgiving, perhaps, or disappointment.

The helmsman began to turn the boat towards the western bank, abandoning the centre of the current.

14

THE BOAT SLIPPED TOWARDS the western shore and this seemed like a positive sign to Metellus, but Daruma's fixed look did not bode well, and Dan Qing's expression was ureadable. The heat had suddenly become oppressive. The damp air rising from the river was suffocating and a line of low, swollen clouds advanced from the west.

A port came into sight, with a great number of ships at anchor. A wide array of vessels were seething with half-naked sailors loading and unloading, sewing and mending sails, repairing and checking oars and helms, yelling out in every language, their calls mixing with those of the gulls that flew low over the surface of the water, swooping after the refuse tossed from the boats.

Metellus scanned all the vessels in search of some shape that looked familiar to him, a ship from Alexandria, for example, which might be persuaded to offer them passage. He thought he could take advantage of his military rank: the captain of a merchant ship might even consider his request an opportunity to jump at, if nothing else for the benefits he would stand to gain once back at home.

Balbus approached him. 'What are we doing, Commander?'

'Going home,' replied Metellus firmly.

'What about him?' added Balbus, casting a sideways glance at Daruma. 'He doesn't seem to see things the same way. Am I wrong?'

'No, you're not. He insists that we escort him and prince narrow-eyes all the way to Sera Maior. China, that's what the

Indian calls it. There's evidently been a misunderstanding, but he'll just have to accept that he can't force us into this.'

'And if he doesn't?'

'What do you mean?'

'He might report us, turn us over to the Persians. What's to stop him doing that?'

'Our guest. He's being hunted by the Persians as well, and Daruma seems to be responsible for his safety. As long as he's with us we have nothing to fear. It could become a problem after we've left . . .'

At that same instant, the voice of the sailor at the top of the mast rang out: 'Warship to starboard!'

Daruma took charge immediately. 'Oars in the water. Men, to your posts! Helm hard aport!' he shouted.

The crew foreman passed on his orders and the rowers thrust the oars into their locks and began to row at full strength. Others unfurled the sail so it would be ready to hoist as soon as they were beyond the river estuary.

Metellus looked to where the sailor was pointing and saw a streamlined vessel manned by at least fifty rowers leaving the port at that moment, with another fifty or so soldiers aboard. The banner being raised at the stern bore a winged creature: the symbol of Ahura Mazda.

He turned to his men. 'Prepare for combat!'

The men shouldered their arms and rushed to the starboard side. Uxal lined up courageously with his comrades, as if he could be of some use in a battle, but Quadratus shoved him back unceremoniously.

Daruma's boat had the current and the impetus of the oars in its favour, but the warship maintained its route and speed, intent on cutting them off.

'Evidently someone beat us here,' said Daruma.

'Are you sure it's us they want?' asked Metellus.

'Who else?' replied Daruma. He watched with dread as the Persian ship advanced at an ever faster speed.

Dan Qing approached him. 'The wind is coming. Raise the sail.'

'But there is no wind!' said Metellus, looking around.

Dan Qing fixed him for an instant with his emotionless gaze and said, 'It is coming.'

'Do as he says!' ordered Daruma.

The sailors hoisted the sail. The great rectangle of cloth hung inert from its yard. Metellus shook his head and went back to join his men. The warship was nearly in the middle of the estuary and Daruma's helmsman continued to haul starboard in the slight hope of escaping to the opposite shore before the approaching vessel completely cut them off.

'Get ready,' ordered Metellus. 'It's five to one.'

'It won't be the first time,' growled Quadratus, 'if I remember well.'

'Ready to prevent the enemy from boarding!' shouted Metellus to his comrades, grasping his sword.

He had not finished speaking when a strong gust of wind hit the boat and inflated the sail. It tensed, making the yard creak and bending the mast. The helmsman withstood the jolt, but couldn't stop the boat from drifting sharply leewards, dangerously close to land. The boatswain increased the rowing rhythm for the men on the left side, who managed to correct the drift. The vessel sailed into the mouth of the estuary, where the wind, no longer buffered by the mainland, hit full force and carried the boat off at great speed.

The warship, which was unmasted, had to cut its mission short and gave up the chase.

'We're saved!' said Daruma.

Metellus sighed in relief as the crew abandoned themselves to exultation. Uxal danced wildly on the deck, making everyone laugh.

The Roman commander approached Daruma and said, 'You're safe now and I'm sure you'll find a way to hire new guards just as reliable as we are as you continue your journey. This is where our paths part. Haul to shore.'

'How?' asked Daruma. 'Look for yourself. The shore is inaccessible, nothing but cliffs. And can't you feel the wind? Don't you know what it is?'

'I'm not a sailor.'

'It's the monsoon that blows constantly east with unstoppable force, day and night, for the entire season.'

'Pull in to shore,' repeated Metellus in a tone of voice that did not allow for objections. 'We'll swim it if we have to. It's just moving air. I'm accustomed to much worse.'

The wind was increasing in intensity and the cloud front was approaching now with frightening rapidity: a wall of black clouds shot through with continuous flashes of lightning, accompanied by the low threatening growl of thunder. The devastating power of such an alien, hostile nature made itself felt all at once. Metellus, used to the mild weather of the Mediterranean, watched the monster with sudden anxiety. A lightning bolt split the sky and plunged into the sea, shattering into blinding streams of fire, unleashing a deafening crash of thunder.

The boatswain shouted, 'All men to their stations! Take in the sails! Bow to the waves!'

Metellus paled at that sight.

Daruma looked at him with a sarcastic smile while a violent gust of wind ruffled his hair. 'What are you afraid of, Commander? It's just a little moving air. Tell your men to find something to grab hold of, and not to let go unless they want to end up in the sea.' He himself firmly gripped the railing.

The sun was being darkened by the menacing clouds, but before it was totally swallowed up it launched a last ray to illuminate the leaden, foaming surface of the waves.

'This is the Ocean, Commander!' shouted Daruma. 'No one and nothing can resist her.'

Dan Qing vaulted over to the bow and seized the lines which bound the foresail to the boom like a horseman gripping the reins of a restive horse. Uxal curled up like a mouse in the forepeak, behind a coil of ropes.

Driven violently by the aft wind, the boat began to pitch,

plunging into the hollows that yawned before it, then suddenly rearing up on the liquid slopes of waves nearly as high as hills.

Then came the rain, in torrential bursts. It flagellated the boat with unbelievable fury, as the waves joined in to sweep the deck from fore to aft. The water began to pour from the only hatchway into the bilge.

Daruma approached Metellus, without ever loosening his grip on the railing. 'I need two strong men at the bilge pump,' he shouted. 'I can't move my men from their stations. Hurry, or we'll go under!'

'Rufus, Septimius, to the pump, fast!' shouted Metellus.

The two men rushed below and started to work the bar on the bilge pump – an exceptional machine, of Roman manufacture, as proclaimed by the brand name. Rufus brought the cloth hose outside and gave the end of it to Publius, who was completely soaked and hanging on to the starboard railing, then went back below and started pumping with all his might.

The pump struggled to expel the water that was pouring in continuously and the two men who were working it took advantage of the rare moments when the storm let up a little to gain a lead. It required enormous effort, and Metellus assigned his men to work in shifts so that the emptying of the bilge was never interrupted.

The storm went on for hours, exhausting the crew, who did their utmost to keep the craft afloat. Every now and then, Metellus would try to make out Dan Qing in the darkness. He never moved, straight as a rod at the bow, and watching him as he gripped the forward railing, Metellus had the strong sensation that it was he who was keeping the boat afloat, he who was guiding them through the tempestuous waves with a mysterious force that Metellus could neither perceive nor understand, but which seemed to permeate the hull and hold the planks and the mast together in that chaos of spray, thunder, wind and lightning. The darkness on board was nearly complete. A couple of lanterns hanging from the stays of the main mast spread a glimmer that made the men's outlines just barely discernible. They seemed more like phantoms, guided by the shouts of the boatswain, who endeavoured to make himself heard over the din of the storm.

It was some time after midnight when, all at once, a wave much stronger than the others swept the deck all the way to the forepeak and dug Uxal out of the corner he was huddling in, dragging him towards the starboard railing. The planking on that side was not continuous; openings about two feet wide had been made to allow the water to drain off the boat. The old man was smashed against the planks by the force of the current and washed out, although he tried to grab one of the railing posts to avoid falling into the sea. He yelled 'Help!' with all the breath he had in him, but it was several moments before Metellus realized what had happened and rushed to his aid.

Uxal was hanging on with his right hand alone, which was slowly slipping. His legs were dangling over the open sea. Metellus seized the old man's hand the instant before he fell, but a second wave took him by surprise and pushed him out through the same opening. He managed to grab the post, encircling it completely with his left arm, while he continued to hold on to Uxal with his right. He started to call out: 'Over here! Fast! Over this way!' But there was such a din, such immense confusion, that his shouts were not heard. A wave washed over the starboard side and ripped Uxal from Metellus's grip. The old man disappeared amid the foaming waves with an anguished scream. Metellus held fast and tried desperately to grab the post with his other hand. He swung against the boat's side, trying to achieve enough impetus to haul himself on board, but the waves hit him one after another and his energy was abating with every new surge. He felt the cold embrace of the Ocean pulling him under. He gave one last yell, before sinking beneath the billows, before falling into death's arms.

At that same instant two steely hands closed around his wrists and lifted him out of the water. Dan Qing was hanging head down, grasping on to the railing posts with his feet. He waited an instant for another wave to arrive, then, exploiting its force, he transferred so much energy to the Roman's body that

Metellus was catapulted over the railing. Metellus grabbed it with both hands and hoisted himself on deck. He watched as Dan Qing gave a backwards spring by heaving the muscles in his back. He flew over the railing and landed squarely on the deck.

Metellus, astonished, managed only to mumble, 'Thank you.'

Dan Qing acknowledged him with a slight nod, then returned to his place at the bow.

The storm did not begin to calm until dawn, when Daruma and the boatswain counted the survivors in the pale light that filtered through the tattered clouds.

Metellus joined his men. 'Uxal is dead,' he said. 'Why did no one answer me when I was shouting for help?'

'Commander,' said Lucianus, 'everyone was shouting, the sea louder than anyone else. There was no way we could distinguish one sound from another in that uproar. We were all hanging on to something for dear life, numb with cold and dazed with the strain, or else we were down below, pumping out the water. I'm sorry . .'

'Poor Uxal,' said Balbus, who had just come up from the hold.

'We owe our salvation to him,' added Rufus. 'Without him, we'd never have got out of that inferno.'

'If I ever get back home to Spoletum,' said Publius, 'I'll raise an altar to him in my courtyard and make funeral offerings to his shade every year, on the anniversary of his death. He was a good man and he'd grown fond of us.'

Daruma approached them. 'I lost two of my crewmen last night,' he said. 'You've lost a man too, haven't you?'

'I did what I could to rescue him but I would have died myself if it hadn't been for him,' said Metellus, nodding towards Dan Qing. 'I still can't figure out how he heard me and how he managed to grab me by the wrists just as I was about to succumb to the waves.'

Daruma gave a slight smile. 'Men like him have been trained in a very particular philosophy that makes them capable of perceiving every force that vibrates in the atmosphere and of distinguishing it from a thousand others. It's extraordinary that he has mastered this skill so young.'

Metellus looked at him in disbelief without knowing what to say, then glanced over at Dan Qing. He had taken off his clothes to let them dry and was sitting cross-legged, dressed only in a small loincloth.

Daruma turned to the boatswain. 'The wind has abated sufficiently. We can hoist the sail. Now we must ascertain what has been spared by the sea water, dry out everything we can as soon as the sun comes up and regain our strength.' He went down to the hold and Metellus followed him. 'Without this pump we would never have made it,' said Daruma, pointing to the bronze machine fastened to a plank.

'Two cylinders, the lift-and-force type,' said Metellus. 'Made for the mines, but it works well everywhere. Where did you get it?'

'I want for nothing! It comes from Alexandria but I bought it at Hormusia. Well, then, do you believe me now when I tell you we can't go west? The monsoon is a constant wind that blows in this direction for six months. No ship can go upstream against the wind, if not by rowing and only for a very short distance. Even someone who isn't a sailor can understand that. In a few days' time, a month at the most, we'll be at the mouth of the Indus. Even if you did decide to go ashore, you'd have to spend the next six months, if not more, rotting in some hole along the coast, amid mosquitoes and mephitic fever, waiting for the wind to change. With no money, no knowledge of the local language and no guarantee that you'll find passage, since you're not capable of paying for it. You might be captured and taken as slaves, just to give an example, or end up in some village of the interior, doing a day's labour in exchange for a handful of rice.'

'What's rice?' asked Metellus.

'Marsh grain. You'll be tasting it soon . . . If, on the other hand, you decide to come with me, you'll see a phenomenal land. You'll cross the highest mountain chain in the world, the

Indian Caucasus, as Alexander's historians named it. We call it the Hindu Kush. And when we have accompanied Dan Qing back home, I promise you that I will bring you back myself, as I've already said.'

'In six months?' asked Metellus suspiciously.

'Well, maybe a bit longer, but it will still be well worth your while. If you attempt it alone, you'll have to stop frequently to earn your passage from one place to the next. Don't think that you'll find a ship that will take you straight to Alexandria, lying out on deck, belly up, enjoying the sun. My proposal is a reasonable one, Commander, the only sensible one, believe me . . . What do you say?'

Metellus sighed. He looked up: the cracks between the planks were pierced by daggers of sunlight. 'I must consult my men,' he said. 'I'll give you an answer before evening.'

Daruma went back towards the hatch to return on deck. Metellus followed him and emerged into the light of day. Ragged clouds galloped through the limpid sky and the deck planks were already beginning to dry here and there. The clothing hanging out everywhere gave the impression of bizarre supplementary sails. The sea had settled into a gentle roll, and it glittered with myriad reflections under the sun. The curved backs of dolphins swelled the surface; they would sometimes make spectacular leaps from the Ocean and then dive back into the white spume.

Metellus thought, 'I must return to my son. I must return to do what I promised my emperor. But I must return alive.' He considered Uxal, sleeping on the bottom of the Ocean, and he felt a lump in his throat. He drew a long sigh and approached his men. 'As you've seen, there was nothing we could do. The wind and the storm have dragged us east.'

'Where are we, Commander?' asked Rufus.

'I don't know,' replied Metellus. 'At a month's navigation from the mouth of the Indus, I believe.'

'The Indus?' repeated Quadratus. 'But that's at the ends of the earth!'

'Not exactly. I think the world is much bigger than we imagine. You've just witnessed the vastness and the power of the Ocean.'

'Well, then, what are we going to do?' asked Lucianus, in a tone that would have earned him an exemplary punishment under any other circumstances.

Metellus pretended not to hear and told them what Daruma had proposed. 'It is not my intention to force anyone,' he concluded at the end. 'Each of you is free to do what he wants. When we land in India, you can decide whether you want to remain with us or attempt to return on your own. As far as I'm concerned, I think Daruma's proposal is reasonable. Actually, it's our only chance of getting home. Late, but alive.'

'But can you trust Daruma, Commander?' asked Septimius with a worried expression. 'We haven't known him for long. He's only a merchant, and there's no one more unprincipled than a merchant, in my book.'

'I think that Daruma is something more than a merchant. I can't tell you what, but I feel sure about this. The fact that he took on the responsibility of freeing the prince of Sera Maior and escorting him safely back to his homeland is no small thing. You must understand that Dan Qing is the equivalent of Gallienus, in a much bigger empire than ours. What's more, Daruma has always held fast to his word and honoured the terms of our agreements.'

'There are ten of us and we're armed,' grumbled Publius.

'We were wrecks when he welcomed us into his camp. Our weapons would have counted for little if he had decided to get rid of us. I'm grateful to him for not having done so and I'm willing to trust him. But, I repeat, each one of you is free to make up his own mind. I'm not going to shoulder the responsibility of giving orders this time.

'The only certain thing is that this wind will be blowing constantly east, at the strength we've seen, for six months or more. Therefore, the only way we could attempt to get back is by land. But I must remind you that Alexander himself ventured out on the same route five hundred years ago. Twenty thousand of his men were lost in that salty desert, without a blade of grass or a drop of water. And he had an army with pack animals, carts for transporting food and water, native guides. I don't know what destiny might await a man who decided to venture off on his own in those desolate lands swarming with fierce marauders.

'The alternative would be to wait on the coast until the wind changes, but that is a risk-fraught choice as well. You decide. You have plenty of time to think it over. If you elect to come with me, you'll see lands that no one has ever explored and you'll experience an adventure that you'll be able to tell your grandchildren about one day. You will be the only warriors in the world to have crossed the two greatest empires on earth, to have reached places that not even Alexander the Great could have imagined.'

A deep silence followed his words. The men had been firmly convinced that they were going home and this option, so unforeseen and unfamiliar, deeply dismayed them. And they were even more dismayed by the option of deciding for themselves, since they had always only received orders from their commander, and carried them out.

It was Quadratus who broke the silence. 'If you go, I'm coming with you,' he said without hesitation.

'So am I,' confirmed Balbus, the other centurion.

'Me too, Commander,' piped up Antoninus. 'Count on me.'

Lucianus and Septimius consulted each other with a brief glance and communicated their decision. 'There's no way we're waiting until the wind changes. We are the wind! We of the Second Augusta, by Hercules!'

'Yes!' exclaimed the others.

Metellus smiled. 'Then we agree. I'm happy that you've decided to come with me.' He went to catch up with Daruma, but then turned. 'Ah, I was forgetting. This is the last decision I'm leaving to your discretion. From now on, we're going back to the old rules: I give the orders, you carry them out.'

15

METELLUS APPROACHED THE PRINCE with a light step, stopping at a certain distance. 'Where I come from, they tell a story,' he began, 'that reminds me a little of what happened last night.'

Dan Qing did not answer but a slight movement of his head let the Roman know he was listening.

'It happened three centuries ago,' continued Metellus. 'A great man among our people, a conqueror, the founder of our empire – his name was Caesar – once had to cross a brief stretch of our Internal Sea, at night, in a little boat. But that arm of the sea was patrolled by the powerful fleet of his enemy, who had massed an army on the other side of the straits. Caesar had to reach his own army on the opposite side and guide them to victory, and he decided to attempt the crossing in total darkness and in dangerous waters. When he was halfway across, a storm broke out and his boat was tossed around by the waves like a fragile nutshell. The helmsman was terrified and exhausted, and could not stay on course, but Caesar approached him and said, "Take heart! You are carrying Caesar to his destiny."

'The helmsman found the strength of spirit to continue his battle against the elements and he succeeded in ferrying his passenger to the other side. Caesar won the battle against the enemy and became the founder of the empire that extends over all the lands of the Internal Sea, which we call "Mare Nostrum", and over all the peoples who live in its vicinity. Every schoolboy hears this story told by his teachers . . .'

'For what purpose?' asked Dan Qing.

'To teach our young people that they should never become

disheartened, because we build our own destiny. With will-power, determination, courage. Last night you saved my life and I've come to thank you. You are safe as well, and with you the destiny of your homeland, perhaps. Like Caesar, that night, when he crossed the storming sea.'

Dan Qing turned. 'What you say sounds like a good omen,' he replied, 'but the road is very long, the threats many and the friends very few. How many men did your leader have waiting for him on the other side of that stormy sea?'

'Fifty thousand,' replied Metellus.

'Not a great number. But not too few either. I am alone.'

Metellus stared into his eyes, trying to decipher his expression. 'Alone?'

Dan Qing merely nodded.

Instead of asking for his help, as Metellus would have expected, the prince turned his gaze to the sparkling surface of the waves.

That man aroused a strange feeling of reverence, while instilling a sense of detachment that was impossible to ignore. When he spoke his words were measured and seemed to come from a great distance, and yet Metellus was attracted by the extraordinary force that pervaded his body and by the seemingly impossible energy that had permitted the prince to pull him from the waves as he was drowning.

'Daruma has asked me to escort you, with my men, to your final destination.'

'Did Daruma explain to you what awaits us?'

'No. But I can imagine.'

'And you accepted?'

'Yes.'

'Why?'

'I'm a soldier. I'm not afraid of such things. And Daruma has promised that he will bring us back. We have no alternative, actually.'

'That seems a good reason.'

'May I ask you a question?'

'You may.'

'Why did you save me, last night?'

'Because you command my escort.'

'An excellent reason,' replied Metellus, and walked away.

NAVIGATION PROCEEDED regularly at a sustained rate and towards evening they saw another boat sailing in the same direction at a distance of perhaps a couple of miles. When night fell, the voyage continued calmly and without obstacles, until around midnight, when the sky clouded over and it began to rain, a downpour that lasted for about half an hour, although the wind never picked up and the Ocean did not rise. The lanterns emitted a dim light and Metellus, lying on a mat on the deck, would open his eyes every now and then and take a look around. Daruma was sleeping below deck, his men above. Quadratus had arranged for a man to stand guard nonetheless; perhaps he didn't trust the company completely, or perhaps it was just the habit of twenty years of scrupulous, disciplined and watchful service.

When he was awake, Metellus thought of the adventure awaiting him and his men in a vast, unknown land, among peoples he had not even known existed. Sometimes he felt he must have been mad to accept such a proposal, while at other times he felt he had done the right thing, the only sensible thing, given the circumstances. But what anguished him most was the sensation of distancing himself with every instant from his world, his son, his mission. He felt a dizziness that took his breath away. He tried to remedy that anxiety in sleep, letting himself be rocked by the continuous lapping of the waves against the keel and by the warm breeze.

At dawn, he was roused by the shouts of one of the sailors from Taprobane who was at the top of the mast. Daruma scanned the horizon before them, then shouted, 'Look! It's blowing, down there!'

They all ran to the bow and saw a spray of steam as tall as the mast of their boat rising from the surface of the sea, and then an enormous curved back and a gigantic two-lobed tail splashing out of the water before sinking down below.

'Over there!' shouted Balbus. 'Another one!'

'And another down there!' echoed Antoninus.

Metellus observed that sight in wonder: monsters bigger than the boat they were travelling on, their backs encrusted with scaling and deposits like the hulls of ocean-going vessels, emerging with nearly half of their bodies out of the water before plunging back in with a resounding plop in a spectacular show of foam.

'What are they, Commander?' asked Lucianus. 'Will they attack us?'

'They are whales,' responded Daruma's voice from behind him. 'Creatures as huge as they are inoffensive. They're playing like little fish do, and grazing. They open their mouths and devour whole shoals of sardines.'

'I've read about them in the work of Onesicritus,' spoke up Metellus, 'Alexander's admiral and pilot of the royal navy, who returned from India all the way to the mouths of the Tigris and Euphrates. But I never thought I would see them.'

'You will not regret making this voyage, Roman. You will finally understand what the world is, and how small the pool you've built your empire around is compared to the immensity of the Oceans that surround the endless vastness of the earth. And I'm sure that this will teach you something, because you seem like a man who is eager to learn.'

Metellus did not reply, and remained in silence watching the dance of those giants of the sea, their gleaming backs, their gigantic tails lashing the waves, the spraying steam that they launched to the sky. One of the monsters emerged at a very short distance from the boat and he could see its tiny eye near the corner of its mouth. A grey, inexpressive bulb that seemed to stare at him for a moment before disappearing beneath the water.

'All those stories about marine monsters that break apart ships and devour the sailors who fall into the water are nothing but legends, then,' observed Metellus when the whales had passed from sight.

'Legends?' replied Daruma. 'Jaibal!' he shouted to one of his Taprobanes. A dark-skinned, half-naked sailor approached. Daruma took something hanging from his neck and showed it to Metellus. 'Does this look like a legend to you?'

'Gods! What is it?'

'A tooth. The tooth of a monster thirty feet long with three rows of these things. Incredibly fast and voracious, an insatiable hunter, seizing anything that moves . . . Turn around, Jaibal,' he said to the sailor.

The sailor turned to show an enormous scar that went from his buttocks to the joint behind his knee.

'This is a memento from that tiger of the sea. Jaibal was lucky. Others are torn to pieces and devoured. Pearl divers run the greatest risk – the waters they dive into are rife with these beasts. And you complain that pearls are expensive! If you found yourself in front of a brute like that at forty feet under, you certainly would not think so.'

'Pearls . . .' mused Metellus. 'I only ever bought one, for my wife, when my son was born on the fifth anniversary of our wedding.'

Jaibal returned to his work and Daruma was served an infusion of herbs, which he offered to Metellus as well.

'I saw you speaking to Dan Qing.'

'I thanked him for saving my life the other night.'

'You shouldn't have.'

'Why not?'

'Because he is a Chinese prince. He is the son of an emperor who is revered as the Son of the Heavens. A man of his rank customarily speaks to no one who has not been introduced to him through a complex protocol. Remember when he landed on the boat? Nothing was said, he merely nodded to me as a gesture of respect. You should have asked me to request permission for you to speak to him.'

'Well, you could have warned me.'

'That's true, but all things told, perhaps it's better this way. If he answered you, that means protocol has lost its meaning for him in this situation.'

Metellus glanced over at Dan Qing. He was sitting on his heels and, as usual, seemed absorbed in his thoughts.

'But . . . what's he doing when he sits for hours in such an uncomfortable position? It would break anyone else's knees.'

'He's meditating.'

'Meditating? About what?'

'His meditation does not have a specific object. He seeks *tao* – that is, the way.'

'The way to where?'

'There is no "where".'

'So he's meditating about nothing and searching for a road that leads no place?'

'More or less, although it's not that simple. It's by virtue of this meditation that he succeeded in leaping from his horse and landing on my boat without faltering. And it's by virtue of this meditation that he can stay in that position for hours, as though his body were weightless. *Tao* is a complex philosophical concept, developed by one of their greatest masters, a man named Kong Fuzi. According to his theories, nature has neither purpose nor intention, but it is invaded by an intrinsic force that governs and informs nature of itself. *Tao* is this universal soul that suffuses the cosmos, the earth and the nature of the human race as well. A man who perceives *tao* and makes it his vehicle and his bearer will forgo trying to bend the flow of events forcibly and abandon himself to its essence, allowing it to pervade his being.'

Metellus smiled. 'We have a saying: *"Faber quisque est suae fortunae."* Do you know what it means?'

Daruma sipped his infusion of dried leaves. 'My Latin is not very good, but even I know that much: *"Every man is the architect of his own destiny."*'

'Precisely. The exact negation of what you were just saying.'

'It doesn't mean that you don't make decisions. Think of that leap. If he had jumped an instant sooner, he would have fallen into the water. If he had jumped an instant later he would have died, run through by a great number of arrows. He flew through the air at the exact moment in which he felt an opening between opposing destinies. At that instant, a small amount of exertion was sufficient to achieve an incredible result. You Westerners, on the other hand, always seem to be rowing counter-current, with the wind against you.'

Daruma was sweating with the effort of explaining such arduous concepts in a language that was not his own. He spoke in Persian, sometimes in *koinè*, and his listener tried to meet him halfway by suggesting appropriate terms himself.

'I wonder how we Romans have managed to build an empire and maintain it for centuries,' replied Metellus sarcastically. 'And how we – a measly crew of emaciated prisoners – managed to survive the insults of fate and the cruelty of our enemies, managed to triumph over crushingly superior forces, managed to cover tens and tens of miles in the dark, eating only what we could find, tormented by thirst and cramps of hunger.'

'I must admit that all this is quite remarkable,' agreed Daruma, 'but it doesn't change the reality of things. The waste of energy is insane, the price paid in terms of suffering exorbitant, and the end result depends on chance alone. But, returning to Dan Qing, it's obvious that he has formed an excellent opinion of you. He would never have risked his life for just anybody, especially for someone he'd known for such a short time.'

'Not so short. I'm almost sure that he remembers first seeing me at Edessa.'

'And what did he see?' asked Daruma, while a galley boy poured more of the infusion into his bowl.

Metellus drank some as well. It tasted slightly bitter, in a pleasant way, and was quite fragrant. 'He saw me in combat, I think. Fighting to defend my emperor. To the death.'

'That explains many things . . .' said Daruma with a deep nod.

Metellus tasted the beverage again, and found that he was beginning to like the curious flavour of those aromatic leaves.

'What was he doing in Edessa with Shapur? And what were you doing at the oasis of Khaboras?' he asked, staring Daruma straight in the eye. 'If destiny has led me to remain with you, it's only right that I should know.'

Cries came from the stern and they turned. The crew had thrown out nets and were starting to draw them in. Metellus's comrades joined in to lend a hand and, as a net was pulled slowly on board, the deck filled with darting fish that were gathered and put into baskets to be cleaned and prepared for dinner.

Daruma drew a deep breath, like a man readying himself for a difficult undertaking, then began to tell his story. 'China is a very ancient empire, perhaps the oldest that exists on this earth, but for decades now it has been afflicted by continuous tumult. The pressure of barbarians from the north, and its own internal strife, have divided that gigantic land into three kingdoms: one in the north, one in the centre and one in the south. Each is governed by a military chief who has proclaimed himself *wang* – that is, sovereign. Each of the three is convinced he has the right and the duty to unify the empire and therefore to kill the other two. This has resulted in an unceasing state of war that has depopulated the once-prosperous countryside, destroyed flourishing cities, reduced trade to less than half of what it had been. The armies are dwindling, due to the impoverishment of the farmers and the fall in population, and so the nomadic barbarians from the steppe, the Xiong Nu, have been enlisted to defend the long wall in the north, and given land in return for their services.

'In this atmosphere of great confusion and decadence, the Kingdom of the North – the biggest and most powerful – has remained perhaps the only point of reference. The capital is grandiose still, and boasts of the biggest library of the country, with twenty thousand students applying themselves to the most diverse studies.'

Metellus was surprised by the many incredible coincidences with the empire of Rome: the pressure of barbarians from the north, the necessity of allowing foreign tribes to settle within the wall of defence, the progressive barbarization of the army and the endemic civil wars ravaging the state.

Daruma continued his story. 'One of the plagues which most greatly afflicted the Kingdom of the North was that excessive power had fallen into the hands of the palace eunuchs . . .'

'That's one thing at least that we don't have,' Metellus couldn't help reflecting.

'Eunuchs? They are frequent in China. The surgeons have become such experts that the number of patients who survive the operation is greater than the number who die. In any case, many of the last emperors were little more than children when they ascended the throne and thus were forced either to allow their mothers to rule the state in their place or to rely on the eunuchs, who often – thanks to their intelligence or their cunning – had succeeded in infiltrating the highest centres of power.

'In Dan Qing's court, the situation was quite unusual, influenced by an event whose implications I've never fully understood . . .'

The wind blew up, filling the sail so forcefully that the mast creaked. A cloud front appeared low on the surface of the waves towards the west and Metellus could hear Antoninus saying to Rufus, 'If this keeps up, we'll have another rough night.'

'Go on,' urged Metellus.

'Three years ago Dan Qing departed for a diplomatic mission to the Persian court, leaving the administration of the state in the hands of the most faithful of his father's ministers, Yangming, who was appointed regent. But when two years – instead of several months – had passed since the prince's departure, someone became seriously worried about his prolonged absence: Dan Qing's master, Wangzi, a wise and pious man who lives in a monastery in the mountains. I have known him for some time, because during my journeys I have often stopped at his retreat, where I have been welcomed with great hospitality.

'It was he who organized this mission. He contacted some Zoroastrian priests who were his friends and gave them a message for Dan Qing, specifying a date for meeting up with my caravan at the source of the Khaburas or at the river port.'

'And now,' concluded Metellus, 'the prince is returning to a kingdom which is no longer his. He has to defeat this minister – who must have betrayed him – and seize power again, without being able to count on anyone but an old monk, if I've understood you correctly. A situation very similar to what my emperor would have found, had I managed to take him back.'

'Did Dan Qing say anything to you?' asked Daruma.

'He told me that he is alone.'

'That must mean that you're right, then.'

'But there must be troops who are still faithful to him. Friends that he helped, officers who have sworn their loyalty . . .'

'If he told you he is alone, that means that he cannot or doesn't want to count on anyone. Or nearly anyone.'

'There's something we must clarify about this, Daruma. We've already clashed once.'

'Ah . . . I think I know what you're referring to.'

'I want to know how far we'll have to accompany Dan Qing, at what point our mission can be considered concluded, and when our voyage of return will begin, as you promised.'

'Don't worry, Commander, I'm neither a hero nor a warrior. We'll enter China from the south and cross the mountains. Once we reach the monastery I've spoken to you about, our roads will part. Dan Qing will go towards his destiny, while we will deliver a load of spices to the plain, pick up a load of silk and then turn back. At that point, you will be able to count the days that separate you from Taqin Guo.'

'Taqin Guo: the Roman empire, for the Chinese.'

'That's what they call it. For them it's a land of legend in the far west, about which they know nothing.'

'It seems impossible,' said Metellus. 'We buy enormous quantities of goods from China, we export many there as well, yet neither of the two empires has ever come into contact with the other, as if they were two different worlds.'

'Distance!' replied Daruma. 'It's the distance, Commander. So great that it becomes necessary to acquiesce to intermediaries. The most curious thing is that the Persians, your implacable enemies, are not always on good terms with their Oriental partners either.'

'True. Two hundred years ago, our emperor Tiberius complained that with the gold the Persians earned in taxes on the silk and precious stones we imported, they financed their wars against us.'

'That doesn't surprise me in the least,' Daruma said sententiously. 'Avariciousness, the desire to accumulate treasure, is another of your most peculiar characteristics.'

Metellus had his answer ready, but a line from Virgil came to mind: '*Quid non mortalia pectora cogis, auri sacra fames.*' The execrable lust for gold did indeed lead men's souls astray. And he bit his tongue.

16

DINNER WAS READY AT DUSK. Metellus and his comrades watched the fish being roasted on the brazier; fish they'd never seen or imagined, brightly hued with blue or metallic green reflections. They tasted delicious, seasoned with an abundance of spices, in particular a condiment that only the very rich could afford in the West: pepper.

Dan Qing sat with the others, slightly apart from them. He was served first, and given the beverage prepared with the infusion of dried leaves that Metellus has tasted that afternoon. The others were served palm wine.

The sun set in a triumph of black-bellied clouds with purple edges, its last rays painting flaming paths on the surface of the Ocean, which stretched out to lap at the boat.

The men chatted, in a good humour. They were talking about women, mostly, and that pleased Metellus. He hadn't heard them talking about women for years, since the last dinners they'd had in their tents on the Taurus mountains as they'd patrolled Edessa. They had never had the time or even the inclination since then.

The topic was proof of vitality regained. Metellus himself felt pervaded by a strength and energy that reawakened his longings. But then the pain came back even sharper, because his desire centred on a person who no longer existed. And yet the thought of her still seduced him: her full lips, the generous breasts that women from the south were so famous for, her round hips aroused visions and sensations that were still very vivid. He remembered the last journey they'd made together, to Italy. A

mission in Sicily. One afternoon in Segesta, in the stone colonnade of the great sanctuary: they were sitting close, watching the
setting sun, talking about what they would do when they were
finally able to come home from the Orient. The house they
would have liked to buy near that marvellous spot, the olive
grove, the vineyard they'd plant, with a garden of roses and
jasmine to scent the evening air. They would raise their little
boy like their ancestors had; Metellus himself would teach him
to make wine and raise bees. They would have more children,
who would grow in peace, who would live serenely in the shade
of these great solitary columns. He even remembered the
chirping of the birds seeking their nest on an architrave that held
up the sky.

It was all gone. Vanished, in a moment of agony, a surging
of blood.

'Aren't you eating?' Daruma's voice sounded at his side.

Metellus started. He looked at the food in his bowl and began
to eat.

'I know how you're feeling, but just wait until we've landed.
You'll really see something then! Landscapes that change from
one moment to the next – cities, villages, mountains, the roar of
tigers and the trumpeting of elephants. India! You will feel so
many new emotions that your life will start to flow again like
the current of a river that has found a new path after a cataclysm
has blocked its original course.

'The sea is different, mind you ... the sea mirrors our
thoughts, unfortunately the deepest and most melancholy ones.
It reflects what is hidden in the depths of our soul, our uncon-
fessed fears. The face of death floats under its liquid surface,
beckons from the horizon that slips further and further away,
without ever allowing you to reach it.'

Metellus smiled. 'You talk like one of us, like one of our
poets. I thought that your philosophy had overcome these fears.'

'Ours has, that is true. But not yours. It's not difficult for me
to see what's passing through your mind.'

'Then you know that you needn't worry about me. I'll survive. And I'll do what I have to do.'

Dinner was soon finished and the moon rose from the sea, illuminating its vast expanse. Metellus remained a while to observe the scaly surface of the Ocean, which reflected the heavenly body in a thousand shimmering facets. He leaned against the railing, abandoning himself to the marvellous spectacle that reminded him so much of the Internal Sea. He realized that he was following the route of Nearcus, Alexander's admiral, only in the opposite direction. He would soon be seeing what the great Macedonian king had only dreamed of. He would have liked to speak with the prince of the oblique eyes, but Dan Qing's haughtiness felt like an insuperable obstacle. He was fascinated by the prince, attracted, even, but he could not help comparing his attitude to the sorrowful humanity of Valerian, and pondering on how the old emperor had died among his soldiers with a dignity and a strength of character that no philosophical searching could match.

He approached Daruma instead, who was still sipping his infusion of dried leaves. 'Do the Chinese truly know of the existence of our empire?'

'Yes, as I've told you, they do. But their knowledge is not much more detailed than or much different from what you know about China. I've heard a very particular story, though. One and a half centuries ago, at the time of Emperor Hedi, a Chinese general named Ban Chao brought his army all the way to the Caspian Sea, crossing the great desert of Central Asia. From there he sent a lieutenant named Gan Ying to try to reach the sovereign of Taqin Guo – that is, of the Roman empire!'

Metellus looked at him in surprise. 'How do you know such things?'

'The monks at the fortress told me about it. They have copies of works and documents that were destroyed in the first fire of the Great Library of Luoyang.'

'Continue. What happened to Gan Ying, then?'

'He reached the shore of an inland sea.'

'The Pontus Euxinus?'

'Perhaps. The description in our sources is not clear. But I think it must have been as you suggest. They say it was only two marching days from the confines of Taqin Guo.'

'Incredible. He must have reached Tigranocerta or Phasis, in Armenia . . . Well?'

'Well, it just so happened that Gan Ying had Persian guides with him, and when they realized that he meant to reach the confines of the Roman empire and speak with the emperor, they told him he could never succeed; that the distance separating him from the border of Taqin Guo was as great as the distance he had left behind him. Gan Ying lost heart and turned back, with nothing to show for his efforts. The Persians did not want the two empires to speak directly.'

'Of course. The taxes that the Persians impose on the silk caravans bring in enormous sums, but perhaps that isn't the only reason. The two empires were too far apart to fear each other, but it might have been in the best interests of both to collaborate, or even ally themselves against common enemies. The Persians, for instance.'

'You hate them, don't you?'

'Hate is a personal emotion. It can't be directed against an entire nation. I hate those who were responsible for the death of my emperor and one of my companions. They inflicted every sort of suffering and humiliation on us. But none of this would have happened had we been ransomed.

'You see, we have a great Greek historian who holds that history is mostly the consequence of chance. The event you've just told me about seems to confirm this theory. What would have happened if, a century and a half ago, the two emperors had established a direct relationship? What would have been the destiny of mankind, the course of history? What happened was that a Persian guide told a little lie and prevented a momentous change from taking place. And so for China we're still Taqin

Guo, a legendary place in the far west, and for us China has remained Sera Maior, the place that produces silk . . .'

Metellus fell still, but Daruma understood what was going through his mind. 'You're thinking that you might be the one to accomplish the task now, aren't you? Why not? Imagine what extraordinary consequences the meeting of two great empires would have. Just think what a turning point in history you would have brought about!' Daruma seemed truly excited for the first time since Metellus had met him.

'I don't want to think about that now,' replied Metellus. 'My only concern is to return as soon as possible. But . . . if I could . . . it's certainly a fascinating idea. I only wonder whether it's possible to establish any kind of relationship with men like Dan Qing. My emperor spoke every day with even the most humble of his soldiers.'

'Because they spoke the same language. If you want to communicate with Dan Qing, you must learn his language. Not just the one he speaks, the one he thinks.'

Metellus looked at him with a sceptical expression.

'I'll help you, if you like,' said Daruma, then wished him a good night and retired below deck.

Metellus took a cup of palm wine and poured a little into the sea, offering up a libation to Uxal's spirit, which rose and fell with the waves, before the moon disappeared behind a cloud.

THEY REACHED the mouth of the Indus thirteen days later. The great river was announced by a wide yellowish patch in the middle of the intense blue of the Ocean. The large estuary was swarming with vessels and the shores were packed with merchants, sailors, labourers and farmers. They disembarked one after another, except for Dan Qing, who stayed on board. Evidently that place held no interest for him. Or, if he was interested, he certainly wasn't showing it. Metellus and his men scattered through the market in their first leave as free men. Because even fear is a form of slavery, and they were finally free from the threat of being followed and hunted down.

Here they breathed the air of a completely different world: the costumes, the clothing, the colour of men's skins. Even the animals were strange: monkeys, parrots, elephants . . . And cows, cows everywhere, roaming tranquilly down the streets. They were very peculiar-looking as well, with a strange hump like a camel's on their backs, just behind their necks.

Daruma, followed by a group of his sailors, busied himself with buying provisions for the rest of the journey. As far as Metellus could understand, the boat would sail up the river for a stretch, taking advantage of the thrust of the monsoon. Then at a certain point, he didn't know where exactly, it would be moored and they would continue on foot, with a caravan, to their final destination.

At a certain distance from the market, Balbus, Quadratus and the others noticed a small crowd thronging around a tree so big that its foliage could provide shade for an entire legion. From its branches hung true columns of vegetation, which were actually roots stretching towards the earth; once they reached the ground they were transformed into supplementary trunks for the boughs that had extended too far outwards. Metellus was even more amazed when he had made his way through the crowd and seen the reason for their gathering. Sitting on the ground with his legs crossed and a turban on his head was a bony man with wrinkly grey skin and a long beard, intent on meditating. He held his hands crossed between his knees with the palms turned up towards the sky. He was so immobile that he seemed a statue and Metellus was reminded of a legendary character of Greek culture, the philosopher Diogenes, a cynic who lived in a barrel and drank from a wooden bowl. This man must have been one of those gymnosophists mentioned in the histories of Alexander. Like the Indian master who had followed the Macedonian sovereign in his journey of return all the way to Persepolis, before having himself burned alive on a funeral pyre. Kalanos . . .

And that bony old man, just like Kalanos, showed that he had no fear of death: a deadly poisonous snake slithered over his belly and wound its way up to his neck, darting his little forked tongue at an inch from his face.

Metellus's soldiers stood there open-mouthed as well.

'This is truly a strange land,' muttered Balbus.

'That it is,' commented Antoninus. 'We'll have lots to tell when we get back home.'

Rufus broke away from the rest of the group. 'I'm going to take a look around the port. You never know . . . I might find a ship coming from our part of the world.'

'Forget it,' said Metellus. 'They'll be blocked here for six months until the wind changes. What's more, we've given our word. I asked if any of you were against it, whether anyone wanted to turn back on his own. You answered that you all wanted to stay with me. And you will, by Hercules! I swear to you that you'll stay!'

'No one wants to back out, Commander,' said Rufus. 'I was just hoping to exchange a few words in Latin, that's all. And to send a message home, maybe. You know, from mouth to mouth, one leg of a voyage to the next . . . It's not certain that every one of us will make it back, after all. We've got a difficult task ahead of us – assaults, ambushes, battles, who knows? It's not going to be plain sailing. So I was thinking, if I could at least manage to get a message through . . .'

'We will make it, Rufus. All of us, together. We'll celebrate to end all celebrations, we'll look back on the dangers and the suffering that we lived through and have a good laugh. Men, it's high time we got back to the boat: Daruma will be waiting for us.'

He cast a last look at the skeletal old man wrapped in the coils of his snake and then he set off, elbowing his way through the crowd.

THEY SAILED UP the Indus for a long stretch, and Metellus tried to recognize the places that Alexander had seen coming down the river in the other direction. Deepest India extended on the right, the India the Macedonian king had never seen. He wondered what Alexander must have felt, watching that fantastic landscape unfolding before his eyes from the railing of the royal ship, seeing the sun rise from that foggy horizon, from the dense foliage of those gigantic trees along with flocks of thousands of birds. He suffered, certainly: his insatiable spirit, thirsting for knowledge, must have suffered when he saw the horizon escaping from him, curving over the ends of the world, denied him by destiny.

Could he manage where Alexander had failed? With his tiny army, would he succeed in reaching the ends of the earth, the waveless Ocean? As they advanced, he noticed that the real world negated the claims of the *Naturalis Historia* and the *De Mirabilibus*, on which he had founded his knowledge of the far eastern lands, but the nature he saw was no less wonderful than the legend.

At night, when they drew up along some swampy bank, Metellus could hear the cries of unknown animals and sometimes even the muffled roar of a tiger in search of prey. The Taprobane sailors trembled at that sound and widened their eyes in fear. Even Metellus's comrades glanced around apprehensively. Only Dan Qing seemed not to know fear. Sometimes, armed only with a knife, he would disembark and set off into the thick underbrush all alone. Metellus would often offer to accompany him, but Daruma dissuaded him. Evidently, a walk through the forest was not an appreciable danger for the prince; in any case, it was just one of his many unfathomable acts.

They saw elephants almost everywhere: the marvellous animals, considered such wild, wondrous creatures in the West that they were put on show in the amphitheatres, here were used as beasts of burden. They moved and lifted huge logs with their trunks or dragged heavy loads on carts or sleds.

Storms would often blow up and then the floodgates of the heavens would open. Walls of water beat down in front of the boat's bow, while bolts of lightning lit up vast areas of land as if it were daytime, followed by fearsome explosions of thunder.

Never in their lives had the Romans seen anything like it. The land on both banks was frequently flooded by the overflowing river and they saw Indian crocodiles lazily paddling through the muddy waters, or fighting over the carcass of some drowned farm animal, flogging the surface with their scaly tails and snapping their mighty jaws open and shut.

At times they would see enormous spotted serpents slithering along the tree branches that hung over the water, or furrowing the muddy quagmires extending beyond the banks, with sinuous, elegant movements. Daruma explained that those monsters were actually innocuous, while others were so poisonous that a man bitten would die in a few moments.

Terrifying, and almost always hostile, the nature they encountered was spellbinding. The men were filled with wonder at every new discovery.

At a certain point, the monsoon wind blew too strongly cross-wise and the men disembarked. Daruma sent the boat back to the port at the river mouth. They would continue on foot.

A month of hard marching followed, until they reached the confluence of the three great tributaries on the left side of the Indus: the Hyphasis, the Acesines and the Hydraotes. It was there that Alexander had built twelve altars to the Olympic gods to mark the outer limit of his eastward march. Metellus sent Daruma to ask after them, thinking it would be interesting to visit the site, but no one knew anything about them. More than five and a half centuries had passed since the adventure of the young Macedonian king and the Greek kingdom of Bactriana existed no longer. It had been wiped out by peoples whom the Chinese had driven away from their own borders.

Metellus spent long hours as they marched with Daruma learning the language of Dan Qing. Daruma had suggested that this would greatly improve relations and foster understanding. For the prince, speaking a foreign language, even one that he knew, was an intolerable humiliation. This, added to his inborn haughtiness as an aristocrat, created a practically insurmountable barrier.

'I'm not doing it for him,' insisted Metellus. 'I'm curious about this language made up of monosyllables, so different from ours. I've always had a natural inclination for learning languages. In Edessa I was the only high officer who spoke an understandable Persian.'

'It's true,' admitted Daruma, 'you have a good ear, and are picking it up very quickly.' Deep down he wondered whether Metellus's curiosity meant that this new world was finding a place in his heart; perhaps learning the language meant that he might stay on for a while. Or even forever.

One day, Metellus asked about the mountains they would be crossing, of which he had heard only vague rumours and conflicting descriptions.

'The Indian Caucasus,' replied Daruma. 'You call them thus, because your Alexander once did. They are the tallest mountains on the earth. Their peaks rise to the house of the gods. Their slopes are covered by cascades of ice. In this season, the warm monsoon wind can set off disastrous avalanches: masses of snow, capable of burying a whole city, go flying down towards the valley with a roar of thunder, destroying entire forests, dragging along boulders as big as houses. As you ascend the mountainside, the air becomes thinner and breathing becomes more and more difficult, step by step, until the strain is intolerable.

'I've heard that some people have insisted on climbing the flanks of these mountains up beyond every reasonable limit, and that the only distance they can cover in an entire day is one hundred steps.'

Metellus was relieved that his men could not understand what Daruma was saying, because it would have terrified them. They were excellent soldiers, exceptional combatants, but they were accustomed to fighting other human beings; the idea of taking on the forces of nature would have filled them with dread, and it troubled Metellus as well. Daruma's calm attitude, which could come only from his long experience, was the one thing that helped to reassure him.

'Are you telling me this to frighten me?' Metellus asked him 'It's usually the opposite: one usually tries to keep the difficulties hidden, so as not to alarm the men.'

'You'll decide how to speak to your soldiers. As far as I'm concerned, I prefer that you know what to expect. I don't want to find myself in an emergency and have to deal with a panic-stricken escort.'

'I imagine that you've already found yourself in the conditions you've described, perhaps more than once.'

'Certainly.'

'And you've come through safe and sound, seeing that you can talk about it.'

'Obviously.'

'So we'll manage to make it through ourselves. We fear neither difficulty nor danger. We have our own high mountains, the Alps, and our legions cross them in any season.'

'Good,' replied Daruma. 'That's the response I expected from you.'

They proceeded in legs of about seven miles a day, stopping now and then in the villages to buy food and replenish their water supplies. Thus they became acquainted with marsh grain. It was much thinner than normal wheat but had a very similar colour. It was eaten boiled, accompanied by vegetables and fish, and they found it very tasty. The men wondered why, with all the cows they saw roaming everywhere, it was impossible to get a piece of beef, and they were told that cows were considered sacred in that land, and that killing them was a crime no less serious than killing a man. The fruit they ate partially compensated for this privation: there was such a wide variety, with flavours so delicious and so fragrant that the men consumed it in great quantities.

They kept their horses and camels at an easy walk. Dan Qing rode at their head on a black horse, silent most of the time, as always. At his side, a little behind him, Metellus was mounted on a sorrel. Then came the two centurions on foot, followed by three men on each side in single file, flanking the camels led by Daruma. Antoninus brought up the rear, with Rufus and his unfailing javelin.

They marched *expediti*, lightly armed and at a cadenced pace, as Sergius Balbus had ordered. Their armour was transported with the baggage of the caravan. The men wondered when it would be time to reassemble and wear it again in the line of duty.

The sky was almost always obscured by dense, low clouds, from which violent downpours would burst unexpectedly. The ground became slick with yellowish sludge run through with rivulets of dirty water, their clothing was sodden and the rain trickled down their backs, arms and legs on to the ground. The village inhabitants, sheltered under rattan lean-tos, watched with curiosity as they filed past, thinking that they must be in a great hurry if they couldn't wait until it stopped raining.

One day the plains became rolling grasslands and their path steepened, heading up towards that ceiling of leaden clouds. The vegetation thinned out and began to change as well. The forest plants gave way to tree-like ferns and then to a kind of evergreen with a majestic bearing. Metellus was reminded of the cedar of Lebanon which he had often seen while visiting the Oriental provinces of the empire.

'They are cedars, in fact,' Daruma explained. 'In our language they're called *deodara*.'

'What does that mean?'

'Tree of God,' replied Daruma solemnly.

'That's strange,' observed Metellus. 'It almost sounds like Greek.'

'You're right,' nodded Daruma. 'In *koinè* it's *diosdendron*.'

'How is that possible?'

'It will seem odd to you, but our language resembles Greek in many ways. Perhaps in ancient times, our peoples lived close to one another.'

'The Judaeans say that at the beginning of time all men spoke the same language, but they committed the sin of arrogance, and their unforgiving God scattered and separated them so that their languages began to differ . . .'

They were so engrossed in their conversation they almost hadn't noticed that the clouds had dropped so low that they had taken on the appearance of dense fog. The men advanced in silence through the thick mist, rather intimidated by the muffled atmosphere which seemed to swallow up every sound. But little by little the shroud of vapours was dispelled and then vanished completely; in the sudden, nearly blinding splendour of the sun the mountains appeared, their summits glittering with ice, their sharp peaks perforating the sky.

17

THE VISION OF THE towering mountain range left Metellus speechless. He could never have imagined such a spectacle, fascinating and dreadful at one and the same time. The mountains rose from a boundless high plain and the tallest peaks looked like crystal pinnacles, sparkling like diamonds. Some were encircled by clouds, while others stood out against a sky so deep blue that it might have been the midnight firmament. Metellus thought of the modest bulk of Mount Olympus, which had inspired the Greeks to imagine the abode of the gods there, and he couldn't help but smile: how minuscule his own world seemed compared to these titanic manifestations of nature!

He understood why Alexander had identified the immense chain with the Caucasus and had imagined it as the scene of Prometheus's eternal punishment. Metellus couldn't take his eyes away from the sight of those lofty peaks, so tall they made him dizzy, and when he looked at his men he saw that their astonishment was even greater than his.

He heard Antoninus saying, 'I'll wager that a person who managed to climb up to the top of one of those mountains could see the confines of the earth on every side, and the current of the Ocean surrounding it.'

'No one can climb that high. Anyone who has got even close has returned with terrible tales to tell. It is impossible to advance beyond a certain limit, if nothing else because the cold is so intense that it would kill anyone who was exposed to it, even for the briefest time,' said Daruma, guessing at the possible intent behind Antoninus's words. 'But also because the air is so rarefied it becomes unbreathable.'

Their conversation did not last long, because all their energies were consumed by the uphill march, which left them light-headed and panting.

Metellus noticed that the natives were rather short, with very wide chests that must help them breathe more deeply. He also noticed several cube-shaped stone constructions, topped by a dome or sometimes a spire, along their route. They looked very old indeed. When they stopped to rest, he asked Daruma what they were.

'In our language they're called *stupa*,' replied the merchant. 'The first one was built to preserve the remains of one of our philosophers. He was a prophet, a miracle-worker – I don't know the word for that in *koinè*. Later they simply became monuments to recall his preaching and his endeavours. His name was Siddhartha, but he has become known as Buddha, which means "the enlightened one".

'His word has reached China as well, and you will find his image in many places. Most monuments portray him in meditation, which is the way he achieved enlightenment.'

'Does Dan Qing's *tao* have something to do with the teachings of this philosopher?'

'Yes, in part. The prince's master is a man who believes profoundly in both philosophies: that of Buddha and that of the Chinese wise men Master Kong Fuzi and Master Lao Tze. You see, Commander, the path of illumination is . . .'

Metellus interrupted him with a sigh of ill-disguised impatience. 'I fear it won't be easy for me to follow you on this ground, Daruma. You ask too much of a simple soldier.'

Daruma smiled. 'Don't let it worry you. I couldn't have gone on much further myself. I'm nothing but a merchant.'

'I'm not so sure of that,' replied Metellus, 'but we'll still have quite some time to get to know each other. As far as philosophers and prophets are concerned, I've always avoided them like the plague.'

'Why?' asked Daruma. 'Are you perhaps afraid to measure yourself up against someone whose thoughts have gone far beyond your own?'

'That could be,' replied the Roman, 'but I'm a soldier. Men like me are given the task of creating enough security and enough peace inside a state so that even the philosophers can pursue their calling, so that the judges can administer justice, so that artists and poets can produce their work. To achieve this, we soldiers have to challenge and fight off people who don't even have enough food to eat, people who don't know how to build a house or till a field. They are primitive beings, animated by a savage desire to conquer . . . the same desire that animated our own forebears at the origins of the first republic.

'You see, Daruma, I think that men turn to prophets and miracle-workers when they become afraid that our swords are no longer capable of safeguarding their lives and their possessions. There is a religion that has been gaining ground rapidly in our land as well. It was founded by a Judaean master called Christ, who they claim is the son of God. This prophet was accused of sedition and executed by one of our governors more than two hundred years ago, and now his word is slowly conquering our empire. Do you know why? He is certainly not capable of guaranteeing the safety of our state, much less of the world, but what he offers the faithful is happiness in the next world, a place that no one has ever visited and from which no one has ever returned. I think that people turn to the gods when they are desperate, when they can't believe in anything else. And if the old gods no longer inspire faith, they simply find new ones.'

'We have a word for men who think the way you do.'

'So do we,' interrupted Metellus. 'We call them sceptics. And even this word comes from a school of philosophy. But remember, Daruma, men like me may not know how to keep up a brilliant conversation, but we have one thing in our favour. We're accustomed to relying on ourselves, and on other men of the same temperament.'

'You mean them?' asked Daruma, nodding towards the Roman soldiers who were busy setting up camp.

'Them,' confirmed Metellus.

'Yet the miraculous leap of Dan Qing impressed you. And it was a real act, achieved by a man of flesh and blood like you.'

'It's true,' admitted the Roman, 'but what good is such ability if he can't even communicate, if he spends most of his time closed up inside himself? What makes him different from a stone or a tree or, if you prefer, from a philosopher, locked into his own convictions?'

Daruma turned for an instant to regard Dan Qing sitting on his heels before a little *stupa*. He answered, 'It's difficult to judge a man by how he appears to us. Silence and isolation may be a punishment that a person inflicts upon himself.'

THEY STARTED marching again the next day. When they had nearly reached the pass, they turned around to consider the long, winding path they had taken; from that height it looked even steeper. They stopped for the night when they found an inn with a pen for their horses and camels. Inside the modest building, constructed of stones and tree trunks, an old man with a thin beard and eyes like Dan Qing's served his customers a mutton stew accompanied by boiled marsh grain seasoned with the animal's fat.

It was certainly not appetizing fare for Metellus's men, but there was no alternative. In a place so far from the rest of the world, they couldn't expect much choice.

At the pass, they transferred their packs on to some Bactrian camels, much more suitable to the terrain, the temperature and the altitude of the mountainous region.

They set off the next day, descending at first down to a vast high plain and then starting to climb uphill again. After a few days of marching, the men had begun to suffer from stinging eyes and nausea. Metellus advised a remedy for their eyes: a black blindfold with two very narrow slits to allow them to see while protecting them from the intense light. The men chewed on salt that Daruma had distributed to fight off their nausea.

Dan Qing seemed not to feel the strain of moving in such a hostile environment, perhaps because he was close to his home. As they advanced, people began to resemble him more in a physical way, although those mountain dwellers had deeply wrinkled skin the colour of clay, due to the sun and the harsh dry air. The Romans, on the other hand, realized with every step that they were becoming the oddities, the object of evident, albeit discreet, curiosity on the part of onlookers.

It was clear that none of the natives had ever seen anyone of their race travelling through those places. The children, inquisitive like in any part of the world, reached out their hands to touch the strange individuals with their bristly faces and round eyes, their arms as hairy as monkeys'. Septimius drew the greatest curiosity with his blue eyes and light blond hair. They got close enough to touch his knees, before they scampered off giggling to hide behind their parents' legs.

After the first pass, they covered another fifteen legs of their journey until they reached the base of another pass even higher than the first. Here they abandoned the Bactrian camels and transferred their packs on to small, strange-looking oxen with very long hair, the only animals, asserted Daruma, capable of enduring the heights that awaited them. They were crossing a landscape of increasingly extraordinary and untamed beauty: the snowy peaks loomed above the caravan like pyramids of ice with bluish reflections. Their narrowing path climbed the mountain slopes, jutting out over precipitous walls, over abysses that took one's breath away. When a stone was nudged by someone's foot and fell off the cliff, the sound of sliding gravel was joined by a chorus of stones rebounding off the sides of the precipice, and everyone understood that taking a false step meant certain death.

They advanced at a slow pace behind the local guides who led the shaggy oxen by their halters. The men became accustomed day by day, nearly hour by hour, to breathing the different air, as they adapted to a light which was ever clearer, an atmosphere ever more transparent.

As they ascended, the cold became piercing and the walls of the chasm closer, until it was clear that they'd soon have to pass to the other side; to do so, they'd have to cross a wooden rope bridge swaying over the precipice between the two rock walls. The men looked each other in the eyes and Metellus could feel their terror. Inured as they were to any danger or adventure, they were not yet acquainted with the harsh demands of such an extreme world. Only the calm resoluteness of their commander and the example of the centurions gave them the sense of security necessary for acceptance and maintaining discipline.

'You must always look forwards,' said Metellus, 'never down. It's just a few steps, in the end. You've been through much worse.'

The most difficult part was getting the animals across. Balbus went first, accompanied by one of the native guides, carrying a rope to be anchored to the other side; the pack animals were secured to the rope so that they wouldn't move too far to the left or right during their transit and throw the entire structure off balance. Then it was the men's turn. Dan Qing crossed without difficulty, ignoring the rope, while Daruma went last, escorted by Lucianus and Rufus, who supported him on either side.

The weather was worsening before their very eyes. A squall was blowing up, cold gusts sweeping the narrow gorge and making the bridge swing back and forth. Metellus feared that even the slightest delay would make their passage impossible. When Daruma had finally set foot on the other side, they immediately began their descent, although the light was rapidly waning. They trudged along until their surroundings were less harsh and the temperature more endurable, and finally set up camp, exhausted with fatigue and numb with cold.

They continued to advance the next day and the day after that, and then for many days more, until they reached a fork with another road that came from the east. It cut into the side of the rocky flank, which was riddled with deep ravines. Here they stopped to exchange the woolly oxen for Bactrian camels and a few horses, small in stature and quite shaggy as well, but very hardy.

Metellus was amazed by this animal-trading system, which reminded him of the horse exchanges that existed in the empire along the *cursus publicus*, the great network of roads that stretched as far as the most secluded Roman outposts in Africa and Britannia. With the difference that there wasn't a single state here, regulating the procedures and the exchanges, but only the needs of the wayfarers and the habits of the local communities.

'Further north,' Daruma told him, 'there are nomadic tribes who raise the best horses in the world. The Chinese call them the "horses that sweat blood", and are willing to pay exorbitant prices for them. Several emperors have given their daughters away in marriage to barbarian chieftains just to have a herd of those fantastic animals. When we are in the Empire of Dragons, you will surely see some.'

'The Empire of Dragons?' repeated Metellus. 'What does that mean?'

'It means China,' replied Daruma. 'It is another of its many names. The dragon is a common mythological figure in the country, taking on a variety of forms, from demon to protector.'

Daruma pronounced many words and expressions in Chinese, in order to force his pupil to practise the language, although he had become resigned to the fact that Metellus's only thought was of getting back home.

In all that time, Metellus had spoken very little with Dan Qing: only brief phrases of courtesy in Persian at the moment of passing food during their communal meals or upon meeting in the morning or retiring at night. But he had never stopped studying the language with Daruma, every night after dinner or when they paused to rest during the day, and his progress had been constant.

During the last legs of their journey through the great

mountain chain, the weather took a turn for the worse again and they soon found themselves in the middle of a snowstorm: an event which they were not prepared for and which sorely tested their endurance. The bitterly cold wind cut through them like a blade, penetrating all the way to their bones. No amount of clothing seemed to help. A dense sleet of piercing crystals fell as the wind whistled and moaned through the mountain gorges. Metellus and his men had to call on all their willpower and resolution so as not to succumb to the cold and their fatigue.

Dan Qing often seemed to be observing them with his oblique glance, and if someone had been able to decipher his expression they would have seen admiration for the perseverance demonstrated by the men of Taqin, for their stubborn determination to overcome the forces of nature.

Conditions continued to worsen. The cold became even more intense, until it froze their limbs and made it difficult to move at all. As they fought their way through the swirling snow, something darted in front of Dan Qing's horse after a bend in the path. The animal reared up violently with a whinny of terror.

The prince was completely taken by surprise and was thrown backwards as the horse fell over, the jaws of a white leopard deep in its flesh.

Dan Qing was pinned between his horse and the edge of the precipice; if he tried to free himself he would fall headlong below. In the meantime, the leopard had spotted him. Releasing the neck of the horse, which was in the throes of death, it lunged towards its human prey instead, baring bloody fangs and stretching out a clawed forepaw. Publius, who had been closest behind the prince, leapt forward and started waving his cloak in front of the beast's face. The leopard, made bold by hunger, continued to roar menacingly and to swipe at those it imagined were after its prey. Publius was trying to draw his sword but it had frozen solid and would not budge from its sheath, as Balbus and Antoninus rushed over and managed to pull Dan Qing to safety. The leopard swiftly lashed out at Publius's arm, sending him right over the side of the precipice.

'Help him!' yelled Metellus, attracting the beast's attention to himself. Just as the leopard had turned on him and was about to pounce, Metellus twisted around and grabbed the javelin of Rufus, who was right behind him, then spun back towards the leopard, running the beast through in mid-leap.

Publius was shouting, 'Help me! I'm here, help me!' and, as Metellus was extricating himself from the animal's inert body, Quadratus, Balbus and Septimius formed a human chain to rescue their comrade, who was clinging to a rock spur.

Septimius managed to grasp his slipping hand a moment before Publius would have plunged into the abyss, and they hauled him up. Metellus drew the javelin out of the leopard's body and contemplated the dying beast: clouds of steam puffed from its nostrils and its blood stained the white snow. He had never seen such a magnificent animal in his life: completely white, with only a few dark spots on its coat to distinguish it from the snow.

Metellus turned around and found Dan Qing standing behind him. Immobile as statues of snow, they stared into each other's eyes without saying a word, then Metellus went over to Publius, who was still trembling with cold and terror, and he embraced him tightly, like a son who had escaped death. They began their march again in the raging storm and it wasn't until after dusk that they reached their resting place: a hut made of tree trunks, flanked by a stable. Famished and almost completely dehydrated, the men managed to push the animals under the roof and drag themselves inside the shelter, where a big fire was roaring in a brazier in the centre of the room, below a hole in the ceiling from which the smoke escaped. The contents of a pot on the brazier were bubbling away and a smoking lamp, burning animal fat, hung from the ceiling beams.

An elderly couple sitting on a sheep's fleece were holding bowls and seemed to be intent on the pot. Daruma said something to them and the old man gestured for them to join them. Dan Qing entered last and sat in a corner, on his heels.

The old woman passed out bowls, then took the pot from

the fire and poured a ladle of broth with a few pieces of mutton into each bowl. The hot food restored a little life to the exhausted men, but also made them profoundly sluggish. No one felt like talking. As soon as they had finished eating, the Romans were undone by the warm atmosphere inside the hut and collapsed on to the sheepskins, one after another, falling instantly into a deep sleep.

More by habit than anything else, Metellus went out for a brief inspection. The moon was just appearing from behind a blanket of dense vapours, illuminating the mountains that were still being scourged by the storm with its ghostly light. The horses and pack animals were calmly browsing on the hay in the manger and in the distance the sobbing of a nocturnal bird wafted up from the bottom of the valley. He returned towards the refuge and found Dan Qing waiting.

'Why did you do it?' asked the prince in Persian.

'I'm paid to do it,' replied Metellus, and, without waiting for an answer, went in.

The next day, the world around them was completely transformed. The dawning sun tinged the snowy peaks pink and made the green fields covering the lower slopes of the mountains glimmer. The wind had dropped and an eagle was soaring through the sky in expansive, solemn flight. Quadratus was the first to rise. He stretched his stiff limbs and walked over to a drinking trough. He broke the ice and washed his face with the freezing water. Little by little, the others came out, last of all Dan Qing followed by Daruma. The drivers prepared the animals and the old couple distributed cups of warm milk. Daruma paid with Indian coins and the caravan set off again. They travelled all that day and all the next until they came to a vast area of level ground where they began to meet other caravans, smaller or larger than their own, proceeding in the opposite direction and loaded down with wares. Almost everyone they met up with resembled Dan Qing and Metellus realized that their destination must be not too far off. Calculating the time it had taken to get to where they were from the mouth of the Indus, he felt that it would be more or less another month to reach the point of arrival, after which they'd be able to undertake their journey home.

They advanced another twenty days, covering about twelve miles a day. They crossed a steppe and then an arid desert, which would have been impossible to negotiate without the local guides, who knew the trails and the location of the wells from which the men and animals could drink.

Now Metellus was certain that they were crossing lands that not even Alexander had encountered during his long march eastward; they had gone far beyond Maracanda and far beyond the last Alexandria. He was sure that they had passed the lands that Herodotus had attributed to the most remote populations, the Issedonians and the Hippomolgians. The very look of the sky and its constellations seemed to have changed. He remembered that Antoninus had served as a land surveyor in the army and wondered whether he might be able to draw a map of their route, but then he realized that they had no instruments, no reference points, no material for writing or drawing. Perhaps when they had arrived at their destination, they would be able to make a measuring instrument, a *groma*, and find the material they'd need to draw a map on their return journey. Such a map would be invaluable: the description of an unknown region, unwinding day by day under the patient, constant steps of his soldiers.

The sensation that dominated his spirit and that of his men was of crossing an endless region, of seeing their own world grow smaller and smaller as they moved away from it, like the sensation one had when looking at people and objects from the top of a high tower or the edge of a precipice.

The immensity of Asia took their breath away: the vastness of the deserts, the flat expanse of the steppe, limited only by the horizon, a land dominated by immeasurable silence or the repeated, monotonous cries of mysterious, hidden creatures. Sunset came abruptly, casting bloody streaks on the golden sands, then immediately yielded to a multitude of stars trembling in the infinite celestial vault. Sometimes, in the dead of night, they would abruptly hear a nearly silent beating of wings like flocks of winged ghosts passing over their heads in the darkness, traversing invisible paths. The moon rose like a great silver shield to illuminate the spectral landscape, awakening the prolonged lament of the jackals. At times, its thin crescent skimmed the wavy profile of the dunes, and when it finally set, the morning star alone remained to guard the threshold of the aurora.

They met other men, other convoys, crossing that vast land in one direction or the other, mostly caravans of camels that advanced with their peculiar swaying gait. Metellus often wondered why they were never attacked. Were there no brigands eager to seize their belongings? He concluded that it must be in everyone's interest for the goods to reach their final destination; the profits to be had were too great for their journey to be disturbed.

During this interminable crossing, relations between Dan Qing and Metellus remained what they had always been, except for those first few days on Daruma's boat. At first, Metellus had tried to make sense of the prince's attitude, and he had come to the conclusion that the man was simply too different: his mentality and his manners were too dissimilar for the two of them to be able to understand each other. The distance between them seemed to become more marked instead of decreasing, and it appeared that not even Daruma was interested in changing the way things were.

One day the prince approached Metellus as they were making their way up to a pass where they had decided to make camp, a saddle between two rocky hills. 'It's time for you to equip yourselves with full suits of armour,' he said. 'The sooner the better.'

'Why?' asked Metellus. 'We've had no problems until now in our light gear.'

'Because we've almost reached the border of China. We must be ready for anything. At our next stop, we'll be able to buy whatever you need.'

Metellus shook his head. 'I don't think we need anything. My men would never use weapons that they're not accustomed to, while they know they can rely completely on their own arms. Don't worry. We have our mail coats and all the segments of our *loricae*, ready to be assembled. We can make our own shields and helmets if we find a blacksmith's shop. But how do you know that we've arrived?'

'Do you see those two formations on either side of the pass?' Daruma broke in.

Metellus had no time to answer. He watched as Dan Qing galloped off towards the spot Daruma had been pointing at. The prince leapt to the ground and bowed several times before an object that Metellus couldn't quite make out.

Only when Metellus had drawn closer was he able to see what it was: at the sides of the pass were two gigantic stone sculptures carved in the rock, in the shape of winged monsters in a terrifying pose.

Daruma looked into his eyes and exclaimed, 'Welcome to the Empire of the Dragons!'

18

THEIR FIRST STOP IN Chinese territory was in a caravanserai where convoys carrying silk habitually stopped. It was a square-shaped construction with four towers, one at each corner, and a four-sided portico inside. A fountain set in a basin of carved stone stood in the middle. The inn was well served by a mill, a bakehouse, a forge and a sawmill, located on its sides. The first and last were fed by a torrent that descended from the mountains; its clear, rushing waters kept the mechanisms turning at a fast, constant rate. Severus and Antoninus were fascinated by those ingenious machines, and drew closer to watch them working.

Metellus joined Daruma, who was negotiating with the man in charge of the four shops to obtain use of the forge for the two Roman *fabri*. He also bought horses for everyone.

Publius and Rufus were assigned the job of reassembling the *lorica* segments and checking the coats of mail. Lucianus mounted the javelins on their shafts, and when Severus and Antoninus had returned from their round of inspection, he instructed them to make shields using wooden boards from the sawmill, and to forge new helmets. Metellus stopped later for a look and lingered to talk with Severus, who was making the shields. He was building them in his own way, in wood and iron.

During the days they remained in the caravanserai, fortifying themselves for what lay ahead, Metellus and his men began to form an idea about the world they were entering, its rules and customs, its currency, the people's habits and ways of dressing and even their religion.

There was in fact a small sanctuary on the premises, built of wood and painted in bright colours: flame red, white, ochre yellow and green. A holy man, a priest or a soothsayer, perhaps, delivered oracles to the travellers who consulted him. Sitting on his heels, in the typical posture of the Chinese, he tossed bones with incomprehensible markings on to the ground. They were mostly animal shoulder bones, whose flat surfaces were suitable for drawing magical symbols.

'It's called ashagalomancy,' explained Daruma. 'Reading bones. Depending on how they fall, one face or the other comes up and the seer draws his conclusions from the symbols carved into them. Dan Qing is an expert in this art. He was taught by his master, the venerable Wangzi.'

'Dan Qing . . .' murmured Metellus. 'It seems like a century has passed since he leapt on to our boat and yet I still know nothing about him. What concept of power do these people have that prevents a ruler from exchanging even the most modest conversation with a common person?'

As he spoke, he was watching the prince ride up the side of a chalky hill that stood behind the caravanserai.

'I don't know much about him either,' admitted Daruma. 'But I've heard stories that hint at something quite unpleasant, some unmentionable secret, hidden in his past. In this country, supreme power is often associated with forms of cruelty that you and I can't even imagine.'

'Power is the same everywhere, but I can see that this land is very different from my own. What is it that you mean exactly?' asked Metellus.

Daruma smiled. 'Well, for example, when the great emperor Huangdi ruled over this kingdom, he decreed that all the schools of philosophy should be closed and all books burnt, except for a single copy of each, to be preserved in the royal library. A certain number of wise men, philosophers and writers, expressed their dissent . . .'

'And?'

'Well, Huangdi had them buried alive, all four hundred and sixty of them, in a common grave.'

'I can see how having to carry out actions of that sort would make even the most communicative ruler a bit sullen,' replied Metellus sarcastically. 'But what's most difficult for me to understand is how a philosophy as advanced as the one you've described to me can reconcile itself with such a profoundly cruel exercise of power. You know, the best of our emperors was a philosopher himself. His name was Marcus Aurelius Antoninus and he was a wise, austere and valiant prince.'

'I believe that his fame reached as far as China, where they call him An Dong,' replied Daruma.

Metellus looked back towards the hill and saw the silhouette of Dan Qing on his horse, scanning the horizon and the forest-covered mountains that followed one another like the waves in the sea, sloping down towards other plains, other rivers, other mountains. This world seemed to have no end.

DARUMA HIRED some porters, a couple of camel drivers and a Chinese doctor, and then they set off again. They marched for a few days until they found themselves in the middle of an oak forest, a place sufficiently isolated for the men to don their armour. They soon looked just like they had when they were on duty in their own units.

Sergius Balbus reported to Metellus, who was awe-struck. The senior centurion's gear was perfect down to the last detail: the insignia of his rank, the horsehair crest on his helmet and the command staff. 'Drawn up in full battle order, Commander,' he proclaimed.

Metellus nodded and inspected them one after another, slowly, looking each man straight in the eye and observing every characteristic of his combat gear, from helmet to large square shield, perfectly reconstructed and even freshly painted, as was the custom the day before a battle. In the gleaming eyes of those veterans he saw a pride and emotion that brought a lump to his throat.

At the end of that brief military rite, Metellus stopped in front of the two *fabri*, Severus and Antoninus, to congratulate them. 'I see you haven't forgotten your trade.'

Antoninus stepped forward. 'We have something for you, Commander,' he said, and uncovered the breastplate they had hidden under a cloak. Fashioned for their commander and befitting his rank, the anatomical *lorica* was made of burnished iron, with the image of a gorgon carved in relief at the centre of the chest. Next to it was a brand-new helmet, made to measure in the caravanserai forge.

It was perfect, and polished as though it had just been crafted by a master armourer, and it took Metellus's breath away. 'But . . . how did you manage . . .' he murmured.

'We've been carrying it under the asses' pack-saddles, half each, and we polished it up for you at the forge. You should have seen how shocked those barbarians were!'

'Incredible!' replied Metellus. 'Help me to put it on.'

Antoninus lay it on his shoulders and Severus fastened the straps at his sides. Metellus could not help but remember the last time that someone had helped him to put on his armour. It had been in his own home, in Edessa, under the portico of the peristyle, as he was leaving to go to the emperor's staff meeting. The home he had never returned to, that he would certainly find dark and empty – or occupied by strangers – if he ever managed to set foot in it again.

He sighed, then put on the helmet that Severus was holding out to him, and he appeared before his little army with all the imposing dignity of his rank. The long marches had toned his body as in the best of times; the muscles of his arms and legs were sculpted by months of continuous exertion and tanned by the sun of the Ocean and of the lofty peaks of the Caucasus of India.

Quadratus approached him, visibly moved. '*Salve*, Commander!' he said, stiffening into a salute. 'We await your orders, as always. If only we had our eagle!'

'The eagle is here, in our hearts,' replied Metellus, 'and will instil us with courage, as it has in the past. We have defied the fury of the Ocean, the vortexes of the Indus, the tempests of the Paropamisus, and we are now only a step away from concluding our mission. As soon as we have accompanied Prince Dan Qing to his destination we shall finally begin our return journey. I am certain that we will see our homeland again, all of us, together, and I am sure that our return will make many tremble and others rejoice.'

He turned to allow them to file past in marching order and found Dan Qing directly before him, staring into his eyes.

'What I have seen is impressive,' said the prince.

'What do you mean?' asked Metellus.

'I have never seen soldiers wear their armour with such pride, or show such a bond with their commander, and so much respect at the same time.'

'Where I come from, no officer can exercise command unless he has earned the esteem and respect of his men. You cannot give orders unless you have proved that you can carry them out. You cannot demand any sacrifice from your soldiers unless you have shown that you are capable of enduring the worst sacrifice yourself. These are the men charged with your personal safety, and I can assure you that none better exist.'

Dan Qing nodded and touched his right palm with his left fist, a gesture of leave-taking that nonetheless avoided contact – it was certainly nothing like the vigorous shaking of hands that Metellus was accustomed to. The Roman replied with a nod of his head and gave orders to begin the march.

They advanced for several days along solitary trails through countryside scattered with bushes, pine shrubs and rattan cane, among which tall, majestic trees would rise every so often, where a depression in the rock held a thicker layer of fertile soil.

As time passed, the vegetation became denser and more luxuriant and streams of clear, quick-flowing water appeared, bubbling between towering rocks and over sparkling gravel beds. They began to see animals as well, mostly brightly coloured monkeys. Their fringed coats were golden and swayed to and fro with their every movement, while their legs were brown, as if they were wearing trousers of another colour. A big male crept close, until he was just a few paces away from them, and considered them with his old philosopher's face, his snub nose, his small, shiny eyes like pin points.

Here and there the rock faces along the banks were carved with figures of animals – deer, bulls, ibexes with huge curved horns – and hunters in the act of tracking their prey with bows and arrows. There were magical symbols at times as well, so ancient that not even Daruma knew how to interpret them. This civilization seemed to be rooted in the very origins of mankind.

The caravan proceeded in single file given the narrowness of the valley; it was without doubt a tedious and difficult route, but for this reason it was little frequented. Before long, Metellus noticed that Daruma seemed nervous, continually glancing about and sometimes stopping as if straining to hear. Dan Qing as well would spin round suddenly, even if only at the rustling of the wings of a bird frightened out of the forest by the intruders' approach.

It felt as if they were entering enemy territory rather than the homeland of their travelling companion. The general edginess spread to the men. Rufus and Publius, who had ventured into the forest, alerted by a strange noise, shouted out in fright as they found themselves face to face with a creature that proved to be completely innocuous. It was a kind of bear, with a black and white coat and spots on his face that resembled a mask.

'Have no fear,' said Daruma, who had run over at the sound of their shouts. 'It eats only cane shoots.'

And yet even Metellus could not shake off the feeling of a foreign presence. He was a veteran of years of combat in the forests of Germany and Pannonia, and his instincts kept him on edge and prevented him from relaxing, even when the others seemed tranquil. The sudden flight of a flock of birds, the sound of twigs breaking under the paws of a fleeing animal, the haunting, insistent cry of a night bird: everything increased his tension, and he ordered his men to proceed with their weapons to hand. Dan Qing seemed more at ease again after a while; his gestures were calm and measured but expressed constant and continuous surveillance, along with the potential for instant reaction.

He wore a sword as well now, hanging from his belt, a weapon that seemed to have appeared out of nowhere; none of them could even remember where or when they had first seen it at the prince's side. It was longer than the legionaries' swords and the hilt was marvellously engraved with refined craftsmanship.

All at once Severus, who was scouting with Martianus about a hundred feet ahead of the rest of the convoy, shouted, 'What was that? Did you see it? What was it?'

Metellus spurred on his horse and caught up with them. 'What's wrong?'

'A bird!' shouted Severus, opening his arms wide to approximate the wing span. 'A bird as big as ten eagles!'

'A monster,' confirmed Martianus.

Metellus rebuked him: 'Oh, come now. No such animal exists.'

He hadn't finished speaking when a sharp swish was heard and an enormous shadow crossed over the ground, looking like the wings of a gigantic bat. Metellus raised his eyes instantly, but saw nothing more than a confused shape flying off over the thick foliage of the trees.

Dan Qing drew up. 'What was it? What did you see?' he asked with apprehension.

'The shadow of a giant bird crossed our path,' replied Metellus. 'Twice. The first time, Severus and Martianus saw it, and I myself the second time.'

'How could you tell it was a bird?' asked Dan Qing.

'Yes, how could you tell?' gasped Daruma, who had ridden up on camelback.

'In the sky there are only clouds and birds,' replied Severus. 'And since I'm certain it was not the shadow of a cloud, it must have been a bird. The shape of the shadow looked like a bird. The commander saw it as well.'

'Are there creatures so large in this land?' Metellus asked Daruma.

Daruma hesitated. 'We are in the Empire of Dragons, don't forget that.'

'We also heard a slight rustling sound, like a swish of air,' added Martianus. 'But it was just for an instant. When I looked up to the sky, whatever it was had already vanished beyond the edge of the ravine.'

'I fear that our arrival has not passed unobserved,' said Dan Qing. 'Perhaps what you saw was someone spying on us ... from the sky.'

'Someone?' repeated Metellus, stunned. 'What do you mean by "someone"? A god? A demon? A winged dragon?'

'A man,' replied Dan Qing darkly. 'And now he knows we're here.'

The prince was quite uneasy now, eyes darting to every leafy bough. All at once, a barely perceptible noise was heard and his sword flashed through the air. A pine cone falling from a tree hit the ground, cut neatly in two, while the squirrel responsible for the false alarm fled squeaking, leaping from one branch to the next.

They all looked at Dan Qing in amazement as he sheathed his sword in a gesture of incredible precision.

'From this moment on, we must proceed with the utmost caution,' the prince said. He then remounted his horse and resumed the journey at a slower pace.

Antoninus, who was marching alongside Rufus, whispered, 'I told you, he's not a man. He must be a god, or a demon.'

Metellus approached Daruma. 'What was the prince referring to when he said it was a man ... I mean, that the shadow that flew over our heads was a man? He can't expect us to believe that men can fly in this country.'

'I don't know what he was referring to. I have heard strange rumours lately. What I can say is that the knowledge of this people is very advanced. Their civilization is over two thousand years old.'

'I'm tired of these mysteries and of him acting as if he were some kind of god. I can't wait to turn back. How much further is it now?'

'I can't say precisely. We haven't taken the usual route. We're journeying along the bottom of this ravine to stay out of sight, but I think I know where we're headed. Let's go on now. Try not to worry any more than necessary.'

They proceeded along the steeply sided wooded valley that bordered the torrent for four more days without anything strange happening. The tension abated and no one thought any longer about that mysterious shadow that had crossed their path. On the evening of the fifth day, when everyone seemed to have nearly forgotten the episode, a suffocated cry suddenly made them all snap to attention: one of caravan drivers tumbled to the ground, run through by an arrow. Another dart whistled past Antoninus's head and stuck fast in a tree trunk.

'Take cover, men!' shouted Metellus. 'Protect the prince!'

Before he could finish giving instructions, a barrage of arrows flew through the air, striking more men of the caravan and piercing the shields of the legionaries, who had raised them in their defence. A swarm of armed men dressed in black rushed out of the forest and fell upon Dan Qing and his defenders, swords drawn.

The Romans were still in marching order at the moment of the attack and could do nothing but turn to face the enemy. They felt vulnerable, in danger of being surrounded and eliminated one by one.

'Retreat towards me, fast! Disengage and retreat!' shouted Metellus. 'Regroup!' But he was already being assaulted full force by a shower of blows.

The agility of these warriors was unnerving, their movements lightning swift. Metellus tried to fend off his assailant's thrusts with his shield and sword, and backed up slowly in an attempt to flank Dan Qing, who, he sensed, was not far behind him. He found the prince at his side at the same moment in which he was attacked by two more of the enemy. They whirled their dazzling swords, more like lightning flashes than blades. Dan Qing responded with the same formidable dexterity. Metellus raised his voice above the fury of that frenetic attack to make himself heard by his men, who were falling back as he had ordered, step by step, bringing their shields up to meet every blow.

He saw Rufus launch his javelin through the air at one of those leaping demons, who crashed to the ground with the sound of shattered bones. Quadratus broke another man's spine with the edge of his shield, while Publius and Severus, back to back, attempted to protect each other from the overwhelming onslaught of the enemy.

'Rufus is wounded! Rufus is down!' Metellus heard all of a sudden, and saw Balbus and Severus tightly closing ranks to defend the fallen man.

Out of the corner of his eye, he saw Dan Qing's arm bleeding, and then his side, and he was pervaded by a fury that he had not felt in a very long time. An awesome energy burst from his chest and spun around his head like a cloud of fire. He smashed the face of the warrior in front of him with a butt from his helmet, whirled and stuck his *gladius* into the back of the warrior attacking Dan Qing, who was struggling to fight on.

'Men, to me!' he shouted, so loud that his voice could be heard over all the shrill, strident cries of the enemy.

As if by miracle, he found them drawing close, one after another, and as they pulled back, the distances between them diminished until they were shoulder to shoulder. Three of the enemy warriors were still assailing Metellus and Dan Qing, but they were cut off now from their comrades, separated by the compact line of Roman soldiers. Six of them walled the enemies off, while Quadratus and Balbus turned to come to the aid of their commander. The three attackers were cut down one after another, but Dan Qing, who had been wounded, was in danger of succumbing. Metellus shouted, 'Close ranks!' and the little army tightened around the weakened prince, enclosing him within the wall of their shields.

The enemy unsheathed other weapons, long pointed harpoons, and launched into spectacular leaps in order to strike from above, but the Romans foiled their intentions by lowering the visors of their helmets to meet the curved tops of their heavy shields and reacting swiftly with their swords. Their defence was impenetrable now. The battle raged on, but this time to the advantage of the Romans. Every time Metellus gave an order the barrier of shields opened and javelins flew out, striking with inexorable precision. All at once, as Metellus raised his head for an instant to take a breath, he spotted some of the assailants up in the trees, about to leap on to Dan Qing behind the lines of his defenders. He shouted, 'Testudo!' The six men took a step back and raised their shields over their heads. The attackers landed on an impenetrable ceiling studded with swords and daggers protruding from between the shields. Their feet and legs slashed, the warriors fell and were immediately finished off. Two more, who had fallen inside the circle, were run through by Roman javelins.

Rufus had been pulled in to shelter beneath the *testudo*. He was alive, but needed urgent medical care.

Daruma, who had managed somehow to find a hiding place, came out with his servants. Their faces were grey with fear and only with great circumspection did they dare to wander among the bodies of the fallen enemies.

Daruma shouted, 'Hey, over this way! One of them is still alive!'

Dan Qing approached, pressing pieces of cloth to his bleeding wounds. 'He must not die,' he said. 'We'll make him speak and he'll tell us everything.'

Daruma ordered his men to seize the wounded man, but as soon as a couple of them got close, he snapped his jaw shut and a trickle of dark liquid dripped from the corner of his mouth. He was shaken by a spasm and, in just a few moments, was dead.

Daruma prised open his mouth and extracted the shattered shell of a quail's egg. 'Poison,' he said. 'This man won't tell us anything.'

19

'Poison?' asked Metellus.

'Yes, of course,' replied Daruma. 'There's no other explanation.' He approached another dead man, the one that Rufus had run through in mid-air with his javelin, and opened his mouth, extracting the fragments of another little black-flecked eggshell. 'They keep this in their mouths,' he said, showing it to the others, 'sealed with wax. It's full of poison. The slightest pressure from the tongue will break it and the poison goes to work immediately. If these men have a secret to protect, there's no chance of them revealing it. Dead men, as we all know, don't speak.'

'Flying Foxes,' muttered Dan Qing behind them.

'What does that mean?' asked Metellus.

'Let's leave here as soon as we can,' said the prince. 'This is no place for conversation. We'll talk later.'

'But you are wounded,' objected Metellus. 'And one of my men has lost a lot of blood.'

'Fine, take care of him,' replied the prince. 'But be quick. And send someone to patrol the surroundings. There may be more of them.'

Martianus went to work on Rufus. He trimmed the edges of the wound with scissors, washed it out with palm wine and began to sew it up with a needle and thread.

'Your medicine is very primitive,' commented Dan Qing, seeing Rufus wince in pain under his comrade's instruments.

'We're doing what we can,' Metellus shot back, irritated. 'We're not in the most favourable circumstances and I don't think there's a hospital nearby.'

Daruma had already motioned to one of his men, who, after a number of low bows, approached the prince and began to uncover his wounds. They were long cuts but not deep ones, caused by the enemy's slashing swords. Metellus picked one of them up and examined it attentively: it was much longer than his *gladius* and had a double edge. The hilt was decorated in ivory and precious stones. Those strange signs that looked like magical symbols were carved into the blade. The grade of steel was excellent: the marks they had left on the Roman swords and the cuts that had scored their shields were proof of that. When he tried to swing the weapon, however, he felt the weight of the blade putting considerable strain on his wrist, confirming his belief that carrying one's own weapon was the best idea: for Metellus his *gladius* was the metallic extension of his arm.

In the meantime, Daruma's men had surrounded Dan Qing, creating a sort of curtain which prevented the Romans from seeing what the Chinese doctor was doing. When Rufus was hoisted on to his horse with his arm in a sling, Dan Qing was ready to resume the journey as well, apparently no worse for wear. He seemed only a bit tired.

They proceeded at a walk, but in full battle gear, carrying their heavy square shields.

Metellus drew close to Severus. 'Nice work, *faber*.'

'Thank you, Commander.'

'The *testudo* worked. The shields held. A technique they weren't expecting.'

'I didn't think an attack would come so soon. I have an idea I'd like to try. At the next rest stop, we'll get back to work.'

Metellus put a hand on his shoulder and took his place next to the prince.

As they advanced, the voices of the forest became more numerous and varied: birds, monkeys, animals of every sort. Once they saw a serpent with a spotted skin slithering up the branches of a tree. The first night after the Flying Foxes' attack, they even heard the low growling of a tiger.

Daruma's men looked at each other with terrified expressions.

'What are they afraid of?' asked Quadratus, watching them tremble like leaves. 'A tiger is only a striped lion and I've seen plenty of lions brought down.'

Daruma smiled. 'Have you ever heard of man-eaters?'

Quadratus's confidence seemed a bit shaken. 'I suppose that if a tiger is hungry, he'll eat what he can find, and if that something happens to be a man . . .'

'You don't understand. Man-eaters eat men and nothing else. Once they have tasted human flesh, there's no going back. And man just happens to be the easiest animal to prey upon.'

'That depends,' replied Quadratus, spinning his sword under Daruma's nose.

'My drivers have seen lots of tigers. And they recognize the man-eaters by their long, low growl, like the one you just heard. If I were you, I'd tell your boys to stay alert tonight. We can't keep fires burning; we don't want other Flying Foxes to be able to locate our position. We may . . .' He broke off as he saw Dan Qing approach Metellus and begin to speak to him. He was visibly moved, as though he was witnessing an event of exceptional importance.

'I owe you my life,' said Dan Qing. 'This time I had no escape.'

'You saved my life as well,' replied Metellus in Chinese.

'How is this possible?' asked Dan Qing.

'My men are the best combatants there are, as I told you.'

'No, I don't mean that. I mean, how is it that you speak my language?'

'Daruma taught me, and I practise with the Chinese porters that we hired when we started down the mountain.'

'That's what your endless chatter was about! I never would have thought that a barbarian could learn our language in so short a time.'

Metellus did not allow himself to be provoked and Dan Qing

continued: 'You and your men . . . I must admit that I did not believe you capable of fighting off an attack by the Flying Foxes.'

'There weren't too many of them and they weren't familiar with our way of fighting. This isn't the first time you've been surprised by what you've seen. It seems that you're often mistaken regarding those who surround you.'

Dan Qing did not react to his provocation either and said, 'In the beginning, I told Daruma that I didn't want you with us, that you'd only be a hindrance . . .'

'You may have been right.'

'I was wrong.'

'Will they be back?'

'I'm afraid so. They move and act as small, independent groups. So we don't know when another attack might take place.'

Metellus had begun speaking in Persian again, feeling that he had not adequately mastered this new language yet, and asked, 'How did they find us? We've always marched at the bottom of a narrow valley, thick with vegetation.'

'From the sky. Remember when your men glimpsed the shadow of that bird? They weren't seeing things. That's the reason these warriors are called Flying Foxes. They glide through the air on wings of silk pulled taut between bamboo canes, using the movement of the wind like a ship does with its sail.'

'That is incredible . . .' replied Metellus in amazement. 'Where we come from, we have an age-old legend about a man who flies with artificial wings. It ends badly: ultimately, he plunges into the sea.' He fell silent for a little while, then added, 'I've never seen a sword wielded in that way, or men vaulting through the air as if they were weightless, like those warriors. And like you, after all. How do you do it?'

'You barbarians from the West are educated to strengthen your bodies. We learn to educate the mind, and the mind goes where it likes.'

'Pretty words, but I still can't understand . . .'

'You saw those men vaulting through the air,' replied Dan Qing, staring straight in front of him. 'As they go through those movements, high becomes low, and low, high, and then low again ... That's the whole secret. That is, nothing is absolute: what is on the right is, at the same time, on the left, and vice versa. If a man is able to convince himself profoundly of this truth, he will be equally at ease in the air as on the ground ... But you are right, these are nothing but words. Prolonged, intense meditation is required to find the way.'

Metellus reflected in silence, trying to comprehend how such a doctrine could influence the movements of one's body, and he felt bewildered, projected into an uncertain, confused dimension.

'In any case,' continued Dan Qing, 'I too have a question to ask you. What energy drives you and your men to fight against enemies much quicker and more expert than you are, masters of a superior military art, without giving in to panic and discouragement? If you do not know the way and cannot balance the natural forces within you, how can you win?'

'It's called *virtus*,' replied Metellus, looking him straight in the eye.

Dan Qing did not even try to repeat the word. 'What is it? What does it mean?'

'It means "virile force", but it's difficult to explain the true essence. It's the force that drives us to give our lives for our families and our homeland, if necessary, without hoping for anything in return except the memory of our honour that we leave behind.'

'Today you risked your lives for me. I'm not part of your family or your homeland.'

'We gave our word and that's enough. This is *virtus* as well.'

'And it's enough to keep that force alive?'

'*Virtus* is a conviction, an image of yourself in which you believe blindly, from the time you're a young boy. You learn it from your father, who learned it from his. A man who possesses this virtue knows that no obstacle is insurmountable, no trial too arduous, no sacrifice too great, not even giving up one's life.

Only a man who possesses *virtus* can bear the weight of *disciplina*, the spirit which keeps our soldiers together, which makes them a single unit, a rock. This *disciplina* instils the strength of an entire contingent in each single man, even when he is alone and surrounded, even when anyone else would give in to the inevitable.'

Dan Qing did not take his eyes off Metellus for an instant, while he was speaking. When he had finished, he said, 'I need you and your men in order to reconquer my empire, which has been usurped by an impostor.'

'I'm afraid that conquering an empire might take more than ten men, no matter how brave,' replied Metellus.

'And yet we will succeed. We will, I can feel it. You must help me. There's no one else I can trust. I must re-establish law and order. I must restore peace. I must reunite my country, which is now split into three parts. Reflect on my words during the time that remains before we arrive at the castle of my master, the Monastery of the Whispering Waters. Think about it, I beseech you . . .'

Metellus was struck by his words, nearly of supplication, words that he never thought he would hear from the prince's lips.

'If you do as I ask, there will be no limit to your reward, and that of your men. If you decide to help me, they will join you, I'm certain of it. They would follow you to the ends of the earth.'

Metellus sighed. 'That's precisely why I choose to exercise my power over them as little as possible. I am responsible for their lives and their destiny, and this responsibility weighs unbearably on my shoulders.'

'Why?' asked Dan Qing. 'They are soldiers and you are their chief. It's what you want that counts.'

'No, you're wrong. It's their lives that count. The wealth of a commander is the lives of his soldiers.'

'I do not understand you, but I accept your way of thinking. In any case, once we've reached the castle of my master, you'll be free to leave. If you go, I will remain grateful to you and remember you for the rest of my life. From the monastery I will contact the forces still faithful to me and we can bid each other farewell. If, on the other hand, you decide to stay, my gift to you will be a new destiny, so great that you cannot even begin to imagine it.'

Metellus bowed his head in thought, then focused his amber eyes on the jet-black eyes of the prince. 'How far is your master's monastery from here?'

'Eight days of marching. Days of unceasing peril, I'm afraid.'

'We will escort you there. And then, with your permission, we will leave with Daruma. He knows the return road and has promised to take us back. Back home.'

Dan Qing sighed. 'If that's what you want, you can go with my blessing and that of my ancestors. But let me hope for the next eight days that you may change your mind ... Now, for having protected me from the assault of my enemies and for agreeing to escort me to my final destination, I wish to name you and your men my personal guard. I will call you the Red Demons, and you, Commander, will have a new name, in my language. This will make you part of the Middle Kingdom, Zhong Guo, and a member of my family.'

'I do not deserve so great an honour, Prince,' replied Metellus, 'but I accept with gratitude, also on behalf of my men.'

'What is the name of your family?' asked Dan Qing.

'Aquila,' Metellus replied in Latin. 'That is the name of my family.'

'What does it mean?'

'It is the largest and most noble of the birds of prey. For us Romans, it is the symbol and the emblem of our combat forces, and it is the animal sacred to the king of all our gods.'

'Then,' Dan Qing began solemnly, 'your name will be Xiong Ying, Resplendent Eagle.'

Metellus replied, 'I will wear this name with pride for as long as I live in your land, and I will keep it in my heart, when I have returned to my homeland, for the rest of my life.'

Dan Qing inclined his head and Metellus responded with the same gesture.

THEY RESUMED their journey, Metellus and Dan Qing riding side by side, Severus and Martianus on either side of them in the forest and the others in a column, preceding Daruma's caravan. They advanced for three days without encountering any difficulties. Rufus was treated every evening by Martianus, even though Daruma had offered the intervention of the Chinese doctor, who instead cared for the prince's wounds with extreme discretion and solicitude. On the evening of the third day, they arrived at a point where the valley opened up all at once, revealing an enchanting landscape.

The wooded banks became less steep, widening out towards open meadows. The water of the torrent split up into dozens of artificial canals that filled wide basins extending over the slopes of the valley like an amphitheatre, one above the other in a descending array of sparkling mirrors, reddened by the light of dusk. Further down, nearly at the bottom of the valley, was a village of roof-tiled wooden houses surrounded by herds of grazing buffalo and flocks of sheep. At the very centre of the village, one building loomed over all the rest: a kind of fortified house in the shape of a tower, several storeys high. Each storey was separated by a projecting roof on four sides, and Metellus noticed that the rows of tiles ended with a decorated antefix, just like the ones used in the temples to the gods at home.

It was a magical vision that left the small group of foreigners at a loss for words. Leaning on their shields, they contemplated that idyllic image, the iridescent colours of the ponds that reflected the dying sun, the wood of cane stalks so tall and flexible that they seemed like a field of rippling green wheat bent by the wind. The cirrus clouds floating through the sky blushed in the sun's last rays and smoke began to rise from the rooftops.

Dan Qing turned to Metellus. 'It is here that I was born, Xiong Ying. My mother was travelling to join my father, who was engaged in a military campaign at the northern border, when she was suddenly gripped by labour pains and had to seek hospitality in this village. That house that looks like a tower was built by the inhabitants as a gift for me and no one can enter unless I inhabit it. The people are loyal and devoted to me, and I think we can consider ourselves safe here.'

Metellus wanted to ask if there wasn't someone from the village who could accompany the prince to his master Wangzi's fortress, so that the Romans could take their leave, but he realized that such a request would seem an insult, since Dan Qing had asked him to reflect for eight days. All things considered, Metellus was a little reluctant to leave so soon. In a place so far from home he found himself in a situation so similar to the one he had left behind: the chaos of the institutions, the disorder and precariousness of the state, which begged to be corrected by an authoritative ruler. By an incredible twist of fate, he found himself once again in the same role that he had held in his homeland: he was the emperor's personal guard, the man the sovereign could trust in blindly.

Dan Qing called Daruma, shaking Metellus from his thoughts. 'Send someone to announce that I am coming. The people will want to pay their respects.'

'I will do so immediately, Prince,' replied Daruma, and sent a messenger on horseback who spoke Chinese to inform the inhabitants of the village that their most illustrious son was about to honour them with a visit.

Dan Qing gestured for them to continue, and Metellus transmitted the order to his men.

If the spectacle of that enchanted village left the new arrivals dumbstruck, their appearance aroused no less amazement in the villagers still at work in the fields. They were bent low over pools in which the marsh grain was cultivated, assisted by buffalo with long, flat horns. The farmers wore curious head-coverings of a conical shape, made of braided wicker or straw. They raised their heads at the passage of that strange procession. Their curiosity was drawn by the soldiers' uniforms. They'd never seen anything like them: their red tunics and polished armour, their embossed leggings and crested helmets. Where could such mighty warriors, so tall and so powerfully built, be coming from?

But some of them had already recognized the person riding erect next to one of the foreign warriors with the crested helmet – it was Dan Qing! They prostrated themselves before him, foreheads to the ground, as he passed. This demonstration of profound respect did not escape Metellus; it was more like adoration, and helped to explain the condescension with which Dan Qing had treated him until that moment.

As they approached the village, they noticed a swarming of inhabitants at the gates, a bustle of people coming and going, of children running to and fro despite their mothers' attempts to stop them. Standards began to flutter in the breeze, weapons gleamed in the setting sunlight, brightly coloured clothes enrobed dignitaries who, until a few moments ago, had been wearing the humble garb of farmers. It was as if a god had descended from the sky to visit that place, and Metellus was struck to see the enthusiasm and the delight of those simple people at the arrival of a sacred figure.

When they reached the entrance to the village they dismounted from their horses. Dan Qing handed the reins to a stableboy who had just run up, and proceeded on foot. Metellus and his men did the same, following him at a certain distance.

The dignitaries, although taken by surprise by such an unexpected visit, were all lined up in the main square awaiting their guest. They wore dazzling silken tunics decorated with dragons or flowers. When Dan Qing stopped in front of them, they all prostrated themselves to the ground, and once again Metellus felt uncomfortable, although not inclined to imitate their behaviour.

Dan Qing made a slight gesture with his hand and they all got up and then, one by one, approached the prince to render him homage personally.

They suddenly heard horses coming at a hard gallop from their left. A group of armed men was arriving at great speed, in a cloud of red dust.

Metellus drew his sword but Daruma sternly shook his head: these were local militiamen, loyal to the prince, otherwise they never would have been able to approach without warning. At a certain distance they stopped, and the man who seemed their commander leapt to the ground, followed by the others.

Their armour was generally not much different from that of Metellus and his soldiers: they wore a particular style of helmet with fins at the neck and on their cheeks, a breastplate of bronze scales linked with iron rings, a knee-length leather tunic, stiff trousers and leather boots with pointed toes. A handkerchief knotted at their throats prevented friction with the breastplate.

At just a few steps from the prince, the squad commander dropped to the ground with his forehead in the dirt, as did all his men, and when Dan Qing motioned for them to rise, he glared at Metellus with a hostile expression and spoke briefly in a curt tone.

The Roman could not understand his words, but their substance was clear.

'What did he say?' he asked Daruma.

' "Why don't the foreign devils prostrate themselves before His Majesty?" '

Dan Qing responded to the officer who had spoken so that even Metellus could understand. 'They will do so, now that they have arrived in this land.' He looked straight into Metellus's eyes with the expression of a man expecting confirmation and a gesture of obedience.

Metellus responded to his look with a respectful but firm expression, and said in Persian, 'A Roman soldier prostrates himself before no man, Prince . . .' As he pronounced those words a memory flashed through the mind of each man and their eyes locked as they had at the moment in which Valerian had been forced to his knees before Shapur. A fleeting image, a painful contraction of Metellus's features. He concluded, saying each word distinctly, '. . . not even before a god.'

Dan Qing said nothing.

20

THE VILLAGE DIGNITARIES accompanied the prince to his residence, where it was their intention to prepare a banquet in his honour, but Dan Qing dissuaded them.

'My esteemed friends,' he said, as soon as they were inside, 'I don't want to put you to any inconvenience or to disturb your work in the fields, which I see is well under way. I desire only to confer with you: to know what has happened in my absence and to decide along with you what must be done.'

They had reached the audience chamber. Dan Qing sat at the centre of the main wall on a silken cushion. The others took their places, one by one, to the prince's left and right, alternating on the basis of their rank and according to the degree of intimacy each individual had with Dan Qing. The officer who had arrived with his squad of horsemen remained on his feet at the entrance door until the prince motioned for him to approach. 'Come forward, Baj Renjie.'

The officer took a few steps, prostrated himself to the ground again, and then got to his feet and drew a bit closer, stopping at five paces from his lord.

'As you will have heard,' began Dan Qing, 'my prolonged absence was due to betrayal. What I do not know is who was responsible. I left more than three years ago for Persia at the head of a legation with the mission of establishing direct relations with Emperor Shapur, but when it was time for me to return I was held back on a series of pretexts that had no justification, except for the fact that – as I imagined it – something had changed at Luoyang – that is, power had passed into someone else's hands.

'I attempted several times to ask Emperor Shapur for an explanation, but it was like speaking to the wind. His responses were always extremely courteous, but just as evasive. My presence was continuously requested at official ceremonies and even on expeditions of war, my treatment was always worthy of the most illustrious guest, but I was never given the opportunity to leave . . .'

A group of servants entered, carrying beverages and refreshments on small rosewood trays. They lay them at the feet of the prince and his dignitaries.

Dan Qing had a sip of the infusion of leaves that he had been accustomed to drinking on Daruma's boat and continued his story, 'It was not until the beginning of this year that I received a message detailing a plan for my liberation. My range of action was quite limited, but I had to find a way to join up with a certain caravan that would bring me back here. It was not easy. I risked my life several times, but in the end I have managed to return and it still doesn't seem true that I am back here among you, after all this time. The merit lies with my faithful Indian friend Daruma and the soldiers you saw at my side.

'Just three days ago, we were violently attacked by the Flying Foxes, and if it hadn't been for those men, I would not be here with you planning the future. They too have survived an imprisonment much harsher and crueller than my own, thanks to a strength of spirit that we may have much to learn from ourselves . . .'

Baj Renjie could hardly contain a disparaging smirk, but Dan Qing continued unperturbed, 'They come from the powerful empire of Taqin Guo, which today finds itself in conditions no better than our own, and I can assure you that they do live up to the legend born at the time of Emperor Yuandi.'

'Are you alluding perhaps to the legend of the three hundred Mercenary Devils?' asked one of the dignitaries.

'I am,' replied Dan Qing.

'With all due respect,' intervened Baj Renjie, 'it's nothing more than a legend, and three hundred years have passed since then. If I may be allowed to express an opinion, My Lord, it does not seem right that you humiliate your own faithful servants by preferring foreigners whom you don't even know, and who are nothing but mercenaries.'

'The great Emperor Yuandi did so. I don't see why I shouldn't. I do not wish to humiliate anyone, but only to honour these men who have risked their lives and suffered injury to save me. You should be grateful to them as well. But perhaps you are blinded by envy, Baj Renjie.'

The officer could barely suppress his indignation, but held his tongue.

'What are your intentions, My Lord?' asked another dignitary.

"To reach the secret refuge of my master, Wangzi, and to consult with him. But I would like you now to tell me what has happened in my absence. Who ordered that I be held prisoner in Persia? I can't quite make sense of what I have learned. You must be privy to other information. Please, tell me what you know.'

The elders and dignitaries glanced back and forth as if not one of them dared to speak first.

'What is it? What stops you from speaking?' demanded Dan Qing.

An old white-bearded man with a venerable appearance finally spoke up. He wore a pale yellow silk tunic, adorned with the signs of the zodiac. He was the keeper of the house, a position that had been created by the empress herself after she had given birth. He knew many secrets of nature and many secrets, also, of the human heart.

'Shortly after your departure,' he began, 'your father's health, already so precarious, worsened. He was confined to the care of his doctors and servants, and was practically never seen outside his palace. The regency, as you know, was in the hands of the sage Yangming but as time passed he too began to appear less frequently in public and the rumour spread that someone else had taken power, certainly someone who enjoyed his trust, someone whom he had protected and whom he esteemed.

There's not much more I can tell you. This village is so isolated that by the time any news reaches us, it is often distorted. What does seem certain is that your father has joined his ancestors in the celestial kingdom.'

Dan Qing bowed his head at hearing those words and only after a long silence said, 'Then you cannot tell me who had me detained in Persia.'

'Whatever I told you,' replied the keeper of the house, 'might not be true and, when in doubt, it is best to hold one's tongue. The only unquestionable fact is that whoever it is, he is your enemy.'

'Three days ago, as I was telling you, I was attacked by a group of Flying Foxes, who would probably have killed me if it hadn't been for the warriors in my service. This event, unfortunately, means two things: first, that the usurper has strong ties with the Flying Foxes or is even their leader; second, that he knows I am back.'

'One of your men betrayed you,' concluded Baj Renjie.

'That may not be so,' the old man said. 'An informer may have seen the prince at some time during his long journey. The Persian emperor may have informed the court of Luoyang of his escape, and thus the border posts would have been put on alert.'

'Your jealousy is ridiculous, Baj Renjie,' said the prince, 'and your attempt to lead me to suspect those who restored my freedom and made my return possible is mistaken and unfair. I will need all those who are willing to help me and especially you, you who have always been faithful to me. But I ask you to respect the round-eyed men, even if they are barbarians and very different from us. Do you understand, Baj Renjie?'

The officer made a deep bow.

'I will stay here no longer than strictly necessary, because I do not want to expose this village, which is so dear to me, to harm.'

'We are willing to face anything for you, My Lord,' said one of the dignitaries.

'I know, but this only increases my responsibility,' replied the prince.

Those present looked each other in the face in astonishment, hardly believing their ears.

'Leave me alone now,' directed the prince. 'I must think things over.'

All the dignitaries left the room.

Baj Renjie approached the prince before leaving. 'Have you any orders to give me, My Lord?'

'None, for the moment.'

'Must I keep an eye on the barbarians?'

'I don't think there's any need for that.'

'And if they should try to leave?'

'They won't do that. They don't know where to go and their only thought is returning home. So you have nothing to fear. I've already arranged for them to be given food and accommodation. Go now.'

Baj Renjie retreated, bowing several times without ever turning his back, until he had reached the door.

Dan Qing waited until he had heard the outer door close, then walked to the staircase and began to go up. With every step, he felt like he was going back in time, to his adolescence, then to his childhood and to his infancy. He remembered the time he had spent in that place among simple people, farmers and shepherds, in accordance with the wishes of his father, who had left him there for long periods of his life. He remembered the first time he had met his sister Yun Shan, a celestial creature with an ivory complexion. She had been his playmate, his confidante, his precious jewel of jade. Then something terrible had happened, a dramatic event that had profoundly wounded her and created a barrier of resentment between them. He had had no news of her since his departure; he wondered where she could be and how she felt about him now.

He reached the top of the house and let his gaze sweep across the valley on which the shadows of night had begun to fall, the contours of the mountains and the sinuous line of the hills, until he found the point he was looking for, a spot marked by an enormous oak and a rocky cliff. He waited, absorbed in his thoughts, until he saw the faint light of a fire at the base of the cliff and a wisp of smoke rising towards the darkening sky. He left the house then, took his horse and rode off towards the place where the fire was burning.

He crossed the village amid the respectful discretion of its inhabitants and took the path that led towards the hill. He advanced at a steady pace, keeping his eye on the reverberating flames which glimmered between the tall, shiny bamboo stalks and the furrowed oak trunks. He stopped when he found himself before the lean, cross-legged figure of the village shaman, who sat in front of a copper pot bubbling over the fire.

'I heard of your arrival,' said the old man, almost without taking his eyes from the flames.

'How did you learn about it so soon? I've only just arrived.'

'Nothing that happens in this village can remain hidden from me. You were gone for a very long time.'

'And now that I've returned, everything has changed. The power of my father is in the hands of a usurper. Do you know who he is?'

'No. But perhaps you do.'

'I told you, I've only just set foot in my homeland. I know absolutely nothing.'

'And yet you have a premonition. Don't you?'

Dan Qing did not answer. His gaze was fixed on the flames, which abruptly seemed to be growing into a fire so immense it could devour the whole earth.

'Don't you?' repeated the shaman.

'What do you mean? That the Heavens have ordained that the rule of the land be taken from my family, as it was taken from the Han dynasty thirty years ago? That what has happened – this *geming* – is the will of the Heavens?'

'You said it, I didn't. The presentiment is yours alone. And this is a bad sign. On the other hand, the blood of the Han still runs in your veins, although their dynasty is lost.'

'What must I do?'

'Look inside yourself. See if there is a cause for all this. If there was an action that violated the harmony, that interrupted the flow of vital energy, and that has brought disorder and confusion, violence and war.'

'I've always dreamed of bringing prosperity and order to my people. I dream of reuniting the country.'

'Then why do you harbour doubt? What strange haste has driven you here so soon?'

'Cast your bones, shaman, tell me who the usurper is. What hides behind his mask?'

The shaman tossed a handful of leaves on to the fire and breathed in the dense yellowish vapour which rose from the flames. He then took the sacred bones from his sack and threw them to the ground three times, near the fire

'What do you see?' insisted Dan Qing.

'I see many lives sacrificed and I see hate that only death can extinguish. But I cannot see where it will strike . . . because you refuse to understand the signs. It is you who dares not look, and thus yours will not be the final blow. It won't be you who cuts down your enemy. Someone else will have to do it for you. One who has done no harm in the Middle Kingdom. As far as you are concerned, if you have the courage to look into your soul, you will also see the face of the usurper. Farewell, Prince.'

He closed his eyes and isolated himself in an impenetrable silence.

Dan Qing remained still for some time as well, trying to make sense of the shaman's message, but he realized that he was not ready to face such a revelation. Only his master, venerable Wangzi, could help him seek the truth.

The prince started at the sound of his horse's neighing. He took him by the reins and led him back to the village. The tower house was illuminated by coloured lanterns in celebration of his return, but there were no other signs of rejoicing. The bad news, perhaps, obscured the good.

He dined alone, as befitted his rank, but it felt awkward after all those months of sharing his meals with his travelling companions, after all the trials they had faced together. He realized that despite the detachment he had insisted upon, there was something about their way of life that had remained part of him. Even something about their language. After dinner, he opened the door to the library and stayed awake until late, perusing an ancient text that had survived the destruction of the library of Luoyang. The text told the story of the 'Mercenary Devils', the foreign soldiers who had appeared suddenly at the western confines of the country three hundred and fourteen years before. No one knew where they had come from.

Emperor Yuandi, who reigned at that time, gave orders to drive them away and to take back the land they had occupied, but his troops were defeated time and time again by those indomitable warriors who engaged battle on the open field and fought with their shields on their heads. In the end the emperor, awed by the valour of those men who had materialized out of nowhere, proposed that they enter his service as his personal guard. From that moment on, their bravery and loyalty became legendary. Many of them fell in combat in a number of military missions, until only three hundred of them remained, and that was the number that went down in history. It was said that if the dynasty was ever threatened with destruction, the Mercenary Devils would return from their tombs to fight their last battle.

Dan Qing lay on the bed in which he had slept as an adolescent, where he had first dreamed of love, imagining the woman he would have at his side one day. His thoughts turned to his ancestors, and he entreated them to show him the way and to help him in an endeavour that appeared more desperate by the day.

'How are you today, Rufus?' Metellus asked his wounded soldier.

'He's much better, Commander,' replied Martianus for him. Rufus was, at the moment, immersed in a deep sleep. 'One of their doctors came last night. He said that the prince had sent him to care for our comrade. I wanted to advise you, but then I thought that it would be discourteous to refuse their help and I gave him permission to examine Rufus.'

'You did well. As far as I can tell, their medicine is probably further advanced than ours is.'

'You could swear on it, Commander. The first thing he did was to pour a liquid on the wound. Then he treated it and sewed it up with a silken thread, with more skill than I've ever seen. Every now and then, I'd ask Rufus if it was hurting him, and he'd answer, "No, not in the least. I can feel the needle piercing my skin, the thread pulling, but no pain at all." Imagine if I'd had something of the sort when I had to put our soldiers' mangled limbs back together after a battle! Their screams, the agony . . . you never get used to it, Commander.'

Metellus nodded his head, then put his hand on the wounded soldier's forehead. 'He has a fever, but it's not high.'

'He's been sleeping for ten hours. It must be the potion that their doctor gave him. It was a dark liquid, very bitter, Rufus told me before he fell asleep, similar to wormwood. Sleep is the best cure for a fever. You'll see, he'll wake up with a roaring appetite, ready to start marching again.'

'I hope so.' Metellus turned to go.

'Commander, can I ask you a question?'

'Certainly.'

'When are we going to change direction? I mean, when are we starting back for home?'

'I can't say. We must have faith in Daruma and in the prince. I think we're not too far from our final destination. A few days at most.'

'And then?'

'Daruma will have to see to his affairs, sell and buy his goods – that may take some time. And we must be certain that Prince Dan Qing is out of harm's way before we leave him.'

'I see. But then we'll be leaving, won't we?'

'Of course. Why do you doubt it?'

'Well, you see, the boys and I have been trying to figure it out. What we're afraid of, Commander, is that by the time we arrive, the favourable winds will have changed, and the weather will be against us again, and we'll have to wait six more months . . .'

Metellus raised his hand and Martianus fell still. 'Your destiny is dearer to me than my own, soldier. That will have to be enough for now.'

'Yes, Commander,' replied Martianus, and Metellus left.

The sun appeared just then from the wooded hills that circled the village to the east and its clear light was reflected in the many ponds arranged in tiers around the town. Big grey herons took off from the placid sheets of water, and flocks of little white egrets left the branches of the trees where they had spent the night and took flight across the valley, like a joyous cortège greeting the morning.

The farmers left their homes and walked down the paths that wound their way around the pools where each one of them had a plot for planting marsh grain, their most common food. They were followed by their dogs and their children, who delighted in playing in the water.

Metellus ran into Publius, Septimius and Antoninus, who seemed very excited. 'Commander, Commander!'

'What's the matter, boys?'

'This place is incredible! Do you know that here the fish, instead of being grey, are the colour of gold?'

'Are you sure? You haven't been drinking already, have you, so early in the morning?'

'No. Come on and see for yourself!'

They took him to a fountain that flowed into a big stone basin. Inside were gorgeous fish of a golden-red hue with long tails as transparent as veils, wondrous creatures indeed. Metellus watched them swimming around for a while, then asked, 'Where's Daruma?'

'He's with Quadratus and the others down there, near those trees.'

'I must speak with him,' he said, and walked, followed by the other Romans, towards the group that was standing around a beautiful tree in a little orchard. Big round fruits, golden-coloured as well, hung from the tree.

'Can you eat them?' asked Antoninus.

'Of course,' replied Daruma. 'Taste one. They're ripe.'

Antoninus picked a fruit and sank his teeth into it, but immediately spat it out, swearing. 'Ugh! It's bitter. It stings my tongue! You've poisoned me!'

Daruma shook his head, smiling slyly. He picked another fruit, peeled it and showed them the inside, a kind of large juicy grape divided into slices which he separated and handed out to the men.

Metellus tasted a piece. 'It's heavenly! The best fruit I've ever had in my life,' he said. 'But what is it?'

'It's an orange. It's the symbol of fairness, because nature has divided it into absolutely equal parts, so that everyone can have exactly what the others have.'

'What about these?' asked Septimius, pointing to a similar fruit with an oval shape and a brilliant yellow colour. 'Are they good?'

'Of course,' replied Daruma again. 'Taste it.'

'You won't fool me this time,' replied Septimius, beginning to peel the fruit.

'I see you learn quickly,' commented Daruma in satisfaction.

Septimius put two big slices into his mouth and his face contracted all at once into a grimace of disgust. 'Ugh! It's awful!' he shouted, spitting it out.

'It's only different,' replied Daruma. 'You just have to get used to it.' He took the fruit from Septimius's hands, detached a slice and ate it with pleasure. 'It's a bit more acidic and a little bitter, but it has many virtues, as do many other bitter things.'

Metellus continued scouting around until he found Severus at work in the village forge.

'Is everything all right?' he asked.

'Fine, Commander. I'm preparing the shields . . . a modification that will make them even more effective.'

'A modification? What kind?'

'You'll know when it's time, Commander. I want to make sure it works first . . .'

Severus was still talking when a youth from the village came running up and told Metellus that Prince Dan Qing wished to speak to him.

21

'YOU HAD ME SUMMONED?' Metellus entered the library accompanied by a servant. Dan Qing was sitting on a mat with his back turned to him. A table was balanced on his knees and he was writing on a sheet which looked like papyrus, although it was much finer and more flexible.

'Why did you not pay me homage yesterday, like all my other subjects? I am the legitimate heir to the throne of this empire and all the inhabitants of this land owe me the act of veneration prescribed by a ritual that is thousands of years old. Your refusal humiliated me before my subjects and Commander Baj Renjie.'

'I am in this land,' replied Metellus, 'but I do not belong to this land. My men and I are not your subjects.'

'You are trying to make me believe that in your country you do not render acts of veneration to the emperor?'

'We burn incense to his *genius* every year, on the day he was born, but we stand on our feet when we speak to him and call him by name. During a military campaign, he eats the same food as us, drinks the same acidy wine and sleeps on the ground like the most humble of his soldiers. That doesn't mean that we're not ready to die for him if necessary. The only relationship that you can have with me is one of equality: one man to another.'

Dan Qing got to his feet and turned to face him. 'Here, a person's devotion towards his emperor is seen as a virtue. It is called *yi*, signifying what is "just". The only relationship we consider in terms of equality is the bond between friends. It is called *xin*, which means "loyalty". I can treat you as a friend, Xiong Ying, but are you prepared to be loyal?'

'I believe I am,' replied Metellus, 'if you tell me that you are.'

Dan Qing nodded slightly, then sat down again and continued writing. Metellus drew closer, curious to see what was taking form on the white sheet.

'Are they magical signs?' he asked. 'They look like the ones carved into the bones that the shaman used to pronounce his oracles in the caravanserai.'

'They are not magical signs,' replied the prince. 'It's the way we write.'

'Complicated. No sign is like another . . . Our system is much more efficient. With twenty-three very simple symbols you can write any word.'

'In what language?'

'In our own, in Latin.'

'And so anyone who wants to understand what you have written has to learn your language.'

'Obviously.'

'In this country we speak a hundred different languages. Each one of these signs expresses a concept of the mind, like "man" or "house" or "tree", and can be recognized by all, although every person pronounces the corresponding word in his native tongue. No one has to bend to learning the terms of a foreign language. These signs respect our freedom of mind, more important still than the physical freedom which is so important to you. Why does it seem so terrible to you to bow before a sovereign?'

'Have you ever heard of a Western king, a great young conqueror named Alexander?'

'Yes, I heard tales of him in Persia, where they call him Iskander and consider him a demon, and news of his exploits reached our land in the past.'

'When he arrived at the confines of India, he had already inherited the crown of the Persians and had decided to adopt their customs as well, so he demanded that his companions bend their backs to him when they greeted him. They refused to do so and an irremediable rift opened between them. Some of them even plotted to kill him. This tells you how important the dignity of a single person, no matter how humble, is to us.'

'Do you have slaves?' asked Dan Qing.

Metellus hesitated a moment, taken by surprise, then answered, 'Yes, we have slaves.'

'Here slavery was abolished by the decree of Emperor Wang Mang more than two centuries ago,' replied Dan Qing, and said no more.

Metellus didn't have an answer and remained to observe the prince as he was writing. 'Where do you find such white papyrus?' he asked after a while.

'I don't know what this ... "papyrus" is,' replied Dan Qing. 'This is paper.'

'Paper?' repeated Metellus.

'Paper,' confirmed the prince. 'We make it by soaking rags. We whiten them with lye and sometimes we perfume them with jasmine or with roses or violets.' He extracted a sheet from a drawer and held it under Metellus's nose.

Metellus breathed in the delicate fragrance, then took it into his hands and held it up against the sunlight, admiring its marvellous transparency and homogeneous consistency. 'Scented sheets,' he said. 'Why?'

'For love letters. Your beloved recognizes your missive from the fragrance it gives off even before she reads it. Charming, wouldn't you say?'

Metellus nodded, his eyes misting over.

'You are thinking of her, Xiong Ying, aren't you?'

'Yes.'

'The favourite among your concubines?'

For a moment, Metellus's gaze and the mysterious anguish evoked by those words were mirrored in the inscrutable eyes of the prince.

'My bride, Prince,' he replied. 'A Roman has only one wife, usually for his whole life.'

'How barbaric,' observed Dan Qing. 'But if it pleases you . . . Do you miss her very much?'

'Terribly.'

'Would you like her to read your words?'

Metellus bowed his head and remained in silence for a few moments. Then he said, 'I'd give anything for that to happen. But I fear it's impossible: there is no message that can reach the kingdom of the dead.'

'Is no one left to you?' asked Dan Qing.

'My son. A boy of seven. I did not even say goodbye. And I do not know what has become of him.'

Dan Qing lowered his head. According to the mechanisms of power that he was accustomed to, that child would already be dead.

Metellus sighed and said no more as Dan Qing began to write again, using a slender brush to draw the elegant signs of his script.

'What does Flying Foxes mean?' asked Metellus after some time.

'They are animals that live in the great forests of the south. They resemble little foxes, but they have a membrane between their front and back paws that stretches out when they jump from one branch to another and allows them to soar and wheel through the air, like birds.'

'But when you spoke of them you were referring to men, not to animals. To the men who attacked us in the valley.'

'Garbed in black,' continued Dan Qing, leaning his brush on a lacquered wooden stand, 'implacable, swift as lightning, peerless combatants, fanatically devoted to their chief and to their mission. Whoever has them on his side can be certain of victory.'

Metellus neared a stone wall on which the shell of an enormous tortoise hung, so large that he had never seen anything like it. He stroked the smooth, shiny surface; it seemed like polished ebony. 'We defeated them, though.'

'Because they did not expect such resistance . . . forces arrayed in a way they were totally unfamiliar with.'

Metellus stroked the big burnished shell. 'We call the tech-nique *testudo*, which means tortoise. A tortoise beat the flying foxes ... Although perhaps our tactics are more like a porcu-pine's. It's strange how men so often compare their behaviour to that of animals ...'

'Don't delude yourself, Xiong Ying. When they have your strategy figured out, they will find a way ...'

'That may be. But you see, we have an ancient proverb, coined by a great poet of the past: "A fox has many tricks. The porcupine just one, but a good one."'

Dan Qing turned to face him and a slight smile crossed his lips. 'That's a good proverb,' he said.

'But who are they, in reality? Where do they come from?'

Dan Qing rose to his feet, uncrossing his legs with the fluid elegance of a serpent or a fish gliding through water. He went to a cabinet built into a wall, opened it and extracted a bundle of reed canes tied with laces. He unwound one of them on the floor and a text written in their script appeared.

'Many centuries ago,' he began, scanning those ancient signs, 'a great master lived in the Middle Kingdom. His name was Mo Tze. It was a dark time, marked by continuous strife between the most powerful families. This master developed a theory wherein the family and its ties of blood were considered the origin of all evil, of all favouritism and all egoism. He designed a society in which each man could be a member of a single universal com-munity, not broken up into families; where every father was the father of all, each son the son of every man, every city the city of all and each citizen a member of each city, without distinction ...'

'We have a master who developed a similar theory as well. We call it *cosmopolitismòs* in the language of our greatest philo-sophers,' Metellus could not help but observe, but then added immediately, 'Go on, please.'

'Master Mo considered war the worst of all evils, the human action most abhorred by the Heavens. He called warriors the fierce mastiffs of the abyss. And thus he decided to oppose war with every means available to him ... including war!'

Metellus shook his head in wonder. 'We also have this concept of the absurd. We call it *paradoxon*.'

'He was convinced that no human action is evil on its own. What makes it such is intent. He organized his followers into a secret sect which was divided into many autonomous groups, governed by iron-clad rules. The sect developed combat techniques of every kind, some purely defensive, others of devastating offensive power, techniques based on control of the mind and its unlimited energies . . .

'If a family fell victim to tyranny, if a community – whether a mere village or even a city – suffered unjustified violence, those men entered into action. They moved in the dark like ghosts, attacked with the speed of a thunderbolt and then vanished, melting into the darkness. They would materialize from out of nowhere, as if answering a call that only they could hear, and their combat units took form as if by magic, in the most unthought-of places.

'They struck with extreme harshness and always left their seal, so that the significance and the targets of their punishment would be evident. If one of them was wounded in combat, he would never allow himself to be taken alive, ensuring that the secrets of the sect would never be revealed . . .'

'Like the men who attacked us . . . But if they fight in the name of justice, then why . . .'

'There is no temptation greater than power. Nothing created by man is free from the risk of corruption, and you should know that well,' continued Dan Qing. 'Could such a formidable tool remain immune to the temptations of power?'

Metellus thought of the legions, the extraordinary military machine of Rome, born to defend her and transformed through time into an instrument of bloody wars of conquest, of mass extermination, of cruel civil conflict.

Dan Qing continued his story: 'Upon the death of Master Mo, the sect stepped back into the shadows. For long periods it even seemed to have disappeared, so that people thought it had ceased to exist. In reality, during those long intervals of silence, the followers not only survived but made continuous progress by refining their fighting techniques and developing sophisticated systems of communication.

'Such efficiency presupposes a completely secret hierarchical order, absolute internal unanimity and blind obedience. They succeeded so well in maintaining secrecy that in certain periods people began to believe that the existence of the sect was pure fantasy, a legend like the many others that circulate in this endless land. It may even be that such a belief was actively spread and sustained by the members of the sect themselves. But at the critical moment they would re-emerge and strike, often in places very distant from one another, and in the most diverse situations.

'From what we know, it seems that, starting about fifty years ago, a momentous degeneration of the sect took place. Those at the top began to use the enormous power and the secrets of their combat arts to support or to oppose one candidate to the throne or another. This was one of the causes that led to the decline and the end of the glorious Han dynasty, which had governed the country for over four centuries ... and to the division of the empire into three separate, rival kingdoms: Wei, Shu and Wu.'

Metellus felt his head spinning: four centuries! A single dynasty had reigned in that land for a longer time than all the imperial dynasties of Rome put together.

'These combatants,' continued Dan Qing, 'who had lost sight of their origins and their reasons for existing became known as the Flying Foxes. Others, a minority, separated from their brothers who had fallen away and took refuge in a secluded place whose location has always remained secret. They founded a community where they live according to the rules of brotherhood, sharing food, natural resources and water, devoting themselves to agriculture and sheep raising, but mainly to meditation, in which they excel.'

'But now,' said Metellus, 'the Flying Foxes have sided against you and want you dead. Why?'

Dan Qing rolled the bundle of reed canes and put it back

into the cabinet, locking it with a key. 'The answer may be very simple,' he said. 'Desire for supreme power.'

'Or?'

Dan Qing fixed him with a magnetic look. 'I don't know why, but I find myself telling you things that I never thought I would tell anyone, and this disturbs me.'

'I would never have imagined that a feeling could disturb you. We can't even hide our emotions: you can see them immediately by the way our faces change colour. But you never blush, or grow pale. Your face is a mask of wax.'

'Yours is a race still in evolution; the material you are made of is still in tumult. We have reached perfection . . . but nonetheless we are subject to the will of the Heavens. And the Heavens can decide to disempower a dynasty – or an emperor – if it has been stained by infamy or tyranny, or by irremediable corruption. What happens then is called *geming* – revocation – and it is followed by a spirit of revolt that nothing can stop. This generates distress that not even an emperor can escape . . . But you will be faithful to me, will you not, Xiong Ying?'

'I could not help my own emperor. I was forced to watch him die like a wretch. If I can help you, I will, but I must know who I am fighting for. Speak to me of your anguish, Prince.'

'My father was a good man, a wise ruler who had the destiny of his people at heart. And I dream of nothing but restoring the unity of the Middle Kingdom. Why should the Heavens have revoked my family's rule? The Flying Foxes are obedient to a dark force, I'm certain of it.'

'Have you done nothing you are ashamed of? Nothing that could cause emotion to flare under that wax mask of yours?'

'How dare you! No one can ask me such a question!' exclaimed Dan Qing. 'Anyone else would already have paid dearly for such impudence!'

'Nothing that has offended justice?' demanded Metellus, drawing closer to Dan Qing.

'What drives you to ask me such a thing? How dare you insist with such impertinence?'

'Because I can sense your insecurity. There's something about you I don't understand. You defend yourself as though you had something to hide.'

Dan Qing glared at him, then, slowly, one word at a time, said, 'I have done nothing that it was not my right to do.' He spun around and retreated into disdainful silence.

Metellus turned to leave but stopped at the threshold. 'We have a proverb,' he said. ' "*Summum jus, summa injuria.*" '

Dan Qing did not say a word.

'It means: "An extreme right is extreme injustice," ' concluded Metellus, and he left.

22

BAJ RENJIE APPEARED after the sun had risen, in fighting order, and asked to be admitted to the presence of Dan Qing.

'My Lord,' he said, 'waiting any longer would be dangerous. The Flying Foxes know you are here and could attack at full strength at any time.'

'I'm ready,' replied the prince. 'Assemble your men.'

'They await your command to set forth, My Prince.'

Dan Qing widened his arms and two servants approached, fastened on his armour and hung his magnificent sword at his side.

'You no longer need the barbarians who accompanied you here,' said Baj Renjie. 'You can give them leave to depart with the merchant.'

'The Red Demons will follow us to our destination, to the castle of my master, Wangzi,' replied Dan Qing.

Baj Renjie did not dare to object, but the expression on his face left no doubt as to his humour.

Outside, the officer found Metellus and his men, armed to the teeth as well, having their breakfast seated on a bench near the fish pool. He did not deign to look at them and joined his unit. There were about fifty men in all, half of them on horseback. They wore breast armour made of bronze plates joined by iron rings, leather tunics, boots and neckerchiefs. They did not have helmets, but wore their hair gathered at the nape of their neck and held in place by long ivory pins and by a ribbon that fell back on to their shoulders, topped by a round cap of dark felt. The horsemen bore bows slung over their shoulders and quivers, while the infantrymen were armed with sword and dagger. Metellus noticed that not even the foot soldiers wore helmets or carried shields. He had already realized that they relied on swordcraft for defence. Dan Qing must have been astonished by the Romans' use of their javelins, shields and short arms.

Dan Qing had reached the square. He raised his hand and Baj Renjie touched his heels to his horse's flanks, urging him into a walk. His twenty-five horsemen followed. The prince joined the column, followed by Metellus on horseback and his men on foot. The Chinese infantrymen brought up the rear. Daruma set off last of all with his caravan, but he did not remain with them for long.

In the early afternoon, the convoy stopped at a fork. The road on the right was wide and smooth, while the one on the left was narrow and steep and they could see how, in a couple of miles, it climbed up a rocky ridge.

Daruma drove his camel forward and caught up with Dan Qing. 'Prince!' he called out, gesturing for him to stop. Dan Qing pulled in on his horse's reins. 'Prince, I'd say that it is here that we must part company. I imagine that you will choose the road to the left, a route I certainly cannot take myself.'

'You have done so on other occasions,' protested Dan Qing.

'Not with a caravan of this size and under such dangerous circumstances. If you are attacked, we would only be in the way. You will give my best wishes to Master Wangzi.'

'I am certain that he wishes to see you, to thank you for having completed your mission.'

'Upon my return, I shall send a messenger to arrange a meeting. Tell him that I have a great desire to speak with him and please extend my most respectful regards.'

Metellus rode up. 'Did I hear you say that our roads separate here? Did I hear you well?'

'Yes, you heard me well, Commander,' replied Daruma. 'Your Chinese is getting better every day. Don't fear, I will stop here on my return journey and we will embark on the westward road together.'

Metellus replied in *koinè*: 'It makes no sense for us to separate. The prince has his own guard. He doesn't need us.'

Dan Qing turned at those words, realizing that they had been uttered in a language he was not meant to understand. Metellus could guess at his thoughts and this made him feel uncomfortable, especially after the way they had left each other the day before.

Daruma replied in the same language: 'Don't panic . . .'

'I'm not panicking.'

'Yes, you are. You think that we'll lose touch in this endless land and never find each other again, or that I will take another route and renege on my promise to take you back home. You are wrong. Listen well: it's obvious that I can't make it up that mule track with this caravan. As far as your journey is concerned, once you've arrived at the monastery the prince will make a decision. Almost certainly, his master will put him in contact with the forces that will support him in his endeavours. If he leaves for Luoyang, you can decide whether to follow him there, where I will be for at least a month. Or, more probably, you may decide to remain at the monastery and wait for me to return.'

'What if something happens to you?'

'This could occur in any case, even if we don't separate. But you may be certain that the prince is no ingrate. He would provide you with guides capable of taking you back. Trust me, Commander, you'll see that the word of an Indian merchant can be just as worthy as that of a Roman officer. We'll meet again at this crossroads in one month's time, or we'll see each other at Luoyang. The prince knows how he can get a message through to me. You will not regret having followed him on this last part of his expedition. He feels threatened and he trusts you implicitly. Don't disappoint him and you won't be sorry.'

Having said this, he approached Dan Qing and bade him a respectful farewell. 'May you have a safe journey, Prince, and may you be destined to have good fortune in your future.'

'I owe you much, Daruma,' replied the prince.

'You'll find a way of returning the favour,' replied Daruma. 'A special concession for silk trading would be a sign of gratitude that I would greatly appreciate, for example, but we will have time to speak about that when we have been able to put all the dangers and vicissitudes behind us.' He made a deferential bow, then urged on his camel and started off down the route to the right, followed by his servants and assistants.

'You may go with him if you like,' said Dan Qing to Metellus. 'You are free.'

Metellus said nothing. He felt his men's eyes upon him and understood how lost they felt in the heart of this boundless land, but he knew that he had to keep his word. He did not want to abandon the prince before their journey's end and he was certain he was serving a just cause, but he didn't want to leave his men at the mercy of someone else's decisions. He said, 'I shall accompany you to your destination, but if I do so, I must have the command of the entire escort, including the Chinese forces.'

Dan Qing expressed astonishment for the first time ever. 'Why? It's best that each commander be responsible for his own men.'

'And thus it shall be. But each one of us will have different objectives, which I shall establish.'

'What do you mean by that?'

'May I speak to you in private?'

Dan Qing nodded, dismounted and the two men walked a short distance away from the others.

'If it's true that the Flying Foxes have located us, they will know exactly where we are now. They have surely kept us in their sights this whole time and may be somewhere close by. If they haven't attacked us thus far, it's because they don't have sufficient forces.'

'That is likely,' admitted Dan Qing.

'They will do so as soon as they are numerous enough to fight us or capture us. This is my plan. We'll all travel together through a stretch of the wood. When we emerge, one of your soldiers will be wearing your garments and carrying your weapons, and he will be riding your horse. You will be dressed like one of the servants who transport the victuals. Your substitute will go down the road for Luoyang with Baj Renjie and the Chinese forces. That is exactly what the Flying Foxes will expect and consider the most logical and rational choice: for the prince to be escorted by his own countrymen, whom he trusts and who speak the same language.

'In the meantime, you will come with us. We'll all be dressed like farmers and we'll cover the path on foot, using our horses as pack animals. We'll only travel after night has fallen, moving in three small groups at a certain distance from each other. During the day we'll stop and remain concealed in the forest. If I'm right, the Flying Foxes will go after Baj Renjie and the man impersonating you.'

'Baj Renjie will gladly sacrifice himself for me.'

'I can take his place, if you prefer. In that case, my men and I will journey with your double and eventually meet up with Daruma, while you climb the path to the monastery dressed as a servant, with your Chinese commander. It does not make much difference to me, but I am sure that there is no other way for you to reach your destination unharmed. I'll wait for your response.'

Dan Qing stood alone in silent meditation for a short time, then approached Metellus again and said, 'We'll do as you say. You will escort me.'

He called his Chinese commander and informed him of the plan. Baj Renjie looked at him with an incredulous expression and tried to object, but the prince cut him off immediately: 'This is my irrevocable decision, Baj Renjie. If you are faithful to me, you will obey. Or leave.'

The officer swallowed his indignation and bowed respectfully. He ordered some of his men to precede them into the forest and arrange for the disguising.

Dan Qing took him aside for a moment. 'Listen, Baj Renjie, I know that this order is bitter for you, but I believe that this is my only chance of escaping attack and preparing my return to Luoyang. May the Heavens protect you. If all goes well, we shall see each other in Luoyang at the tavern of the White Mulberry.'

Baj Renjie bowed, then mounted his horse and rode off at the head of his unit, flanked by the servant impersonating Dan Qing.

'The route they will cover is mostly in the open,' observed Metellus. 'Whoever is watching them will have to remain at a certain distance so as not to be seen. They will not be able to distinguish your double from you.'

The Romans and the prince entered the thick underbrush and prepared for their journey. The men removed their armour and loaded it on to the horses, then dressed in native garb and found shelter under a huge oak, where they could rest before setting off.

The days of their imprisonment were long past; they were in excellent physical shape and in a good humour as well. Accustomed as they were to long military campaigns, they felt quite at ease with their mission. The journey had not been taxing or particularly perilous. Rufus's wound had healed well and had not suppurated, proof that Chinese medicine was far superior to the Roman. As the prince stripped with the help of two servants, Metellus noticed that he still wore bandages on his arm and chest, but they were not stained, a sure sign that he was healing as well.

They ate before nightfall: boiled marsh grain with pine nuts and pieces of squab that had been prepared by the prince's cooks in the village. The men still had the spoons that Uxal had carved for them and they consumed their meal hungrily, stopping now and then to steal a look at Dan Qing, who brought tiny quantities of food to his mouth with his sticks. Metellus had tried to use them once or twice with little success, and had gone back to the wooden spoons that his soldiers used.

An hour after darkness had fallen, Quadratus cautiously left the forest and reconnoitred the trail to make certain that no one was around. He reported back to Metellus, who gave the men their marching orders: they all set off on foot, leading the horses by their halters as though they were simple pack animals.

The dirt path was well trodden, its few rocky stretches worn by thousands of years of passage. The breeze barely ruffled the leafy boughs of the thick forest which extended along both sides of the road. The moon had not yet risen and they advanced very slowly to allow their eyes to become accustomed to the darkness.

The men chatted softly to keep each other's spirits up in that atmosphere which became gloomier and more foreboding with each step they took; every tree, every spur took on a threatening appearance.

'Commander Metellus,' said Balbus, 'has decided to adopt the same strategy as when we were escaping from Aus Daiwa, journeying by night and covering less ground but staying out of sight.'

'The Flying Foxes would have to have eyes like cats,' added Quadratus, 'to be able to spot us on a night this black.'

'They'll be headed after the fake prince with the Chinese escort anyway.'

'Well, probably so, but the commander is no dupe, that's for sure. He's just hoping the trick will work long enough to give us a good start.'

'Just five more days,' said Balbus, 'and we'll be on our way back. Can you believe it? I'm counting every moment that separates me from home. Have you ever been to Spain? To Saragoza?'

'Don't think too hard,' replied Quadratus. 'Anything could happen before we get home. Do you have any idea of how far away we are? Can you imagine what we'll have to deal with on our way back? Did you see how worried the commander looked when Daruma went off on his own? He's thinking that the old guy won't show and that we'll find ourselves in the middle of this endless country with no clue about which way to go.'

'That won't happen. In any case, the prince would send

someone back with us. After all, he owes it to us that he's come this far.'

'Well, I hope so. I just can't shake this feeling that something will go wrong, and I've never seen Commander Aquila so troubled.'

A long howl echoed from the mountaintops, a kind of lament that greeted the slow rising of the moon from behind the peaks. A wolf, perhaps, or maybe a jackal, or some other unknown animal from this land so full of surprises.

They marched accompanied only by the sounds of the forest and by the rustling of the leaves at every gust of wind. In the distance, over the tops of the mountains, they could see lights flashing and illuminating enormous black clouds from inside the lurking storm. The dull rumbling of thunder reached their ears from time to time, dashing against the sides of the valley like waves.

Prince Dan Qing advanced with Metellus at the head of the column all night in silence, matching their pace to the sharp rise of the mountain trail.

Dawn surprised them at a little clearing dotted with tiger lilies and marvellous blue flowers similar to gentians. Metellus ordered his men to retreat to the forest and find a place in the shade of the thick vegetation to rest for the day.

THEY ADVANCED for four days, resting as soon as the sun appeared and marching at night by the ever lighter glow of the waxing moon. The forest was intensely scented and populated by flowers they had never seen before, with fleshy petals and gaudy colours. That stretch of the mountainside was practically deserted. They rarely encountered other wayfarers, and only in the hours that preceded the dawn or just before sunset: woodsmen bent under loads of enormous bundles of sticks gathered in the forest, or shepherds leading their flocks towards mountain pastures.

On the morning of the fifth day, the monastery came into

sight on the slope opposite a deep ravine, perched up on a rocky peak. It was a massive complex, with a tower at each of its four corners, the same grey colour as the surrounding mountains.

Towards the east, the mountain sloped down towards wooded hills which descended towards the plain. The place seemed like a peaceful, serenely isolated retreat. It stood out against an opal sky which was paling into the rosy hues of the aurora. The mighty structure was surrounded by green fields dotted with colossal trees, solitary giants whose bulk seemed conspicuous even from that distance. It was a celestial castle, an abode of the spirit whose existence Metellus would never have been able to imagine. A similar construction in such a dominant position in his world would have been a gloomy fortress, posted with armed men and war machines.

'Who lives up there besides your master?' he asked the prince, who was absorbed in contemplating that sublime vision.

'A community of monks who spend their time in meditation and study, in the education of the spirit and the body, in the search for universal harmony. Master Wangzi is their spiritual guide, but they venerate him as if he were their father, admire his ascetic gifts and love him as a person.'

'What is a monk?' asked Metellus.

'A person who chooses to separate himself from the society of men to become an intermediary between the Earth and the Heavens. A man who makes searching for his true self and for the higher forces of the cosmos his reason for being. A humble man who does not pretend to be the repository of truth, but embodies the desire to seek the way and to walk the way, along with whoever is willing to follow. This man, for me and others like me, is Master Wangzi. If it had not been for him I would still be a prisoner of the Persians and my mission would have no chance of success.'

'How did he know you were a prisoner?'

'Before I left, I came here in secret to bid him farewell, and I promised him that I would be back before the year was out to tell him of my experiences. When he saw that I hadn't returned after a year, nor after two, and he realized that power was passing from one hand to another at Luoyang, he activated all of his contacts in China, in India and in Persia itself, to learn what had become of me. When he had located me, he sent two messages, one to me and one to Daruma, to organize a meeting between us. It was almost a miracle, and this made me think that the Heavens had destined me to bring peace back to the Middle Kingdom and to restore the state.'

Metellus said nothing.

'Let us go forth now,' exhorted Dan Qing. 'I can't wait to see him again!'

'Not yet,' replied the Roman. 'We've got this far unscathed because we have followed my plan rigorously. It would be foolish, now that we've nearly arrived, to let ourselves be swept away by impatience. I'm surprised at you, Prince. Patience should be one of the fundamental virtues of your education.'

'It's not a question of patience, Xiong Ying,' retorted the prince. 'The ravine that separates us from the castle can only be crossed using a rope bridge. An endeavour difficult enough by the light of day. By night it would be suicide.'

'We'll have the moonlight,' replied Metellus.

'The moon is not enough. Her light is too dim to illuminate the bridge.'

Metellus stared into his eyes. 'All right,' he replied. 'How far is it from the bridge to the castle?'

'Two hours of marching,' replied Dan Qing.

'That's an acceptable risk,' replied Metellus. 'But we'll cross the bridge tomorrow at first light. The sun is too high now.'

'As you wish,' replied Dan Qing, and melted back into the forest.

Some time later, Metellus saw him absorbed in meditation with his legs crossed, his back straight, hands one upon the other to form a circle with his arms. He remained immobile in that position the whole day and before night fell he appeared before Metellus suddenly, as if he'd materialized from another world. 'I'm ready,' he said. 'Let us go.'

'Let us go,' repeated Metellus, and signalled to his men to prepare for setting off.

His two centurions drew up alongside him: Sergius Balbus and Aelius Quadratus. Quadratus, higher in rank, spoke: 'Commander, I propose that we don our armour. Once we enter the castle we will be in a closed place, susceptible to an ambush.'

Metellus smiled. 'That place is a refuge of the spirit, Centurion, an oasis of peace inhabited by pious men who have given themselves over to meditation. Our arms must never be shown. If it makes you feel better, you can carry your sword beneath your cloak.'

'May I tell the others to do so as well?'

'Yes, as long as you keep them hidden.'

Quadratus nodded without great conviction. It was hard for him to believe that an apparently impregnable fortress was only a place of meditation.

They marched off just after sunset, a flaming sunset that set afire the cirrus clouds scattered throughout the immense vault of the heavens, and then pressed on until they found themselves before the rope bridge.

Metellus went to see whether they could cross it immediately, despite the dark, but he risked falling into the abyss and turned back to tell his men to wait for dawn.

23

At sunrise, Dan Qing was the first to advance along the rope bridge, a structure as fragile as it was daring, flung across an abyss thick with vegetation from which the intense aroma of musk flowers rose. An invisible torrent rumbled far below, flowing fast between rocks and boulders. He walked backwards, holding his horse by its halter, after having blindfolded it. He could thus keep the animal in the centre of the bridge, distributing its weight in the best way possible.

When Dan Qing had arrived at the other side, Balbus went next, imitating the prince's example. Severus, Publius, Rufus and the others followed, one after another in the same manner, followed by Quadratus at a certain distance.

Metellus was the last to cross, along with his horse. At every tiny oscillation, the animal, despite being blindfolded, showed signs of nervousness and fear. Metellus realized that the slightest side-step would unbalance the bridge and throw him into the damp, sweetly scented abyss that yawned beneath him. But he trusted in the protection of his ancestors, who had always been propitious. They would certainly not abandon him now, with so little time remaining until he could start back home again. When he finally set foot on solid ground, he felt as if he had overcome the very last obstacle, and it didn't even occur to him that he would have to face the same difficulties, perhaps even worse, on his way back.

'All is well,' he said. 'And now on to the castle.'

Dan Qing removed his horse's blindfold, as did the others, and the men mounted their steeds and rode towards the monastery.

They found themselves on a brilliantly green high plain, scattered with purple crocuses and spikes of white flowers that looked like asphodels. In the distance, to their right, a herd of deer grazed tranquilly under the vigilant gaze of an old male with enormous horns. Flocks of birds took flight as they passed, escaping the great oaks that rose majestically at the edge of the meadow in the fluttering early morning mist.

Metellus urged on his bay and neared the prince. 'Everything seems calm,' he said. 'It would appear that all has gone well.'

'By this time they will have seen us,' replied Dan Qing. 'Soon my master will come out to greet us, I'm certain of it.'

The climbing sun illuminated the bastions of the majestic structure and the statues of two griffons on top of the highest tower. The main gate slowly began to open and a tall, slender figure stood out against the light at the centre of the opening.

'Is that him?' asked Metellus.

Dan Qing shook his head without removing his eyes from the dark shape that stood at the centre of the gate and replied, 'No.'

'Did your master know of our arrival?'

'I don't think so. There was no time to inform him.'

'Could there be any danger?'

'I don't know. We'll find out soon.'

'I'll go ahead with a couple of my men. I'll make myself understood.'

'No. There's no reason to fear. Master Wangzi may be intent on his meditation, or may be teaching the novices. In any case, it would make no difference.'

He hadn't finished speaking when the low, prolonged sound of a horn blared from one of the towers and echoed repeatedly on the slopes of the surrounding mountains.

'What does that mean?' asked Metellus again.

'Nothing. It's the signal for prayer. Life in the monastery is measured by these sounds.'

'Do you know that man?'

Dan Qing continued to advance without answering, then

said, 'There's something familiar about the way he looks, but I can't make out his features against the sun.'

Metellus noticed a certain apprehension in his usually imperturbable gaze.

They were now just about a hundred feet from the gate and Metellus gestured for his men to stay alert, but at that very instant Dan Qing spurred on his horse and rode straight towards the gate. Metellus set off after him and caught up in time to hear him say, 'I'm a disciple of Master Wangzi. Please announce my presence. You can tell him that the person he has been expecting has arrived.'

The tall, slim figure bent into a deep bow. 'Every passer-by and every pilgrim is welcome between these walls. The master is meditating at this moment but I will announce your arrival as soon as possible, so that he may receive you.'

Dan Qing considered him for a moment in surprise, as if something were escaping him, but the youth who had come to welcome him gestured graciously towards the inside of the monastery, saying, 'Enter, please.'

Dan Qing went in, followed by Metellus and his men, but every now and then he seemed to be casting a furtive glance at the monk who preceded them.

'How is the master?' he asked.

'Well,' replied the other. 'Thanks to the Heavens. But who are these foreigners who accompany you, if I may ask?' he said, gesturing at Metellus and the others.

'They are my servants. I made a long journey westward, and it is from those lands that they come: from Taqin Guo, the great Western empire.'

'Taqin Guo . . .' repeated the monk. 'Very few men have gone so far and returned to tell their tale. They say that the distance is enormous . . .'

As they crossed the large slate-covered courtyard, Metellus took a look around. There was a busy coming and going of men with their heads shaven, dressed in long, wide-armed tunics. Some carried fruit in wicker baskets, others bore musical instruments. He noticed that Dan Qing turned every time one of them passed, following them with his eyes.

'Here is the master!' said their guide all at once, indicating a priestly figure wearing a long ochre-coloured tunic, standing at the top of one of the two rear towers of the castle, which was covered by wooden roofing. 'I will go presently to announce your arrival and that of your round-eyed servants.'

Metellus noticed that the monk was attracted, or made curious, by his appearance and that of his comrades. Evidently, he had never seen anyone who came from the West. He would certainly have liked to ask more questions about them, but probably held back so as not to seem tiresome or discourteous.

They had reached the opposite side of the courtyard, where several doors led to interior rooms. Dan Qing met his escort's eyes once again. 'I have the feeling that I've seen you before.'

'That's certainly possible,' replied the youth. 'It's not the first time that I've come to this monastery, and if you are a disciple of Master Wangzi, it is very probable that we met some time ago in this very place. Please take a seat. I will have tea brought, if you would like to share a cup with me.'

'I would gladly have some. They make excellent tea here in the monastery, if I remember well.'

The young man nodded his head to accept the compliment and motioned towards the entrance.

Dan Qing glanced over at Metellus and the youth noticed his gesture. 'Your servants will be served refreshments as well, naturally. One of the brothers will accompany them to the servants' quarters,' he said, beckoning to a monk who was approaching them.

Dan Qing nodded to Metellus, indicating that he could follow the other monk, and Metellus nodded his assent. He made a bow and went off, followed by his men, who were holding the horses by their reins.

Dan Qing entered a room which he had already visited during previous visits, and he felt reassured by the strong sandalwood smell of the furniture and the fragrance of tea brewing in the nearby kitchen. The hospitality of that sacred place required that tea be ready at any hour of the day, from the first light of dawn until late at night, so that wayfarers and visitors would be welcomed by the warmth of that refreshing beverage. The monk disappeared for a moment and returned with two steaming bowls on a tray, which he set down on a red lacquered table. He sat opposite the prince, served him and then took the other cup and brought it to his lips.

Dan Qing noticed his eyes over the rim of the fine light blue ceramic and he felt his gaze pierce him. He took a sip himself and said, 'My name is—'

'Dan Qing,' completed the other with a deep bow. 'My Prince.'

'Then you know who I am . . . but you haven't yet told me your name.'

The youth continued to stare with a gaze that, under any other circumstances, would have seemed brazen if directed at a prince of imperial blood, but was not out of place in that refuge of the spirit, where humility reigned. 'Do you truly not recognize me?' he asked with a suddenly serious expression. 'Can it be that the memory of your cruelty has become so unbearable that you have succeeded in cancelling it from your mind?' Saying thus, he leapt to his feet. 'Must I open my tunic and show you the mutilation so that you remember?' he shouted.

Dan Qing was deeply stricken by those words. He murmured, 'Wei, you must be Wei . . . It's not possible . . .'

'It is I. And I am here to take my revenge.'

METELLUS, BALBUS and the others passed under the archway of the northern tower, an imposing structure of carved, painted wood, following the monk who was accompanying them towards a large oak door.

Something fell from above on to the head of Rufus, who was the last in line. 'Blasted birds!' he swore, raising his hand to wipe it away. He was shocked to see a red stain and showed it to his commander. 'It's . . . blood!'

An image flashed into Metellus's mind: the rigid, immobile figure of Master Wangzi on the top of the tower, the one directly above them. He lifted his eyes towards the ceiling and saw blood dripping through the planks.

'Your weapons, men!' he said instantly. 'Return to the prince!'

A sword materialized in the hand of their escort and cut through the air like lightning. It would have neatly decapitated Metellus had he not been forewarned and dodged it just in time. Antoninus had already pulled a knife from his belt; he threw it with deadly precision and it sank into the monk's forehead. He folded to the ground without a cry.

'Back to the prince, quickly!' shouted Metellus, and he lunged with his sword in hand towards the visitors' quarters, followed by his men. He kicked open the door and rushed inside, shouting, 'Prince! It's a trap! Beware!' but he drew up short at the sight of Dan Qing, immobilized by armed men.

The man who had received them at the door was obviously their leader. He motioned to one of them, who brought a sharp blade to the prisoner's throat. 'Drop your weapons or I'll have him slice it open,' said the young man, and his gaze was no less cutting than the knife pressing on the prince's skin.

Metellus tossed down his *gladius* and so did the men who had entered with him.

'Your servants are quite perspicacious,' said Wei sarcastically. 'I wonder how they could have imagined what was happening here.'

'As we were passing below the northern tower,' said Metellus to the prince, 'a drop of blood fell from above. What's on the tower is the corpse of your master.'

Dan Qing howled in despair, struggling to get free, but his captors forcefully twisted his hands behind his back, forcing him to his knees.

'I had no choice,' said Wei impassively. 'That crazy old man refused to listen to reason and was about to react in an ill-advised manner. You well know that he can be quite dangerous, despite his age. Only a sword is harder than those bony hands of his.'

'You rabid dog!' shouted Dan Qing. 'Curse you! You will pay for this infamy!'

'More than I've already paid?' replied Wei. 'Don't you think you're exaggerating a bit, My Prince? Do you have any idea what castration means to a boy of sixteen? Do you have any idea of the atrocious pain, of the horror, of the agony that seized me that day?'

Metellus stared in bewilderment at Dan Qing, who would not meet his eye.

'It was only the desire for revenge that kept me alive,' continued Wei. 'And now I shall have what I have so long desired. I've taken your kingdom, and I'll help myself to everything else before I condemn you to eternal desperation. You cannot imagine how eagerly I have awaited this moment.' He turned to his men. 'Take them away.' As they were carrying out his order, he added, 'Their weapons as well. There are more of them hidden under their horses' saddlecloths.'

Metellus and the others followed the men, who led them to the middle of the courtyard and chained them to the hay crib. Dan Qing was conducted inside the monastery. As he was being dragged over the threshold, the prince turned towards Wei and asked, 'Where's Yun Shan?'

Wei replied with a smirk, 'She's here. And she will soon be in my hands. Who knows, maybe she still loves me. What do you say?'

'Leave her in peace!' replied Dan Qing. 'She has nothing to do with this. It's between me and you!'

Wei looked hard at him, his eyes full of hatred and anguish. 'Yun Shan has everything to do with this, Prince. It was because of her that you had the most cruel humiliation inflicted upon me.' Although he spoke from the bottom of his throat, his adolescent's voice was shrill, in a disturbing contrast with the virile fury of his gaze.

Wei's features were extraordinarily beautiful. His skin had the smooth transparency of wax, his slightly pronounced jaw gave him a wilful, unsparing expression. His neck was straight and muscular, his shoulders wide, his waist narrow, his legs long, his fingers as slim and tapered as those of a girl, but as steely as tiger's claws. Dan Qing felt his heart sink as they dragged him away.

WEI WAS PACING back and forth in the large empty room, alone. Then he leaned his elbow against the wall and his brow against his hand, standing perfectly still.

He jumped at the voice of one of his men: a tall, lean Manchurian with eyes as narrow as slits. 'My Lord, we have searched everywhere, but we have not found her.'

'That's simply not possible!' shouted Wei. 'You haven't looked hard enough. Find her, do you understand that? Find her, if you want to keep your head. I know she's here! I'm certain of it!'

The Manchurian made no visible reaction: his grey stone face remained impassive as he bowed and left the room. He was soon heading back underground to order his men to continue the search. He descended a spiral staircase which led to a vast subterranean chamber, stepping over the bodies of the monks who had given their attackers a tough fight. They were scattered along the stairs and the black streams of their clotted blood stained the grey stone. He found himself before a bronze door opening on to a large room illuminated by bronze lamps. A colonnade of dark stone lined the walls. On one of the short sides, two bronze dragons flanked a stair that led to a large statue of Buddha in meditation. An enormous tripod of finely embossed bronze was full of lustral waters on which purple lotus flowers floated. Five armed men were striding out.

'Where are you going?' the Manchurian demanded. 'Our lord said we are to keep looking.'

'There's nothing here,' replied the patrol leader. 'We've scoured the place.'

'There may be secret hiding places,' replied the Manchurian 'Continue your search. I'll go to the eastern wing to check on the rooms there. We're not leaving until we find that cursed viper '

The five men turned back and began to inspect the floors and walls, the part of the sanctuary behind the statue and then the statue itself. They tapped their spear shafts against every stone slab, every inch of the wall, the bases and shafts of the columns.

'It's no use,' said the patrol leader in the end. 'There's nothing here. Even if we stay here all day we won't find a thing. Let's go.' He lifted his torch high one last time to inspect the ceiling beams, then shook his head and went out of the door. His men followed him one by one.

At that same moment, a slim figure dressed in black leaned out from behind one of the big joists, slipped over to one of the columns and dropped down along its polished shaft, touching the ground instantly without making a sound. She caught up with the last soldier before he crossed the doorway and cut his throat with a razor-sharp dagger, accompanying his lifeless body to the floor with her other arm, with the same grace and ease as if she were laying a baby in its cradle. She swiftly put on his tunic and boots and pulled his helmet over her head, lowering the mask-like sallet over her face. She grabbed his bow and quiver and went up the stairs to join Wei's men, but a hand encircled her ankle, immobilizing her.

'Yun Shan . . .'

The girl bent over a dying monk. 'Bao Deng! My poor friend . . .'

'Flee this place, save yourself. Find the men of the Red Lotus. Only they can protect you.'

'They don't know me . . . I've never met them. The master wanted to put me in contact with them but it's too late now.'

'Go to the capital . . . the tavern of the Green Dragon. Give the owner this pendant I wear at my neck . . . Take it.' He collapsed with a slight gasp.

Yun Shan dried a tear and slipped the leather lace from the monk's neck; hanging from it was a silver pendant with a red enamelled lotus blossom at its centre. She closed his eyes and then, with a few agile leaps, caught up with the end of the small column that was heading up the stairs.

The Manchurian officer who had just arrived from the eastern quarters could see in his men's eyes that they'd had no success and he went straight to Wei to report on the negative outcome of his mission. 'We looked everywhere, My Lord. We even checked the corpses one by one to make sure that she hadn't accidentally been killed in the fray. Nothing. She is nowhere to be found. Either your information was not correct or she managed to escape in the initial confusion after we broke into the monastery.'

'That is not possible, Commander Zhou. I trust my sources and what I tell you is always correct. Remember that, unless you want to face unpleasant consequences.' He left the room, went to the centre of the courtyard and for a few moments stood watching the ten Western barbarians chained to the feed crib with ill-concealed curiosity. A short distance away his men were passing around the barbarians' weapons with great interest.

The sky over the monastery began to darken, as a strong north wind picked up, carrying rain-laden black clouds with it. Thunder rumbled in the distance.

Wei turned to the Manchurian commander. 'Have all the villages in the vicinity searched. Post guards at all the roads and trails, bridges and fords. I want that girl at any cost.' He turned back to consider Metellus and the others. 'Tie them to their horses. We'll take them with us.'

One of the guards unchained them, while others brought their horses and forced the prisoners to mount them, tying their hands to the saddle pommels.

Dan Qing underwent the same treatment, as the rest of Wei's men were gathering in every corner of the monastery courtyard. Some of them, the prince thought, were surely members of the Flying Foxes, like those who had ambushed them towards the end of their long journey. He recognized those formidable combatants by their light bearing, the intensity of their gaze, and by the way they kept their hands on the hilts of their swords. Metellus passed without even acknowledging him and Dan Qing felt humiliated.

'You have no right to judge me,' he said. 'You know nothing.'

'I think I know enough,' replied Metellus. 'What I heard is enough for me. What you did is atrocious and incomprehensible. Not even the maddest of our emperors would have done such a thing.'

The column prepared to start off, with Wei at its head on a black charger. Dan Qing's and Metellus's horses were tethered behind the last chariot, followed by those of the other Romans.

The clouds had clustered into enormous black thunderheads fringed with grey, flashes darting through them like snakes of fire. The dull roar of the oncoming storm reverberated into a thousand echoes on the rocky sides of the valley. Rain began to fall.

Dan Qing watched as Wei dismounted his horse and entered the first carriage and then answered Metellus: 'The solidity of our state depends on exemplary punishment.'

'That is not punishment. It's savage cruelty that nothing can justify. What had that boy done to deserve such horror?'

One of the Manchurian horsemen from Wei's escort passed alongside Metellus and stared into his eyes for a moment with particular intensity. A gaze that reminded him of Dan Qing's, when he had seen him for the first time outside the walls of Edessa. He forced himself to look away and to listen to what the prince was saying.

'I did not give the order.'

'Oh no? And who did, then?'

Dan Qing felt humiliated at the idea of having to provide explanations to a subordinate, something he'd never done in his whole life. But he could not help himself from continuing: 'Wei was trying to seduce my sister, Princess Yun Shan, but I never even met him. My father learned about it from one of his ministers. He was told that the youth was very ambitious and wanted to use his charm to bind the princess to him and enter thus into the royal family. It was rumoured that someone was using him to infiltrate new blood into our noble lineage.'

'Two adolescents in love . . . Good gods, he had only fallen in love with your sister! That doesn't seem such a serious crime to me. It happens every day where I come from and no one is surprised by it.' The end of the column had begun to move, and Metellus turned around to encourage the others. 'Take heart, men! After what we've been through, this certainly shouldn't worry us. The journey will be lengthy and anything may happen. The prince's Chinese troops will come to our aid.'

Dan Qing interpreted that interruption as another intentional sign of scorn, but he had agreed to accept a different relationship with the Roman he'd called Xiong Ying, and he realized that his attitude was meant to put him to the test, to examine his motives before deciding whether to carry on with their friendship. It was a trial he had to submit to and he continued as if nothing had happened: 'Yun Shan was promised by my father to a prince of the state of Wu, a kingdom which had broken away from the empire. It was a way for him to reunite the state without bloodshed. He told the minister to dissuade Wei from his intent, but to no avail. The minister felt that an exemplary punishment was necessary so that nothing of the sort might happen again, so that in the future no one would ever think of attempting such a thing.'

'And he had him castrated.'

Dan Qing nodded.

'Contemptible,' said Metellus without even looking into his eyes.

'I did not give that order.'

'That doesn't change things. He who holds power is responsible for what his subordinates do. Even in the fury of battle, even under the most precarious circumstances, my men know that they must respect the rules that their commander upholds. In any case, I am responsible for every action of theirs, no matter how contrary it may be to my principles. This is what we call *disciplina*.'

Dan Qing fell silent. Only the snorting of the horses and the rumbling of the thunder could be heard in the mist-covered valley.

24

'SHE'S ALIVE.'

Dan Qing turned towards Metellus. 'What are you saying?'

'Your sister is alive.'

'How can you say that?'

'I can still tell a woman's gaze when I see it. A woman disguised as a Manchurian soldier . . . who else could that be?'

'You're probably right. Where did you see her? Where did she go?'

'I don't know. She looked at me for a moment, then rode off. She might still be here, or she may have gone off into the forest.'

The wind was blowing up even more strongly, with furious gusts, until the clouds split and the rain hammered down in a violent downpour, flooding the ground at their feet and transforming the trail into a muddy stream. The Romans bent their backs under the lashing storm, accustomed to bearing up silently under adversity, under the hostility of men, nature and the elements. Every now and then Metellus would turn to check on them, and it broke his heart. He had convinced them to follow him on this adventure, which had just concluded in reimprisonment perhaps no less cruel than the one they had escaped from.

He feared that destiny, this time, would not be giving them a second chance. He had not exploited their new-found liberty as he should have, and he tormented himself by thinking of thousands of ways of escaping. When he stole a glance at Dan Qing, he could feel his fury and humiliation, his frustration and impotence, but what came across most strongly was his need to talk, his need to share the anguish that oppressed him.

'Who do you think betrayed you?' Metellus asked, eyes pointed straight ahead.

'I don't know. It could have been anyone. So many people saw me in the village. Perhaps not all of them are loyal to me.'

'But the attack of the Flying Foxes came from the same men who are holding us prisoner now, wouldn't you say?'

'That's possible.'

'And so your enemy already knew when we crossed the border . . . Daruma?'

'Impossible,' exclaimed Dan Qing. 'Why would he have freed me, facing constant danger to bring me back to my homeland? My master trusted him, and no one knew a man like my master did.'

'Your master is dead, unfortunately . . .'

'By now the storm will have washed away his blood. Those black clots have dissolved in the water flowing over the bastions and down the stone steps . . . The man who killed him must die.'

'You seek revenge for a vengeance. That's absurd.'

'I was not responsible for his misfortune. Don't make me repeat it again.'

'That doesn't change anything. Nothing can heal Wei's wound. He has become a war machine, a concentration of hatred and resentment that can find relief only in the grief and pain of others; in his determination to inflict more suffering than what he has been made to bear.'

'From what you've told me, you evidently feel the same way . . . towards the man who killed your wife and took your child. Am I wrong, Xiong Ying?' Metellus did not answer, and Dan Qing brought his argument to its conclusion: 'That's why I have to kill him. For one reason or another, Wei is no longer a human being: he's a ferocious beast, a rabid dog. He must be eliminated.'

The storm seemed to be abating after the enormous violence

of its onset. The clouds galloped off towards the plain, leaving frayed traces of their passage. A dense mist invaded the valley and the rain continued to fall in occasional downpours. The column was now making its way through a vast clearing covered by a luxuriant blanket of grass.

'Is there any hope for us?' asked Metellus.

'Hope is always the last to die, says an ancient proverb of ours,' replied the prince.

'We have a proverb that says the same thing. But what do you think?'

'Do you remember when I told you about the Flying Foxes?'

'As if you'd just spoken.'

'The followers of the true way indicated long ago by Master Mo still exist. They are the most tenacious adversaries of the Flying Foxes. They are warrior monks, bound to each other by an oath, capable of any feat, ready for any sacrifice. They are the men of the Red Lotus. They are the only ones who can save us from this situation.'

He had just finished speaking when a shriek echoed through the valley, as high and grating as the cry of an eagle. Wei leaned out of the carriage and twisted repeatedly, scanning the slopes to his right and left, prey to a strange agitation.

'What was that?' asked Metellus.

'A signal,' replied Dan Qing. 'A message to let us know that we are not alone. Perhaps you are right: Yun Shan is alive and thinking of how she can free us.'

'Yun Shan means . . . Swathed in Clouds, doesn't it?' said Metellus, translating into Persian.

'That's right.'

'Do all of your women have such fascinating names?'

'Yes, almost all of them. What was your wife's name?'

'Clelia.'

'What does that mean?'

'It was the name of an ancient heroine. With her last breath, my wife beseeched me to take care of our son, and I don't even know where he is . . . or if he's still alive. And the direction of my march continues to take me away from him.'

'Not forever . . .'

Metellus was quiet for a little while. 'I don't know what to think of you,' he said all at once, as if concluding a thought that had remained in his mind.

'You will have to overcome your diffidence,' replied Dan Qing. 'If you care to, that is. In any case, if you think about it, I'm the only person you can count on, whether you like it or not.'

Metellus fell silent again.

'We must unite our forces now and try to survive,' began Dan Qing again. 'We'll decide about the rest later. You'll have the time to learn who I truly am.'

Metellus looked back again at his men, trying to judge their mood. Had being taken prisoner again broken their resolve? They were riding along, speaking softly to each other. Perhaps they underestimated the danger, or perhaps they just didn't want to brood on it because they knew fretting was useless.

They set up camp towards evening at the edge of a village perched on a green hill. The prisoners were unbound and gathered into a single tent, watched over by armed guards. Dan Qing was brought to another tent, alone.

Metellus spoke briefly to his men. 'I know what you're thinking: that it would have been better to wait for the spring monsoon in India and that this time we may never win back our freedom. If that's what you're thinking, you're wrong. The decision we made was the best one, even if all seems lost now.'

'But . . . what's happening, Commander?' asked Balbus.

'The youth who met us at the castle gate is the man who has come to power in Dan Qing's absence. They hate each other, implacably, but we're no part of their duel to the death. No matter what happens between them, I think we'll survive. I want to make one thing clear: until this affair is over with, we're on Dan Qing's side, even at the risk of death. We've given our word and will keep it.' Antoninus shook his head, but Metellus pretended not to have seen him. 'Stay on the alert and don't lose heart. I'll see to it that you get back home, even if it costs me my life.'

THEY RESUMED their journey the next morning, crossing the valley eastward for three more days. They rode with their hands bound to the saddle pommels and their feet tied to the stirrups, closely watched over by Wei's armed guards, fierce-looking Manchurian mercenaries who carried long curved swords. At the head of the column advanced the men in black, armed with double bows and long, heavy arrows. To attempt to escape under those circumstances would be suicide. After the first day, Dan Qing journeyed separately, tied behind Wei's own carriage, an elaborate vehicle with a luxurious sedan at the top, decorated with bronze and lacquer ornaments.

After four days of marching, the valley began to open into a vast rolling plain crossed by a wide, muddy river navigated by boats travelling downstream. They had big trapezoidal sails and were laden with goods of every sort. The fields all around were flooded with water for the cultivation of marsh grain, which even the prisoners ate every day, along with goose meat and eggs. The men could not help but wonder at this unusually generous treatment, which even included a fermented drink that resembled wine.

'The commander is right,' said Quadratus. 'We're not part of their internal conflicts. Perhaps Wei wants us to serve in his army and doesn't want us to become debilitated.'

'That's possible,' replied Antoninus, the highest in rank after the two centurions. 'I think you're right about that, for sure.'

Their complete uncertainty about their future made them want to believe the most reassuring hypotheses. Metellus, on the contrary, had a bad premonition, but he kept his feelings to himself.

They advanced for three more days and the landscape continued to change. They saw endless rows of trees with big dark green leaves on which small yellow or red berries, which looked much like brambles, grew. It seemed strange to all of them that there would be such extensive orchards of plants that produced only tiny berries, but they ascribed it to yet another of the many oddities that made this boundless land so different from their own.

As they proceeded, the villages became more numerous and more populous and their paved roads were teeming with people. After every day's leg, there was a rest station where they changed their horses, which offered hot food and lodging for wayfarers. The convoy would set up camp in a separate clearing which was always ready to accommodate important guests. Metellus was sure that they were headed for the capital. A name kept coming up: Luoyang.

And Luoyang appeared before them one evening towards dusk after many days of journeying from the place where they had been taken prisoner. It was, for these people, what Rome was to them, and Metellus could not help but admire the large city surrounded by imposing walls and mighty towers made of huge blocks of stone cut with exceptional skill. Grandiose buildings of a different style rose inside the walls as well: temples, perhaps, or aristocratic palaces. Great leafy-boughed trees loomed up everywhere, lit by the last rays of the setting sun. The sky had been overcast and the sun was veiled but, nonetheless, that enormous disc descending at their backs behind the crests of distant mountains spread a sanguine glow over towers, palaces, spires and pinnacles, igniting continually changing reflections in the painted wood, in the bronze, in the multi-coloured ceramic.

Metellus and his men, despite the worries gnawing at them, were awe-struck, realizing that they were probably the only ones from their world ever to have seen such wonders. But the thought immediately occurred to them that they might never have the chance to tell anyone about them. Their isolation was compounded by a lack of information. Separated even from Dan Qing, the only person who could help them interpret events or decipher signals that meant nothing to them, they felt totally at the mercy of chance. On the other hand, the passing of the days and the long hours of their forced march, during which nothing ever happened, had given them a sense of tranquillity and normality that in the end had inspired a certain unconscious optimism.

Before entering the city, the column stopped and Metellus noticed a brief scuffle near Wei's carriage. Soon after he saw a hooded horseman come forward between two armed men. It must be Dan Qing. They had covered his head in a black cloth bag so he wouldn't be recognized.

The column set off again and continued at a steady pace until they found themselves before the western gate of Luoyang. It was still open, and guarded by an armed military unit. A dispatch rider must have advised the guards about Wei's arrival, because an imperial cavalry squadron appeared immediately in a cloud of dust to escort the carriage of the young eunuch into the city. This seemed strange to Metellus: the new emperor's power in the capital must not yet be consolidated if he needed an escort of that size.

At least fifty soldiers on horseback lined up on both sides of the carriage with swords in their hands, while others lit torches to illuminate the darkening roads of the city. The prisoners remained at the end, along with the rearguard.

Plump-cheeked children hung out of the windows overlooking the street to admire that impressive parade, but the voices of their parents calling them back in sounded worried. Rare passersby hurried along, and an unreal silence seemed to have fallen on the city. Metellus exchanged an uneasy look with his centurions and they passed the word on to the men: 'Be careful. Anything could happen at any moment.'

'I've managed to loosen my bonds,' replied Antoninus. 'If I can get free, I'll help the others.'

'Good,' replied Quadratus, 'but don't take any initiative without the commander's orders.'

The column had arrived at a point where the road narrowed under an archway which rested on thick stone pillars. The horsemen had to regroup into a single file, since the passage was not wide enough for two men to ride through side by side. Just when Wei's carriage was proceeding under the archway, several men wearing red armbands, dressed in grey tunics and trousers, dropped swiftly from the top, sliding down silk ropes. They landed on the roof of the carriage and tried to slash it open with swords and axes. Fierce fighting broke out between the escort and the aggressors as Wei's men climbed on to the top of the carriage to fend off the attack.

Metellus and his men were forced to remain at a distance, closely guarded by a group of mercenaries of the rearguard with their weapons drawn. They must have received strict orders indeed regarding the prisoners, because they didn't take their eyes off them for a moment, as if nothing were happening just a few short steps away; as if the very survival of their leader were not at stake.

The assailants moved with deadly speed: their weapons flashed like lightning bolts, their sudden movements were imperceptible and unforeseeable, until the moment they struck.

Metellus saw Prince Dan Qing writhing violently at the heart of the clanging and fighting, his head still covered by the black hood. It was as though the fury of the battle that raged around him had invaded him as well, but the knots that held him only dug deeper into his skin. Metellus also caught a glimpse of Wei, stock still inside his carriage, paralysed by fear, possibly, or seized by a sudden desire to die. Or perhaps he was merely totally unmoved, his mind far away from the scuffle.

Everything happened in a few moments that seemed to stretch on infinitely. The group at the head of the escort, which had already passed under the arch, spun back around. When their horses reached the archway, they catapulted from their saddles, vaulting over the suspended span and landing firmly on the carriage roof.

Flying Foxes.

The first defenders, mostly Manchurian mercenaries, had already been killed or driven away, but the battle was on even terms now. The exchange of blows became so fast and so flawless that Metellus and his men nearly forgot that they were prisoners, becoming completely absorbed in the spectacle of a struggle that seemed more like the clash of demons animated by infernal energy than of human beings.

The men with the red armbands abandoned the roof of the carriage, springing to the ground so they could fight more freely, but in no time the numerical superiority of the Flying Foxes had won the upper hand. One of the assailants fell dead, then a second and a third: the first run through from front to back, another neatly decapitated, their comrade hurled against the wall with such force that his skull shattered. A fourth was taken alive and disarmed before he could manage to kill himself.

Only then did Wei leave the carriage and look around. The surviving Manchurian mercenaries approached with their lit torches and the scene of the massacre appeared in all its gruesome reality. The warrior who seemed to be the leader of the Flying Foxes approached the prisoner they'd taken alive and ripped the kerchief from his face, revealing a boy of perhaps twenty. 'You'll be sorry you didn't die when I get to work on you,' he snarled.

'Who are those men, Commander?' asked Publius.

Metellus tried to read meaning into the scene he saw before him, cut by deep shadows and bloody light. 'Wei was attacked by a group who must be against him taking power, but he won out in the end. You've seen for yourselves: the Flying Foxes are invincible.'

'We beat them,' replied Rufus.

'Well, we did, thanks to Severus's shields, and also because they weren't prepared for our style of fighting, but . . .'

Metellus's words were interrupted by a yell and a loud chorus of cursing: the captured rebel had been struck in the middle of his forehead by an arrow loosed from above, and he crumpled to the ground. All around the arrow shaft blood gushed copiously, covering the youth's body, which cramped up in violent spasms, as if he were refusing to surrender to the death that had already taken him.

Metellus turned in the direction from which the arrow had come and distinctly saw, on the rooftop of the house opposite him, a dark figure holding a bow. Two more arrows flew in rapid succession and two of the eunuch's guards dropped dead.

Only then was Wei's apparent impassivity perturbed. He shouted, 'Seize that man, damn you! Get him!'

Another arrow whistled by, missing Wei by a hair's breadth and sinking instead into the leg of one of his Manchurian mercenaries. The man fell to the ground, twisting and moaning in pain. The archer then took off, springing from one rooftop to another with incredible leaps.

In the confusion that followed the assault, Dan Qing, still hooded, had been forced back and was now only a few steps away from the Roman prisoners. Metellus whispered just loud enough to make himself heard: 'Prince, we're here.'

'Is that you, Xiong Ying? What has happened?' asked Dan Qing. 'What was all that uproar? Are you all right? Is anyone hurt?'

'We're fine. The men who launched the attack were after Wei, not us.'

'And what happened?'

'They were defeated. Three of them are dead. A couple of them got away. A survivor was taken prisoner but killed by one of his comrades posted up on the rooftops. The Flying Foxes are after him now. They've got their bows drawn . . .'

The heavy arrows that the Flying Foxes had nocked into their bows were more like harpoons, with silk ropes at their tails. Their purpose became clear to Metellus: they were shot into the beams under the eaves, where they stuck fast. The archers swiftly hoisted themselves up on the ropes and took off after the fugitive.

'He has a red lace on his arm, like the others did,' continued Metellus. 'He's moving fast, but Wei's men are close behind. It looks like they're flying! Gods, what is this place?'

'The Red Lotus,' murmured Dan Qing. 'Not all hope is lost, then. Can you see anything else?'

Metellus glimpsed the fugitive as he dropped behind the edge of a rooftop, reappeared briefly inside a terrace and then vanished entirely.

Wei was giving insistent orders to his guard, and half a dozen men shot off at a gallop in different directions. He then signalled to the escort, who regrouped in a compact formation. The corpses were gathered and loaded on to a wagon, then Wei re-entered his carriage and the convoy started up again.

Antoninus turned towards Metellus. 'What's going to happen now, Commander?' he asked.

'I don't know,' replied Metellus. 'But you try to stay alive. Whatever happens, try to stay alive.'

25

THE FULL MOON HAD RISEN behind the mountains, illuminating
the rooftops of Luoyang, glittering with the evening dew. Dark
shapes ran as light and fast as shadows after another figure who
jumped from one terrace to another, climbed nimbly up steep
pinnacles, leapt on to the branches of the great trees waving
their foliage over hidden gardens, and then scurried like a squirrel
towards the top of another building.

The Flying Foxes gave the fugitive no respite. They hunted
him down from the left and from the right, trying to drive him
towards a point where the city's houses sloped down towards
the walls. But the runaway appeared and disappeared continually,
taking cover whenever possible and then darting off in another
direction as soon as his pursuers had passed. At a certain point,
he managed to get enough of a lead to shin up a tower and
establish his stalkers' bearings, unseen by them. As soon as he
saw one of them sailing from one rooftop to another, he drew
his bow and ran him through in mid-leap. The lifeless body
plummeted to the road below. The resulting confusion allowed
the archer to disappear under a hatch and to descend a staircase
to the atrium, from where he reached the street. A dark archway
offered the fugitive refuge for long enough to allow the Flying
Foxes to scatter in the distance, like a pack of bewildered
bloodhounds who had lost the scent of their prey.

When all was calm, the mysterious figure removed the
kerchief that covered his face, revealing a delicate, feminine oval
shape and jet-black eyes that sparkled for an instant in the light
of the moon like a young tiger's. She opened the door at her

back with a light touch of her hand and found herself in an inner courtyard where a horse waited, its reins tied to an iron ring.

She loosened them and glanced back outside. She strained to hear, until she made out a slight buzz at the end of the street: a place with a lot of people, she hoped, where she could blend in unnoticed ... She walked at a fast pace in that direction, leading the horse by its reins, heading towards the dim light she could see at the road's end. She soon found herself at the edge of a little square bounded on the opposite side by a caravanserai. A confused babble emerged from the vast enclosure: people's voices joined with the loud snorting of Bactrian camels, the huge beasts that accompanied caravans for immense distances, bringing goods from one side of the world to the other. The girl was about to step out into the open when a cavalry squad passed by at a gallop with their unsheathed swords pointed forward. She drew back into the darkness and waited until their furious galloping faded into the distance. She checked that no one else was coming and crossed the square, facing the courtyard of the big caravanserai.

She took a look around as she tied her horse to a crib. The inner part of the enclosure was illuminated by a number of coloured lanterns that spread a warm light under the arches, over the baled merchandise, on the servants tending the animals and on the colourful characters who came from every part of the world, wearing costumes of every sort, conversing in a multitude of languages and getting ready to sit down for their dinner after concluding deals with the other merchants who frequented the place.

The girl realized that she was still wearing the red ribbon on her arm and she slipped it off as soon as she heard voices behind her. She tucked it under her belt and turned her head away, to avoid meeting anyone's eye.

'Easy on that crate! It's fragile, I said, damn you!' croaked the voice with a strong foreign accent.

The girl moved a little to let them by and a corpulent, dark-skinned merchant passed alongside her, accompanied by two servants who were dragging a wooden crate on a wobbly cart.

A Chinese scullery boy approached the man. 'Very honourable Daruma,' he said, 'your most honourable colleague Wu He awaits you for dinner.'

'I'll be there straight away, my boy,' replied Daruma, and he moved his bulky frame towards the entrance to the tavern at the end of the caravanserai.

Behind him, the girl reached out her hand and deftly snatched a swatch of cloth resting on top of a bale of raw wool. She draped it over her shoulders to hide her grey tunic and entered the tavern herself. She went to sit down at the end of the smoky room just like any other regular customer, in a dimly lit corner near the table where Daruma and the Chinese merchant were sitting.

A group of Mongolian musicians sitting under an archway were playing string instruments, producing low-pitched sounds that they accompanied with voices just as resonant. The soloist had a voice so deep that the girl could feel it vibrate inside her.

'It has been a terrible year . . .' started up the Chinese merchant.

'. . . production was down, parasites nearly wiped out the silk worms . . .' Daruma finished his words with a knowing air. 'I've heard this story before, Wu He. You're looking for an increase of 10 to 20 per cent. There has never been a good year since I've known you and your prices are always going up.'

'Ah! You mustn't complain!' retorted Wu He. 'Who knows how much those Westerners earn when they sell our silk to the foreign devils. Oh, by the way, do you know that some of them showed up in the city just a short time ago? Strange-looking characters with bizarre clothing. They were with the convoy of the eunuch Wei, may the gods preserve him, and they seemed to be prisoners.'

The girl overheard his words and unobtrusively slipped along the bench to get as close as possible to the two merchants, who were seemingly intent on their conversation.

Daruma noticed her move but didn't react and continued speaking with Wu He. 'Foreigners, you say? What did they look like?'

'Round eyes, beards as thick and dark as a boar's bristles, hair on their arms and legs like monkeys . . . wearing metal bracelets at their wrists. That's how a servant of mine described them to me. And then there was another prisoner, Chinese it seemed, to judge from his clothing, whose head was covered by a hood.'

The girl could not hold back. 'I could not help but hear your words, honourable gentlemen,' she said, 'and I would be very curious to see these foreigners, because I have never seen one in my whole life. They say they are truly horrible . . . Do you know where they've been taken?'

Wu He considered her in surprise, while Daruma shot her an enquiring look: that sudden remark from a stranger who had been listening in on their conversation seemed quite out of place.

Wu He began to speak nonetheless: 'As far as I know, it seems they were taking them to . . .'

He hadn't finished what he was saying when a group of imperial army soldiers entered the tavern. The girl immediately lowered her gaze and turned her head towards the wall, and that didn't escape Daruma's attention either. He grabbed her by the wrist and pulled her close to speak to her so that the others could not hear. 'Too slight a wrist to be a man's, but very strong nonetheless,' he thought. Aloud, he said, 'And now, if you don't tell me why you're interested in those foreigners, I'll tell those soldiers to search under your belt, where they just might find a pretty red ribbon . . .'

The girl's free hand slipped under her tunic, seeking the haft of her dagger, but Daruma's next words stopped her.

'There may be some friends of mine among those foreign devils, friends I care about deeply.'

The girl's hand slid off the dagger's hilt. 'Friends?' she repeated.

'Friends,' confirmed Daruma. 'Can we talk about it?'

'We can talk about it,' replied the girl.

'What's your name?'

'I can't tell you for the moment.'

'Why can't you tell me?'

'Because it's not the right time and because I don't know you well enough. You're a foreigner, after all.'

'All right, but now you'll do as I say. Go and wait at the caravanserai near the arch by the fountain.'

The girl nodded.

Daruma raised his voice and, pointing to a large jug in front of him, said loudly, 'Offer some pomegranate wine to these valiant soldiers! They will be tired and thirsty. Landlord! I'm paying!'

The girl obeyed and went to pour some wine from the big jug, helped by the tavern keeper. She handed it out to the soldiers, who tossed it down without giving her a second glance. When she had handed them their mugs, she slipped casually out of the tavern towards the caravanserai. The soldiers left shortly afterwards, mounting their horses and riding off at a gallop through the deserted city streets.

Daruma's bulk filled in the space of the open door. He was still accompanied by his colleague, who had taken up his litany again: 'As I was saying, honourable friend, the year was a very bad one, many mulberry trees dried up in the drought and . . .'

'All right,' replied Daruma. 'All right, I said. How much do you want for the whole lot?'

'Seven thousand five hundred *dariens*,' replied Wu He swiftly.

Daruma considered him with an appalled expression, then said, 'You are a thief and a bloodsucker. This is highway robbery, but I have no alternative.'

'No, don't say that, honourable friend! I'm certain that you'll be able to pass on this small increase to your clients, who will be calling you thief and bloodsucker before long. It's the law of our trade.'

'Fine, all right, but you really must excuse me now. I'm very tired and I would like to retire early this evening.'

Wu He bowed respectfully and left through a side door. The

girl stole a look at him, then walked over to her horse as if to untie the reins, but Daruma's voice sounded as if in her ear: 'I wouldn't do that if I were you.'

Yun Shan turned and was amazed to see that Daruma was still on the other side of the caravanserai, at a distance of at least thirty paces, and seemed to be meditating, his head leaning against the tavern wall.

His voice echoed even closer, in a completely natural tone: 'You heard what I said. There's something we still have to talk about, isn't there?'

The girl dropped the horse's reins and walked towards him, crossing the courtyard. 'How did you do that?' she asked.

'A little trick. You see, if you speak into this little niche in the door jamb you can be heard on the other side of the portico.'

'Interesting. What is it that we have to talk about?' asked Yun Shan.

'Why did you ask about those foreigners? And what are you doing here?'

'Why do you want to know? I don't know you.'

'It's very simple. Wu He's description leads me to believe that the prisoners he was speaking of are none other than Prince Dan Qing and his guard: men who come from the distant kingdom of Taqin Guo, the furthest to the west. When I heard you asking about them, I could not help but wonder whether both of us were interested in the same people. You are a girl dressed as a man, you wear the bracelet of the Red Lotus and you were running from the imperial guards.'

'Supposing that were the case,' she replied, 'who tells me that you're not a spy?'

'The fact that I didn't report you to the soldiers. You would have had no way out and I would have earned myself a pretty sum of money – enough to cover at least a part of the increase that Wu He has demanded on the consignment of silk I'm buying from him.'

Yun Shan looked askance at him without saying a word. She seemed to be studying him, and he was free to observe her freely as well now. The girl had thin but beautifully shaped lips, eyes that were bigger than usual and a little wrinkle between her forehead and nose.

'You're still not convinced?' asked Daruma.

'My master always told me that there is no better way to deceive a person than by winning his trust.'

'He's right. And you certainly have your wits about you. What can I do to make you believe me?'

'You won't have long to convince me. I'm about to leave.'

'You greatly resemble your brother, Prince Dan Qing,' Daruma said then. 'I'm the man who brought him back home from Persia.'

'Give me proof of what you are saying.'

'Only your brother can prove it to you, but first we must find him. We were supposed to meet in this tavern, but many days have gone by and he hasn't shown up, and what Wu He said makes me think that he may very well be the hooded prisoner. There's no doubt that the foreigners with the round eyes and bristly beards are his bodyguard. I recruited them myself in Persia. There are ten of them, but they're worth a hundred men. Formidable combatants: without them your brother would have never made it back, Princess Yun Shan.'

Yun Shan seemed to accept the evidence. 'He is their prisoner. I was there when Wei captured him. What I was trying to learn from Wu He was their destination . . . How did you know I was his sister?'

'I didn't know. It was a guess, based on how much you resemble him. Shall we go and sit over there?' he said, motioning towards a couple of woollen cushions and a carpet beneath an arch in the corner of the caravanserai. He blew out the lamp, so that the enclosure was lit only by the light of the moon and they could continue their conversation safely in the darkness.

Daruma drew a long sigh. 'How did it happen?' he asked.

'Wei seized the Monastery of Whispering Waters. He killed Master Wangzi.'

Daruma bowed his head, bringing a hand to his forehead.

'Did you know him?' asked Yun Shan.

'It was with him that I organized your brother's escape from Persia. Dan Qing and I separated at the foot of the climb that leads up to Whispering Waters. My caravan could never have passed the bridge over the chasm. But I left him in good hands: he had his guard, and the hospitality of Master Wangzi . . . So you were there as well.'

'Yes, I was there.'

'And now you belong to the Red Lotus. For how long?'

'A month. I had no one I could count upon and one of the monks at Whispering Waters told me to go to them.'

'Why were those soldiers after you?'

'We tried to free my brother.'

'And you failed.'

'We nearly succeeded. Did you learn anything more from your friend the merchant?'

'No. But we can try to get more information. How long ago did the attack take place?'

'Two *dan* after sunset.'

'And you were able to escape immediately?'

'We were forced to withdraw: the enemy forces overwhelmed us. They had a group of Flying Foxes with them. I'm not ready to fight them yet.'

'So if Wu He has learned about it, it means that his informer must have seen them not too far from here. And no longer than half a *dan* ago. The only place they could have been taking them, in an area so close to the caravanserai, is the Palace of the Bronze Tripods.'

'That's possible,' replied Yun Shan. 'That is a reasonable deduction.'

'It's more than possible,' countered Daruma. 'The Palace of the Bronze Tripods, as you know, is an ancient structure built in the era of Emperor Wudi that your father had restored, replacing most of the mud-brick enclosure walls with squared stone, but it still has a weak point. The problem will be how to inform the prince that we are preparing to free him, so that he'll be ready when the time comes.'

'I think I can find a way. The Red Lotus has many informers, even in the most inaccessible places.'

'Tell me what happened to his escort. They are remarkable men and must be saved as well, at any cost. I owe them, and I've made a promise I mean to keep. Were they all alive when you last saw them?'

'I didn't count them. But there seemed to be about ten of them.'

'Their commander is a man of exceptional character, and he's succeeded in winning your brother's trust, and perhaps his esteem as well. He's a tall man, quite muscular, with dark hair and amber-coloured eyes that look right through you . . . Did you see him among them? I mean, did you see a man who looked like that . . . alive?'

'Yes, I saw him. I think so . . .'

Daruma let out a long breath. 'I hope you're not wrong.'

Yun Shan hesitated. 'One of them looked at me . . .' she said.

'Please the Heavens, I hope Xiong Ying is alive. He's a famous warrior in his country, but he's also a man who has greatly suffered. He has seen the people he loved die without ever losing heart. A man who is true to his word, should it cost him his life. He doesn't deserve to finish his days racked by torture, nor do his men.'

Yun Shan thought of those deep, amber eyes which had fixed hers with the penetrating intensity of an eagle's gaze. The eyes of Xiong Ying . . . 'Why does he have a Chinese name?'

'Your brother gave him that name after he'd saved the prince from the Flying Foxes. You couldn't even pronounce his real name.'

'How do you intend to free him?' asked Yun Shan.

'We'll have to gather as much information as possible, as fast as we can. Every passing instant may be his last. This will be my headquarters. You can send me messages here when you like.'

Yun Shan stood to leave.

'Just a moment,' said Daruma.

The girl stopped.

'Is there any truth in the story that's circulating about you and Wei?'

Yun Shan tried to speak but her voice died in her throat and her eyes filled with tears. She rushed back to her horse and took shelter in the silence of the shadows.

Daruma remained alone. 'It's true, then,' he murmured to himself. 'It's all true.'

26

Yun Shan moved forward cautiously until she could see that there was no one on the road. She covered her face and flew off at a gallop. She raced like a ghost through the silent streets of Luoyang, bathed in moonlight. Her horse's hoofs seemed to barely touch the earth, as if it bore no weight at all on its back, as if the rider were one with its flashing legs and contracting muscles. It soared through deserted squares, leapt over enclosure walls, streaked past hidden gardens and shadowy courtyards, under sculpted porticoes, along avenues lined with big tripods, amid the dimming flames of pale lanterns.

She raced to escape her own thoughts, the painful memories of the past and the anguish of the present. To free herself of the shades of the dead, ghosts who galloped as swiftly as she did, veiling the light of the moon.

A shadow.

The shadow of a horseman at the end of the road.

She pulled up short, yanking the reins to one side, and spurred her horse on in the opposite direction, no longer recognizing the places she passed, not knowing where the wild galloping of her mount would take her.

A shadow, again.

A horseman, immobile under an arch, blocking the road that led out of the city.

Yun Shan spun around, certain she'd find the roads barricaded by bands of imperial soldiers, but she found them empty.

That horseman summoned her to a solitary challenge. And she would accept.

She pulled on the horse's reins and felt, behind her saddle, for the sheath that enclosed Tip of Ice, the sword forged three centuries earlier for her ancestor Xung Zhou, by a master from Yue. She leapt to the ground and unsheathed the weapon, which glinted blue in the light of the moon.

The horseman dismounted as well and drew his sword. He was dressed all in black, a deep blue silk scarf covering his face.

Step after step they drew close, until they were near enough for a lunge to transfix one or the other. Their blades cast iridescent reflections, gave off azure flashes, sliced through the air, at first with soft whispers. Their bodies moved in a dance in which their limbs sought perfect equilibrium, the concentration of strength from which death would spring.

Then the blades collided furiously in an argentine blaze, in a ringing out of clean, pure, increasingly rapid strokes. The lethal edges of the swords glided over steel and grazed human flesh, swooped down towards their eyes, or their brows, or their hearts, only to be deflected by a sudden flash of the other's mind, of the other's hand, of the other's blade.

All at once, both of them stopped, tips pointed forward, to prepare a new, meditated attack.

Yun Shan could tell that the force of her adversary was intact, while her own had been cracked by the breathless chase, by too many emotions, by the fear of her enemy's growing energy. She had to overcome the feeling that was weakening her: she had to spring forward with an eagle's shriek, a tiger's pounce. She would vault through the air to strike him from above like lightning, with a clean blow between his shoulder blades, reaching his heart from on high.

Reach the heart from on high.

She realized that those words were passing through the other's mind in that very instant. He dodged her blow by pirouetting on the tips of his toes, spinning like a child's top that skitters off across the floor. Tip of Ice plunged into the ground and Yun Shan fell to her knees next to the sword, her right hand still gripping the hilt, her left resting on the earth. Her adversary's blade struck, slicing the tie that fastened the veil around her neck. Off fell the veil, revealing her face in all its waxen perfection.

Her enemy would have been able to finish her off with a single swipe, but he stopped as if the vision of that face had pierced him to the depths of his soul. 'Princess Yun Shan . . .' he said, and bared his own face.

'Wei . . .' replied the girl. 'What are you waiting for . . . Wasn't it me that you wanted? Strike!'

'So it was you who wanted to kill me,' said Wei as if he hadn't heard her words.

'I wanted to free my brother.'

'Your brother has made you miserable and has driven me to despair,' he said, moving in a circle around her. 'He must suffer a wound that nothing can heal, on his own flesh. He must be made to suffer all that a man can suffer.'

'That will not restore anything you have lost.'

Wei did not stop Yun Shan from pulling Tip of Ice from the ground. His own sword was pointed downward as were his eyes, while he continued to walk round Yun Shan, who wheeled to face him.

Yun Shan stepped away from the centre of that imaginary circle, narrowing the space between them. She thrust out her sword towards her adversary's neck. 'You killed my master, Wangzi. And I will avenge him.'

'He wasn't your master. He was your brother's master. And I hold him responsible as well. Bad teachers must pay for the bad pupils they have spread through the world to cause the unhappiness of others.'

Tip of Ice was very close now to Wei's neck, a neck as white and pure as that of a maiden.

Wei raised his bowed head then and showed his tears. They fell freely from impassive eyes on to perfect cheeks. 'Only from you could I accept death. Only from you could I have peace, for I could not have love. Strike now, Yun Shan. You will never have another chance.'

Yun Shan delivered her blow, straight and true, but Tip of Ice glanced off Wei's forehead and withdrew, leaving a drop of vermilion there where the steel had penetrated his flesh, a bead as small as a drop of dew. The sword then vanished into its sheath.

'Consider this my last act of compassion towards you,' she said. 'You have chosen a road that leads to an abyss, a road that only the evil can follow. Free my brother and I will forget what you have done. Free my brother and the men in his escort. Retire to a monastery and no one will ever hurt you again. I give you my word.'

Wei drew close until his face was just a breath away. His eyes glittering with tears touched her heart but his voice was icy and cutting as he said, 'I will annihilate this cursed house that the Heavens have repudiated and I will found a new one. But if I should fail, I will go towards my final destiny without regret.' His voice seemed to break as he added, 'I am accompanied by a memory, Yun Shan, the memory of a feeling that not even the cruellest blade could cut from my flesh. Farewell, forever.'

He sheathed his sword and made an incredible leap on to his horse's back, landing lightly on the saddle. He spurred his mount off in the direction of the countryside and soon disappeared from sight.

Yun Shan's gaze followed him for a while, then she crumbled to the ground in tears.

THE HORSEMAN entered at a gallop from the main entrance of the imperial palace between the two rows of guards posted on watch until dawn and continued at full tilt all the way to the base of the majestic staircase that led to the main pavilion. He left his horse then to the care of the grooms, who had promptly rushed up, and bounded up the stairs to the atrium, which was illuminated by six large lit braziers in monumental bronze tripods.

An elderly palace official came to greet him with deferential solicitude. 'Noble Lord.'

'What happened today is unheard of. I was attacked in my own city. I risked death at the hands of the Red Lotus!'

The old man bowed, confused. 'I'm aware of what happened, honourable Wei, and we are doing everything possible to . . .'

'I don't want everything possible,' shouted Wei. 'I want those men destroyed! Where are your spies? What are your informers doing? My life is in danger between the walls of my own palace!'

'The Red Lotus enjoys the complicity of a great number of people, My Lord, many of whom profess fidelity towards the imperial house. It is nonetheless fortunate that you have managed to capture Prince Dan Qing.'

'Fortune has nothing to do with it. I've captured him thanks to my ability, and thanks to the fact that I saw to matters myself,' retorted the eunuch. 'I am surrounded by bunglers and imbeciles. I can trust no one but myself!'

The old official continued speaking as if he had not heard this outburst. 'The emperor is dead, although no one has been told, and his son is your prisoner. You have only one remaining goal to attain: winning over the people and, with them, the favour of the Heavens.'

'What do you mean to say?' asked Wei, suddenly calm.

'You must convince the people that you are an instrument of the Heavens, sent to punish an unworthy dynasty. At that point there will be no limits to your power. Perhaps you will even succeed in reuniting the three kingdoms, and unifying our entire country behind a single border, as is right and just.'

'And found a dynasty that will die with me . . .' Wei observed sarcastically.

'That's not so. A lineage can be created. Don't you realize how often empresses who had no children of their own deceived their husbands by presenting them with the son of a slave? If sterile mothers can beget heirs, why can't the same be true for a father? Believe me, Powerful Lord, what you have to do now is to win the public favour.'

'How can I do that? They do not love me. That much is certain.'

The silence of the night was so deep that the soft sputtering of the oil lamps could be made out, and the light, intermittent breath of the northern wind. For a moment, footsteps could be heard crossing the outer courtyard, then nothing.

The old man seemed to have finally found a suitable answer. 'Because they have built up an image of you that does not correspond to the truth.'

'In the sense that I'm much worse than what they can imagine. And there's no doubt about that either. But tell me what you have in mind.'

'It will soon be time for New Year celebrations. For many years now, due to the turbulence that has saddened our people, the festivities that they were accustomed to no longer take place.'

'Festivals, lights, dragons of coloured paper that puff smoke from their nostrils . . .'

'And combat between prisoners.'

'Don't tease me with your riddles. Get to the point.'

'They say that those barbarians you captured along with the prince are formidable fighters. Is it true that they come from Taqin Guo?'

'It seems so. And their looks confirm it.'

'I have consulted the secret texts saved from the fire of the Great Library of Luoyang. It seems that in their country they practise a rather barbaric but interesting custom. They say it is their most eagerly followed spectacle. Prisoners, or professional warriors, do battle before the public in large constructions with tiered seating.' He stopped a moment, for emphasis. 'Have them fight in the great courtyard of the palace, at the foot of the staircase, and open the courtyard to the people.'

Wei seemed to fade away for a moment, his gaze lost behind distant visions.

'Doesn't that seem like a good idea?'

'Yes, perhaps. There's a group of fierce, savage Xiong Nu, recently captured near the Great Wall, who could serve as their adversaries.'

'With all respect, Powerful Lord, I believe that the battle would be even more spectacular if their adversaries were much more fearsome.'

'Aren't the Xiong Nu fearsome enough? Who are you thinking of? Who else is worthy of facing the barbarians from Taqin Guo?'

The old man frowned and lowered his eyes before saying, 'The Flying Foxes.'

'You know very well that that's not possible,' replied Wei after a moment's hesitation.

'Why not, Powerful Lord? What prohibits it?'

'The common sense that one should have at your age. The Flying Foxes are, and must remain, without faces and without bodies, in order to inspire as much terror as possible. Showing them in public combat in the light of day would make them seem like flesh-and-blood human beings. Therefore vulnerable.'

'I understand your point of view, and I appreciate your great wisdom, but seeing them in action against the most fearsome warriors of the West would make everyone realize that it is impossible to oppose such a force.'

'The spectacle would be for the men of the Red Lotus, you're saying.'

'I'm certain that a great number of them will be present in the crowd.'

Wei began to pace backwards and forwards down the huge atrium, his figure standing out as he passed before the spectral light of the moon. 'And you think this would win me the people's approval?'

'Without a doubt.'

Wei shook his head, perplexed.

The old man started speaking again: 'The barbarians should be dressed in their armour and carry their own weapons to make the fight even more exciting. And you will promise them their freedom if they should win. Their fury will be boundless! There's another reason why the Flying Foxes are their only worthy adversaries . . .'

'Another reason? What?'

'You may not know this, My Lord, but they are not the first to arrive in our land.'

'What are you saying?' asked Wei in surprise.

'Have you ever heard of the three hundred Mercenary Devils?'

'Of course. But it's only a legend.'

'It's the truth. The three hundred Mercenary Devils truly existed. More than three centuries ago they appeared on our western frontier as if they'd come out of nowhere. They occupied a redoubt on the border and showed no signs of wanting to leave. The head of our garrison, a good man who was entirely loyal, attacked them with the forces he had available but they proved to be such fearless adversaries that they could not be driven back. The chronicles of the time report that they used a strange combat technique, with their shields raised above their heads, arranged like fish scales . . .'

'What kind of story is this, old man?' interrupted Wei. 'It seems completely ridiculous to me. And how is it that I have never read of them in the texts that have survived the fire of the Great Library of Luoyang?'

'Because those chronicles have been kept secret. Only those who have seen the inscription on the rock of Li Cheng know their story.'

'Continue . . .' said Wei, and the old man thought he could see a fleeting, mysterious weakness in his eyes. He motioned to a servant who stood at the end of the room like a statue. He disappeared and shortly thereafter came back with a steaming pot from which he poured a tawny infusion into two embossed golden cups.

The two men sat back on their heels and drank, and then the old man continued his story. 'Emperor Yuandi learned of this episode and was greatly angered. He had the garrison commander's head cut off and sent a younger man with fresh troops with a definitive order to crush the barbarians. But the second man failed as well. The enemies came out into the open field, dragging machines no one had ever seen before which launched darts of frightening proportions. They then sallied forth unexpectedly and attacked in a closed formation, putting our soldiers to flight.

'This time, the astonished emperor asked just how many combatants there were and how many of our own would be required to wipe them out. He was told that five thousand men would surely be sufficient to crush those barbarians like disagreeable insects. But that was not to be. When the new contingent attacked they found themselves up against a fortification so innovative that all their efforts to take that modest dried-mud redoubt were foiled. The army became bogged down in the autumn rains, then froze in the chill of winter, while that trifling outpost – which had become a powerful fortress – gave no sign of intending to surrender . . . Must I continue, My Lord?'

'Continue,' replied Wei.

'Our commander then decided on an all-out attack, weary of waiting for them to surrender because of hunger. He ordered his men to storm the walls, but even this endeavour ended in disaster. Trenches which had not existed opened under the attackers' feet, walls of flame rose before them, boulders fell from the sky and lethal darts mowed down their ranks. When our forces finally managed to open a breach, they found a second wall of hewn stone before them. And side towers, from which more arrows rained down . . . The assault was transformed into a bloodbath.

'The emperor realized that he had no choice but to unleash a vast offensive, but he didn't feel he could destroy men who had defended themselves with such valour. Instead of sending a new army, he sent a teacher.'

'A teacher?'

'Yes, My Lord. A teacher of Chinese, who was welcomed and treated well by the barbarians, who proved to be much less barbaric than anyone had imagined. By the end of the winter, their leaders had learned our language well enough to be able to hold an elementary conversation. At that point, the teacher asked them a number of questions suggested by the emperor himself: who they were, where they came from, why they had stopped in that place and why they had fought so fiercely.

'They replied that they came from a distant land which they considered the greatest empire on earth. An empire with over ten thousand cities, an empire that contained a sea even greater in size than itself, crossed by thousands of ships . . . All of the evidence pointed towards the fabled Taqin Guo.'

'The same people, then . . .' murmured Wei, as if talking to himself.

'The same,' confirmed the old man. 'They said they had participated in a great battle against the Persians. They had fallen into an ambush and most of their comrades were slaughtered after strenuous resistance. Their unit alone succeeded in breaking through and making its way to safety. All roads were blocked except those that went east, so that was where they headed. They marched for a year until they reached our borders.

'Upon hearing their story, the emperor asked them to enter his service as his personal guard. They accepted, and in the missions entrusted to them they showed such valour that they came to be considered invincible and nearly immortal. After many years in the emperor's service, he discharged them and gave them lands to farm in a village called Li Cheng, where it is said that their descendants still live. The emperor decreed that only they were worthy of accompanying him for all eternity, when his time came.'

'Why have you told me this story?' asked Wei in the end.

'Because those men became legendary, and they still are today. Only a legend can defeat another legend: the Flying Foxes against the warriors of Taqin Guo.'

'And you truly believe that this would win me the people's approval?'

'Without a doubt. Seeing the Flying Foxes in action and realizing that men of such incredible ardour and ability have vowed to serve you would leave no doubts about the legitimacy of your power. And there will be no limits to your ascent. One day you will unite the three kingdoms under a single sceptre and go down in history as the saviour of our country.'

'Do you imagine that I care about any of that?' asked Wei, an almost absent expression on his face.

The old man bowed his head with a slight sigh and did not reply.

The wind had picked up and a window shutter creaked somewhere. A dog howled in the distance and the flames in the braziers seemed to be dying away.

'It's late,' said Wei all at once. 'I wish to retire. See to it that their weapons are restored to the warriors of Taqin Guo. Their armour and ornaments as well. They will fight the Flying Foxes in seven days' time.'

'I shall do as you say, My Lord. You will not regret it.'

Silence fell again between the two men, sitting on their heels facing one another.

A song passed through the night, or perhaps the sigh of the wind. It was the last sound to be heard before the hush that precedes the dawn.

27

METELLUS SPENT THE DAYS of their imprisonment agonizing over what destiny held in store for him and his men. Might help arrive from outside, and if so when? Although he was alone in a cell, he tried to stay in contact with his men by calling out to them or by knocking against the door with his knuckles to let them know he was there and to keep them from giving up. He knew how much his own attitude affected theirs. He had promised that he would bring them home, and he devoted the long hours of solitude to imagining and planning how he would succeed, but the bare walls of his cell, interrupted only by a high window near the ceiling, through which a dim light filtered, seemed to preclude any hope.

There was no situation in the world so bad, he thought, that a worse one could not be found. Compared to this harsh isolation, the atrocious conditions at Aus Daiwa seemed almost preferable. There at least he'd had contact with his comrades, and the chance to give a little assistance and help to those who needed it. He thought of Uxal, of his rough show of friendship, and he wondered what he would have done or said had he found himself in this prison with them.

Every night, before sleeping, he turned his mind to his ancestors and to Clelia, and in the dark he tried to give shape to her face, to her dark, shiny eyes, to her soft, full lips. And her features, recalled by his melancholy, made him think of those of his son – so far away, so lost. Alive, perhaps, or dead, defenceless, a victim of uncontrolled power. And he thought too of Aurelian, his brave and loyal friend, and hoped that he would be a bulwark, both to his homeland and to his son.

At times, among these sensations emerged another, unexpected and disturbing: the feverish eyes and enigmatic gaze of Yun Shan, the girl with whom he'd exchanged a fleeting glance at the monastery before being dragged away along with Dan Qing. The thought of her gave him a strange feeling, a confused sense of fascination and even attraction.

But then he realized that his thoughts could go nowhere in that desolate, silent place, and he tried to keep his mind occupied with other activities – calculations and memory games. He tried to recite the cantos from Virgil's *Aeneid* by heart, calling upon his youthful studies, or the first chapter of Xenophon's *Anabasis* in Greek, which he had so often read aloud from his desk in school.

His only contact with the outside world came when food and water were passed through a slot in the door and he could see the face of his jailer for a few moments: an old man, with a long white beard. One day he realized that he'd lost contact with his comrades. They weren't answering him any more; he inferred that they had been transferred somewhere else, and he was seized by profound despondency. Now he was surrounded only by silence. The whole building seemed to be empty and his voice calling out to them was swallowed immediately in the darkness.

After a few days of this non-living his mind began to waver. He realized that these conditions might last for months, even years, or perhaps forever, and he would not be able to bear it. He tried to imagine what he would do if he were in the place of those holding him prisoner, but every hypothesis seemed unlikely because he could not guess at how their alien mentality worked. He decided that when he could no longer bear that absolute nothingness, he would take his own life, honourably, as a Roman. But up until that time he was resolved to keep his mind sharp and his body fit. The strangest thing about the prison was the relative abundance and variety of food, the excellent quality of the water and even of the amber-coloured infusion that every so often was served along with a meal.

One night, shortly before dawn, he heard noises – doors creaking, bolts being rattled. Then silence fell once again.

He tried to feel his way to the door but he realized that he was no longer in the place where he had always been. He soon found the door on another wall. How could that be? He felt anguished and disoriented. Was he really losing his mind?

He heard the same sounds again. He leaned his ear against the door to hear better and, to his enormous surprise, the door gave way under the pressure and fell open. Metellus found himself in a corridor dimly lit by a bronze oil lamp and started to advance cautiously. The corridor was quite short and led to a large room lined with other cells. There appeared to be no way out. How could he make sense of this absurd situation?

He went to one of the doors and touched the bolt.

A voice in Latin asked, 'Quis est?'

He recognized Martianus's voice. 'Is that you?' he asked.

'It's me, Commander! What are you doing out there? And where did you go to? We haven't heard your voice in days.'

'I don't know,' he answered. 'My door was open.' He tried to draw the bolt. And found Martianus standing in front of him, incredulous.

'What's happening?'

'I don't know,' answered Metellus. 'I don't know.'

'Hey!' came the voice of Quadratus. 'Commander, is that you?'

'We're here!' other voices exclaimed.

Metellus unbolted the doors one by one and liberated his men. They embraced. It seemed impossible that they should find themselves together again after such total, distressing isolation.

Balbus slapped a hand on his shoulder. 'What a pleasure, Commander. But now what happens? It doesn't look like we can get out of here.'

'I think not,' replied Metellus. 'But at least something will happen. If they've reunited us, there must be a reason.'

Lucianus started to inspect the walls painstakingly, swearing in Greek as he realized that the building was a box of stone without entrances or exits. 'Does anyone remember how we got in?' he asked.

Rufus scratched his reddish hair. 'May I drop dead if I've ever seen a single corner of this hole before.'

'It was dark when they brought us in,' recalled Septimius.

Publius approached Metellus. 'Commander, how can you explain this situation? None of us recognizes the place we find ourselves in. No one remembers how we got here and there's no apparent way to get out. Yet someone left the door of your cell open. Whoever that was must have got in and out somehow.'

Metellus reflected in silence, then said, 'There's only one explanation: we've been transported to a different place from where we were brought at first.'

'Commander,' replied Antoninus, 'I wake up if a cockroach crawls across the floor.'

'Not if they've narcotized you,' retorted Metellus. 'It wouldn't have been at all difficult for them to put something in our food or water.'

He hadn't finished speaking when they heard a sound coming from one of the open cells, a kind of squeaking like stone rubbing against stone, and a man appeared dressed in a long green silk tunic. It seemed to all of them that he had materialized before them in that very moment, like an apparition.

'Which of you is Commander Xiong Ying?' he asked.

'I am Xiong Ying,' said Metellus, stepping forward. 'How do you know my name in Chinese? Has the prince sent you? Have you come to free us?'

The man in the green tunic did not answer his questions, but motioned for him to follow and went back into the cell he'd come from.

Metellus and the others followed him into the cell where Septimius and Rufus had been locked up and saw that the back wall was open: the entire wall had rotated upon itself on a hinge, like a door, and opened up on to another space beyond it. Having crossed the stone threshold, they stopped short and considered the amazing vision before them. Lined up alongside each other on wooden hangers were their suits of armour, in perfect condition. The red crest and shiny metal of Metellus's helmet made it stand out from all the rest.

'What does all this mean?' asked Metellus in Chinese.

'That I'm here to offer you your freedom,' replied the man, saying the words one by one so he was certain to be understood.

'Explain yourself better,' Metellus insisted. 'Do you mean that we're free to leave?'

'Freedom is a precious possession,' replied the man, 'and must be earned.'

Metellus understood that they could hope for no good to come out of this strange situation.

'Tomorrow we celebrate our New Year. Our lord, the most honourable Wei, has decided to revive an ancient custom from the first years of the dynasty: foreign prisoners fighting in a contest against our best combatants. If they win, they are granted their freedom. If they lose, they are buried in the cemetery of foreigners with their armour and their weapons.'

Metellus drew a long breath.

'What is he saying?' asked Rufus.

'He's saying that we'll have to fight against their best warriors if we want to regain our freedom. In a kind of gladiatorial battle.'

'Tell him we're ready,' said Quadratus. 'We're not afraid of anybody.'

'That's right. Better the quick blow of a sword than rotting away in this hole,' confirmed Publius.

All the others nodded.

'We're ready,' said Metellus. 'What are the rules?'

'No rules,' replied the man in the green tunic. 'It's a fight to the death. There will be no interruptions until the last of you, or the last of your adversaries, is dead.'

Metellus translated these words and looked into the eyes of his men, one by one, the best men he'd ever had under his command. He studied them as if he were inspecting them for the first time: the senior centurion, Aelius Quadratus, centurion Sergius Balbus, *optio* Antoninus Salustius, legionaries Martianus, Publius, Septimius, Lucianus, Rufus and Severus, good with their swords and with their javelins, fine marchers, undaunted by hardship, lovers of wine and women, tough-skinned and tough-souled. Soldiers.

He had no doubts when he turned to the man in green and answered, 'We accept.'

The man nodded in acknowledgement of his decision and left. A massive bronze door opened at the end of the room and he disappeared through it.

'That's why they were feeding us so well,' said Martianus. 'I don't know whether the rest of you have noticed, but we've been given a fighter's diet: marsh grain, meat, vegetables, fish, eggs.'

'I noticed that it was all good, but that had me worried. A man condemned to die can usually expect a good meal,' commented Rufus.

'What shall we do, then?' asked Severus.

'We'll prepare for combat,' replied Metellus. 'Don't be deceived. They're going to put their best up against us, and you've already had a taste of how indomitable they are.'

'Are you talking about the Flying Foxes, Commander?' asked Balbus.

'I'm afraid so,' replied Metellus. 'Listen, the only reason they'll have us fight is because they are sure we won't win. They may very well pitch us against a superior force. We may be outnumbered, or their martial skills may be far better than ours, or perhaps both things together. But we're soldiers and we're not afraid of death. Refusing to do battle would certainly not save us, while we can't rule out the possibility of surviving the fight and regaining our freedom. Our only option is to fight with courage and tenacity. The worst that can happen is that we'll sell our lives dear and have been granted a soldier's death. The best that can happen, as I've said, is that we walk away from the battle free men. Does anyone have anything to say?'

Balbus and Quadratus looked at their men and replied, 'I think we all agree with you, Commander.'

'Fine. Then you centurions will prepare your men for battle.'

Quadratus nodded and turned to his comrades. 'First of all, each man must inspect his armour, his sword, his long arms. Everything. We can't exclude some hidden trick on their part. Then we'll have to establish a battle plan. I fear that the most difficult test of our lives awaits us.'

Severus and Antoninus, the two *fabri*, picked up the shields and examined them.

'Good,' said Severus. 'It seems they haven't noticed anything.'

'What do you mean?' asked Metellus.

'We told you we had a surprise for you when we rebuilt our weapons in the caravanserai at the border. Here it is: a little improvement that we finished when we were at the prince's village. See this small lever behind the straps?' he asked, turning to the other soldiers. 'Well, all you have to do is pull it and eight steel spikes poke through the leather exterior and stud the whole surface. Our enemies won't know what to expect because they've never seen us in action, and this will really take them by surprise.'

Balbus was about to pull the lever but Antoninus stopped him. 'Don't do that now, Centurion. It's a spring mechanism that can only be used once. When the leather is pierced, you can see the hidden spikes and then, "Goodbye, surprise." At that point we'd have to take the shields apart and replace the leather. All we can do is hope that our trick will work when it's time to use it.'

'I see.' Balbus nodded. 'All right, men, as soon as you've inspected your arms, we begin training. We'll form two units and fight each other. We must prepare for the incredible speed of our adversaries. Our defence must be impenetrable. Remember the words of the poet, whose name I can't remember just now: "A fox has many tricks. The porcupine just one, but a good one."'

'Archilocus,' suggested Metellus.

'Right,' replied Balbus. He went on: 'It's not important that each blow be lethal. Every wound inflicted is an advantage for us because it will disable the enemy, slowing down their movements and their reaction time. It will weaken them and make them more vulnerable. I don't think we'll be able to use our bows, but our javelin-throwers will strike whenever the enemy tries to attack from above. Rufus, you're the best. Every throw must hit its mark.'

Metellus watched them all day from a corner of the room. Towards evening the bronze door opened again and two servants came in with food. He signalled for the training to cease and the men sat down for their meal.

'Why do you suppose they transferred us from one place to another after narcotizing us, if that's what actually happened?' asked Martianus.

'To prevent anyone from noticing us during the transfer. Our appearance attracts a lot of attention,' replied Metellus. 'That makes me think they were afraid that someone might try to free us. Perhaps we haven't been forgotten. We must not lose hope. And what we've been asked to do, men, is what we've been training for our whole lives: combat.'

The man in the green tunic appeared later and accompanied them to another room beyond the bronze door, where beds had been prepared for the night.

The men lay down one after another and Metellus listened at length to their subdued conversations. Martianus and Antoninus were very quietly playing *mora*. Quadratus was pacing back and forth along the external wall, his hands folded behind his back, while Balbus ran a whetstone up and down the length of his sword. He wore the stone at his neck, hanging from a little iron chain, as if it were a pendant.

Metellus thought at length about the ups and downs of fortune over the last years: how fate had inflicted defeat and imprisonment upon him, then offered him his freedom, only to cast him into prison again, and demand this final test of him. The last, perhaps. But who could say? He knew that he would go into battle accompanied by the thoughts of those he loved and had loved and that there could be no better *viaticum*. He would face destiny under the protection of his ancestors, the

Aquilas, renowned for their virtue and their devotion to what they believed in. It was they whom he asked for assistance and protection, not the gods, to whom he hadn't prayed since he was very young. There were too many of them, almost as many as there were men, and this meant, for him, that if God had to hide behind so many faces, he didn't deserve to be sought out. He fell asleep, finally, and slept peacefully until dawn.

A servant brought them breakfast and they all sat on the floor to eat, conversing in a relaxed fashion as if this might not be their last meal.

Metellus stood up first and began to put on his armour, but Antoninus came to his aid and helped him to fasten his shoulder straps and his *lorica*. He slung the baldric over his commander's shoulder and hooked on the scabbard. Metellus hung the second *gladius* from his belt: the finest of weapons, passed on from father to son for seven generations, made of excellent steel with an oak hilt. It made a hard metallic sound when Metellus slipped it into its sheath. Last of all, he put on his helmet and tied the cheek-pieces under his chin.

The others donned their armour as well, helping each other to do so, and when they had finished they picked up their heavy curved shields. Martianus and Rufus took their javelins and clutched them to their shoulders. They were ready. Septimius kissed the amulet he wore at his neck. Severus, who had once been Christian, made a hurried and almost secretive sign of the cross. Antoninus lay his forehead against the wall, softly murmuring words of ancient magic. Then the bronze door opened and the man in green motioned for them to follow him.

They marched down a long corridor two by two, behind their commander and the centurions. The rhythmic sound of their nailed boots made their courage rise within them. Roman soldiers on the march: who could stop them?

Another door opened suddenly at the end of the corridor and they were momentarily blinded by the sun. Then they came out into a square flooded with light. And full of armed men. There were two rows of soldiers on horseback decked out in full armour, bows slung over their shoulders. Metellus recognized the mercenaries who had escorted them to Luoyang.

As they proceeded down that garrisoned path, they neared a massive gate with three doors through which they could see a blackish blur and hear a loud hum of voices. Many people were still trying to get in, but the arena seemed to be packed. When Metellus arrived at the entrance he felt a shiver run down his spine like the first time he went into battle. It seemed strange but then, as he looked around him, he realized where the sensation was coming from. He locked into two dark, shiny eyes with a penetrating, enigmatic gaze. The same gaze that had moved him at the monastery before they had taken the road to imprisonment: Yun Shan was here!

He exchanged her look with soulful intensity, without understanding what message he was transmitting, without knowing whether her presence represented hope or the final seal. For an instant, he had the feeling that she was trying to get closer, but he soon lost her from sight.

Contrary to what he had expected, they were not led directly into the vast arena that could be seen beyond the triple door, but taken to a side entrance inside a kind of a guardhouse adjoining the big square, from which they could watch what was going on through large windows.

They saw dancers enter in marvellous silk costumes, waving long coloured banners tied to poles that they twirled to create beautiful designs in the air. Cloth dragons then made their appearance, twisting as though they were alive and blowing smoke from their nostrils.

The square seemed huge. It was flanked on either side by tiered seats and closed off at the end by a large stage on which they could make out a figure dressed in black seated under a red canopy. Standing alongside him were more men, dressed in black as well, wearing gowns that came down to their ankles, topped by short, long-sleeved tunics.

Once the swirling of the dancers and dragons had finished, wrestlers were led in. They performed a number of spectacular holds with great flair and skill. This was followed by sword duels between Chinese warriors and barbarians from the north, the notorious Xiong Nu. Almost all of the duels ended with the deaths of the barbarian combatants and Metellus and his men had the chance to closely observe how the Chinese used their swords, how they feinted, how they struck and how they managed to dodge their opponents' blows.

After the last battle was over, a gigantic Mongolian seized a mallet and forcefully struck a big bronze bell. Upon hearing that sound, which echoed throughout the whole city, the officer who had been guarding Metellus and his men pushed them towards a door that led into the square. Metellus understood that the time had come, and signalled for his men to follow.

Suddenly they found themselves in the immense courtyard of the royal palace, which was crammed with spectators. Metellus looked around in a daze as the buzzing of the crowd died down almost completely, and was replaced by an unnerving, unreal silence.

He started at the sound of Sergius Balbus's voice. 'They were waiting for us, Commander,' said the centurion.

'I'd say so,' replied Metellus. 'And now the party can begin.'

28

THEY ADVANCED TOWARDS the centre of the large rectangular space, glancing around at the crowd, feeling all eyes upon them. Metellus was in the middle, with Quadratus, Severus, Lucianus and Martianus to his right. To his left were Balbus, Publius, Septimius and Rufus. The two centurions took positions at the sides, as if they were commanding maniples of hundreds of men. They were the flanks of that minuscule army, the anchors of that little prow. Antoninus, the only *optio* and Balbus's lieutenant, held the centre.

Metellus wore only his two swords; all the others bore their heavy shields in their left hands, holding them close to their shoulders, so that for someone watching from the side, they looked like a single shield, while they were barely visible from the front.

The air was cool, the light clear, the silence so deep it was eerie. They had expected a loud roar from the crowd and were disoriented by that breathless hush. The voice of the announcer sounded quite clearly: 'Our great benefactor, the most honourable Wei, has the pleasure now of offering you a spectacle that you would never have been able to imagine. An ancient, long-forgotten custom that once served to invoke prosperity in the new year: a ritual in which the Sons of the Heavens did battle against ferocious barbarians, the enemies of the Supreme Order of our land. You have seen the savage Xiong Nu annihilated by the warriors of our imperial guard. Now you will see ten foreign devils, men who have come from the remote land of Taqin Guo, hairy, frightening creatures with round eyes, armed with terrible weapons, so strong that they have subjugated all the nations of the West, pitted against the most valiant of our combatants, the heroes who keep watch over our peace, day and night: the Flying Foxes!'

Metellus turned to seek the eyes of Yun Shan, a *viaticum* for this last journey, but he saw only a disorderly throng. He said to his men, 'We'll have the sun in our eyes, but it's high enough so that it won't trouble us too much. Stay ready.'

Yun Shan had not lost sight of him for an instant. Her eyes were fixed on the Roman commander's magnificent breastplate, on the crested helmet that gleamed in the sun and on the drawn features of his face.

A voice very close to her ear startled her: 'Princess.'

'Daruma.'

The Indian merchant was behind her. 'It's all ready, Princess Yun Shan. Baj Renjie, the commander of the guard, is on our side, fortunately. He has found five horses-that-sweat-blood, the swiftest that exist, and promises to bring your brother to safety. My little beast is ready as well. Afterwards, there will be a boat waiting for the two of you, hidden in a bend of the Luo Ho river, just after the ford. Everyone will be occupied here, watching the fight, at least for a while. But tell your friends we have to move fast. This battle will be over soon.'

Yun Shan couldn't take her eyes off Metellus. Daruma, at her side now, noticed. 'Forget him, Princess. He's a dead man. There's nothing you can do to save him.'

Yun Shan lowered her head and started to make small gestures near her chest which someone, standing on the other side of the square directly opposite her, was capable of deciphering. A red ribbon waved through the air for a moment and the princess turned towards Daruma. 'Our men are ready. They will be at the appointed place by the time you arrive. You can go now.'

'Aren't you coming?'

'Later,' said Yun Shan.

Daruma said nothing else and walked off in the direction of the exit, while Yun Shan pushed her way through the crowd to get as close as possible to the foreign soldiers, who were advancing slowly shoulder to shoulder. A drum began to roll, obsessively, with a thunderous boom, then went silent all at once.

Balbus was dripping with sweat under his helmet. 'How often I'd go to see the gladiators fighting! I never even wondered what those men might be thinking as they went to their deaths. Now I know.'

'Oh, really?' replied Rufus, clenching his teeth. 'And what were they thinking?'

'That everything is useless and nothing makes sense.'

'We've looked death in the face many times.'

'That was different. Then we were fighting to live. Now we're fighting to die.'

'Maybe it's just entertainment for them. Maybe they'll let us go when it's over,' said Septimius.

'Why should they?' retorted Publius. 'Death is the most exciting spectacle, after all, anywhere in the world. And that bastard down there decked out in black doesn't look all that warm-hearted.'

'That's enough,' said Metellus. 'If we have to die, we'll die as soldiers. All we must think of now is how to spend our energies as wisely as possible. No one can say what fate has in store for us. We don't have many javelins and our swords are too short. All we can do is defend ourselves.'

Lucianus took a sling out of his pocket. 'I've saved this,' he said. He opened his fist to show some lead shot. 'And these,' he added.

'Better than nothing,' nodded Metellus.

Publius pulled a couple of knives crafted from two big carpentry nails. 'These will be good for throwing.'

Smiling, Metellus marvelled at how ingeniously they were hanging on to life. 'Excellent. Now, get ready to close, at my command.'

Before he could go on, a terrifying shriek emerged from the mouth of one of the bronze dragons under the stage and out jumped a warrior of the Flying Foxes, armed with a sword.

Metellus breathed in deeply and drew both of his *gladii*. The cold hiss of the unsheathed steel cut through the unmoving air.

'Closed order,' he barked out, and the men moved their shields to a frontal position, walling themselves off in front and on the sides, with only the tips of their swords protruding. 'Get ready for the *testudo* if they decide to start flying.'

Another scream burst out and another warrior sprang from the jaws of a second dragon. Then a third, a fourth, a fifth, until the number of combatants was identical: ten against ten.

'All right. We can get started,' growled Metellus. 'An even fight.'

Their adversaries were very close now and brandishing their swords, which whistled through the air so fast they seemed almost invisible. Then one of them suddenly made an incredible leap and, as he was landing, his feet cracked into one of the poles from which the imperial banners flew.

Metellus saw his move and shouted '*Testudo!*' just in time. The pole crashed on to them and would have slaughtered them had not the roof of shields stopped it.

'Careful!' shouted Metellus. 'Their feet and hands are their most formidable weapons. Be ready the next time one of them jumps.'

Lucianus stepped back behind the line formed by his comrades and, as soon as Metellus ordered him to stop, placed his shield on the ground and started to twirl his sling. Rufus, on his knees, was weighing his javelin.

The circle of adversaries pressed close and their blows showered down from every direction with no forewarning; only the total closure of the Roman formation afforded them protection.

'They'll try to get in now!' shouted Metellus. 'Careful, careful!' And as he was shouting, one of the Flying Foxes vaulted up, rebounded off a comrade and went soaring through the air, followed by a second.

'Open up!' shouted Metellus at that very instant.

Lucianus's shot streaked through the air and hit the Chinese warrior full in the forehead. He dropped lifelessly to the ground in their midst. The other's assault was aborted when Rufus's javelin forced him to twist aside.

The furious response of the Flying Foxes was immediate: two of them flew through the air, whirling their swords, and tried to catapult into the centre of the enemy formation, but before they landed, the *testudo* closed up again and Severus shouted out an order. Eight steel spikes sprang from the leather which covered each shield and pierced through the feet of the two flying warriors at the moment they touched down. They fell to the ground screaming and were promptly finished off by Lucianus and Septimius, who ran them through with their swords.

Then the formation closed up again in a tight seal.

'We can make it, men!' said Metellus. 'We're already ten against seven. Don't let up. Stay shoulder to shoulder! Brace yourselves with your feet!'

Wei, livid with anger on his throne, turned to his adviser. 'If this continues, a new legend will be born. The foreign devils must die, immediately. But not all of them.' He gave a signal and four more warriors sprang from the dragons' mouths, wielding arms no one had ever seen before: jointed axes that they whipped through the air with a shrill whistle. In a moment they had joined the other seven.

'They've already admitted defeat!' shouted Metellus, trying to encourage his exhausted men. 'Fourteen of them against ten of us. Hold out! We can still beat them!'

The Flying Foxes exchanged understanding looks. Brief guttural sounds flew between them and, before the Romans had a chance to react, the four fresh warriors were upon them, flying over their heads. A lob of Rufus's javelin eliminated one of them and one of Publius's knives wounded another, but the other two landed on the *testudo* and hacked through the raised shields with their axes. The others were already managing to catapult inside the Roman formation, flourishing their swords. They finally broke through the obstinate resistance of the small contingent, forcing the compact group to do battle individually.

Those who remained outside started to advance in a semi-circle, whirling their swords faster and faster until their whistling turned into a dull roar in the spectral silence of the immense arena. When they were very close to the Romans, a cry as shrill as a falcon's echoed through the square and the man dressed in black sitting between the two bronze dragons on the stage got to his feet. He let his long robe slip off and he flew into the arena wearing only a light costume of black silk, brandishing a razor-sharp sword that glittered with blue reflections.

From her vantage point, Yun Shan shuddered. Wei was entering the field to lead the assault of the Flying Foxes himself! Her hand grasped the hilt of Tip of Ice under her cloak, but she stopped herself. She knew full well that if she were found out, it would be all over.

Wei shot in like a bolt of lightning and the assault was transformed into a violent onslaught. The Romans' shields yielded one after another to the Flying Foxes' deadly weapons and their cuirasses were ripped to shreds. The Flying Foxes coordinated their actions as precisely as if they were obeying a single brain: a single mind that contracted their muscles and stretched them into superhuman leaps, that commanded their swords to strike invisibly, piercing and slashing.

And now the crowd cried out, exploding into a roar as if liberating energy long suppressed. As if some mysterious fear or strange indecision had kept them silent until that moment.

Metellus fought alongside his men like a lion, dripping blood from every part of his body. He parried and returned blow after blow with his two *gladii*, but it was like fighting off a monstrous hydra with a thousand arms and a thousand swords. He saw Severus, his ingenious *faber*, fall, and then Publius, just after one of his flying knives had plunged deep into the shoulder of a

Flying Fox. He saw Rufus, the red-haired Sicilian, disembowelled by the swipe of a sword; he collapsed to the ground, holding his guts in his hand, futilely defended by Lucianus, daring slingsman, who was himself finished off by an enemy slash. He saw Septimius, blond Septimius, the great hunter, battling on with a maimed arm, howling like a wounded beast, blood spraying from the stump on to his assailant, until he was run through simultaneously by three swords. He saw Antoninus, who had lost every weapon, in a clinch with the enemy, sinking his teeth into the other's shoulder like a wolf, before taking stabs to the stomach and neck. He watched as Martianus dropped his broken sword to grasp his dagger but was stopped by hands and feet as hard as stones, and the sound of his shattering bones accompanied the rattle of death. Quadratus and Balbus were the last to fall: Balbus's chest caved in under a devastating kick and he was nailed to the ground by a dagger's blade, and then Quadratus was struck from behind and on his side by four adversaries as he tried to shield his fallen comrade. He crashed to the ground like a slaughtered bull.

Then silence, again.

METELLUS SWAYED on his feet, exhausted. His blood flowed copiously from many wounds: a single red stain covered his body. He felt that death was moments away, but time, in that grievous solitude, seemed to stretch out infinitely. He should have been dead and he couldn't understand why the final blow hadn't arrived. He ripped off his helmet and tossed it away, and then his breastplate, which fell to the ground at his feet.

Wei dropped his sword.

Metellus was panting. He wiped the blood from his eyes to see black death looming over him: the beautiful youth, with his raven hair and cruel eyes, who paced around him from left to right and from right to left and who could have made him fall just by looking at him.

Yun Shan, very close now, knew how the warrior of Taqin Guo would die: the tiger's blow, the secret handed down from generation to generation from Master Mo himself. A blow so fast that it was invisible. She knew that she could fend it off by absorbing a part of its lethal power. Yun Shan concentrated all of her energy into the chest of the wounded warrior, who still gripped his *gladius*. There, he was lifting it suddenly to strike, but Wei stopped him. His left hand slashed down and broke the arm that held the sword; Metellus let it drop with a groan of pain. At that very moment, the death blow descended, invisible, from the right. Yun Shan stiffened into a painful contraction, her eyes rolled up into their sockets and her heart stopped beating.

When she could see again, Metellus was stretched out on the ground lifeless while the crowd deliriously cheered the victor, who climbed the staircase between the two open-mouthed bronze dragons. Wei turned for just a moment, his gaze searching for something, and Yun Shan realized that he was looking straight at her even though he could not possibly recognize her at that distance. Her chest ached terribly, but she forced herself to make her way through the thronging crowd.

Wei, on the stage now, was relishing his triumph, while a group of servants removed the dead bodies and loaded them on to a cart.

'As you see, My Lord,' said his elderly counsellor, 'I was not mistaken. The people are with you.'

Wei nodded. 'Fine,' he said. 'You know what you must do now.'

The adviser motioned for a Manchurian mercenary to approach. He whispered something in his ear and the officer hurried off.

THE GIGANTIC ELEPHANT charged in a fury, goaded on by the Indian mahout, while Daruma watched closely from behind the corner of a nearby house. The animal drove his iron-plated tusks and headgear into the brick wall before him, producing a wide rent. Several Red Lotus fighters dropped into the breach and found a bewildered Dan Qing inside. They tied two ropes to the iron rings which bound the prince and urged on the elephant again. He pulled back, ripping the chains from the wall.

A moment later, Dan Qing was in the saddle of a swift horse, bolting off at a gallop with the comrades who had freed him right behind. Baj Renjie and several of his soldiers had stayed in place momentarily to take care of the guards who had rushed up, shouting, to give the alarm. From his observation post, Daruma saw a group of Manchurian horsemen arriving at full tilt from the area of the palace where the combat had taken place, and he realized that they had spotted Dan Qing breaking out. He had to stop them by some means, even at the cost of cutting off the escape route of Baj Renjie and his comrades, who were still occupied with the guards. He stuck two fingers in his mouth and whistled hard. A herd of camels, asses and mules was instantly driven into the middle of the road, obstructing it completely. The Manchurian mercenaries struggled to get through but even more animals flocked in to block their passage.

Dan Qing and his comrades disappeared at the end of the street, while Baj Renjie, trapped along with his soldiers, was captured and disarmed. Daruma, flattened against the wall of his hideout, breathed a deep sigh. He had had no choice, but at least he'd acted in time. Another instant of hesitation and the plan to free Dan Qing would have failed.

A NIGHT OWL perched on a skeletal trunk hooted mournfully, then suddenly took to the air, frightened by the arrival of a cart. Wings silently beating, it vanished into the dark.

The two cart drivers pulled on their mules' reins, stopping them short. They dismounted and opened the unhinged gate that led to the foreigners' cemetery, where a wide, freshly dug ditch was waiting for the corpses of the foreign devils. They hung a lantern from a tree branch, then grabbed the bodies by the feet and shoulders and dragged them to the edge of the pit, piling them up on top of each other. They stopped a moment to catch their breath and, as they were stretching their tired limbs, they saw a ghostly apparition that left them dumbstruck. It was a warrior – his face covered and a red ribbon on his arm – standing in front of them with a drawn sword. They took one look and spun around to run for it, but their heads, detached from their shoulders, fell directly into the ditch, while their bodies still lunged forward, driven by the impetus of the race they'd just begun.

The warrior's face was exposed now, revealing delicate feminine features. Yun Shan gave a long sigh and bent over the inert bodies of the Romans, turning them over one by one until she found the man who had led them into the arena for that desperate battle. She placed a hand on his heart and on his jugular vein, then bowed her head disconsolately.

She remained still, but a breath answered hers and a barely perceptible voice murmured, 'Yun Shan . . .'

The girl's head snapped up and she saw the foreigner turning his eyes to the martyred bodies of his fallen comrades.

'My soldiers . . . my brothers. I vowed to bring them home, and I led them to death . . .'

Yun Shan felt tears rise to her eyes. 'You're alive . . .' she whispered, passing her hand over his tumid features. 'You're alive . . .'

Metellus embraced her for an instant, letting the warmth of her body pervade his.

Yun Shan looked into his eyes. 'We haven't a moment to lose. Please, you must try to get up. We have to leave!' She helped him to his feet and supported him for the few steps that separated them from the cart. She set him down gently and hid him under the bloody rags that had covered the cadavers.

Just then the gravedigger who was to bury the dead bodies approached. He dropped down behind a bush before anyone could see him, trembling with fear.

Yun Shan sensed a presence, but when she took the lantern and looked around, her other hand gripping her sword, she saw nothing. She grabbed the hat of one of the cart drivers and threw his cloak over her shoulders before urging on the mules.

The cart swayed and squeaked its way off, soon disappearing into the darkness.

The gravedigger, finally free to take a breath, ran as fast as his legs could carry him to report that a girl had killed two live men to carry off a dead one. Most thought him mad; someone else, on the other hand, took him seriously.

29

Baj Renjie was brought into the presence of regent Wei that evening by a dozen Manchurian mercenaries. The first things he saw were the instruments of torture, and the thought of the savagery of those skilled in inflicting pain made him tremble. He knew he was completely at the mercy of an extraordinarily intelligent and incredibly cruel enemy, a man who hated the world for what he had suffered. Waves of panic washed over him and he had to restrain himself from falling to his knees and begging for mercy.

'Where are they headed?' asked the eunuch.

Baj Renjie drew a long breath and then said, all at once: 'I can't tell you anything you don't already know.'

'Then they're making for Li Cheng.'

Baj Renjie did not answer.

'And how does one get to Li Cheng?' asked Wei, unperturbed.

Baj Renjie could very easily imagine the monsters that were crouching in the apparently immobile swamp of the eunuch's soul. He called on his courage and said, 'I do not know, and even if you torture me I cannot tell you what I do not know. None but the initiated members of the Red Lotus know where Li Cheng is.'

'Do you take me for a fool?' shouted Wei. 'Even if you don't know where Li Cheng is, I'm sure you know someone from the Red Lotus.'

'Of course. But none of them has ever revealed the location of their hideaway. Much as your Flying Foxes won't speak if they are captured.'

Wei bowed his head and the fact that he would not show his face deeply alarmed Baj Renjie. He tried to imagine what expression the eunuch would have when he looked up again. But at that moment one of Wei's bodyguards walked in and, after prostrating himself, whispered something in his ear.

Wei raised his eyes and stared at Dan Qing's officer with an icy look. 'The body of the adversary that I defeated in the arena has been stolen . . . and two faithful servants of the country were indecently beheaded while they were attempting to give a decorous burial to those valiant barbarians. Can you explain why?'

Baj Renjie looked bewildered as the torturer took a step forward with every word that Wei uttered.

'What it means, in all probability, is that he wasn't dead, unfortunately. Otherwise why would he have been carried off?' Baj Renjie couldn't quite hide a scowl of disappointment.

'I understand how you must feel,' continued the eunuch. 'Your prince preferred a foreigner over you. A barbarian come from far away, a stranger. Isn't that so? I've been told that you regarded him with envy when he rode on Dan Qing's right, in the position of honour. I've even heard say that he was not required to bow in the presence of the prince: a privilege quite unthinkable.'

'You're mistaken. What you've heard has nothing to do with me. I never . . .'

'It's understandable. You've always been loyal to him. Who knows . . . perhaps you even cherished a hope, a dream, deep down in the heart of a faithful old soldier. The dream that he might have given you the hand of Yun Shan . . . and why not? Who would not desire that sweetly scented rose, that morning star? After all, you were the only one he could trust. Don't tell me that you weren't counting on it . . . And then this foreign devil walks in and takes your place. That's what happened, isn't it? And she – for it could have been no one else – goes off searching for his butchered body, runs the risk of dying herself to save his life. And she may very well succeed . . .' The torturer had stopped and was watching him without any expression, like an automaton. 'I, on the other hand, would certainly recognize your true worth, if you were to help me. Look at me, Baj Renjie. Look into my eyes and tell me that you are indifferent to this offer of mine.'

Baj Renjie did as he asked, and it felt as if he was staring into the eyes of a cobra. He felt ensnared by that look, depleted, crushed.

'How does one get to Li Cheng?' repeated the eunuch.

Baj Renjie hesitated, then spoke: 'All I can tell you is what I've heard. Rumour has it that the place is inaccessible. It seems that it can be reached by sailing up the Luo Ho river, but the boats which venture there vanish into thin air in the middle of the night. It is said that only a bird can reach the rooftops of Li Cheng.'

Wei half-closed his eyes. 'Only a bird. Perhaps you're right. Perhaps that is the only way.' He made a gesture with his hand and the torturer retreated silently, along with his acolytes, to a dark corner of the room. The eunuch stiffened, as if he had been seized by sudden pain, or by a thought. Or perhaps by a demon. A strange vibration ran through the large, shadow-filled room, intensifying into a soft argentine ringing; weak and barely perceptible at first, it became more distinct, as if carried in on gusts of the west wind that blew under the arches of the portico outside.

YUN SHAN watched the small bronze amulets hanging from a cord stretched over the entrance door. They jingled with every passing breeze, raising their voices to the wind that carried them far away.

A voice sounded behind her: 'Come inside now . . . It's raining.'

Yun Shan was sitting on the steps at the threshold. She answered without turning: 'What are you saying, nurse? The moon is out and the sky is clear.'

The old woman came to the door. Her face was the colour

of baked clay, her eyes were like slits and her grey hair was collected in a bun at the nape of her neck. 'An evil aura is raining down,' she said. 'I can feel it. Quickly, come inside!'

Yun Shan passed under the amulets and went to sit next to a copper brazier that spread a soft glow and a pleasant warmth through the room. She sat on her heels and looked the old woman in the eye. 'Will he live?' she asked.

'I've done what I could,' she replied.

'Help me, Shi Wanli! I don't want him to die.'

'He fought in the arena against the Flying Foxes and against Wei the eunuch, without any experience,' replied the old woman. Her words seemed a death sentence. 'It is difficult to survive such a trial. He has many broken bones. Even if he lives, he will be a wreck, not a man.'

Yun Shan's eyes brimmed over. 'I saw him fight with such desperate courage, protecting his companions in every way he could . . . I . . . I took some of the blows meant for him.' As she spoke she bared her chest, showing a dark bruise between her pure-white breasts.

The old woman widened her eyes. 'You used the energy of the hidden heart for him . . . You did, didn't you?'

Yun Shan nodded.

'You shouldn't have done it!' said Shi Wanli. 'That energy was given to you only to save your own life when there was no other choice. Years and years will pass before you can accumulate it again, understand? Long years of meditation and harsh discipline.'

'I don't care. I couldn't let him die.'

'He's a foreign barbarian. Beware.'

'Why?'

'Because he will go, and break your heart. If he ever heals, he will leave.'

'Perhaps he will, perhaps he won't. You've seen me, nurse. Do you think he would spurn me?'

The old woman sighed. 'Any pretender would hand over all of his riches merely to be able to glimpse you without veils, daughter . . . but the past of a man you do not know can hold a bottomless abyss . . .'

A moan was heard. Yun Shan got up hurriedly and went to the next room, where Metellus lay on a mat on the floor. He was awake and his breath came in painful wheezes. He was naked, an arm and a leg confined by bamboo sticks. His body was covered in wounds, which Shi Wanli had stitched up one by one with silken thread. His lips were split and covered with clots of blood. His eyes were puffy and almost sealed shut and his right cheek was grossly swollen. His limbs seemed disjointed. He was a mass of aching flesh and almost unrecognizable.

'Is that you?' he murmured.

The girl bent close, seeking his eyes. 'I'm here,' she answered. 'It's Yun Shan.'

'Swathed in clouds . . . *sicut luna*,' said Metellus in a breath.

'What did you say?'

'I spoke in my language,' he replied.

'And you? What's your name?'

'Marcus . . . Metellus . . . Aquila. In your language I'm called Xiong Ying,' he managed to say before drifting back into semi-consciousness.

'Resplendent Eagle . . .' sighed Yun Shan, brushing his arm with her fingers, 'but your wings are broken.'

AS THE DAYS PASSED, Shi Wanli seemed increasingly nervous and worried. Every now and then she would go down to the village nearby to buy provisions and to wait for a message, or a signal. She would always leave after dark so as not to be noticed. One night she returned in great haste, much earlier than usual. 'Finally!' she said as soon as she was in the house. 'I've learned that the person you were waiting for has arrived. You will depart this very night. We must be quick. The evil aura is mounting in intensity – I can feel it.'

Yun Shan fell silent for a few moments, then said, 'Help me to move him. We'll drag the mat to the door and then pull him on to the cart. You will drive the cart to the ford. I'll ride on ahead to make sure that the way is clear, and to see my friend, if he's there waiting for me.'

'Let's leave now, then,' said Shi Wanli. 'Every moment lost could prove fatal.'

Yun Shan nodded and together they began to pull the mat Metellus was lying on over the floor to the entrance portico. Yun Shan yoked the mule on to the cart and had him back up until the platform was at the same level as the portico floor. They slipped the mat on to the cart and wrapped Metellus, still unconscious, in a woollen blanket. Shi Wanli got into the driver's seat, while Yun Shan leapt on to her mount and spurred him through the oak forest that extended in front of the house. The wood soon gave way to a grove of willow trees that stretched to the banks of the river. Yun Shan stopped when she saw the silvery glittering of the waters between the willow boughs.

She dismounted and waited, scanning the other bank. Shortly afterwards she heard a rustling of leaves and the cry of a scops owl. Once, twice, three times. She jumped on to her horse and crossed the ford in a cloud of silvery spray.

'Yun Shan . .' a familiar voice greeted her.

'Daruma!'

'Thanks the Heavens you're well. The foreigner?'

'He's alive. But just barely.'

'It's still remarkable. No one has ever survived an attack from Wei.'

'Did you bring what you promised me?'

'By this time the boat should be anchored down there, round that bend. Trusted friends have taken care of this for me. I'll wait as long as necessary. If you don't come back, it will mean that all has gone well and you are on your way.'

'Thank you. This may be the only way to save him. The bumps and jolts of a journey over land would surely kill him.'

'There's no need to thank me. I've known Xiong Ying for much longer than you have.'

'How can I repay you?'

'By saving his life.'

'I will. But isn't there anything else?'

'And by conveying my regards to Prince Dan Qing, your brother.'

'That won't be easy for me. My brother has wounded me deeply. And not only me.'

'This will be your opportunity for reconciliation. Much time has passed. He has suffered himself: a long imprisonment and exile from his country. He needs you, and he needs friends. But go now, please, before you're discovered. Wei's men are on your track.'

Shi Wanli arrived and Yun Shan tied her horse to a willow tree, then got into the seat next to her nurse. The horse whinnied, trying to free itself.

'Forgive me, Breath-of-Fire,' said Yun Shan, and whipped the mule drawing the cart.

They travelled upriver towards the bend and found the boat anchored there. They gently eased Metellus on to the bottom of the little vessel, and loaded a big jar of spring water and a sack of supplies into the boat. Yun Shan signalled to Daruma that all was well, then embraced her nurse. 'Please take care of Breath-of-Fire for me,' she said.

'I will. You needn't worry,' replied Shi Wanli, and pulled on the mule's reins to return down the path.

Yun Shan had begun to cast off the moorings when she heard a step behind her and swiftly drew her sword. She found an unarmed man carrying a bird cage.

'Daruma forgot to give this to you,' he said. 'It's a gift for the prince.' He held out the cage with a dove inside.

Yun Shan took it, got into the boat and began to row. From where he was standing, Daruma could see her leaving the hidden cove, reaching the centre of the current and slowly moving off along the silvery wake cast by the moon.

He continued to watch until she had disappeared round a bend in the river. He breathed a long sigh and retraced his steps back to the village.

IN THE LIGHT of dawn, Yun Shan was better able to observe her second passenger: a dove enclosed in a beautifully crafted silver cage. A scroll at the top said that it was a gift for Dan Qing. At least having this creature along would distract her from her worries.

An enchanted landscape was opening before her eyes: she was crossing the surface of a lake from which many little islets emerged, some low on the surface of the water, others taller and craggy, all covered by thick, lush vegetation. Each one of them was mirrored in the clear water, creating a play of images that multiplied into a thousand different perspectives as the boat advanced through the tranquil waters, carried along by a barely perceptible current. A light mist was rising at that moment from the lake, enveloping every shape and form in a fluttering veil.

The boat slipped along silently, and whenever it passed alongside one of the little islands it was greeted by the cries of cormorants, which took to the air in search of food.

Yun Shan followed the current with the motion of her oars. Every now and then she would turn to gaze at her travelling companion, who lay fitful and feverish in the bottom of the boat. She would dip a cloth in the water and wet his forehead and temples. Metellus would sometimes open his eyes and even say a few words, but his look was full of anguish. Perhaps in the changing reflections of the water he saw the bloodied faces of his murdered friends.

Long silences followed, accompanied by the slow dipping of the oars and the tranquil cooing of the dove in its silver cage.

They sailed on for three days, crossing the lake and then going downstream again. The river was wider now, with several tributaries flowing in. They would meet up with other boats at times, mostly belonging to fishermen or merchants, but then, after a certain point, there were no more. The river became strangely deserted and Yun Shan had the distinct impression of being watched by someone hidden in the dense wood that lined the banks. Metellus woke rarely and always asked for water.

They stopped on the evening of the fourth day at the foot of a towering cliff covered in cascading greenery. Trickles of water furrowed the surface of the rocks and flowed into the river, creating a concert of different sounds, depending on the size of every rivulet: soft whispering, gurgling, swishing, as the water rushed through the branches and leaves of so many different plants.

To the west, where the waterline met the horizon, the sun was setting, enflaming the river and the clouds as they drifted slowly through the sky. Yun Shan drew the boat in as close to the base of the cliff as she could, where the current was practically nonexistent. She took from under her gown a long roll of red silk which she unwound into the water, creating a vermilion trail that lengthened out on the surface of the river like a streak of blood.

Metellus opened his eyes and watched her as she performed this strange act. He had only enough strength to ask, 'What do we do now?'

'Nothing,' replied Yun Shan. 'We wait.'

And they waited, until they saw the full moon slowly rising, enormous, through a screen of light blue vapours; it hovered like a magic lantern over that dreamlike landscape.

Then a cloud advancing from the west obscured the face of the moon and the surface of the river turned into a leaden expanse. The shriek of a bird of prey pierced the night and the frightened dove beat its wings against the walls of the cage. At that same instant they heard a sudden splashing: four ghosts shot out of the water and landed on the boat, two at the fore and two aft. All that Metellus could see were the dripping shapes of steel limbs moving with extraordinary agility, weightless bodies that seem to barely touch the deck. Vermilion bands swathed their hips and razor-edged blades flashed silver in their hands.

Yun Shan brought her hands together at her chest and bowed to them as a sign of respect. No one spoke.

Metellus could hear noises: iron scraping on rock and then a metallic clinking. He felt the boat swaying strongly and then heard an unmistakable dripping. The vessel had been lifted out of the water by cables secured to the railings and fastened to a metallic trestle at the top of the cliff; it was swinging through the air. The moon appeared again and illuminated the scene, and Metellus watched the rock wall covered with bushes, creepers, outstretched trees passing before his eyes as the boat rose. He saw, or heard, birds disturbed from their rest taking flight and abandoning their nests with a whirr of wings at the passage of that strangely suspended object, outside its own element.

The boat was stopped, pulled to the side and set down at the top of the cliff. The four warriors leapt out and others arrived with a bamboo cane stretcher, on which they laid the wounded foreigner. Torches were lit to illuminate the scene and Prince Dan Qing arrived.

'Sister,' he said as soon as he saw Yun Shan.

The girl bowed her head and stood mutely before him.

'I've long awaited this moment. All these years I've dreamed of the instant that you would throw your arms around me again ... but ... I understand. But I beg of you, do not close your heart, and give yourself time to think. You will realize that, even if I was wrong, I thought I was making the right decision. And there must be a reason that the Heavens have reunited us here after these long years of separation.'

He turned to Metellus. 'Xiong Ying!' he exclaimed.

'Prince,' Metellus managed to respond, trying instinctively to prop himself up on his elbow. He fell over on his back with a groan of pain.

Yun Shan took the silver cage and handed it to her brother. 'It's a gift from Daruma.'

'A gift ...' Dan Qing smiled. 'As if he hasn't done enough already! That man freed me from prison when I had lost all hope.'

'At the cost of many men's lives,' said Yun Shan.

Her brother did not answer. He ordered the litter-bearers instead to transport Metellus to where he could be cared for. As they took him away, the prince saw the bloodstain in the bottom of the boat and watched his sister's eyes following the Roman until he disappeared in the darkness.

He went to the place where Metellus had been taken and entered. A group of monks had already gathered around the battered man. One of them was heating water, while another was dissolving a dark-coloured substance inside a bronze bowl over the fire. Others were preparing bandages, surgical instruments, bamboo splints.

They peeled off the blanket wrapped around Metellus, which had stuck to the clotted blood in many places, causing some of the wounds to open up again. Dan Qing was dismayed at the sight of Xiong Ying's tortured body. He raised an inquisitive glance towards the surgeons.

'The person who stitched his wounds certainly increased the possibility that he might live,' said one of them, 'but what we must do tonight will put him sorely to the test. He is extremely weak, but we have no choice. Waiting any longer would be condemning him to certain death.'

'Proceed, then,' said Dan Qing.

One of them walked to a cabinet and took out a silver case filled with a great quantity of slender needles. Metellus saw them and clenched his jaw, bracing himself to suffer more pain. He knew from experience what to expect from the needles of military surgeons, but Dan Qing was smiling at him, like an old friend trying to encourage him to take heart.

'Let us proceed,' said the surgeon. 'First of all we must isolate the pain centres.'

He took the needles, one after another, and began to stick them into various parts of the battered body. They were inserted just under the skin, with quick, precise gestures, and soon a forest of silver needles was marking out mysterious paths.

The surgeon made a gesture. One of assistants, unseen by Metellus, brought the flame of an oil lamp close to his foot; the Roman showed no reaction whatsoever. The surgeon nodded, took the bowl from the hands of another assistant and brought it to the patient's lips.

'Drink,' said Dan Qing. 'It is incredibly bitter, but it will help you to slip into unconsciousness. You will feel no pain.'

Metellus slowly drank the infusion, more bitter than poison, and sank back on the mat. He saw the faces of the men leaning over him and then nothing.

30

METELLUS ENTERED INTO a state of mind that he had never
experienced before in his whole life. A suspended, rarefied
dimension, like a dream but deeper; hazy awareness alternated
with a complete disengagement from any reality known to him.
He thought that he was dead, and that this inkling he had of his
frail spirit was the afterlife. What the poets had described. Hades,
with no divinities but thronging with spectres.

The first to appear were those of his comrades who had
fallen in the fierce battle. They approached him with their faces
bloodied and disfigured by the beatings they'd taken, limbs
maimed, guts spilling out. And then they'd vanish like mist in
the wind, without saying a thing, without responding to his
pleas. But he knew that they were appealing to his fluctuating
yet heedful conscience: they were demanding revenge. The
restless shades of men who had been denied the fulfilment of the
promise he had made them, denied funeral rites as well.

And then there was the shade of Clelia, gentle spirit, so small
she seemed a child. She watched him, caressed him with the
gaze of a devoted, loving wife. It seemed that she wanted to tell
him something: her mouth moved, but no sound came out.
And he cried out, invoking her name, weeping. In vain.

She faded away.

At times he felt that he was on the verge of understanding;
close, very close to a revelation. But of what? Of the meaning of
life, perhaps, or the meaning of death, but that sensation spun
around on itself, spiralling faster and faster, creating a vortex that
sucked him upwards like a leaf at the mercy of the autumn wind.

There were sounds he wanted to hear, sounds he mourned for: the voice of his son, which he imagined must be different after all this time; but he couldn't hear it, as hard as he tried! He thought it must be a good sign: Titus was alive and thus could not appear to him in Hades. But he still missed him intensely and he realized, he was sure, that he'd never again see him or hear his voice. That the emotions that made him feel like a father would be denied him forever.

In such a state, time no longer had any meaning: there was neither light nor shadow, day nor night, nothing that allowed him to place the flow of events or to perceive a duration or an end or an interruption. The only sensation that reminded him of existing was a scent: light, almost constant. Which became faint, at times, only to pervade him again. Unable to associate this fragrance with any creature or image or concept, he ended up believing that it was the scent of the afterworld.

The asphodel meadows? He could see them: long, slender stalks with spikes of white flowers, stretching out as far as the eye could see in every direction, without a horizon, without limits, traversed by a mysterious pulsing, the wind perhaps, or an interior light of their own, that vibrated absurdly in that diffused, shadowy, empty atmosphere.

And his essence became that fragrance, and with the passing of time, the fragrance became warmth and then both things together. He felt like he was floating, he felt the sensations that reminded him of life. And he was conscious of remembering . . . Then, in a single event that he could not place in any particular moment of his being, there was a caress.

A caress.

He knew it must be one of the cycles of his bodiless existence. What else? And yet he'd never had such a sudden, concrete sense of the truth. And the next sensation was that of light.

Soft.

Without colour. Without edges but growing, constantly, throbbing abruptly, taking on an impetuous rhythm. Until he could feel that he had . . . eyes.

And tears.

'Xiong Ying . . .'

The tears were running down his cheeks into his mouth and he could taste them. He saw dark, shining eyes, and smelled the fragrance, now connected with a look, a body, an expression.

'Yun Shan.'

'You're back.'

'And . . . I'm alive.'

'You are, but . . .'

'How long?'

'Many days and many nights.'

'And you've always been here with me?'

'Don't speak.'

'Why?'

'Because you don't have the strength.'

SHE BROUGHT HIM a drink with a strange flavour, slightly bitter, and then some nearly liquid food. His strength did return, day by day, and with it the pain. Acute. In his arms, his legs, his chest.

'You will feel pain,' Yun Shan had told him.

'Pain is . . . life, at least. A life that I owe to you.'

'To the physicians.'

'Yet I know that it was you who saved me from certain death. But I don't know why.'

'Each one of us knows what our heart tells us.'

'What did they do to me? Why don't I remember anything?'

'They prevented the pain from reaching your mind while they opened your flesh and reassembled your bones. It is there that you feel pain, not in your hands or arms. They enclosed your mind in a web of slender needles.'

'I don't understand.'

'And then they put you to sleep.'

'Will I go back to being what I was?'

'Yes. But it will take time.'

'Days? Months?'

'Whatever is necessary.'

Metellus fell silent, absorbed again in his thoughts.

'And when you are healed, what will you do, Xiong Ying? Will you return to your home . . . to your family?'

'My homeland, Taqin Guo . . . It's been so long since I've heard anything. I saw my emperor die in prison like a slave. I left my city at the mercy of the enemy . . . I saw my wife murdered before my eyes and my son . . . I have had no news of my son.'

'And these are the reasons why you want to return . . . It's only right.'

'I don't know what's right any more. I don't know what world awaits me . . . And my comrades, contemptibly slaughtered . . . their shades demand justice.'

'Is that what matters most?'

Metellus searched for her eyes. 'No . . . When I look at you, my thoughts are different. My life is measured by the beating of your heart.'

Yun Shan bowed her head.

'Lately I've been having the same dream. I find myself in the big courtyard of the imperial palace. My comrades' dead bodies are all around me and my enemy stands in front of me, about to deal the death blow. But when his hand darts into the air you put yourself between us and you receive the blow for me. There, where your heart is.'

'Xiong Ying . . .' murmured the girl, 'dreams are only dreams.'

'Right there . . .' His hand neared her breast. 'It's as if you gave a part of your life to save mine. It's true, isn't it? I don't know how, but I know it happened.'

Yun Shan said nothing. She continued to keep her eyes low.

'Why did you do it? I will be grateful to you for all the time I have left to live. But please, tell me why you did it.'

She lifted her head and looked at him. No language could have expressed what her eyes were saying in that moment: her answer went straight to his heart. Emotion that burned with arcane power, with fervent passion.

He saw those eyes shining with tears while her face remained composed in supreme dignity, in sublime harmony. All in the blink of an eye, in a heartbeat. Yun Shan got up, bowed her head ever so slightly, and left. Metellus fell back on to the mat and closed his eyes, as if to imprison her look inside him and seal it in his heart.

HE DIDN'T SEE HER again for many days, but he did receive a visit from Dan Qing, who showed him the gift Daruma had sent. The upper part of the cage was activated by a mechanism which made it revolve like a miniature firmament, marking the months and the seasons on the rim of the base, as well as the zodiac, which bore strange names in Chinese: the monkey, the mouse, the rabbit. The ingenious mechanism was rewound by the movements of the dove on his little swing.

Metellus was finally able to rise from his sickbed and to begin walking. In a few days' time he felt ready to start running. He didn't have any idea of where he was, except that the citadel was called Li Cheng. His rehabilitation took place in a vast room roofed with beams of enormous oak logs. The floor was of polished pine and the walls of white-plastered bricks.

At times he was given access to the garden, a place of divine perfection where paths had been marked out to allow visitors to walk without breaking a branch or causing a leaf to fall. There were plants of rare beauty, in dreamy hues, and the branches and leaves had been trained into fantastic shapes. There was one, in particular, overhanging a pond, covered with very big, fleshy flowers, pink with hints of white. How could such a celestial plant, so harmonious and noble in bearing, grow outside of Elysium? Its flowers were so numerous that they created a cloud, and not a single leaf opened until the last petal had fallen.

The flowers of the red lotus blossomed in the pond; they were the symbol and emblem of the sect of monks who lived there. The bottom of the pond was an artful mix of grey and white pebbles, and it was populated by marvellous red, blue and iridescent green fish.

That natural perfection, fruit of the most sophisticated arti-
fice, gave him a sense of profound peace on one hand, but on
the other a strange excitation, a thrill that he could feel under
his skin. The garden's natural terrace overlooked the jutting face
of the cliff, and from there he could see the river bend and
beyond it an expanse of forests and marshes from which flocks
of birds took wing at dawn, passing in front of the disc of sun,
which was immersed in the dense cloud of vapours that rose
from the wetlands.

Once, from his room, he saw Yun Shan strolling in that
enchanted garden, enveloped in a gown of light blue silk that
gracefully sheathed her body. He watched her passing among
the flowered branches as though she were ethereal, as light and
vaporous as a cloud.

He would have liked to speak with her, to look into her eyes
to see if they were still burning with the light that had enraptured
him that day. But he knew that the garden was a shelter of the
spirit, and that its delights had to be savoured alone, in solitude. It was a taste of the hereafter in which those extraordinary
beings prepared their souls for undisturbed happiness, for the life
without end.

THE DAY CAME in which Metellus began to learn the secrets of
the ancient arts of combat which Master Mo had taught his
followers: both those who had chosen the righteous path and
those who had fallen away from it.

'You'll learn to move like me,' Dan Qing told him, 'like the
Flying Foxes. But you can even surpass them if you are convinced, if you are certain of the road you must take.'

'Tao . . .' said Metellus.

'A philosophy, more than mere physical discipline. A deep
conviction, a leap of faith, of the mind. We call it Go Ti.

'You will move in harmony with nature, perceive its breath,
let it run through your body. There is nothing that you cannot
achieve. But you must not strain convulsively towards the goal.
You must allow yourself to be transported by the current of life,

by the energy of the cosmos that flows through a blade of grass as it does through your body, through a grain of sand or through the stars that pulse in the eternity of the sky. You will have to learn meditation, as I have learned it from my master, Wangzi. And you must forget everything that you learned in your country, because what you knew led you to defeat and to the massacre of your men.'

'There's one thing I won't forget,' replied Metellus. 'The force which pushed the valour of my men beyond every limit. The courage that can lead a man to sacrifice his very life because of his faith in the values handed down to him.'

'If that's what you want, may it be thus. Perhaps it is only by remembering the sacrifice of your comrades that you will be able to fight the demon who destroyed them and hope to defeat him. But you can unite your destiny with ours, learn a different life, a world that you've never even imagined, a civilization built on an unparalleled intensity of thought. I'm not saying that you'll attain truth – truth always flees from us like the horizon from the weary traveller. But you'll live your life with the maximum intensity that a human being is capable of. Do you want to learn all this, Xiong Ying? Will you join us and fight our battle?'

'I will,' replied Metellus.

'Then thus it shall be. But on one condition. You must promise me on your honour that what you learn will never leave our realm.'

'This I promise,' said Metellus. 'But how will you convince me that you are less blameworthy than your enemy? That his cruelty is not the consequence of your cruelty, of your unrestrained thirst for power? In your search for perfect harmony between the force of the body and that of the spirit, have you perhaps forgotten that none of this makes any sense without virtue? If you give me an explanation, I will accept it because I am your friend, and friendship, like love, does not observe propriety.'

Dan Qing looked deep into his eyes and smiled. 'You are starting to think and talk like the Chinese, Xiong Ying ... but

I'm afraid there's not a single word that I could tell you at this moment that would be capable of convincing you. At that time I was too young to resist the corruptive force of power. I reacted to what I felt was a threat in an extreme way, but in the atmosphere of supreme authority, it seemed completely normal. A wise measure, even, a way to protect the dynasty from disorder and from disruptive forces.

'It is only now that I have fully realized the suffering I caused by brutally destroying the love of two adolescents, shattering the utmost harmony of a universal emotion with the utmost violence. At times I wonder if it is not for this reason that our land has been mortally wounded, split into three separate warring bodies. But all I can do now is to try to repair the damage by rebuilding the country. By fighting without sparing my strength and without fleeing from any danger, and by healing the wound that I myself inflicted on Yun Shan's heart. I think she loves you.'

'What are you saying, Dan Qing?'

'Yes, I believe she loves you. That's why she stays away from you . . . because she fears you. She fears abandoning herself to an emotion that will once again be denied her. I'm telling you this because it will be Yun Shan who will train you. She will be your teacher and your unrelenting adversary in fencing and the martial arts. Take care, for she may strike you much harder than necessary. But you must understand that we have no choice. I'm afraid that neither I nor Yun Shan can defeat Wei, because neither of us is truly capable of hating him. As you have said, I am to blame for part of his cruelty and his fury. And Yun Shan . . . loved him with the innocent, perhaps unconscious, love of a young girl, and she would not be able to kill him even now with a staunch heart and a steady hand. Only you are capable of defeating him and of restoring the harmony of this country.'

'In the West, in Taqin Guo, the harmony of the land has been shattered as well, by a chain of brutal crimes that has broken my heart. Who will save my country?'

'Don't think of that now, Xiong Ying. Now you must keep

343

the promise you just made to me and to your comrades, butchered so mercilessly by those monsters. I will try to get information about your country for you. I swear it. Only then can you make your decision.'

'So be it, Dan Qing,' replied Metellus. 'Let's begin now. I can't wait any longer.'

THE SPRING PASSED, and the summer, in continuous and exhausting sessions. The masters who took turns in training him were increasingly swifter and more expert and harsher in their blows. Only when they had profoundly transformed him, and he was capable of sensing the intentions of his adversary before he sprang to the attack, was he brought to the great *palaestra* where the duels were held. It was the first morning of winter of that year of the Dragon, the third day of the second month.

The relentless drum roll that filled that huge room immersed in semi-darkness died away and a shrill cry burst out all at once. A kick struck him full on the left shoulder and sent him rolling to the ground.

'Defend yourself!' shouted Yun Shan. 'If I had wanted to, I could have killed you! Defend yourself!' she shouted again as her foot flashed through the air.

He fell again and tumbled between Dan Qing's feet.

'You must forget she is a woman!' he told Metellus. 'She is not a woman: she is an adversary who can kill you. Remember when you used your two swords? You have to use your hands like you used your swords, understand? It's the only way to beat her.'

'Let's get down to work now,' said Yun Shan, and she lunged forward, her hands stretched out taut and ready to strike.

But Metellus was already back on his feet and he'd understood. He had to put into practice the art he'd been taught by these saintly monks to avoid being wounded by the sword. His naked hands were his weapons. And they darted through the air now, faster and faster: parrying, thrusting, slashing, jabbing.

But Yun Shan had more surprises. She suddenly dropped to

the ground and swiped at him with her foot. Metellus was down again.

Dan Qing was very close now. 'You still fight like a barbarian. The force of the spirit is much stronger than that of the body. Watch!'

Under Metellus's astonished eyes, Dan Qing put his hands to the floor, kept his head down and stretched his body up, stiff as a rod. He detached one hand from the floor and remained supported by the other. Metellus couldn't believe his eyes as Dan Qing began to lift one finger after another of the hand still on the floor, until his entire weight rested on his index finger, rigid as a steel bar.

'Teach me,' he said. 'Teach me *Go Ti*.'

Dan Qing returned to a standing position. 'This is our most powerful weapon, our most precious secret. No barbarian has ever been instructed at this level of knowledge. Give me a reason why I should do so.'

'Because I'm your friend,' said Metellus. 'Because by binding my destiny to yours I lost my comrades. Because I want to avenge them and bring peace to their spirits by killing Wei with my own hands.'

'Will you still insist on judging me?' asked Dan Qing.

'No, I won't.'

'And you, sister?'

Yun Shan bowed her head, still breathing fast and said, 'Nor will I, brother.'

'Remember,' said Metellus then, 'now it seems that I am the needy one, but there will come a time, when you are ready to reclaim your throne, that I will have many things to teach you and your men, things unknown to you that may well decide the fate of the battle.'

Dan Qing smiled. 'Why didn't you save your emperor, then? I saw him on his knees before his enemy. Have you forgotten?'

'It was deceit that defeated us,' shouted Metellus, beside himself. 'Not valour! I don't need you, or your secrets. I will regain my strength on my own, I'll find that demon and I'll kill him like a dog. And if I have to die, I will.' Indomitable passion burned in his eyes.

Yun Shan approached him. Dan Qing regarded him in silence. In the Roman's gaze, the prince could see, and perhaps even understand, the virtue of that barbarian.

'Follow me,' he said.

31

A BLADE OF LIGHT carved out their profiles as they sat face to face on their heels. Metellus was no longer uncomfortable in that position, as he had been when he first attempted it in Daruma's tent at the oasis of Khaboras. They remained like this in silence for an indefinite time, as the light slowly waned away. Until the darkness was total.

And more time passed, in the absence of sound, in the dearth of light. Metellus no longer needed references; he felt complete within himself. He knew also that he was alone now and he didn't need to reach out his hand to be able to tell that the space in front of him was empty.

Dan Qing's voice rang out, seemingly miles away: 'Where is your spirit, Xiong Ying?'

'It's here, within me,' he answered.

'Where?' a voice reverberated again. A different voice, which sounded much like Yun Shan's. At that same instant, a ray of light spilled in from above. Within the cone of light was a monk dressed in black with a red band on his arm who moved like lightning, striking Metellus's side.

'No!' Dan Qing's voice sounded again. 'It's in your side, there, where the blow has fallen. Beware! Be careful!'

The ray of light went out. The figure disappeared.

'Where is your spirit, Xiong Ying?' cried out Dan Qing again.

'You said that Yun Shan would be training me!' shouted back Metellus.

'She has indeed! She is behind everything you've done. You

347

may not see her, but it is she who sets you against your adversaries. Or perhaps she is your adversary. Beware!'

Metellus thrust his hands out to ward off the threat, whatever direction it was coming from. Another ray flashed in the dark, another figure suddenly appeared and struck him hard from behind.

Metellus fell.

The ray was extinguished.

'Try to remember, Xiong Ying! It's night-time, you're a young recruit, you're on guard. Where will the enemy's arrow come from? Careful! Careful! Your instinct will tell you. Follow your *tao*, there!'

A third ray revealed another assailant.

'Remember, Xiong Ying!' rang out Dan Qing's voice once again. 'Remember: clay is shaped to make a vase, but it is the emptiness inside that makes the vase what it is!'

Hands darted like claws, but Metellus's arms fended off the blow, just as quickly. The adversary disappeared.

A whistle, two dull thuds. Two *gladii* plunged into the ground at a short distance from each other. Only the polished edges of their blades were visible. Metellus had just enough time to seize them before two adversaries appeared. A dim glow illuminated the limited area of combat, although its source was not evident. The two were armed with long Chinese swords, decorated with fine engravings.

The drum started up a pounding roll and the assailants were upon him with cleaving blows.

Metellus spun round with feline force, parrying then thrusting his *gladii*, their flinty power contrasting with the sinuous flexibility of the slender Chinese swords, which intertwined like steel serpents. All at once the four blades collided over the combatants' heads in an inextricable clash, jammed one against the other by the unrelenting strength of the arms wielding them. A brighter shaft of light lit up their tips.

Metellus's two adversaries broke away abruptly, blades shrieking, and they melted back into the darkness.

The light went out and flared again elsewhere. A cone of white light flooded the floor and at its centre was Yun Shan, brandishing Tip of Ice. An intermittent flashing began as if an unknown mechanism were screening the light and then releasing it in a rhythm so quick that the image was shattered, splintered into indistinct fragments. Yun Shan broke free of that whirlwind and pounced at him like a tiger, blade outstretched. The fight burst into flame: the swords were tongues of fire, screeching against each other, steel biting into steel, blades gleaming like the eyes of the combatants, sudden flashes of wild energy. The swords blazed in that white light like burning meteors sparking. Clanking steel tore through the silence of that immense, bare room with its pulsating lights.

Yun Shan suddenly shot backward, rebounded and flung herself at her opponent, delivering a downward blow of tremendous power. Metellus's two *gladii* rose up to cross over his head and trap Tip of Ice in a steel vice.

They looked into each other's eyes, panting.

'Would you have killed me?' asked Metellus.

Yun Shan did not answer.

Metellus moved even closer. 'Would you have killed me?'

'Yes,' replied Yun Shan. 'Because the death that Wei will give you will be a thousand times more painful.'

Metellus dropped his *gladii*.

Tip of Ice descended inexorably but stopped at a hair's breadth from his head.

Metellus moved her arm away and got even closer. He could feel the heat of her breath. 'But you couldn't do it,' he said.

Yun Shan sheathed Tip of Ice.

Metellus clasped her to him and kissed her. A long, ardent kiss, while the last flash of light went out.

They had fought all day long.

AT THAT MOMENT, Dan Qing was entering his quarters. He closed the door behind him. He heard a sound that had become familiar, the ticking of the mechanism that rotated the roof of the silver cage that Daruma had sent him. Then he heard a click, so clear that it made him turn. The door of the cage had opened and the dove was flying out of the open window. Dan Qing watched as the bird soared across the courtyard towards the darkening sky; it was flying in circles, confused. The prince hoped that it would return, as house animals do when it gets dark, but the dove took off towards the forest that covered the surrounding hills and in just moments had vanished from sight.

THE NEXT MORNING Metellus was woken by one of the monks, who informed him that Princess Yun Shan was waiting for him in the *palaestra* courtyard, and that he should bring his riding gear. Metellus washed, dressed and went as quickly as he could to the courtyard. He was anxious to see what she had in mind. If they were truly going for a ride, that would be the first time he had been allowed to leave his quarters since he'd arrived at Li Cheng.

Yun Shan did not even wait for him to greet her but leapt on to her horse and spurred it on. Metellus did the same and the two of them galloped through the gate that opened on to the village.

It was a small settlement of houses scattered on the hillside, clustered around a road paved with grey stone. Although they were moving quickly, he noticed that there were no monks to be seen, so all of them must live inside the fortress. The people walking along the road had a very particular appearance, their features noticeably different from the other Chinese he'd seen up till then.

They'd soon ridden through the village gate and found themselves in a dense forest of giant canes stretching south over rocky hills that sloped down towards the open countryside. Beyond the forest was an area of vast rolling meadows edged by a line of green knolls where a narrow river flowed, flanked by trees that were certainly ages old. Towards the west an imposing group of grey cliffs jutted up from the terrain. Their colour and shapes contrasted so sharply with the rolling greenery that they seemed a sort of natural monument.

Metellus followed Yun Shan in that direction and caught up with her so that they were riding side by side, until the girl pulled on her horse's reins and jumped to the ground, leaving the animal free to graze. Metellus did the same, but he tied his own mount, which he was not familiar with, to a woody plant. When he turned, Yun Shan was leaning against a big tree which had grown in a crevice between the enormous rocks. He walked close and sought her eyes.

'How do you feel?' she asked him.

'Like someone who has risen from the dead. Like a new man,' replied Metellus.

'I imagine that must be a pleasant sensation.'

'It is in part, although it's not easy to forget the past . . . Why did you stay away from me for so long?'

'I wanted you to face your memories, as I struggled with my own. Now perhaps we can look one another in the eyes without wounding each other every time.'

'Do you still think that Wei will destroy me?'

'He knows all the secrets of a centuries-old art . . .'

'And I've just had a few months of initiation.'

'But you have been training in the *palaestra* designed by Mo Tze himself. Few have had this privilege.'

'How do they produce those beams of light in which the adversary suddenly appears?'

'I don't know. It's a machine of some sort.'

'Who does know? Dan Qing?'

'No, I don't think so. The eldest of these monks must know. He is a venerable old man. My master, Wangzi, was his disciple.'

'I will be using the arts you have taught me to defeat Wei . . . but I can't stop thinking that he himself is a victim.'

Yun Shan bowed her head. 'It's true,' she said in a whisper, 'but Wei has chosen a road that can lead only to destruction. To cruel, unlimited power. The Flying Foxes are a confraternity of bloodthirsty fanatics who are blindly obedient to him. But, you know, there's something even more alarming about them . . .'

'I do know what you mean,' replied Metellus. 'There was a moment, as we were fighting in the arena, when I had the clear sensation that the Flying Foxes were moving like limbs of the same body, commanded by the same mind.'

'I think you're right. You've hit upon the truth. But to achieve this, he's lost all respect for the human condition.'

'There are some wounds that never heal,' observed Metellus.

Yun Shan looked up at him and Metellus saw that her eyes were full of unfathomable sorrow. He touched her hair.

Yun Shan turned away and walked towards a cave that opened at the foot of the towering grey cliffs. She entered.

Metellus knew that if he followed her into that cave his life would change and nothing would be as it had been, but he also knew that he desired Yun Shan more than life itself. The fragrance which had pulled him back from the other world, her fragrance, was stronger than any other memory. He entered slowly and looked around. It was a big natural cavern and the white limestone-streaked walls were full of carvings: hunting scenes, herds of fleeing animals, galloping horsemen loosing arrows. Images of inconceivable antiquity in a land already so ancient.

The floor was covered with clean, golden sand and on the sand were the blurred prints of bare feet.

She was in front of him, her raven-black hair loose on her shoulders, gazing at him with a look so feverish that he felt his body and soul take flame. He forgot everything when she enveloped him in her embrace and her hair caressed his neck and shoulders. They let themselves fall, clinging to one another, on to the bed of sand, entwining with impatient frenzy, seeking each other with trembling hands. Metellus was engulfed in that intense fragrance – he could smell it in her hair, on her lips, on her smooth, arching stomach. He kissed her everywhere, while she abandoned herself to the panting heat of his breath, opened her virginal body to his tumultuous desire.

They made love endlessly, passionately, and then more gently, with languid exhaustion. When they finally fell back, spent, they could hear the voice of the wind blowing through the forest of giant canes.

'Will you stay with me, Xiong Ying?'

'I will stay with you,' said Metellus. And he was sincere as he pronounced those words. A deep calm had followed the storm of sense and spirit and he was pervaded by a melancholy awareness that a destiny had been carved out for him in that limitless land, in that territory guarded by invisible dragons whom none could flee.

'You will forget,' said Yun Shan. 'When you have won, you will forget. You will learn to rise with the sun each morning.'

THEY STARTED BACK before dusk and stopped to contemplate the walls of the citadel, which were illuminated by the sun setting behind the mountains. The road paving at that point was as smooth as marble and quite slippery. They continued on foot, leading their horses by the reins.

'Li Cheng is the only centre of resistance to Wei,' Yun Shan explained. 'It has never been conquered only because no one knows how to get here. There's a rock wall on the river side and a thick bamboo forest on this side that hide the fortress from sight until you are very close.'

Metellus watched a dove tracing wide circles in the paling sky. 'Only that bird up there,' he said, 'can see it all and count the houses one by one.'

'Yes,' replied Yun Shan, 'but he cannot speak. And so no one can ever be told.'

They passed a boy with two buckets of water hanging from either end of a pole who stopped to look curiously at the stranger.

Metellus looked back in surprise: the child's nose was straight, his eyes big and dark. He bent down for a closer look but the boy, frightened, dropped his buckets and ran off.

'Wait!' shouted the Roman. 'Wait, please, I won't hurt you!'

The child turned, saw Yun Shan's reassuring smile and slowly retraced his steps. Metellus knelt so that his gaze was level with the boy's. His features were not Oriental! A strange, involuntary emotion gripped them both as they looked into each other's eyes and recognized their mysterious similarity. Metellus brushed the boy's cheek with his fingers.

'He reminds you of someone, doesn't he?' asked Yun Shan.

'Yes,' replied Metellus with shiny eyes. 'Yes.'

Intimidated, the boy backed off, picked up the pole and buckets, and took to his heels.

'How can that be?' asked Metellus. 'How is it possible? Those features, the colour of his eyes . . .'

He hadn't finished speaking when a man came up to the boy and took the two water buckets. His father, probably. A man much taller than normal, with a thick, bristly beard, a square jaw and an aquiline nose. He reminded Metellus of Sergius Balbus, his faithful centurion.

Metellus couldn't take his eyes off them as he continued: 'How is that possible? That man has . . .'

'His features, do you mean? His eyes and beard?' They remounted their horses and proceeded at a slow place as Yun Shan began her story: 'There's a tale that's told around these parts . . .'

'What tale?' urged Metellus.

'The story of the three hundred Mercenary Devils. You see, during the reign of Emperor Yuandi, a strange thing was said to have happened on our western border. At that time, about three hundred years ago, we were subjected to continuous raids by the barbarians of the north, whom we call the Xiong Nu. The emperor finally managed to get the upper hand by sowing discord among them and setting their tribal factions against one another . . .'

'*Divide et impera*,' murmured Metellus.

'What did you say?'

'Divide and rule,' he replied. 'We do that as well. Evidently all empires must use the same methods. But go on, please.'

'Well, what happened was that one of his marshals, who had pushed westward to ensure the security of the Silk Road, had learned from a scout that a group of foreign soldiers had taken possession of a fortress on the border.

'The emperor gave orders to evacuate them, and sent a robust detachment of infantry and cavalry to wipe them out. But they returned in a sorry state after suffering severe losses. The supreme marshal had the inept commander executed for losing to a handful of barbarians, and sent out another, more numerous detachment of seasoned troops with the order not to come back until they had accomplished their mission.

'The second detachment attacked but were once again repulsed by that obstinate bunch. The scouts returned to describe those foreign devils: they were hairy, with round eyes and square jaws. Just horrible . . .'

Metellus smiled, looking at the black hairs on his arms and stroking his chin.

'They did battle lined up like fish scales, and sometimes fought with their shields over their heads.' Yun Shan pronounced those words with particular emphasis, not hiding the emotion she felt: in her mind's eye she saw Metellus and his men in their desperate resistance against the Flying Foxes.

Metellus felt the same sensation pierce his soul, but he tried to dispel thoughts that were still too painful. 'Go on,' he said.

'The supreme marshal was furious and decided to besiege the fortress, but big boulders rained down from inside the walls, and steel arrows of incredible dimensions, as if they had been loosed by the hands and bows of invisible giants.'

'*Ballistae* and catapults,' thought Metellus, becoming increasingly excited by the story.

'Terror was sown among the troops,' continued Yun Shan, 'and they failed to do battle with their customary ardour. News of the catastrophe reached Emperor Yuandi, who decided to go personally to the outpost to see these foreigners.

'He was so impressed and moved by their extraordinary valour that he asked to meet their commander, but there was no common language in which they could converse. And so the emperor sent a teacher who taught them Chinese and, when they were able to understand each other, they negotiated.

'Yuandi allowed them to remain in the fortress they had occupied, as long as they agreed to defend that stretch of the border from any invaders. And so it was. But three hundred of them agreed to become his personal bodyguards and they served him faithfully on innumerable occasions. When the emperor died, he bequeathed them the right to found a *tituan*, a colony, and to live as free men right here at Li Cheng. That's why the people of the village look the way they do. They resemble you, in a way, now that I think about it . . .' she concluded, looking at him as if she were seeing him for the first time.

Metellus almost had tears in his eyes.

'What's wrong, Xiong Ying?' asked Yun Shan.

'When did you say this episode happened?'

'If I remember well, it was the twenty-second year of the reign of Yuandi, so that would make it . . . three hundred and fifteen or sixteen years ago, more or less.'

'They were Taqin like me, weren't they?'

'It's possible,' replied Yun Shan. 'When I mentioned their way of fighting with their shields over their heads I thought of you that day in the arena.'

'Translated into our time . . . three hundred and fifteen years ago . . . would mean . . . seven centuries from the foundation of our City . . . of the capital of Taqin Guo. Oh, gods in heaven! It's the Lost Legion!'

'What do you mean?' asked Yun Shan.

'Just two years before these events you've told me about, one of our armies was annihilated in a great battle against the Persians. Just a single unit, just one legion, managed to break through the encirclement and escape, but they were never heard of again. No one ever knew what had happened to them . . .'

The sun had dropped below the red-tiled rooftops of Li Cheng and the clouds faded from flaming red to orange to blue-grey as the sound of the horns inviting the monks to meditation echoed in the valley below.

'In the rest of the country,' continued Yun Shan, 'those men are legendary. It's said that they were invincible. And it's said that they will reappear, rising from their tombs, if a single descendant of the Han dynasty should ever be threatened . . .'

Metellus looked into her eyes. 'Did they leave no sign of their presence? Have you ever noticed anything strange around the village or outside it?'

Yun Shan bowed her head as if suddenly struck by his words, then said, 'Follow me . . . the great green stone, perhaps . . .'

'What is it?'

'Follow me,' she repeated. 'Perhaps you'll be able to understand.' She swerved to the right, urging her horse up a paved ramp that led to the high part of the village, and Metellus followed.

They soon reached a large rock wall that gave access to a wide staircase. The lower part of the wall seemed to be hand-hewn. Yun Shan dismounted and approached a spot of the wall completely covered by creeping vegetation that hid it from view. She turned to check that Metellus was behind her, then pushed aside the climbing plants to reveal a worn inscription carved into the stone.

It was in Latin!

Metellus felt tears rising uncontrollably to his eyes and he hid them by drawing closer to the rock. He ran his fingers over those time-weathered signs and he imagined he could still feel the heat of the hands which had inscribed them. The hands of the men who had escaped the massacre of Carrhae, the men of the legendary Lost Legion!

'Was it them?' asked Yun Shan anxiously. 'Did they truly come from your country?'

Metellus nodded deeply without taking his hand off the wall. 'Yes, three hundred and fifteen years ago. Not one of them ever came home. None of them ever saw their wives or children again.

They carved this inscription and then they decided that they would never again speak their mother tongue, not even with each other, so as to forget . . . so as not to suffer. That's what it says here,' he concluded, placing his index finger on the last lines of the inscription.

ITAQVE LINGVAE MAIORVM ELIGIMVS OBLIVISCI
NE POENA AMISSAE PATRIAE INTOLERABILIS FIERET

' "And thus we decided to forget the language of our fathers so that our nostalgia for our lost homeland would not become unbearable" . . . They wrote this for me,' he said, leaning his head against the wall. 'No one before me could have read this.'

32

THE DOVE ENTERED from the little window in the western tower of the imperial palace of Luoyang and went to perch upon a swing where fresh water and food awaited him. The servant in charge of the dovecote noticed him immediately but did not move. He let him eat and drink, and only when he heard him cooing tranquilly did he approach and skilfully grasp him between his hands.

He hurried down to the ground floor, stood before the entrance to the audience chamber and spoke to the guards. One of them disappeared inside and returned almost immediately to admit the servant to the eunuch's presence.

Wei cupped the dove between his hands and brought him to his cheek, murmuring soft words to his ear: 'You're back, finally! And now you'll take us to where you've been all this time. Now you'll take us to Li Cheng, won't you, little one?'

The servant took his leave, backing away towards the entrance. He was absolutely convinced that that man could make himself understood to animals, and understand their language as well.

Wei struck a bronze disc hanging between two columns and a loyal follower soon appeared: one of the chiefs of the Flying Foxes.

'My Lord,' he said, bowing.

'Do you see this dove? He has just arrived from a long journey and he is still quite tired, but when he has rested and regained his strength he will take us to the fortress of the Red Lotus at Li Cheng. We will destroy them just as we did the disciples of Wangzi at the Monastery of Whispering Waters. Draw up your comrades immediately, all those who are available, in the inner courtyard. I'll be there soon. While you're leaving, send in the superintendent of the security forces.'

The man bowed again and left.

Wei, all alone now, leaned his head to look at the dove he held in his lap and he began to stroke it slowly, passing his waxy hands down its back with grace and delicacy, almost affection, one would say. Then he brought the bird close to his face. He cupped its belly with his right hand, its claws inserted between his index and middle finger. His left hand held its head between his thumb and index finger so that the bird's eye was a palm's width away from the tip of his nose.

Superintendent Zhong Wu entered, stopping at twenty steps from Wei's chair, and bent over into a deep bow.

'We have finally learned how to reach Li Cheng and destroy the refuge of the Red Lotus,' said the eunuch, still stroking the dove and without any excitement in his voice, as though he were speaking of a perfectly normal event.

Zhong Wu bowed his head as if to honour he who had achieved such a feat, though in reality to hide a grimace of disappointment. Such an important discovery on the part of his leader was humiliating for him, as it highlighted his own failure.

'From this moment on, all those whom you cannot completely trust must be put under strict surveillance. At the least hint of anything suspicious you must take immediate action. Arrest and imprison any spies. Eliminate them, simply, or have them followed discreetly at a distance to learn what connections they may have. There's no need to teach you these things, I suppose.'

The superintendent bowed again. 'Your advice is always precious and I am eager to take it to heart, My Lord.'

Wei nodded without commenting on that expression of servile adulation, continuing to stroke the dove. His hands had such a perfect hold on the wings and claws of the animal that it could move nothing but its head. And it did so continually, as if seized by extreme agitation.

Zhong Wu spoke again: 'Once the corrupt imperial lineage has been done any with and the last heir is out of the way, you can declare the reigning dynasty abolished forever. You will be proclaimed Son of the Heavens.'

Wei sighed, then said, 'I had given you another job.'

'I know, My Lord.'

'Well?'

'I have restricted the choice to a very few candidates: very young children who are without parents, or whose families are willing to give them up for a reasonable sum of money or an exchange of favours. We are considering their aptitude and natural inclinations, their intelligence, quick wits and daring – all qualities which are not easily identified in children as young as you have specified.'

'The chosen one will have to consider me and recognize me as his father in every way. And once we have taken Li Cheng, the little one will have a mother as well. Go now. Do as I've ordered.'

The superintendent took his leave and reached the exit. Wei got up from his seat next to the imperial throne, which he had decided not to use just yet, and walked towards the door that led to the inner courtyard of the first pavilion, holding the dove close to his chest.

As soon as Wei appeared, the commander of the guards promptly ran up to hear any orders he was mindful to give.

'Summon a team of horsemen,' Wei ordered. 'The fastest we have. Now.'

The officer rushed towards the guard post and gave curt instructions to his underlings. A squad of horsemen, auxiliaries from the north-west regions, presently rode up on their mounts, indefatigable horses of the steppe, even more costly than the tiger cubs from Siam that were gifted to sovereigns. They were called the horses-that-sweat-blood, for their extraordinary speed and resistance.

'You'll have to follow the flight of this dove,' Wei explained to them. 'Unlike any other animal of his species, he has been trained to return to a place where he has remained for at least six months. Woe to you if you lose sight of him! You will suffer an exemplary punishment. I'm sure you can imagine what that entails.'

The horsemen listened, sitting perfectly still on their shaggy steeds, covered by heavy leather tunics crossed over at the chest.

'Every evening,' continued Wei, 'one of you will return to the garrison at Luoyang to communicate the location of your detachment. The last messenger will inform me of the position of Li Cheng. At that point, the expeditionary force will be ready, and we shall set out to conquer the city and the fortress. Have no fear: your mission will not be a difficult one. This creature will guide you, and I am confident that you will never lose contact.'

Wei opened his hands and released the dove. He stood still, eyes trained on its first uncertain burst of flight. The bird soared off then in a wider sweep, straight towards the luminous midday sky. The horsemen left at a brisk gallop, following their winged guide.

Wei re-entered the big silent room and immersed himself in profound meditation. His mind sought the solitary place that sheltered his implacable enemies, where – he was certain – Yun Shan was hiding with the foreign barbarian, who, he felt sure, was still alive; he had survived the blow of the tiger and the massacre of all his companions. Did Yun Shan love him? The force of his suspicion made the pain caused by the thought intolerable. Doubt gnawed at him like a worm. He knew deep inside that Yun Shan had forgotten the feeling that had united them when they were little more than children. She had forgotten the agony he had suffered. He remembered her last words, the night of their duel at the walls of Luoyang.

His powers of concentration and the hatred streaming from his mind like a jet of poison were not sufficient to reveal to him what was happening in the place where Yun Shan had devoted herself to another man and had, perhaps, opened her heart to him. He felt he could see images, scenes of secret looks and caresses, simmering desire. He yearned for the death of his adversary with all the intensity he was capable of, and it seemed impossible that the blow he had inflicted upon him had not then crushed his heart.

FOR DAYS he remained in that state, fasting and drinking only an infusion of bitter herbs. At times, his prostration was so extreme that his mind fabricated an idyllic scene: a family, where he and Yun Shan had a child, a creature that he had chosen to raise in the palace so he could found a new dynasty. He saw himself teaching the child the basics of universal knowledge and his mother the rituals that could bring a man close to the Heavens. But in the end those scenes left him with nothing but a sense of burning frustration and a furious ire that only blood could atone for.

He would interrupt his meditation when a rider came to report on the flight of the dove, on the legs of the journey that would bring him to Li Cheng. Each time, he felt invaded by an almost infantile apprehension.

Sometimes, to calm the pangs of hatred, he would practise calligraphy on a fine ivory-coloured silk fabric, the same that had been used to compile the classic texts that had survived the fire of the Great Library of Luoyang. He painted the ideograms of an ancient version of *I Ching*, the Book of Changes. His hand seemed inexorably attracted to tracing out the changing lines of a coupled hexagram that reproduced the image of a funerary stele, obsessively, insistently. He searched for a response from the oracles carved into the shoulder blades of bulls and rams, which he cast furiously over the floor of the throne room, again and again.

A funerary stele. An omen of death. Whose death?

That evening one of the servants entered his living quarters; his expression made it clear that he had bad news.

'A man is waiting for you in the audience chamber, My Lord,' he said, and withdrew hurriedly.

Wei got up and went to the audience chamber, where his

initial impression was confirmed. It was one of the horsemen of the imperial cavalry and fear was painted on his face.

'We've lost contact with the dove, My Lord,' he said, his terror growing as he spoke. Wei's face twisted into a sneer of disgust and rage. 'We've searched everywhere. We split up and went in every direction, but the bird had taken off over impenetrable territory where our horses could not follow. No one had considered the possibility of this happening, My Lord, the chance that . . .'

The words were not out of his mouth when Wei's arm flashed through the air, striking the base of his neck. The man crumpled to the ground without a sigh. Then the eunuch turned and went back to his quarters. He sat down, picked up his brush and began to draw the signs of an ancient oracle on silk.

His hand moved with supreme grace, with measured, elegant gestures. The ideograms took shape as if by magic, blossoming like flowers in a meadow. His arm was almost immobile and suspended; only his wrist moved, commanding his hand and his brush. The ink seemed to flow directly from his body on to the fabric, in a black haemorrhage of evil humours. He laid his brush down at last on a rosewood stand and withdrew into himself, seemingly dozing. The features of his face slackened, his limbs relaxed, his lids drooped until his eyes were nearly closed.

He remained in that state of apparent unconsciousness for some time without moving and the entire palace plunged into a leaden silence.

One of the handmaids assigned to his personal care entered his rooms every so often, carrying a tray with a steaming cup of the infusion he usually took at mid-morning and afternoon. She would remain for a few moments at a respectful distance, unmoving, eyeing him furtively with a timid but admiring glance, perhaps taken by the fierce beauty of her master. She would then place the tray on a table and walk away with an imperceptible step, vanishing amid the indigo silk curtains that fluttered in the light breeze always wafting through the palace, produced by its clever architectural play of secret passages and polished surfaces.

Finally, one day, another messenger was announced and Wei got up, shook off his torpor and walked towards the audience chamber. He immediately recognized the man as one of the Flying Foxes.

'My Lord,' he said, 'our chief has instructed me to advise you that he was so bold as to take the liberty of having the cavalry followed by several of our men, with instruments adequate for a hunt over impenetrable terrain, should the need arise. He hopes that you will pardon this initiative undertaken without informing you, because it has produced a positive outcome. The dove was followed, in flight, where the horses could not venture, and now we know the exact location of Li Cheng. The horsemen have been informed as well, and they are now camped at a suitable distance from the fortress, silent and watchful. From there, they will be able to send information in time for us to make adequate provisions and take the necessary measures.'

Wei was exultant although he did not let his excitement be seen. 'Tell your brothers to be ready to leave as soon as possible, in full battle order. The best units of the imperial army will accompany us, in sufficient numbers to guarantee the certain success of our mission.'

IN THREE DAYS' TIME, the army was ready to move. Wei led them in person, at the head of the Flying Foxes. He mounted a horse from Xixia, black and shiny as the wing of a crow, a gift from one of his marshals in the south-west.

The long convoy of cavalry, foot soldiers, carts and pack animals set off at the first light of dawn through the silent streets of the city, but their departure did not pass unobserved.

Daruma was awakened by the scuttling of many hoofs on the cobblestones as he slept a less than tranquil sleep in his room at the caravanserai, where he had been settled for some time. He dressed hurriedly, went down to the courtyard and crossed it to access the area where his warehouse and pack animals were.

A voice resounded at his back: 'How is it that you're such an early riser this morning, Daruma?'

33

THE SUN WAS SETTING on the valley, illuminating the cliffs that loomed over the village of Li Cheng on the west, and opposite them the rooftops of the monastery of the warrior monks of the Red Lotus, perched on the rocky plateau that rose steeply over the bend in the river.

Dan Qing was looking at the façade of the tomb of Emperor Yuandi, which was guarded by winged dragons with gaping jaws and preceded by a majestic staircase. From that dominating position he could see even the path that led towards the access ramp at the southern gate and his attention was drawn to a small cloud of dust moving fast in the direction of the citadel. Before long, he could make out a horseman approaching at a full gallop, spurring his horse on with great urgency.

He watched as the man crossed the gateway, leapt to the ground and exchanged a few words with a guard, who pointed out the paved road that led towards the great imperial tomb. In just a few moments, he was standing before the prince. He was covered in dust and sweat.

'Prince, a signal has arrived from our observers. Wei is marching on Li Cheng.'

Dan Qing scowled. 'How can they say that? How far away is he?'

'About two weeks' march from here, but his outriders have already been spotted nearly at the base of the rise. We can't see where else he could be headed. If we're mistaken, all the better, but it seemed wise to warn you.'

'You've done the right thing. Do you know how many men there are?'

'About three thousand, plus the Flying Foxes, at least two hundred of them. Wei himself is riding at their head.'

'Then I fear there's no doubt about their destination. Have the guards give you a place in the stables for your horse and a room for yourself for the night.'

Metellus and Yun Shan arrived almost immediately, informed by the guards that there was an emergency.

'Bad news?' asked Metellus.

'The usurper is marching on Li Cheng. He's just two weeks' march from us. He has a great number of men with him and the Flying Foxes. We have very little hope of survival. Perhaps it's time that you go, Xiong Ying.'

'Go?' asked Metellus with a bitter smile. 'Where?'

Dan Qing glanced back towards the monumental staircase and asked him, 'Are you ready?'

Metellus nodded and motioned for Yun Shan to follow.

'No,' said the princess. 'You go alone.'

Dan Qing took a torch from its stand on the enclosure wall and began to climb the steps that led to the emperor's tomb. 'Yun Shan has told me you've seen the carved green stone.'

'I've seen it,' replied Metellus.

'Did they really come from your country?'

'There's no doubt. The words on the stone are written in my language.'

'Did she tell you about the legend?'

'Yes, she did,' he replied.

Dan Qing stopped and looked straight into his eyes. 'Would you like . . . to see them?'

Metellus stared back uneasily. 'Are you making fun of me?'

'Not at all,' replied Dan Qing. 'Emperor Yuandi wanted to be buried here at Li Cheng and he wanted the three hundred Mercenary Devils to mount guard at his tomb for all eternity. That's how the legend was born.'

'I don't . . . understand.'

'Follow me, then. If you choose to remain in this place and risk your life here, it is only right that you meet those who came before you.'

They had reached the top of the staircase and Dan Qing lit the torch from one of the votive tripods burning before the entrance. He then pointed to one of the dragons guarding the mausoleum and said to Metellus, 'Turn that statue towards the left, while I turn the other one in the opposite direction.'

Metellus did as he was asked and what seemed to be a wall of smooth stone shifted aside, revealing a corridor behind it.

The sun had already sunk behind the mountains and Dan Qing, after having raised his eyes for a moment to the darkening sky, entered, followed by his companion.

They advanced for about thirty steps between two walls of solid rock inscribed with texts from ancient oracles, until they found an opening on the left and a flight of about twenty steps that led down into a crypt. Dan Qing lifted his torch to illuminate a vast underground chamber and a phantasmagorical vision appeared before Metellus's incredulous eyes. The sarcophagus of Emperor Yuandi was carved from a single block of jade shot through with tones that ranged from green to golden yellow. It was guarded by three hundred statues. Although crafted in a Chinese style, they unmistakably represented Roman legionaries from the Republican age, wearing authentic armour. Their helmets and *loricae* were still in good condition despite the passage of time and they reflected the torchlight here and there with a metallic gleam.

'Gods . . . O powerful gods . . . I can't believe it,' murmured Metellus, wandering among the ranks of immobile warriors in the timeless atmosphere of the great tomb.

Hanging at each man's chest was a *titulus*, the lead identification plate on which Metellus could read off their names one by one, in a choked voice: name, rank, division, decorations. He walked along the files of those disquieting figures as though he were inspecting an army of ghosts.

Then, all at once, the torchlight drew a figure different from all the rest out of the shadows. It was not a soldier: he was sitting, dressed in a long tunic and a cape, and he held a little case on his knees. The object was authentic, not modelled in clay like the rest of the statue. There were words written on the case:

CORNELIVS AGRICOLA, PRAEFECTVS FABRORVM

'Do you understand what this means?' asked Dan Qing. 'Many of our wisest monks have tried in vain to decipher . . . these.' He opened the case, revealing a number of scrolls inside.

Metellus opened one with great care and brought it close to the torchlight. There were symbols, formulas, drawings, construction plans and assembly instructions in Latin and Greek.

'I . . . just can't believe this,' he repeated, completely taken aback by what he was seeing, unrolling one scroll after another.

'What are they?' asked Dan Qing. 'What do the drawings represent? They look like machines, but our technicians have not been able to interpret them.'

'Because the instructions are written in an old military code and the sequence of drawings is in reverse order. This man was the greatest designer of war machines of his time. He disappeared quite suddenly and no trace of his work was ever found . . . Do you understand what this means? These papers will show us how we can win our battle, even though we are outnumbered. You'll realize that every civilization, even the most advanced, has something to learn from others. Tell me this: are there any other exits from this tomb that lead to the surface?'

'Yes, more than one.'

'I must know exactly where they are located and where they come up.'

'What do you mean to do?'

Metellus scanned the steel armour, the swords hanging from the statues' baldrics. 'You'll know soon enough,' he replied. 'Let's go immediately. We haven't a moment to lose.'

When they emerged at the top of the outside staircase,

under a starry sky, Metellus turned to the prince. 'You must give me the authority to enrol and train men here at Li Cheng and in the surrounding countryside.'

Dan Qing nodded. The imperious light of a commander of armies shone in Xiong Ying's eyes. He was ready to take up the challenge.

'Yes,' he replied, 'I'll give you one of my adjutants. But remember that your own training must never be interrupted, not even for a single day. Yun Shan awaits you in the *palaestra* even now.'

'I know,' replied Metellus.

'Xiong Ying?'

'Yes, Prince?'

'Listen to me. What is about to happen was unforeseeable, and I must be sincere with you. Unfortunately, we don't have much chance of surviving. Wei's forces are crushing, and our walls will not be able to hold out for long. What's more, he has the Flying Foxes with him. You know what that means, don't you?'

'I do,' replied Metellus.

'Then think it over, while you still have time. This is not your war. You've done everything you could do, and you've paid a high price indeed. You can go now, if you want. The only thing I ask of you is that you give me your word as a soldier that you will never reveal to anyone what you have learned here. I trust you.'

Metellus smiled. 'I think it's already a little too late for that. I have a piece of my heart here at Li Cheng, don't I? You mustn't worry. Doesn't the legend say that when your dynasty is in danger, the three hundred Mercenary Devils will rise from their tombs and put the enemy to rout? Sleep well, Prince.'

'You too, Xiong Ying.'

Metellus vanished into the night.

FOR TWO WEEKS, the southern quarter of Li Cheng resounded day and night with strange noises. Incessant hammer strokes, wheezing bellows, rhythmic shouts guiding the common and coordinated efforts of many men. But not a thing was visible. The foreigner whom everyone called Xiong Ying had been given the use of a big storehouse usually used for threshing marsh grain and that was where he had established his base.

The men who had reported for service could never be seen coming or going. They left the place long after dark and by daybreak were back at work in the old warehouse.

Then one day the doors of the big building were opened and strange wheeled machines were dragged out, although it was difficult to discern their shape under the heavy canvases that covered them.

When Dan Qing and Yun Shan saw them later, uncovered, they were amazed at the huge dimensions and ingenious construction.

'What extraordinary machines!' observed Dan Qing. 'But what do they shoot?'

'Stones, bolts, jugs of burning pitch,' replied Metellus.

'I think our monks know of something even more effective than pitch. I'll see to it that they prepare your ammunition.'

Metellus had the machines towed between two wings of the gathering crowd towards the section of the walls that faced south on to the highlands, the only point from which the citadel could be attacked.

The machines were hauled up already-positioned wooden ramps on to the battlements and then disguised with wooden screens. The once-futuristic plans of *praefectus fabrorum* Cornelius Agricola had taken form in wood and iron and were in perfect working order.

But Metellus had another weapon in reserve, this one completely clandestine, which he worked on every day after sunset in a clearing west of the tall grey cliffs that towered over the plain. No one was admitted, not even Dan Qing or Yun Shan, and Metellus's men were solemnly sworn to secrecy.

One night, just a few hours before dawn, Yun Shan joined

Metellus up on the battlements. He was intent on scanning the darkness for signs of enemy approach.

'Eagles cannot see at night,' said Yun Shan.

'No, they can't. And yet in the many nights that I guarded the great wall on the borders of our empire, I developed a sort of secret sense. I learned to hear the enemy approaching before I could see them.'

'You also have a wall defending your borders?'

'Yes, certainly. In the north we control a vast island called Britannia. At the point where the risk of invasion was greatest, we built a wall right across it, from sea to sea. It takes nine days of marching to get from one end to the other.'

Yun Shan smiled. 'Ours protects the entire northern border and it takes six months to cover its total length. It's so wide that there is a road on top that chariots and entire armies can use in both directions.'

'It must be extraordinary,' said Metellus. 'I'd like to see it some day.'

'You will . . . We will survive this.'

'I hope so. For you . . .'

There was a long silence, then Metellus asked, 'What do your wise men say to ward off the fear of death?'

' "When death comes, we shall acquiesce and allow ourselves to be taken inside the mystery," ' replied Yun Shan. 'And yours?'

'One of our emperors wrote, "When your time comes, go in peace, for there is peace with he who calls you." Similar concepts, I see. One of our poets wrote, "Banish the fear of death with love." '

Yun Shan clasped him close and embraced him. Metellus could smell the fragrance that had made him feel alive in the time of his unconsciousness and he felt an intense wave of emotion fill his chest. He kissed her and the warmth and softness of her lips made him feel he was kissing a goddess. He took her hands in his and brought them to his face. 'It doesn't seem possible that hands like these can give a caress or impart death with the same light touch.'

Yun Shan pulled away from him and sought out his eyes in the darkness. 'I will not let them take me alive, Xiong Ying. You know that, don't you?'

'I know, Yun Shan, and the thought of it chills my heart. How is it possible that we've found each other, that you wrenched me back from the other world, only for us to be called towards death once again? Why do the Red Lotus want to defend this place at any cost? Isn't there somewhere else they could go?'

'No. Wei would find us anywhere. Facing him is the only solution. He is bent on soothing his own suffering with the suffering and death of others, and there is nothing that can turn him away from this road.'

'Not even you?'

'I've thought about it. If I could save Li Cheng by handing myself over to him, I would do it. But it wouldn't be enough, I'm certain of it. He is obsessed by a desire that cannot be satisfied, by an unconsumed love that burns stronger than any real love, because it lives only in his imagination, generating bloody ghosts, demons who infest his nights and pollute his meditation.

'There is no peace for Wei. He wants to turn himself into a nightmare, into one of the monsters he calls up every night when he closes his eyes.'

Metellus held her until he could feel the beat of her heart becoming one with his own. She threw her arms around him and kissed him again.

'I want this night to never end,' she said. 'I want the darkness to cover us and hide us, I want time to stop, I want all of your memories to disappear except for those that we've experienced together.'

'My memories only make my feelings for you deeper, Yun Shan, because they're the memories of a man who has nothing to hide . . .' He broke off. 'Listen . . . they're coming.'

Yun Shan strained to hear.

'Horsemen and foot soldiers ... a great many of them ... thousands and thousands.'

The wind carried a barely perceptible buzz that faded when the breeze diminished in intensity.

'You have the ears of a fox.'

'I told you that I spent long hours as a border guard. I saw many of my comrades fall because they hadn't heard the enemy crawling through the dark with a dagger between his teeth. Look now,' he said, pointing to the horizon.

It was swarming with lights. Thousands of flames quivering in the dark, swaying as if moved by the same gusts of wind that blew through the silent alleyways of Li Cheng. The front was narrow, but then slowly broadened into an ever wider line, until the entire expanse of the high plains was covered by trembling lights.

The men came into sight as dawn crept over the sky; rare stars pierced the cobalt dome with a light as pure as a diamond's. Then the sun sent a blade of light between the hilltops and a thin strip of clouds.

Wei's army was revealed.

There were foot soldiers advancing with long yellow drapes tied to the shafts of their pikes, warriors from the steppe wearing leather helmets with long horsehair crests, Manchurian horsemen with bronze breastplates and spears decorated with onager tufts. The imperial cavalry carried long banners of red silk on which the golden monogram of the Han dynasty was still embroidered; they wore breastplates of leather and bronze and helmets of the same shining metal.

At the centre was the black heart of the army: the Flying Foxes. Black they were, on black horses, arousing fear even at this distance.

Metellus heard a beating of wings over his head. He saw a dove fly over the rooftops and alight on one of the windows of the monastery, the quarters of Dan Qing.

'How strange,' he said. 'Did you see that? Your brother's

dove is back. Doves may fly back to their homes after they've been deliberately transported far away, but I've never heard of the opposite. Go tell your brother what's happening. I'll stay here.'

Yun Shan ran to the monastery and was soon back with Dan Qing, armed with a bow, bludgeon and sword.

Dan Qing let his gaze sweep over the army that was now drawn up in full battle formation, stock still on the plain. Only the standards fluttered in the morning breeze, shot through with shivers of light.

'What are they waiting for?' asked Metellus.

'I don't know. Perhaps for someone to open the gate.'

'Come now. Here? That's hardly possible,' objected Metellus.

'It wasn't possible for an army to get this far either. It's never happened.'

'Someone has betrayed us,' said Yun Shan.

'Have you had any further news of Baj Renjie?' asked Metellus.

'He took part in my breakout, but he never showed up at the meeting point afterwards. I fear he was captured. He's probably dead.'

'Does he know how to get here?' asked Metellus.

Behind them they could hear their soldiers rushing to the bastions to prepare to defend the citadel. The machines creaked noisily as they were put in position and freed of their heavy canvas covers, revealing huge firing arms, powerful scorpions with multiple bows.

'No,' replied Dan Qing. 'No one but the members of the Red Lotus knows where this fortress is located. And no member of the Red Lotus has ever betrayed it.'

'What if the traitor were your dove?' Metellus asked again. Yun Shan looked puzzled. 'That cage had a kind of mechanism that released its occupant after a certain number of cycles. There must have been a reason for that ... Where did you get that cage, Yun Shan?'

'As I told Dan Qing, Daruma gave it to me. It was his gift for the prince.'

'Daruma . . .' muttered Metellus. 'Daruma . . . is that possible?'

'It was Daruma who organized my escape,' said Dan Qing. 'Why would he ever . . .'

'Look out!' shouted a voice. 'They're advancing!'

A unit of enemy archers was running towards the walls. They drew up at the bottom of the ramp and took position.

'Take cover!' shouted Metellus.

A cloud of arrows shot upwards, described a wide parabola and landed inside the circle of walls. One of the warriors who had not found shelter collapsed to the ground, run through by a number of arrows, as did all the domestic animals wandering through the square: three dogs and a trained monkey.

Metellus turned to Dan Qing. 'No one assaults a fortress with archers. They want to keep us busy on this side, so they can attack from another. Watch out!' he shouted. 'Over there!'

A second barrage of darts rained down on the rooftops, the towers and the sentry walk on the walls.

There was silence, several interminable moments of deep silence.

Then a whistle pierced the sky.

34

'FLYING FOXES!' someone screamed. 'Alarm, sound the alarm!'

Metellus raised his eyes to the sky and saw, in utter astonishment, what he had never been able to see clearly in the past: a swarm of flying men, hanging from huge wings of silk, gliding on the wind, skimming the treetops.

'Archers!' shouted Dan Qing. 'Loose!'

The archers turned their sights away from the advancing troops and trained their bows upwards without striking their targets, who were moving quickly and still too far away. A second volley took off, but many arrows were intercepted by the tree branches and fell to the ground without causing harm. Two of the soaring raiders were hit and fell headlong to the ground. Several more were injured, but the rest landed safely in great numbers and immediately engaged in furious battle with the monks who surged around them.

Metellus could see the army charging the walls from outside and had his men load the machines. He had put together a formidable array of field artillery: catapults with several arms, multiple-bowed scorpions that hurled steel bolts, *ballistae* that flung jugs of flaming pitch to which Metellus had added the mysterious concoction prepared by the monks, one of their most jealously guarded secrets.

'Fire!' he shouted. 'Now!'

The various *ballistae* shot, at brief intervals, four heavy boulders each, opening frightening voids in the ranks of the Manchurian cavalry. The bolts came next and then the jars of burning pitch. They flew like flaming meteors over the wall and then, to Metellus's utter amazement, exploded in mid-air with an earth-shaking boom, scattering a rain of fire on the troops below. Many tried to run off, but the Flying Foxes, positioned at the wings, stopped them cold with the deadly aim of their bows: the punishment reserved for cowards. Wei's voice could be heard, as shrill as a falcon's cry. The troops reunited in a compact front and charged forward again in attack, shouting and shooting volleys of thousands of arrows against the besieged citadel and against the war-machine posts. Many of those who manned the machines on the bastions were hit and put out of action.

Those who survived remained at their posts and fired again in quick succession: first, second, third, fourth station. Their bolts shrieked through the air and mowed down the enemy archers and foot soldiers in great numbers. Other meteors streaked across the sky, strewing globes of fire that exploded on the ground, this time in the middle of the infantrymen, slaughtering tens of them with each blast. Wei rode furiously on towards the fortress as if nothing could stop him, as if the arrows were deflected by the fierce aura that surrounded him. He was yelling with his strident, penetrating, inhuman voice and no one dared any longer to retreat. The enemy continued to advance under the hail of missiles, racing up the access ramp to the southern gate. Behind him Metellus could hear the shouts of the combatants and the raging of the battle. He imagined that Yun Shan had joined the fight, no longer seeing her at his side, and he was tormented with anguish, but he held his position and went on coordinating the relentless firing of his machines.

Wei, from outside, realized that his men would never reach the gate as long as those machines remained in position and he ordered his archers to let fly with barrages of incendiary arrows. The darts stuck into the wood of the machines' mobile frames and set them on fire. Many of the artillerymen were forced to leave their posts to attempt to put out the flames.

A second and third wave of Flying Foxes descended inside the citadel, coming to the aid of their encircled comrades and reversing their odds. Dan Qing and Yun Shan, flanked by their best combatants, counterattacked vigorously, hurling themselves into the fray. From his vantage point on the battlements, Metellus could see that the Flying Foxes were trying to open the gate from the inside. He ordered several of his archers to aim in that direction and to bring down as many as they could. Several were hit and fell, but many others amazingly dodged the arrows and continued to advance, spinning their swords with remarkable rapidity and making dizzying leaps. They seemed to be animated by inextinguishable ardour, coordinated by a single mind. Metellus had already seen this approach in the great courtyard of Luoyang and he was flooded by panic. His brow dripped with cold sweat. Now a large group of assailants was racing up the stairs towards the battlements, spreading themselves around the entire perimeter. Metellus and his men met them, the Roman brandishing his two *gladii* and plunging furiously into the battle.

He had never been able to test his new combat skills on the battlefield and he realized that the incredibly fast hail of blows, the glint of steel narrowly missing his face, his head, his heart, produced a delirious excitement he had never felt before, not even at the peak of the fiercest battle. He was concentrating so intensely on his adversaries' movements that he could deconstruct them in time and space and understand the direction they were coming from as if they were three times slower than in reality. The two *gladii* flashed and struck with massive power, they intersected high and low, parrying, deflecting, stabbing, whacking, slashing.

In the eye of the storm, each combatant sought a single adversary, and the battle fragmented into myriad individual fights, with a victor and a victim at every instant. Metellus shouted out at the top of his voice, 'Yun Shan! Yun Shan, where are you?' and knocked his adversaries back down the stairs, making them fall in clusters. He himself seemed an unstoppable war machine. A sword sliced into the flesh of his right shoulder, another grazed his left thigh, but he kept advancing, indifferent to the pain. A fresh wave of Flying Foxes swooped down very close to the gate and, before the Red Lotus combatants had time to react, managed to open it.

Wei and his men stormed through the gate but Metellus, from the battlements, ordered the artillery to wheel their machines around and aim them inside. The invaders were greeted by relentless volleys of steel bolts, boulders and balls of flaming pitch pouring down upon them, spreading death and destruction. But Wei was their soul: black on his dark steed, he drove on without pause, dragging the others behind him. They seemed possessed, trampling on their own fallen in their fury to advance. Waves of assailants came spilling through the open gate now, like a river breaking its banks.

Watching this happen from above, Metellus understood that the situation was hopeless. He shouted to his men, 'Resist at any cost. Cover me from behind!' and ran along the battlements in the direction of the staircase leading to the mausoleum of Emperor Yuandi. He suddenly vanished as if the earth had swallowed him up.

In the big courtyard, Wei's warriors had fallen upon the monks of the Red Lotus, led by Dan Qing and Yun Shan, who fought on with desperate valour. Wei had dismounted and was doing battle with his sword in his hand, cutting down anyone who tried to get in his way as he neared the centre of the enemy ranks. He had spotted Yun Shan and it seemed that nothing could stop him.

But when it appeared that all was lost for the Red Lotus, a thunderous clap of bronze resounded through the courtyard, reverberating again and again. An explosion flared on the vast terrace of the mausoleum up high behind them, then another and a third. Many of the warriors turned to look in bewilderment as they heard the mighty roll of a drum beating out an invisible step.

More explosions, and a thick curtain of smoke spread along the entire façade of the mausoleum, slowly wafting down the stairs as well. The drum roll was loud, pounding, and as the cloud began to thin a spectral vision was revealed: one hundred and fifty clay warriors decked out in Roman armour were descending those stairs in step, shoulder to shoulder, shield to shield, an impenetrable wall of iron. Marching at their head was Marcus Metellus Aquila: Xiong Ying, the Resplendent Eagle!

A voice seemed to thunder from the bowels of the earth: 'The Mercenary Devils have risen from their tombs!'

Panic spread among Wei's troops, who began to pull back in a disorderly manner. The army of spectres suddenly seemed to have stopped. Another clap of bronze thunder was heard and a barrage of darts was loosed from the wall of ghost shields, falling like hail on the rows of Wei's men and decimating them. The army advanced again, loosing a second barrage and then a third, opening huge gaps in the enemy ranks.

Dan Qing shouted, 'The Mercenary Devils have returned from the tomb to save us! The prophecy has come true! Forward, men! Victory is ours!'

At that sight and upon hearing those words, the warrior monks felt their waning strength surge up and they charged Wei's baffled, disoriented troops, pushing them back towards the lower ground.

The din of the drum was deafening and the vision of those ghosts of clay advancing with the jerky movements of automata struck terror into the men, and even the Flying Foxes seemed to no longer heed the cries of Wei goading them on.

Another frightful noise was heard, as if the earth were heaving, then another roar and a curtain of smoke. One hundred more warriors, moving iron-clad statues, emerged from the other world and began to march forward, their weapons levelled, towards the undefended right flank of Wei's army.

One of the enemies yelled, 'They're the Mercenary Devils! They'll drag us under the ground!'

Wei lopped off his head with a single blow of his sword, but the terrorized Manchurian troops were already fleeing out of the still-open gate, followed by a great number of foot soldiers routed by Metellus's spectral army.

A crack of thunder was heard yet again, a thick screen of soot hid the side of the hill and yet another maniple of clay warriors burst out of the ground. The earth shook under their heavy hobnailed boots as they marched forward, a terrifying sight, shielded in impenetrable armour. Anticipating the attack from that side as well, Wei's men, decimated and completely unnerved, took to their heels behind their comrades already rushing outside the walls.

Only Wei, with a band of Flying Foxes, battled on with savage energy. They were held off with great difficulty by Dan Qing and his warrior monks.

All at once, Metellus sensed that Yun Shan was in danger and he shouted out her name. Wei wheeled around at the sound of his voice, spotted him and flew at him, spinning his blood-soaked sword.

Metellus defended himself, returning blow after blow, joining his formidable skill at wielding two swords with the secrets of combat art learned at Li Cheng. But after his initial surprise, Wei reacted with awesome violence. He took a spectacular leap and landed behind the Roman, instantly dealing a blow to his loins. Metellus spun around, dodging the blade, but he could not avoid a long cut on his side, from which blood began to flow. Wei's foot struck his leg and made him fall to his knees. At that moment, Metellus saw his comrades falling one after another in the arena and Wei's leering face looming over him as it did now.

'Your comrades were devoured by the dogs,' Wei shouted, 'and now you will meet the same end!'

Metellus felt those words pierce him like a flaming blade and he flipped back with a powerful contraction of his back muscles. He then attacked with all the force he was capable of. The eunuch wavered and backed off at that unexpected assault, and found himself at the rim of the opening from which the last of the Mercenary Devils had emerged.

Metellus tried to push him in, but Wei swerved to the side and it was the Roman who fell into the void.

Yun Shan, who had not taken her eyes off their duel to the

death, thought that Metellus had been killed. She let out a cry and ran as fast as she could to the spot where she had seen him disappear. Wei dived in after his enemy without a moment's hesitation. He vaulted down to the bottom of the underground stairway and rushed along the corridor to a second staircase, which ended in a grandiose portal. Before him was the enormous tomb of Emperor Yuandi, guarded by a throng of mute ghosts.

Metellus, hidden behind the sarcophagus, saw Wei standing out against the entrance in his black suit, gripping his bloody sword. He could hear him approaching and backed into the darkest corner of the mausoleum, from where he could attempt an ambush. He moved cautiously among the spectres of the Lost Legion, unmoving and staring with their unchanging smiles of stone.

Yun Shan had arrived as well and she descended the steps warily, without making a sound. She soon found herself in front of the arched entrance to the mausoleum, almost totally immersed in darkness. She drew a long breath, then slipped inside, settling in a shadowy corner. Only a few oil lamps hanging from the outer walls gave off a dim, trembling glow. The others had burnt out their oil and were smoking.

Another lamp went out. Metellus realized that it was Wei who was extinguishing them. He was stealing along the walls and blowing on those that were still burning. The huge room was plunged into darkness. The only pale reflection to enter the portal was caused by the complex interaction of refracted light from outside. Metellus moved among the statues, nerves as taut as steel, his heart pounding. He knew that the threat could come from any direction.

Dan Qing's voice sounded inside him: 'Beware Xiong Ying! You are a sentry in the darkness! Where will the enemy's arrow come from? Where will the dagger strike?' The memory made his arm dart like a lightning bolt towards the hint of a shadow that had materialized in front of him. The tip of his *gladius* flashed towards the throat of . . .

'Yun Shan!'

At that very instant, Wei had sprung from the darkness behind him, implacably thrusting his sword forward.

Yun Shan managed to say, 'Xiong Ying, no   !'

But the Roman was turning, slowly, towards the enemy standing stock-still behind him, Metellus's other *gladius* sunken into his chest up to its hilt.

Metellus extracted the sword while Wei let his own drop, making the floor and walls of the chamber ring with argentine echoes. He slumped to the floor, his eyes still wide in an incredulous expression. Yun Shan knelt beside him and received, in the darkness, his last look. She then closed his eyes, whispering, 'Rest now, finally, young Wei. May oblivion descend upon your soul . . .'

Metellus knelt and picked the body up into his arms and carried it outside.

The combatants saw him thus, ascending the stairs with the body of the youth in his arms, white with the extreme pallor of death, his long tapered fingers swinging inertly with every step.

Combat ceased. The survivors turned tail and bolted through the open gate towards their camp.

Metellus deposited Wei's body at the foot of the great staircase and joined Dan Qing, holding Yun Shan by the hand. There was no exulting, no cries of victory. The ground was scattered with dead bodies clutching at one another in a final show of violence, while the survivors sought out their comrades, separating them with measured gestures from the grip of the enemy.

Dan Qing had his horse brought to him and led his men out to chase the fugitives who were fleeing to their camp. Metellus and Yun Shan also leapt into the saddle and galloped out behind him. The camp was completely surrounded and the soldiers of the imperial army dropped to their knees before the prince, declaring their subjugation and begging for clemency.

The warriors of clay vanished after winning the battle, just as they had appeared.

Yun Shan did not stop. She rode through the camp at full speed as though she were looking for someone, until she got to the animal pen and found Daruma trying to get on to a camel. She grabbed him by the arm and, indifferent to his protests, had him dragged into the presence of Dan Qing.

'He's the one who betrayed us. It was he who had me carry the dove to you.'

Daruma seemed astonished. 'Dove? What dove are you talking about?'

'Don't pretend you don't know! I'm talking about the dove that led Wei to the walls of Li Cheng and that you arranged to have put into my boat as a gift for Dan Qing.'

Daruma widened his eyes but Yun Shan pressed on: 'I should have known that it was a trap. Only you knew where I was headed.'

Metellus stepped forward and stared at him with a calm look, but his voice was hard when he asked, 'Why?'

Daruma looked at him through watery eyes, with a pathetically defenceless expression. 'I'm a merchant, Metellus, and it is my nature to buy and sell . . . everything, even myself at times. But I did not betray you. I would never have done so. I truly do not know what you are talking about, but in any case it was Baj Renjie who prepared the boat.'

'Why didn't you tell me it was Baj Renjie?' Yun Shan insisted.

'There was no time for long explanations. I told you that trusted friends had made the arrangements, remember? Baj Renjie reached me one night at the caravanserai. He was in tatters, deeply upset. He told me that he had managed to get away from Wei's men. He asked me about you and I told him that we absolutely needed to find a boat and help you reach safety along with Metellus, and that I didn't know how I could get one. He offered to help me. He assured me that he would get a boat, with everything that was needed, to the bend of the ford on the Luo Ho river. I thanked him. What else could I do?'

'But it was one of your men who gave me the cage with the dove in it,' retorted Yun Shan.

'One of my men?' protested Daruma. 'That's impossible. I was alone.'

Yun Shan hesitated a moment and then demanded, 'If you had no role in this whole story, then why were you just trying to escape when I caught up with you?'

'Because I didn't want to be found in the wrong place at the wrong time, fearing that my presence here might raise suspicions, which is exactly what has happened. But it's not how it looks, you must believe me. I'm here against my will. I was about to leave the caravanserai, fifteen days ago, when I was stopped and arrested by Wei's guards. At the time, I was certain that Baj Renjie had betrayed me. He was the only one who knew, the only one I'd trusted. As far as this bird cage is concerned, even if I'd seen it, I'd have had no reason to be suspicious about it. How could a dove reveal the whereabouts of Li Cheng?'

'Perhaps because rumour has it that no one who has tried to reach Li Cheng in a boat ever returned to tell about it. If Wei had had their boat followed, he might have captured Yun Shan and Metellus, but he would never have found Li Cheng, and that was his true obsession,' Dan Qing said, his head hanging dubiously.

'I believe him,' said Metellus.

'I'd like to, but I can't,' retorted the prince. 'Who warned Wei about our re-entry into the country? How did the Flying Foxes manage to attack us right after we'd passed the border? Only Daruma knew where we were headed.'

Daruma, who up until that moment had seemed more bewildered than worried, began to change expression. 'You can't seriously believe such a thing . . . Prince, but why would I have saved you to then turn you over to the enemy? It doesn't make sense!'

'Yes, it does, I'm afraid,' replied Dan Qing, 'and it fits in perfectly with a diabolically cunning plan. The only way to attract all the different components of the resistance was to have me return after a period of imprisonment. All those who were opposed to Wei's tyranny but who were scattered throughout the country would join around me. And Wei would be able to wipe them all out in a single blow. And that's what was about to happen, thanks to the idea of using someone who was above suspicion: you. Only you knew when we would be crossing the border, and when we were about to go up to the Monastery of Whispering Waters, you abandoned us, because you knew what awaited us there. Then, at Luoyang, you managed to free me, regaining credibility and my trust. But then you used my sister to find this refuge and you brought Wei's army here. Your presence in the camp is the proof of your guilt.'

'But . . . that's nothing more than a series of coincidences!' protested Daruma.

'That may be,' replied Dan Qing, 'but I cannot run the risk.' He turned to his men. 'Take him away.'

Metellus approached. 'Please reconsider. Don't let yourself be swayed by the demon of suspicion. You have already committed one atrocity that you came to regret.'

Dan Qing turned away without answering and walked towards his horse.

Daruma shouted to Metellus, 'Help me!'

Yun Shan neared him. 'Unfortunately, I'm afraid my brother is right. When I found Daruma, he had found a camel and was trying to escape.'

'He admitted that himself,' replied Metellus. 'And I would have done the same. He couldn't risk being found here.'

At that moment, one of the monks ran up, panting. 'Come quickly!'

Metellus and Yun Shan followed him and were taken inside one of the pavilions, where Baj Renjie was dangling from the pole that supported the centre of the tent. Metellus looked at him in consternation.

'I think this may be enough to exculpate Daruma,' he said. 'Let's go and tell your brother.'

'Yes,' agreed Yun Shan. 'I'll run and stop him.'

'My Lord!' rang out another voice nearby. 'Look! We caught him as he was trying to get away!' Four of his men were dragging a man dressed in the Persian style.

'Who are you?' demanded Metellus, in Persian.

The man did not answer.

'I'm the Roman commander who broke out of Aus Daiwa with nine of my men. Can you imagine what I'll do to you if you do not speak?' he said, pronouncing the words in a tone that left no doubts.

'I was sent by the great king, Shapur, to warn Wei of the escape of the man with the piercing eyes. I could never have imagined that you had run off together!'

'We did not, in fact.' Dan Qing's voice sounded behind them. 'It was by chance that we met.'

'Are you convinced now?' asked Metellus.

Dan Qing lowered his head.

'Where is Daruma?'

'He's alive,' said Yun Shan, running back into the tent. 'Just in time!'

'Just in time . . .' repeated Metellus. 'One must always take one's time before judging a man guilty. And before taking his life.'

Dan Qing approached him. 'Come, let us go back to Li Cheng. It has been a long and difficult day. Tomorrow everything will appear in a different light.'

They mounted their horses and headed towards Li Cheng, proceeding in silence for a long stretch. They crossed the gate of the citadel and Dan Qing turned towards the mausoleum of Yuandi and then towards Metellus. 'How did you do it?' he asked.

'Nothing strikes terror into the hearts of men like the unknown,' replied Metellus. 'Even the most courageous are afraid of what they cannot understand. I brought an ancient legend to life. There are many men in this city who resemble us Romans. I chose those among them who had the most Western features, I trained them in our combat techniques and at the crucial moment I had them appear wearing the armour I'd taken from the statues, with their faces and hands coated with clay. When I'd achieved the desired effect, I had them disappear. For a brief time, legend became reality, history. And then history faded back into myth. This day will never be forgotten.'

35

Out on the monastery balcony, Metellus observed the spectacle of the sun sinking behind the forested mountains amid flaming clouds that slowly changed colour and from bright red faded into azure blue and then the intense indigo of the West, where the evening star already sparkled. From the garden, where once, during his long convalescence, he had seen Yun Shan passing like an apparition, the song of a nightingale arose. The song echoed with shadows and he was moved as it aroused distant memories and present emotions that were no less intense. His hand instinctively fell to his belt and found a wooden elephant with a jointed trunk, the toy that he had hoped to bring his son after his imprisonment . . .

He heard her footsteps approaching and she was standing in front of him. 'Do you know what kept the tip of my sword from your throat, down there in the mausoleum of Yuandi?' he asked her. 'Your fragrance . . . the scent of your hair, the only sensation that I remember from the time I was unconscious. That fragrance is a part of my soul and my senses now.'

'And your heart is a part of my heart, Xiong Ying.'

'I know. The power of the hidden heart saved me in the arena, and perhaps even down in the mausoleum, a moment before Wei could run me through with his sword.'

'No, that can't be,' replied Yun Shan. 'My energy was surely not capable of stopping him.'

'Then it was your presence. I know I couldn't have been faster than he was, I'm sure of it. Wei sensed you, even in that deep darkness. He felt that you were close and that made him hesitate . . .'

The girl dropped her head to hide her tears.

A long silence followed and when Yun Shan raised her eyes she saw that Metellus was turning a little object over in his hands. 'May I ask you what you're thinking of, Xiong Ying?'

Metellus gazed at her with eyes full of sadness.

'What are you thinking of, Xiong Ying?' she repeated softly.

Metellus opened his hand and showed her the wooden elephant. 'It had been hidden in my belt for so long that I'd forgotten about it . . . I bought it for my son . . . I . . . I have to go back, Yun Shan.'

'Go back? But why? Here you have the love . . . of everyone.'

Metellus replied, 'I love you, Princess, more than my own life, but I must go. I've felt the need to return inside of me ever since I read that inscription on the green stone . . . the words of men who had given up everything, even their own language, in a vain attempt to forget the land of their fathers and the loved ones they had left behind . . . They never returned, it's true. But I made a promise, to my dying emperor, that I would return to prevent the ruin of that world, and to my son, that I would not leave him alone.

'I couldn't live like this, Yun Shan. Can you understand? You would see me bend under the weight of these unkept promises, day after day, thinking of my son, who continues to trust in my homecoming, not knowing that this will never happen. Forgive me, my beloved, my dream, my soul . . .'

Yun Shan ran away in tears.

Dan Qing saw her as he left his quarters, and approached Metellus. 'When a woman cries, a man loses a part of his heart, says an ancient proverb.'

'It's the truth, Dan Qing.'

'The love that you have for my sister has healed a part of my own blame. It makes me very sad to think it may end.'

'It will never end, Prince. I will love Yun Shan as long as I breathe, and no other woman will ever replace her in my heart.'

'You speak like a man who is preparing to leave.'

'You're right. I must leave. Too much time has passed. I

promised my emperor that I would return to keep my homeland from ruin. A promise made to a dying man . . .'

Dan Qing considered him with a bitter smile. 'Do you remember when I told you that I would seek news about Taqin Guo, your country? Well, the news has arrived. Bad news, I'm afraid. My messengers wore out their horses riding back through all of Asia to report that Taqin Guo no longer exists. The rivalry between the heads of the army has dismembered the country into many parts which have gone adrift like the wreckage of a vessel destroyed by a storm. Just like what has happened here.

'You would be going back to nothing, Xiong Ying. But here you have everything. You will be the commander of my armies, titles and honours will be bestowed upon you, and you will become my brother by marrying Yun Shan. We will rebuild the unity of this land together. We will bring peace and prosperity.'

Metellus replied with a melancholy smile. 'The Heavens know how much I would like to be part of this future, but I can't . . . I can't. I've tried. I thought that my love for Yun Shan would make me forget all else, even my son . . .' Tears streaked down his face. 'But I have not succeeded, Dan Qing. I tried but I have failed.'

Dan Qing stared at him, greatly moved himself. 'Don't go, Xiong Ying . . . Please stay . . . I beg of you.'

The prince of the royal blood of the Han, the legitimate lord of the Middle Kingdom, implored him in tears.

Metellus dropped his head in silence.

FROM THE HILLTOP, Dan Qing and Yun Shan watched the dark figures of Daruma and his convoy and Metellus on horseback silhouetted against an enormous red sun, veiled by distant clouds as it set over the steppe.

'Don't forget us, Xiong Ying!' shouted Dan Qing suddenly, overwhelmed by emotion. 'We will always carry you in our hearts!'

The wind brought his words to Metellus's ear. He waved his arms in the air and shouted back, 'I will not forget you!'

Dan Qing turned to face his sister, tears that he could not curb running down his cheeks. 'I don't think that you could ever make any man in my kingdom happy, or any man in the neighbouring kingdoms. Do as your heart wills, my sister . . .'

Yun Shan respectfully bowed her head and then turned her eyes to her brother as she had not done for a long time, with a look full of intense, sorrowful love. 'Farewell, then, brother. May the Heavens grant you all that you desire. You will remain forever in my heart.'

'And you in mine, sister. Go now, before I start crying like a child.'

Yun Shan spurred on her horse and flew over the slopes of the hills that bordered the caravan route.

'Look!' said Daruma. 'Look, up there!'

Metellus turned and saw the little Amazon racing over the ridge in a cloud of red dust and his heart missed a beat. He spurred on his own steed and raced towards her, pushing the animal as fast as it could go. The two lovers jumped to the ground and ran into each other's arms while the desert wind whirled around them, intermingling their hair and their cloaks as if they were a single creature.

'Do you know what awaits you, Princess?' Metellus whispered into her ear. 'Sorrow, hardship, mortal danger. Think, while you still have time.'

Yun Shan stepped away and touched his chest with the tip of her index finger. 'Half of my life's energy is here, have you forgotten? If we separate, the other half will be extinguished. Is that what you want? Take me with you, Xiong Ying, if you love me.'

Metellus held her close in a long embrace, then they leapt on to their horses.

Dan Qing was still visible in the distance. He had reared up his horse and raised his hand in a final farewell.

FOR MONTHS and months they journeyed in the blazing sun and the blinding snow, along winding rivers, across desolate steppes, around the shores of huge salt lakes surrounded by dazzling white wastelands, until the moment came to separate from Daruma. His caravan would turn left towards the pass that Alexander had crossed five centuries before to invade India.

'I prefer to entrust you to guides I know I can rely on rather than put you on a ship full of unknown sons of bitches ready to sell you off at the nearest market on the pirates' coast. But I'll send news of your return with the first ship leaving for the West, and I'll see to it that it's delivered. I have correspondents as far as Alexandria and Antioch who will be glad to do me a favour.' He put his hands on Metellus's shoulders and looked deep into his eyes. 'You have saved a great kingdom, but above all you have delivered a man from the corruption that threatened to overcome him. You gave him the gift of self-respect and a sense of virtue. Once I told you that you seemed like one of those Romans who were inflexible, intrepid and even a little stupid.'

'I remember as if it were now,' said Metellus, smiling.

'Well, I was wrong. May your gods protect you, Commander Aquila.'

'And may they protect you as well, Daruma, my friend. I'll think of you whenever I hear the rustling of a silken gown.'

Daruma embraced him and kissed both of his cheeks, then departed.

Metellus and Yun Shan sat straight-backed on the saddles of their horses, watching as the caravan wound its way up the snaking path that rose towards the pass, against the majestic backdrop of the immaculate peaks of the Paropamisus, until it had vanished between the colossal wrinkles of that titanic land.

THE NEXT LEG of their journey brought them to Aus Daiwa, three months later. Metellus managed to pitch their tents close to the camp in a visible position, in order not to arouse suspicion or curiosity, so that they'd look just like any caravan of merchants heading west to the oasis of Khaboras.

On the second day, he saw a small group of Persian soldiers approaching at a couple of dozen paces. He lifted a hand to greet them and even sent a servant to offer them something to drink. They thanked him with a wave of their own and rode off at a gallop back towards the camp, where they would report on the small caravan of an innocuous merchant.

That night, Metellus told Yun Shan of everything he had suffered in that camp. He felt exhilarated at the thought that he was free, and at such a short distance from people who would do anything to sink their claws into him. They lingered for a few days until he was sure that no one was keeping an eye on him any longer, and then he went to the spot, marked with a stone, where he had hidden Valerian's ashes. He easily dug out the clay jar buried under a few spans of sand and hid it among the implements he was carrying with him. All of the emotion of their break-out rushed back into his mind, along with the hopes that he and his comrades had shared of all returning together.

He was returning with nothing more than a handful of ashes, but he had kept one promise, and this made him hopeful that he could keep the others as well. Every time he looked at Yun Shan, he knew that he already had with him an invaluable treasure.

THEY REACHED Nisibi in Upper Syria six months later, burnt by the sun, their lips cracked and skin parched by the interminable desert, but Metellus's eyes glowed with a magical light that seemed to come straight from his soul.

'This is my land, Yun Shan,' he said. 'This is the land of Rome that you call Taqin Guo.'

'I am happy for you, Xiong Ying. Your homeland will never disappoint you. It can never disappear like the constructions of men. What will you do if your country no longer exists?'

'We'll know soon. Tomorrow, when we reach the gates of my city, where the headquarters of the Eastern army are located.'

'And what if you find foreigners there or, worse, enemies?'

'I'll think about it when it happens. Each day has its worry.'

They dismissed the guides and continued alone until evening fell and then for all the next day until, towards dusk, they came within sight of Edessa.

Metellus stopped to contemplate the massive line of walls and splendid towers and he turned his thoughts to Clelia, his gentle wife, who perhaps rested in the shade of those walls. Then he spurred his mount in the direction of the big stone entrance arch which bore an inscription by Trajan, in the hopes that the garrison's guardhouse would still be there.

Two legionaries crossed their spears to deny his entry.

'*Consiste!*' ordered the youngest, warning the stranger to stop.

Metellus realized what a lowly impression they made: his clothing was dusty, a turban covered his head and swathed his face, leaving only his eyes visible. An impression no doubt compounded by the mysterious air of his companion. He got off his horse, bared his face and approached the men on foot, speaking Latin for the first time in a very long time: 'Who has the authority over these lands, soldier?'

'Lucius Domitius Aurelian, Emperor of the Romans.'

'Lucius Domitius . . . was an excellent officer and a great soldier when I left here, many years ago.' He realized that he had lost count of how many. 'What has become of Gallienus?'

'You have been away for a long time, my friend! Lucius Domitius had him executed for having abandoned his father to the hands of the barbarians. Aurelian is now preparing to march against the last rebels still barricaded at Palmyra, in order to definitively restore the unity of the empire. But who are you who knows nothing of all this?'

Metellus took off his turban and showed him the little terracotta urn that he held close to his chest under his cloak, thus exposing the titulus hanging from his neck, with his name, rank and unit. 'I am he who shared the bitter imprisonment of Emperor Valerian until his death, and have now brought his ashes back to his homeland as I swore to do. I am Marcus Metellus Aquila, Legate of the Second Augusta Legion, Commander of the army of Syria.'

The two legionaries looked at each other with stunned expressions, then stood aside and stiffened into a military salute.

'Welcome back, Commander Aquila,' said the older of the two. 'We have never forgotten you. The emperor will be pleased to embrace you and to reinstate your rightful high command so that you may join in the fight to restore the unity of the empire. And your son will be no less happy to see you.'

Metellus responded to his salute, remounted his horse and set off in the direction of the city, Yun Shan at his side.

Metellus smiled at her, then looked over at the sun sinking into the highlands.

'Let's hurry,' he said. 'I promised my son I'd be back before nightfall.'

And away they raced at a gallop.

AUTHOR'S NOTE

This novel is the fruit of imagination, as are its main characters, except for the great historical protagonists of the age in which it is set (Emperor Licinius Valerian, Shapur I of Persia, Gallienus, Aurelian, Chinese emperors Huang-di and Yuandi, as well as famous thinkers such as Lao Tze and Mo Tze), although it is inspired by the recently debated hypothesis that Roman soldiers may have been present at some point in ancient China.

The problem was officially raised for the first time by Homer Dubs in his 1942 publication which considers a passage from the annals of the Han dynasty that speaks of a battle which took place in a locality on the Talas river, near the city of Zhizhi in Gansu (today Dusanbe in Tajikistan) between Chinese troops and the forces of a local chief who had rebelled against the empire. Among the rebel forces were foreign soldiers, probably mercenaries, who fought using fish-scale formation. This suggested the traditional Roman *testudo* formation to Dubs. Moreover, these soldiers, before the battle, were entrenched in a camp built with large wooden poles – a type of *castrum*, that is.

Dubs later discovered the existence in the Fanmu district of a city called Lijian, which in that era indicated the lands of the West in general, including Rome. He conjectured that it may have been founded by the Roman soldiers who had fought on the Talas river. The most commonly accepted explanation is that the toponym Lijian comes in reality from Alexandreia, a place name that generically indicated all the cities that Alexander the Great had founded in Bactriana and central Asia – that is, any settlement of Westerners. Chinese sources nonetheless report that Lijian remained independent for six hundred and twelve years, a very strange and absolutely singular occurrence.

If this story were true, who might these Romans have been? Many have thought, given the chronological correspondence, that they may have been Roman prisoners who survived the massacre of the battle of Carrhae in 53 BC, deported by the Parthians to the extreme eastern regions of their empire. These men may have been the origin of the tradition of the legendary Lost Legion. It is a well-known fact that when Augustus negotiated peace with the Parthians in 20 BC, demanding the restitution of the Roman insignia and prisoners, the former were returned, but there were never any traces of the latter. What could have happened to them?

Homer Dubs's response – and later that of many other researchers both in China and in other nations – was that these soldiers, after long wanderings, reached the Chinese border and established a settlement there.

Recent investigations and archaeological surveys at the locality of Zhelaizhai have convinced a number of researchers that they are dealing with the legendary Roman settlement of China; genetic analyses have suggested that the inhabitants possess Western traits.

It should be noted that, in general, the evidence adopted to support this thesis is rather weak. The arrival of ancient Romans in such a distant land cannot be excluded a *priori*, but certainly requires much sounder evidence.

That doesn't mean that the Romans did not know about the Chinese, and vice versa. Not only Horace, Pliny and other authors, but also the greatest cartographic document of antiquity – the *Tabula Peutingeriana* – indicate Sera Maior at the extreme eastern part of the world. Sera Maior is the Land of Silk – that is, China.

Regarding this subject, an extraordinary episode, mentioned in this novel, should be recalled here. In the era of Emperor Hedi, between AD 97 and 98, the Chinese marshal Ban Chao, sent westward to restore order and security along the vital Silk Road, journeyed as far as the Caspian Sea. Ban Chao was the brother of the famous historian Ban Gu, and may have been inspired by his brother to send a delegation (led by an adjutant, Gan Ying) to seek out the sovereign of Taqin, the legendary empire of the far west: the Roman empire! Although Gan Ying actually arrived at a short distance from the border – from exactly what direction is not clear, although it might have been from the area of Mesopotamia or Syria or Caucasia – the fact is that the Parthian guides, who had realized his intentions, discouraged him from going on, raising any number of problems and difficulties, so that the Chinese officer was persuaded to cease his efforts. The Parthians earned enormous profits from the taxes they levied on consignments of silk crossing their territory, and would certainly not encourage the Han empire to enter into direct contact and establish direct dealings with the Roman empire, cutting them out as middlemen.

If the mission of Gan Ying had been successful, the consequences would have been unthinkable. The two greatest empires of the planet, too distant to find themselves in competition, might have discovered the benefits of collaboration. History might have followed a completely different path had Rome and Luoyang spoken!

Perhaps because all great empires resemble each other in the end, Rome and China had many things in common: the organization of their armed forces, their system of streets, the custom of founding military colonies, their methods for measuring and parcelling lots of land, the concepts of borders and of fortified walls, and even the habit of settling barbarians inside such confines in order to naturalize them and use them to defend the territory against other barbarians. They also had enemies in common, if it is true that the Xiong Nu named in Chinese documents were the Huns of Roman sources.

In the end, China has survived, transmitting its traditions, civilization and state structure intact over more than four millennia of history, all the way to the present day, while Rome collapsed a long time ago. This novel wants to tell the story – as if it were a dream – of the marvellous experiences that a westerner, like Commander Marcus Metellus Aquila, might have had if he'd managed to reach that remote planet called Sera Maior, an event not entirely impossible, one of the many that would have been forgotten or lost in the turbulent vicissitudes that have characterized the story of humanity.